Cover Design by CoversbyJules

Interior Design by Feel-Good Smut

Editing by Dave Holwill

A ROMANCE
NOVEL

TOO HARD

Hayes Brothers Series Book Five

I. A. DICE

Also by I. A. Dice

HAYES BROTHERS SERIES

A sries of interconnected standalones

Too Much

Too Wrong

Too Sweet

Too Strong

Too Hard

Too Long

BROKEN DUET

Broken Rules

Broken Promises

DELIVERANCE DUET

The Sound of Salvation

The Taste of Redemption

Playlist

"All the Things I Hate About You" by Huddy
"Bad Drugs" by King Kavalier, ChrisLee
"Lately" by Allan Rayman
"HELLGIRL" by Ari Abdul
"How Dare You" by MaRina
"SLIDE" by Chase Atlantic
"Numb to the Feeling" by Chase Atlantic
"i hate u, i love u" by gnash, Olivia O'Brien
"Good Enough" by Allan Rayman
"Contaminated" by BANKS
"I Do" by MaRina
"WITHOUT YOU" by The Kid LAROI
"Flesh And Bone" by MaRina
"Train Wreck" by James Arthur
"The Therapist" by Foreign Air
"Hellfire" by Barns Courtney
"Gods" by Nothing But Thieves
"Casual Affair" by Panic! At The Disco
"Alone" by HIMALAYAS
"Just Pretend" by Bad Omens
"You Know Me Too Well" by Nothing But Thieves

Dedication

To the girls who daydream about hate-fucks.

ONE

Cody

There's only one thing I absolutely hate—packing.

Packing a suitcase is mildly annoying, but boxing up my entire life? Well, that's another flavor of fucking torture.

It took me three days to vacate my room at Nico's.

Three days.

I had no idea how many of my things hid around his mansion. Turns out the seventeen boxes I filled clearing the bedroom I called mine for the past four years were only half of the shit I accumulated. The rest, scattered around the obscenely large house, filled another van.

Add furniture into the equation, and transporting everything from Nico's to my condo took three trips last night. Good job I have six brothers unafraid of heavy lifting.

It's also a godsend that Nico's fiancée and my younger sister are exceptionally organized. They didn't just help me pack but labeled the boxes so unpacking would be easier.

While I considered moving into the same condominium as my brother Conor and his girl—Vivienne—I couldn't get on board with no ocean view.

I coughed up a bit more cash, trading hypothetical two-bedrooms in Conor's building for a one-bedroom, third-floor with an unobscured view of the ocean. My place, like Conor's, is brand new, brought to life by the construction company headed by my older brother, Logan.

It's a simple but functional design—Logan's go-to style. The kitchen is to the right, separated from the main entrance by a coat closet. Straight ahead is the combined dining and living area. The master bedroom, complete with spacious bathroom and walk-in closet, is to my left.

The panoramic living room windows look out onto the patio, framing my favorite sight in the whole wide world: the ocean. Nothing beats this when the sun's edging over the horizon, painting the calm blue waves in dawn pinks and purples.

Not only did I get a hefty discount, but I also spent the last few months working on this place outside college hours. Every fixture, power socket, and cabinet was installed by yours truly, so if anything falls off the wall, I'll know exactly who to blame.

I rake both hands through my hair, gathering it into a bun as I inspect the airy living area. I groan inwardly at the prospect of spending the entire day making this place livable—free of clutter, mess, and trip hazards.

My wristwatch tells me it's half eight in the morning. I should be asleep still. Why the fuck am I up already?

Probably because my brain buzzes with the list of tasks I should get done today. Wasting precious daylight hours in bed isn't an option this fine Friday morning.

Well, not the bed, technically. The couch. My bed hasn't arrived yet.

Glancing at the three-high box-stacks by the crisp white walls, I let out a long, defeated breath. I should've accepted Vee, Mia, and Rose's offer to help unpack this mayhem because I lied.

There are two things I hate, and right now, unpacking is a fate worse than packing.

Only the massive vivarium housing my pet albino python, Ghost, stands where it should be. It takes up the living area's entire left wall, where a dining table would go had I bought one.

Instead of a traditional dining setup, I asked my architect brother to tweak the blueprints and incorporate a kitchen island with a breakfast bar into the design.

It's not like I'll host dinner parties here.

Pulling my phone out, I scroll to *B* for *Bug*, then tap the screen twice—once to dial, once to activate the loudspeaker.

"Up already?" Mia sing-songs, her good mood almost infectious. "How was the first night in the new place?"

"Uncomfortable," I admit, shooting a glare at the couch. "If the bed doesn't show up today, I'm crashing in your guest bedroom."

"I don't want to sound rude, but I did suggest you stay with us."

That's her subtle way of saying *I told you so.*

"Yeah, I know, Bug. You were right. Happy?"

"Not really. I miss you already. Have you changed your mind about letting me and Rose lend a helping hand?"

"God, yes." Without a second thought, I slump onto the nearest box. I should've checked Mia's neat writing on the side before sitting my ass down. The crunch of glass doesn't bode well. "When can you get here?"

"Good news, we're already on our way. Won't be long."

"I love you." Relief rattles through me as a lead weight lifts off my shoulders.

I'm a touch dramatic, but you should fucking see this place... it's the stuff of nightmares.

"Hey! What about me?!" Rose's theatrically wounded tone hits my ears. "Who the hell stayed up with you until stupid o'clock unpacking your clothes?"

That she did. The walk-in closet is my only box-free room. My t-shirts are neatly folded, accessories organized in display drawers, and my jeans, jackets, and shirts hang in tidy color-coded rows because Rose is a stickler for the tiniest details.

"I love you too, sis."

"Yeah, you do," she trills, her voice painting a picture of the grin undoubtedly stretching her lips.

A knock on the door has my eyebrows meeting in the middle. "Are you guys here already?"

"No, that's probably Conor and Vee."

"Have you called in the whole family?"

"Pretty much. You need all the hands you can get. Start with the box labeled *coffee*, okay?" Mia pleads.

"Is that an indirect order to get off my ass and get you a coffee, Bug?"

"Make that two," Rose chimes in. "Will be there soon. Bye."

In true Rose fashion, she hangs up the call before I say another word. I've grown fond of her over the past five months. She's easygoing, down-to-earth, and fits our quirky family dynamic like she's always been a part of it.

Every part of her character mirrors one of us. She's as moody as Nico, but still carefree like Logan and me. She's effortlessly funny, like Theo and Conor, though with a slice of

Colt's smartassery. To top it off, there's a hint of Shawn's rational thinking to balance out her obvious carelessness.

She's an explosive mixture, all bundled into a package that's unmistakably Hayes. Well, not entirely. Her looks are more centered than her character. While she does resemble us all, she looks closest to Nico: black hair, black eyes, a golden complexion. I think she connects with him the most, too. Probably because she grew to *besties* status with Mia within a month, which means she spends a lot of time around Nico.

"Come in!" I shout when another knock shakes the door.

Conor and his Little Bee enter the condo dressed in sweats, ready to work.

"I see you've made progress," Conor muses, gaze drifting over boxes that remain exactly where he left them last night.

"Rose was here until two in the morning helping me unpack my clothes. I was too tired to do much else after."

"Good thing we're here. Dibs on the bathroom," Vee says, then stops mid-step, horror flooding her face. She falls into a momentary daze, murmuring under her nose. *'What if there are hundreds of condoms? Or toys...'*

"No toys, *Little Bee*. I prefer my vaginas real not rubber. Though, I might have some condoms. Need any?"

She snaps out of the trance—something the whole family has grown used to. Vee has ADHD and speaks to herself whenever her thoughts get too busy to stay inside her head.

"I'm on the pill, thanks."

"That's more information than I needed, Vee."

She pulls a face, big eyes sweeping across the boxes, searching for one labeled *bathroom*.

"Coffee first," I say, carefully shaking the box I sat on, listening for a telltale rattle. "I might've broken the cups with my ass."

Conor fetches his car keys, using one to slice through the tape. Within minutes, the coffee maker is plugged in, ready to go. It's not as fancy as Nico's, but I've ordered an identical machine. It's only a matter of time before I'm drinking the best coffee one can brew at home. Until it arrives from Italy, I have to make do with what I have.

By the time my sister arrives with Mia in tow, the breakfast bar is lined with five steaming cups, filling the condo with a rich, bittersweet aroma.

It's two weeks before graduation so we're all off college, and Vivienne doesn't start her new job as Nico's administrative assistant until Monday.

Turns out, Conor's *Little Bee* has an exceptional knack for numbers. She completes complex calculations in her head faster than most people could type the numbers into a calculator. Not even Conor knew that until Nico was almost pulling his hair out last week, searching for a mistake his assistant made in a client's account.

He had about thirty pages of stock transaction data strewn across the breakfast bar, tirelessly cross-checking figures until I'm sure he was seeing double. It took Vee five minutes to find the blunder among the sea of data.

Five fucking minutes.

Needless to say, Nico immediately offered her an entry-level position, with a promise he'd sponsor any courses she'll need if she ever decides to climb the career ladder.

So yeah, she's between jobs and can spend the day helping her boyfriend unpack my shit.

Perfect timing.

"When's the rest of the furniture getting here?" Conor asks while the girls lock themselves in the bathroom.

I seriously doubt it needs all three of them to line the shelves with my toiletries, but I keep my mouth shut.

Who am I to interrupt their gossip time?

"Soon, I hope. The driver called at eight, saying delivery should be by eleven."

"Alright. We should clear some space then." He grabs his coffee, taking a slow, measured sip, inquisitive gaze scanning the room. "You know what you desperately need?"

"Beer?"

He laughs, nodding. "Yeah, but gentlemen don't drink before noon, so put a pin in that. I meant your flat screen. That's what we're starting with. You want it mounted on the wall?"

"Not like I have a choice. I threw the stand away last year," I sift through the boxes, hunting for the one labeled *tools.*

Once I have it and Conor locates the TV, we measure the wall, drill it, and secure the bracket. Half an hour later, the girls move on to the kitchen stuff—most of which they bought last week using my card—and Conor flicks through the channels till he finds ESPN so the practice run for Spanish GP can serve as background noise.

An hour whizzes by. We've unpacked just five of over thirty boxes. Rose brews another pot of coffee as a knock reverberates through the condo.

Colt stands in the hallway, cradling the largest case of beer available. I'm surprised he's here this early. I didn't expect him to show up until at least late afternoon, when we'd have done most of the work, reducing his job to fuck all save for delegating the remaining task.

"A bit early for that, isn't it?" I point at the Coronas he's protectively clutching.

"Think of this as a pre-housewarming party and live a little." He points his thumb over his shoulder at the boxes, furniture, and mattress leaning against the wall behind him. "Looks like my timing couldn't be better. The rest of your stuff's here."

Narrowing my eyes, I throw a skeptical look at the white bookshelf and a mattress that can't be the King-size I ordered.

"I don't think that's mine..." I say, glancing down the hallway where two men carry a three-seater, navy-blue couch.

And then all hell breaks loose. Figuratively, of course, but it feels like the Cerberus was let off his leash and charges right at me, all three wide mouths baring their long fangs.

My breath falters as a familiar figure rounds the corner, a large green plant in hand, a black designer purse slung over her shoulder to complement her tiny black dress and red-soled heels. I can't actually see the red soles, but that's all she ever wears.

"No fucking way," I mutter, prompting Colt to check what got my panties in a twist. "This isn't happening."

A stifled snort flies past his lips. "Oh-oh," he hums, amusement palpable. "Just your luck, huh?"

I clench my jaw so hard my teeth start cracking when none other than Blair Fitzpatrick—the instigator of Mia's long years of bullying—locks eyes with me.

Her smile slips, and those striking, dark, stormy blues of hers narrow, roving up and down my body, her nose scrunched in disgust. Just like my breathing, her steps slow.

A shadow crosses her face, but as fast as it appears, it's gone. She lifts her chin a notch, seemingly unfazed that fate, karma, heaven, and hell are shitting all over us right now.

Looks like I lied again...

There are three things I hate, and Blair Fitzpatrick takes the top fucking spot.

I'd rather be sentenced to a never-ending Promethean cycle of packing and unpacking than live across the hall from *her*.

Grabbing my smirking brother by the arm, I yank him inside the condo hard enough that he stumbles over his feet and swears at me, catching both his balance and the case slipping from his grip just in time.

Ignoring his *calm the fuck down*, I slam the door shut, ticking like a bomb about to go off.

"Guess who's moving in across the hall as we speak?" Colt summons everyone's attention. "Cody's favorite person." He wiggles his eyebrows, the sarcasm almost dripping from his voice.

"Blair?" Conor immediately supplies, well-versed in my *favorite* people. "No way."

"*Yes* way."

"Shut up," I snap, grabbing my phone. "I've got a bone to pick with Logan. You'd think he'd give me a heads-up."

"Logan doesn't deal with sales, Cody," Colt says. "What will calling him do? You already bought this place, bro. It's done."

I pinch the bridge of my nose as reality settles in.

Fuck. My. Life.

TWO

Blair

"What are the chances?" I snap at Brandon, who's chuckling at my oh-so-amusing misery on the other end of the line.

"Actually, pretty high if you think about it. His brother built that place, Blair, and you knew Cody was moving out of Nico's, right? I did tell you. I'm sure I did."

"No, you didn't." I pat a mover on the shoulder, before showing him where to leave the boxes. "Even if I knew, I would've expected he'd buy a mansion like Nico's, not a condo."

"The triplets are loaded, but not *that* loaded. Nico's house is worth like, I don't know... twenty-five million or something."

I slump onto the sofa, using my hands to shield my eyes from the space quickly filling with furniture and boxes.

The instruction to carry everything back outside and re-load the van sits unspoken on the tip of my tongue.

"He'll be growling at me any chance he gets," I whine. "I don't want to live here."

"Babe, you're overreacting. Cody's cool."

"Cody hates me."

I don't know what's worse. Staying here with the man who hates me more than I hate myself, or running straight back to my money-obsessed father.

Home is worse, I decide, swallowing hard. Cody can bark, growl, and glare all he wants, but I can bark, growl, and glare right back. There's balance. Equal distribution of power. Something entirely absent in any dealings with my father.

"You have a point," Brandon drawls in amusement. "But you know he won't attack unprovoked. That's more your style."

"Thanks," I mumble, his words striking a nerve.

He's one hundred percent correct, but I've been working on myself for a long time now... alone.

Which—according to my therapist—is why I hadn't made substantial progress until I started sessions with her. Now, with her help, I'm emerging out of the darkness, gradually finding ways to feel in control without projecting my hurt onto others.

"I recall you saying I'm not such a bitch these days."

"Two points to you, babe. Still, attacking unprovoked is much more your style than Cody's." He pauses, then chuckles when I groan. "What? You're backing down on your *call it as you see it* request?"

"No, not at all. It's just... I wanted to be on good terms with my neighbors, you know? I wanted to bake cookies, introduce myself, exchange numbers and keys for emergencies like they do in the movies."

"You can still do that. Suck it up. Take the initiative. Say *hi*, say *sorry*, say *I hope we can leave the past where it belongs and just be civil.* I happen to know Cody likes cookies."

"I'm fresh out of cyanide."

Brandon bursts out laughing in my ear. "You'll be fine. If Cody could give me another shot, you'll get one too."

That won't happen, but I don't bother voicing my thoughts. Brandon only got a second chance from the triplets because of Mia. She forgave him for putting up a price on her virginity. Forgave him for being a relentless, *clueless*-in-his-pursuit asshole with an ego the size of the Grand Canyon. She forgave him because her petite frame hides more strength than it should ever be expected to hold.

Brandon made *one* bad call. One mistake fueled by how much he wanted her without realizing he was in love.

Still is in love.

Pure intentions, bad decisions.

With Mia's forgiveness, the triplets followed, reluctantly giving Brandon a chance to prove his worth.

I don't deserve the same treatment. Brandon's one mistake pales compared to the years of bullying Mia endured at my hands. It doesn't come close on the forgivability scale.

A second chance won't happen, but I've made my peace with that. Not everyone deserves a second chance.

I most certainly don't, even if my therapist has a different take on the matter.

"Either talk to Cody and clear the air, or if you're afraid he'll lash out, stay out of his way," Brandon continues. "I guarantee he'll return the favor."

That he will.

Like Brandon said, Cody's not the type to attack unprovoked. It's been almost a year since that dreadful night when Jake cornered Mia. A year I spent on the sidelines, wondering how to rebuild my life and reputation while the majority—rightly so—blamed me for Jake's actions that night.

I may not have played a direct part in that, but I hurt the girl time and time again over the years, using her as a means to gain something I never had.

As one of the primary sources of humiliation and pain for Mia—the girl who became the topic on everyone's lips overnight and the girl the Hayes triplets regard as their little sister—I paid the price for years of bullying.

Again, rightly so.

The social pariah status was long overdue.

I wish it had happened years ago instead of people idolizing me and fueling the destructive cycle. Maybe I would've taken a long, hard look at myself sooner, but no one ever held me accountable.

They treated me like royalty. Like their queen, and the intoxicating rush of control, validation, and having my voice heard was too enticing, too important to consider the monster I'd become...

Until my senior year of high school, when a man more than three times my age opened my eyes on his luxury yacht.

For a while, through the murkiness of my past and the nightmare he put me through, I glimpsed clarity. I recognized my wrongs and chose a different way to make myself seen and heard.

I replaced bullying with promiscuity, diving headfirst into a maelstrom of meaningless sex.

Not the best way to recover.

My therapist labeled me self-destructive during our initial session last year. She wasn't wrong.

I swapped one addiction for another, but my resolve wasn't strong enough. I relapsed. I went back to bullying, humiliating Mia with fabricated nudes... and then I went off the deep end when I set her hair on fire.

I clench my teeth, shoving the memories aside, but as always, they claw their way back.

A lot has changed since Jake cornered Mia in the restroom last year. A lot of *people* have changed, including me.

My worshippers turned away, leaving me with nothing but determination to escape the vicious cycle my life had become.

Knowing what Jake did to Mia was hard to stomach, but there's a big difference between knowing about it and having to watch it with my own two eyes.

The video Jake recorded while assaulting Mia was leaked. Watching her fear-stricken, tear-stained face, hearing the malicious delight in Jake's voice as he preyed on her...

It hit so close to home I couldn't sleep for days.

No woman should ever go through that. No man should ever abuse the power he holds.

After seeing the video, I understood there was no hope for me if I couldn't let go of the hurt ripping me apart.

That's when I took that long, hard look at myself. I didn't like what I saw. I still don't. Maybe I never will.

People blamed Brandon on par with Jake and me. After all, it was his stupid prize Jake wanted to win. But no one blamed Brandon more than he blamed himself. It took months before he composed himself enough to look in the mirror without smashing it to pieces. Months before he crawled out of the ditch he'd dug himself that night.

I've never seen a man fall from grace so fast. From the very top of the college hierarchy to the very bottom. From a king-of-the-world attitude to a complete wreck. Until then, he lived his lavish life in the fast lane without a care, then crashed into a brick wall that appeared out of nowhere.

That's what love and an ocean of blame do, I guess. Brandon hadn't realized what he wanted from Mia was more than physical. It was emotional, deep... *real.* He didn't realize he was in love with her until it was too late.

He crumbled under the weight of regret, shame, and self-loathing. Therapy and countless hours crying in my arms saved him. Once he regained his footing, earning Mia's forgiveness became his new mission.

Not an easy task when she's dating the most ruthless man in town. Maybe the entire county. The man Newport looks up to. The man everyone respects.

But he managed to pull it off. With persistence and sheer fucking stubbornness, Brandon earned himself a second chance. He got his friends back and shed a portion of his pompous attitude along the way.

A bittersweet victory. No matter what he does, he'll never get to play his cards right with Mia.

That girl is taken. Claimed by none other than my new neighbor's older brother—Nico Hayes.

And he is obsessed with his girl.

Come to think of it, all the Hayes brothers go a bit Looney Tunes when they find the love of their life.

"I should start unpacking," I tell Brandon, perfectly aware I've been silent for at least a minute.

He's used to my long pauses. I've been zoning out, lost in my thoughts, for months.

The initial shock that rocked me when I saw Cody bought the condo across the hall has gradually eased off.

That's not to say I'm looking forward to enduring his hateful stares for however long we'll be neighbors.

A long time, I bet.

"Oh, and... it might be better if I skip your graduation party. I'll have enough of Cody's attitude on a daily basis now."

"No, you're not missing the party," Brandon says, and the bed creaks on the other side of the line as if he snapped upright. "This is my last ever college party, babe. I've planned a bunch of fun games. Don't stand me up. You're coming. I've already ordered your favorite wine. Besides, it's still two weeks away. Maybe you'll work shit out with Cody by then."

A sweet, sarcastic chuckle falls from my lips. "And maybe hell will freeze over."

"You never know but, if nothing changes, dress to impress and fuck the haters."

Easy for him to say. He salvaged his reputation. Mine's still trashed. I may be on speaking terms with most people, but not the way I was. And no matter how many friends I win back, I'm ostracized wherever the triplets are present.

Brandon nagged me into crashing their Halloween party and I got booted the moment Cody saw me talking to Justin. The most humiliating night of my college career.

There've been many more humiliating and degrading situations in my life, but none this public. None caused by my peers.

I won't be kicked out from the seniors' last college hurrah, since Brandon's organizing it, but it doesn't make things any easier...

My old friends, the girls on the cheerleading squad, barely acknowledge me beyond a quick *hey* whenever we cross paths. I'll likely be glued to Brandon's side, hanging out with him, Finn, and Justin—the two guys who had Brandon's back last year.

It's a given the triplets will be there.

I don't need their glaring on top of everything else I'm dealing with.

But I know Brandon. If I say *no* he'll be here in a heartbeat and won't leave until I say *yes*. A little white lie is in order.

"Okay, we'll talk more when I see you," I say, driving the point home with, "You better have ordered more than one bottle."

"Three sound good?"

"Perfect."

"Perfect," he echoes with a drown-out sigh. "I'll swing by soon." With that, he hangs up.

The movers are gone, and my new condo is filled with boxes waiting to be unpacked. Not one person ready to help. Unlike across the hall, where I'm sure half the Hayes family is helping Cody.

Must be nice.

THREE

Blair

Life has a cruel way of stealing happiness at the least appropriate moment. Fridays used to be my favorite day of the week. I loved hanging out with my girls, trailing from one boutique to another, coffee in hand, chatting, laughing, and gossiping about boys.

Now, as I haul two shopping bags from my car, I feel like an impostor. Gone is the easy air. Gone is the carefree vibe and joy I felt surrounded by friends.

Maybe because they're not my friends anymore. They've let me back into their close-knit circle, but it feels like I'm on probation. Like my every move and word is scrutinized, judged...

They're on guard, always coming up with some excuse to stop me joining them for drinks.

Last week Kelly-Ann excused herself from the group, then came back saying drinks were canceled because her grandmother surprised them with a visit. This week Mikaela got a call from her brother, Toby, begging her to babysit his son.

It's been happening for months. At first, I believed the stories, but one evening Kelly-Ann's excuse didn't quite add up. So, after parting ways, I drove past the cocktail bar we love most, and sure enough, there they were, at a window table, laughing and drinking margaritas.

I couldn't hold back the tears trailing down my cheeks the whole ride back home. I almost skipped our shopping spree the following week, but... I hate feeling so lonely.

This past year was the worst of my life. I locked myself in my father's mansion for weeks on end, drowning in tears, regret, and fear.

There is an upside: I grew as a person. I grew as a woman. But I'm only human and I join the girls every Friday, craving any form of interaction.

So what if I'm not sipping margaritas with them right now? At least I wasn't locked in my condo all day, like every evening since I moved here.

It's already been a week. Seven whole days of living across from Mr. Hayes. After the conversation with Brandon, I spent the rest of the evening unpacking and pondering how to navigate the Cody situation. The following day, heart in my mouth, I said *hey* when we bumped into each other in the hallway.

His shoulders tensed, jaw clamped shut, and my greeting flew over his head, not a word in return.

I expected a rude comment out of his mouth, so the silent treatment felt like a small victory. But after five more days of no reaction, no words, not even a glance, I started feeling stupid.

All the more so because, every day, I left my condo as soon as I heard his door open, hoping he might finally bark out *hey* if I was persistent enough.

Wrong thinking.

I was forced to admit defeat and stopped *accidentally* crossing his path yesterday.

The lock on my red Porsche—an eighteenth birthday gift from my dad—clicks as I make my way toward the building, two bags swinging from my wrist. My brows furrow when I spot a girl on her phone, propped against the wall next to the main entrance.

I haven't seen her around here before. I would've remembered the blonde pixie cut and tiny, pierced nose. Her large silver hoop earrings sway as she shakes her head, rubbing a hand down her patchwork jeans.

I'm about ten steps from the door when her face crumbles and she closes her eyes as though holding back tears.

"Cody, please let me in, baby. I just want to talk, okay?"

To say I freeze mid-step doesn't paint the picture. I come to such an abrupt, screeching halt I almost give myself whiplash.

My inner gossip girl takes over. Slowing my pace, I creep just enough steps closer to overhear Cody's response.

Biding my time, I set down my shopping bags and fumble through my purse for my keys. You can't get in without a six-digit code and a key unless someone inside buzzes you in.

"Go home, Ana." I barely hear Cody's stern voice coming through her phone's speaker. "You can't keep doing this shit. How did you find out where I live?"

"I followed you," she admits like it's so obvious.

Like it's so normal.

Instead of shame heating her cheeks, she looks proud. "You promised we'd talk," she adds as I locate the keys and slide one into the lock.

Her eyes flick open at the sound, sparkling as her gaze idles between me, the key, and my finger hovering over the keypad.

"Oh, hey," she greets, a bright smile stretching her lips. "I'm visiting my boyfriend. Could you let me in, please?"

"Jesus, Ana, what the—" Cody snaps but she cuts him off, finger jammed against the volume down switch.

"It's okay, baby, don't worry. I'll be up in a minute." She ends the call, pulling a concerned face. "He's not well," she sighs. "Can't get to the door. I think he caught the flu."

I've been playing different roles my whole life, and her acting skills wouldn't fool anyone. Cody obviously doesn't want this girl here, and the fact she followed him home raises all kinds of red flags.

"I'm sorry, but I don't know you. I can't let you in," I say, dropping my hand from the keypad.

I think she'll bulldoze her way in if I open the door.

She beams, showing off her teeth as she extends her hand. "I'm Ana Johnson. Cody's girlfriend. Do you know him? Cody Hayes. He moved in a few days ago."

"I do know Cody," I admit, less and less comfortable around her. "If he says it's okay to let you in, I will."

"It's okay, honestly. He's just not well, and—" A movement inside the building stops her talking.

We both peer through the glass door at Cody crossing the entryway, his shoulders drawn back, eyes narrowed, fingers flexing as he clenches and unclenches his big hands. He's been doing that since I can remember—a telltale sign of nerves.

The heavy door swings open, and Cody blocks the path, snatching my shopping bags off the ground.

Without so much as a cursory glance my way, he hands them over, stepping aside to let me through, then zeroes in on Ana.

"I'm taking you home. We'll talk on the way."

The last thing I see before he drags her toward his Mustang is the elated, dreamy look on Ana as she stares at Cody's fingers cinching her arm.

She's not far off melting into a puddle at his feet.

I can easily relate. There's no denying that Cody is handsome. He's a Hayes. They're all hot, but Cody is just... more.

Broad shoulders, the expanse of his muscular back, the way he always wears his long, dark hair in a bun, short beard trimmed. And when he's in his white sleeveless tank top and gray cargo joggers for the gym like I've seen him the past week... *yes please.*

When Conor, Colt, and Cody were younger, they wore their hair and clothes exactly the same, making it nearly impossible to tell them apart. But as they entered middle school, they began to differentiate themselves. By high school, their sense of fashion evolved, and there's no mistaking one for another anymore.

And no overlooking Cody every time I see him in the hallway. It's not a secret I've had a crush on him since high school. Half of the school lusted after the triplets.

My innocent crush turned not so innocent when I moved to college. I hadn't seen Cody for a year, since he graduated earlier, and when I caught a glimpse of him after all that time, my insides somersaulted backward.

Cody was always good-looking. Always a catch, as the girls called all the Hayes. On top of his looks, he was funny. Clever. Careless in an adorable, boyish way. But in that one year he changed a whole lot.

He was no longer a boy.

He was a man. Big, toned, ripped, his jaw chiseled, intricate tattoos running from his wrist all the way to his neck.

My crush intensified, swelling out of all proportion, then died quickly when I saw him with Mia. I didn't stand a chance. The triplets were so protective of her, and Cody took his big brother role one step further than Colt or Conor.

Once my mom died, life became that much harder, and my crush was forgotten.

Until—apparently—now.

FOUR

Cody

Ana might just top the list of my worst mistakes, and I've made a shitload, so that's saying something.

We met at *The Ramshack*, a rundown bar not far from the pier, when Conor was busy chasing after his soon-to-be fiancée, Vivienne. During the first hour or so, Ana was into Colt, batting her eyelashes and trailing her fingers down his chest.

I was stuck with Ana's friend, Gracie—not my type in the slightest. She drove me insane with how forward she was, licking my ear and grinding into my lap.

Girls like her are much more Colt's type. He likes when they give him attitude. When he can tame them... and Ana sure wasn't that. She oozed obedience—*my* type—so it seemed we both ended up with the wrong side of the stick.

The evening was doomed from the start with Conor's head in the clouds and my foul mood, but after a nose-powdering break, the girls switched places.

One loaded look between Colt and me was enough to say we preferred it that way. Ana took Gracie's spot on my lap, her personality exactly what I enjoy. Snappy, confident, but moldable like clay. I don't mind a sharp tongue in an effortlessly submissive girl, but the brat mentality oozing from Gracie's pores was an immediate turn-off.

Not for Colt though. He loves when they give him shit.

Once the switch happened, Ana and I spent the evening dancing, drinking, talking, and making out like a pair of hormonal teenagers. She was amazing. Easygoing, funny, pliant. She checked every box on my mental list, and for the first time, I tried Colt's approach: keep one longer than one night.

And *that* was a mistake despite precautions.

I laid my cards out right away. Honesty is key. I learned a long time ago that certain questions have to be asked and certain information has to be divulged so both parties can make an informed decision whether to go ahead with the night.

Taking the new approach with Ana, the last thing I needed was to accidentally give her false hope. I told her exactly how I wanted our no-strings deal to go down.

Zero romantic dinners. Zero late-night strolls down the beach. Zero conversations. Zero expectations. Zero phone calls. Zero texts. Nothing.

Just sex.

Ana was fun but not the kind of girl I'd consider dating—no ambitions, clueless with kids, no passion, no knowledge besides the basics. Kind with a big heart, but that's not enough for me.

She agreed, and added a rule of her own: no sex in bed. It boded well, but I still made her confirm she understood we were both agreeing to a no-strings and no-feelings deal. Just good fucking whenever the mood took us.

Things were running smoothly for about a month before she caught feelings. I sat her down, reminded her of the rules we set in place, explained that a relationship was out of the question, and we went our separate ways.

She took it like a champ. Kept at a distance for a while, but two weeks ago, my brothers and I ventured into *The Ramshack* again to see Vee's friend, Abby, perform with a band she joined recently. She plays electric guitar, and as an amateur guitarist myself, I was curious.

Ana was there, hanging on some guy's arm. I mentally cheered that she'd moved on. She seemed perfectly fine. Drunker and writhing more expressively than usual around the guy on the dancefloor, but overall *fine*. She gave me no reason to worry and even stopped by our table for a drink. Not a trace of those feelings she caught, as far as I could tell.

It all went to shit when we were leaving the club. Me with a long-legged surfer girl, Ana by herself. God knows what happened to the guy she was with. He was MIA, unable to stop Ana making a scene. A jealous hissy fit. She screamed at me for being a heartless jerk who promises the moon and stars then takes them away. Needless to say, she scared off the surfer girl.

And it only went downhill from there.

The next day, Ana arrived at Nico's doorstep, apologetic, tearful. She blamed her behavior on too many drinks.

We all do stupid things when drunk so I believed her. Until she texted me later that night, saying she saw how I looked at her. Whining that she missed me...

No matter how many times I explained or pleaded, she wasn't getting the message. She kept showing up at Nico's unannounced, but I was moving out soon, so didn't worry much.

I should've known she'd figure out my new address.

Now she's veering into *stalker* territory and I'm seriously debating calling Shawn for advice.

The thing is, Ana isn't throwing herself at me. She's not causing trouble. She's just... annoying, so I'm trying not to be an asshole. I keep telling her she should move on, hoping it'll stick.

If push comes to shove, I'll ask my Chief-of-Police brother for help.

"You can't keep doing this," I tell her, pulling out of the parking lot, barely keeping my temper in check.

It's not just Ana's stalking tendencies and selective hearing that got me on edge tonight. It's Blair. She's been grating my nerves since she moved in, leaving her condo whenever I leave mine, muttering *hey*, like we're best fucking friends.

Every time I see her, my muscles seize. My spine turns rigid, skin clammy, *itchy*, and my lung capacity halves every second until I can't draw a single breath.

The intensity is staggering. Unlike anything I've ever experienced. It's been growing, and growing, and gaining momentum, making me feel so raw that her voice, sweet coconut scent, and presence cause physical pain.

"Baby—"

"Enough, Ana. I'm not your baby and I'm tired of repeating myself. I know you're sensible, but right now you're acting batshit crazy."

She pouts, fidgeting her fingers, each short, labored breath bringing her closer to a full-blown sob fest. The thing is, Ana's not upset. She's channeling her efforts to manufacture crocodile tears: *acting* upset.

I fell into that trap one too many times.

She knows I'm a sucker for a damsel in distress. My savior

complex makes it impossible to ignore a distressed woman.

"Don't even start." I flip the indicator as I stop at traffic lights. "You'll get yourself in trouble, you know that?"

"How? I didn't do anything wrong. You should be flattered, Cody. At least I have the courage to act on my feelings."

"You should also have the decency to understand I *don't* have the same feelings. How many times do I have to say we're done?"

She looks out the window, pinching her lips like she wants to add something but can't find the right words.

It wouldn't matter if she could. Nothing she'll say will change a damn thing. I know she's having a rough time. Her brother took his life a few weeks ago and she's mourning, struggling to accept he's gone. It's the only reason I give her chance after chance to get her act together.

She's a little lost, I get that, but it doesn't mean I should indulge her imaginary feelings and ignore the stalking. She's not my responsibility. Still, whenever I think about calling Shawn, I remind myself that drastic measures should be my last resort.

There's still time for cops.

"Can't we start over?" she finally suggests. "As friends."

We've been through this already. It was her fallback the third or fourth time she showed up at Nico's house. Seeing how vulnerable she was, I agreed.

Our friendship was a whole ten minutes old when she threw herself at me, shoving her hand in my pants to grab my dick.

Nico, Mia, and Colt were in the room with us...

Not fucking cool.

"Too late for that." I take another turn, speeding down her neighborhood. "No friendship. No relationship. No sex. Nothing, Ana. Stop coming over."

"But I love you! We were so good together! Why are you fighting this so hard? I'm not asking for a ring, Cody. We can take things slow!"

Am I too soft?

I think so. Any other guy in my predicament—and I know because I consulted Colt, Conor, and Logan—would've taken out a restraining order by now.

The fact she followed me home, lurked outside the building and called me back every time I hung up is enough grounds to worry. She hasn't shown signs of being unstable enough to do something reckless, but I can't completely rule it out given how fucking tone-deaf she is to everything I say.

I park by the curb in the sketchier part of town where Ana lives with her mother and two younger sisters. Four women under one roof might be why their house looks the least neglected out of the lineup. Their lawn isn't as overgrown as their neighbors', and no broken bottles or discarded trash litter the narrow, paved pathway to the front door.

"Goodnight, Ana. Don't show up again, or you'll be walking home. We're done, understand?"

I might as well be talking to a brick wall. She stares at me with hooded eyes as her tongue peeks out, moistening her lips. She's turned on. I've seen that look before.

I spent the last few minutes rejecting her, and she's ready to vault over the middle console, pull my dick out and ride me outside her house while her sister peeks through the curtains from the second-story window.

"Don't even think about it. Get your ass home," I warn.

Her sultry gaze slides from my lips down my chest until the burning intensity focuses on my groin. The corner of her mouth quirks as her eyes jerk back to mine. "You're so full of shit, baby. Your dick is hard. Doesn't look like you're not interested. I don't know why you're fighting me, but I'll find out."

She doesn't wait for me to speak. I'm glad because it's fucking pointless. She hauls herself out of the car, closes the door, then taps a goodbye against the window.

The second she steps back, I floor it, peeling out of there and tearing through Newport at too many miles an hour toward *Tortugo*. A few drinks will help me take my mind off Ana's accurate observation.

My dick is hard.

Though Ana is not the reason.

FIVE

Blair

Cody's playing guitar again.

The sound is distant, but if I sit with my ear glued to the door, I can make out the melody. It sounds like Hozier's "Movement" today. Cody doesn't sing, and with two doors and a hallway between us, deciphering the title is not always easy.

Still, I try. I'm growing attached to the soothing strum of his guitar. He's played every day since he moved in, and when he didn't last night, after taking Ana home, I was so disappointed I couldn't sleep.

He didn't mention Ana when I stepped out at the same time he did this morning. This time it wasn't planned. I was pushing out a box full of clothes I decided to donate after the endless boredom drove me to reorganize my wardrobe.

I said *hi*.

I promised myself I wouldn't, but when he glanced at me over his shoulder, the word bypassed my brain and sprung out without permission.

He didn't reply. Obviously.

He's been giving me the silent treatment for a year now, unless he has a reason to scream like the time he kicked me out of his Halloween party.

He didn't say *hi* back. He didn't say *fuck off* or *stop talking to me* or *do you need help...?* but he *did* grab the box I was struggling with, hoping to push it all the way down the corridor, into the elevator, then outside, and somehow load it into my car.

Without a word or a backward glance, holding my box, Cody marched away. I followed, my heart beating a wild rhythm. I half expected him to toss the box—and me—down the stairs, but no.

Cody isn't spiteful.

He holds grudges, hates me, and makes it known, but he's not spiteful. He wouldn't hurt me for the sake of it.

Not wanting to jinx this tiny progress, I quietly asked if he could load the box into my car, pointing out my Porsche to save him asking. I opened the trunk, and once he deposited the box inside, he walked away, without so much as a nod.

Progress is progress.

Helping me is a gesture louder than *hi*, so I took it as a good omen. I also stood watching his biceps and triceps shifting and pulsing as he yanked the door to his Mustang open.

Now, with a heavy sigh, cradling a cup of hot tea in both hands, I slide down my door until my butt hits the cool marble floor. Eyes closed, I listen to the melody.

He's good. I've imagined what he looks like with that guitar in hand a thousand times. I never knew he played until I moved here, but during the past week, I learned many things about Cody Hayes.

He plays guitar and he's damn good at it.

He hums along to music when he's got earphones in.

Metallica is his favorite band judging by how many of their songs he plays.

Oh, and let's not forget the obvious—he has a stalker.

Not me. Though I admit, I ponder timing my condo exits to run into him again, but my intentions are not to earn a night.

As hot as Cody is, there's too much foul history and hatred between us to hope he'd ever look at me like anything but a waste of space. What I want is a chance to apologize. Really apologize, not just throw him a quick *sorry*. Forgiveness would be best, but it's a stretch. I can't expect people to forgive me when I can't even forgive myself.

I'll take *civil* from Cody, as Brandon described it. If we can be civil, maybe somewhere down the line I'll have a chance to apologize to Mia too. So far, all attempts have been futile.

Even with that goal in mind, I am *not* stalking Cody. Ana is.

She was here again today. Or maybe she still is. When I came home an hour ago from my therapy session, she stood by the door, scrolling through her phone, large shades concealing half her face. She didn't ask me to let her in, so I guess she decided to ambush Cody when he leaves. Which I'm sure he will.

It's Saturday. He usually hangs out with his brothers, but they don't meet until seven or eight in the evening, so Ana has a good six-hour wait ahead.

The notes Cody plays right now grow angrier with every strum, but it takes nothing away from the melody. If anything, it gives it a raw, gritty edge that sends shivers down my spine.

My fingers twitch as I spin a pencil between them. I've been sitting on the floor, back against the door, sketchpad in hand every day, but the pages are blank. I'd love to sketch him with his guitar, engrossed in the music, but I can't seem to start.

I shouldn't be thinking about Cody at all. I shouldn't imagine how he looks right now. I shouldn't listen to him play.

He's not said one word to me in over seven months—since the Halloween party—but now we live across the hallway and I see him daily, the stupid crush has resurfaced.

I know I'm just trying to break the loneliness somehow, and I know Cody's the last person I should lust after but it's hard not to think about someone you see every day...

A loud knock on the door almost has me spilling tea all over myself. I know that knock. It's so distinct there is no mistaking who stands on the other side.

KNOCK knock-knock-knock-knock KNOCK-KNOCK.

My muscles pull taut when, a second later, he knocks again, an angry boom. Before I scramble to my feet, a tight ball of nerves settles deep in my stomach.

He knocks again, measured annoyance reverberating through each thump of his fist as if I'm purposely making him wait.

I cast a quick glance in the mirrored coat closet doors, making sure I look decent. I purposely leave the scrunchie holding my hair up intact—a tiny blade in his back. Mom always wore her hair up and he hates that I remind him of her so much.

"Hey, Dad," I say, stepping out of his way as he strolls inside, loosening his tie as if it's choking him.

Stopping in the middle of the living room, he assesses the space, delaying the moment when his gaze will inevitably land on me. He has no problem using me, but looking at me when I'm not playing a role is a hard pill to swallow. Even standing ten feet away, I notice his breathing hiccup when our eyes lock.

It doesn't last long.

After a fleeting glance, he returns to the safety of scrutinizing my new condo. "You're not dressed," he clips, two angry creases lining his forehead. "And this place is a fucking mess, Blair."

Other than my sketchpad on the breakfast bar and a single Victoria's Secret bag hanging over the back of the stool, nothing is out of order. He could eat off the floor it's so clean.

"I didn't have time to put the sketchbook away. I was—"

"Excuses," he snaps, his eyes quickly appraising my body as he pinches the bridge of his nose in clear exasperation. "What is this?" He points at a wooden stand housing a few plants I bought to give this place a less clinical vibe.

This is my father's idea of small talk—belittling me and finding faults in things I enjoy to reinforce the sky-high wall between us. Not that it needs reinforcing.

We barely speak unless I'm required to play a role in his schemes. Outside that, he usually contacts me through his assistant.

During the past year, I've seen him a dozen times at the many banquets and business meetings he organizes, but only twice outside the "work" environment, even though we lived in the same house the whole time.

I saw him at my mother's funeral, then again when he handed me the key to this condo. A subtle way of saying *I can't stand having you under my roof any longer.*

I share the sentiment. Spending my days alone in his house made me feel lonelier than I already was. Here, the space is smaller, no echo from my solitary footsteps in the grand entryway, no deafening silence.

I'm still on my own, but the sounds filtering in from outside keep the loneliness at bay.

Dad met a woman not long ago—something I learned from Brandon. Our fathers do business together, and apparently, Dad introduced his new girlfriend to them three weeks before handing me the key to this place.

It must've been increasingly inconvenient, avoiding his mansion to keep me away from her, so I was evicted.

"They're plants," I say, crossing my hands over my chest, my tone emotionless. It's my only line of defense.

His eyes snap to me again, and I shrink in on myself under his belittling stare. "Why aren't you ready?"

"Ready for what?"

"Lunch with Mr. Anderson!"

Lunch means it's starting all over again. My father's voice booms in my ears, drowning out the melody Cody's playing. An invisible hand grips my throat, tightening the hold. *This* is why I hate seeing him. Because in nine out of ten cases, it means a few weeks of crying myself to sleep.

Lunch is the first meeting. Casual but professional so Dad can test the water. Three hours of polite conversation tinged with weighted questions to figure out Mr. Anderson's weaknesses and the most effective bait.

And then, if he considers it the best strategy, he uses me to reel in the catch. Bait and hook. Keep Mr. Anderson coming back to discuss business until he's in my father's grasp, dancing on his strings like a lifeless puppet.

"Are you listening to me?" Dad barks, and my stomach tightens, coiling around my spine. "I told you yesterday that I'd pick you up at one o'clock sharp."

He didn't tell me. I've not spoken to him all week but he'd never admit he forgot to mention the meeting or instruct his assistant to do so. It doesn't matter who's at fault.

He's right, I'm wrong, and end of story.

I play along.

It's easier that way. Less painful.

"I'm sorry. I'll be ready in five minutes, I promise."

"Three. Not a minute longer. Red dress, high heels..." He leaves the remaining demands that I know off by heart hanging in the air unspoken.

His hands are clean if he doesn't voice them. He can pretend it was my initiative to wear a slutty, revealing dress, even though Dad was the one who bought all my red dresses. He can pretend I purposely chose one that doesn't accommodate a bra.

That it's *my* idea to flaunt my body in Mr. Anderson's face so Dad can gauge his reaction.

He can pretend I'm a slut, happy to tease older men until they sign contracts, making my father richer and richer and richer...

As if the millions he makes aren't enough.

That's all we've been doing in the Fitzpatrick household for years—pretending everything is fine. *Normal.*

Nothing about our family has been fine or normal since my mom was diagnosed with schizophrenia when I was five.

She started having random episodes even earlier. My earliest clear memory is from when I was about four. Mom and I were sitting in the living room watching a Disney movie late into the evening. Dad wasn't home; it was just us two there when she started talking to herself. Her hands shook as she looked at things I couldn't see, and when I tried to get her attention she yelled at the wall.

I remember how scared I was the louder she screamed. No matter how hard I tried, I couldn't get her to look at me. I couldn't understand what she was yelling. Words jumbled together, her face paled, eyes turned bleak and fearful. She sprang to her feet, frantically pacing the room until she collapsed to her knees by the coffee table, tears streaming down her cheeks.

"Why did you kill your daddy?! You killed him!" she accused.

She said I stabbed him in the neck. Kept yelling about blood. Kept pointing at the floor as if Dad lay there bleeding out.

I begged her to stop. I cried and promised that I didn't do anything, that Dad wasn't home, that she was wrong...

She wasn't listening.

Scared, I ran to my room and hid under the covers until Dad found me hours later. Mom had stopped screaming by then but never came looking for me.

Dad didn't believe me when I told him what happened. He said I made it all up because I watched too many cartoons.

He witnessed one of Mom's breakdowns firsthand not long after.

From then on, the episodes were more and more frequent. Once she was diagnosed, after months of psychiatric evaluations, the real battle began: testing different medications to find a combination that worked, changing them because of side effects, hallucinations, delusions, screams, tears...

I was alone with her for days on end. Dad quickly withdrew from us. He still came home every night, but slept in a separate bedroom from Mom, and fled before we woke up in the morning.

There were weeks when I didn't see him at all. Days I spent crying under the bed, hungry and scared of the one person I should feel safe with.

I was just a little girl. I didn't understand that my mother had no control over her delusions, that she didn't mean to scream or accuse me of doing awful things. She was sick, Dad was absent, and I felt utterly powerless for years.

My home became hell, but it wasn't always bad.

There were good moments when the doctors found the

right meds to keep Mom relatively sane. She was functioning better. The delusions subsided if she remembered to take them on time... until my father realized the potential of her disease.

"Fucking *move*, Blair. You're running out of time!" He barks the order, shoving me toward my bedroom.

One foot after the next, I move. I pull out one of the many red dresses he bought me for the events I attend on his arm—the only color I'm allowed to wear and the one I despise most.

The dress is tiny: two delicate silver chains acting as shoulder straps and a bit of fabric circling my ribs. It just about covers my ass, so there's that. It's ludicrously, inappropriately short. Backless. Deep cleavage.

Most women at my father's "work" events wear beautiful cocktail dresses, whether long or short. They're elegant, exquisite, and I... I'm dressed like an expensive hooker. The dress is a gold label, and the soles on my heels are red.

Cheap whores don't wear Louboutins.

Not even the escorts my father's associates bring with them tip the scales as far to the *expensive* side as I do.

Shitty consolation, but I grab what I find.

"Wear bling," Dad's voice booms. "Lots of bling. This is an important meeting, Blair. You need to do good."

All these meetings are important. He always tells me I need to do good, or he'll cut me off. The last time I misbehaved, slapping an old man's hand away when he squeezed my butt hard enough to leave a bruise, Dad took away my car.

I was sixteen. Untouchable. *Illegal.*

But inconvenient facts didn't matter to my father, the great Gideon Fitzpatrick. Consent was a meaningless word while he paraded me around, using my young body to taunt sleazy businessmen, melt their perverted brains, and close lucrative deals while they salivated at my every move.

I rebelled the first few times. I cried, begged, and threatened him with the police, but he quickly found a way to cease my tantrums—as he called them—by confiscating Mom's meds whenever I caused any trouble.

Watching her succumb to the hallucinations was worse than feeling the heated gazes of much older men roving my body.

I gave up fighting pretty quickly.

Either play along or be played.

Dad prefers option three, one not available to me: play *them.* Play everyone. That's what he does best: manipulates people until they chase the carrot on the stick using any means available, and while that's not always me, it happens often.

Though not nearly as often as before I turned eighteen. It's been a while since the last event. A month at least. Enough that I started hoping, yet again, that maybe I'm too old to appease the degenerates he feeds off.

Apparently not.

"Ready," I say, joining him in the living room, the tight dress rolling up, showing off too much skin. I tug it down every few steps, or else my ass will be on display.

Which is kind of the point.

"Hair down," Dad clips, looking me over like a piece of meat. "And do your makeup darker. You have one minute."

Obeying the order, I retreat into my bathroom, do a quick smokey eye, and fan my hair out so I don't remind him of Mom as much as I do with my hair up.

"Red lips!" Dad yells, his voice shaking the door.

He must've forgotten I no longer live in his mansion. I still can't believe he let me move out. I begged him for my own place since I started college, but the answer was always a resounding *no* until three weeks ago when he gave me the key to this place.

I find my red lipstick, coat my lips, and grip the sink with both hands, hanging my head low. Time for a quick pep talk.

I can do this. I've done it many times. This is the last stretch. Just one more year before it stops.

Once I'm independent, once I can access my trust fund, I'll take my life into my own hands. No more relying on Dad. Even if I don't get my dream job, I'd rather do anything else than play the lead role in Dad's puppet show.

I could find a job now. Work as a cleaner or at a retail store. I could sleep in a cheap motel until I save enough for rent. It's plausible. *Doable.*

The problem is that the friends I'm slowly earning back will turn on me if I'm broke. I won't fit in their circle once I can't afford pointless shopping sprees or late-night cocktail bar gossip sessions—something I hope they'll soon invite me to join. Though if I'm driving anything less than my Porsche I can't see that happening.

No matter how much I hate meeting my father's expectations, I'm stuck for another year. I came this far already... throwing away the long struggle to keep my head above water wouldn't make sense now that I almost see the finish line in the distance. One more year in exchange for a condo, stuffed bank account, and a trust fund isn't that high a price.

Survival of the fittest.

Exhaling all the air from my lungs, I glance at my reflection. "You've got this," I whisper, pushing away from the sink.

SIX

Cody

My finger hovers over *Shawn,* my patience hanging by a thin, flimsy thread.

Ana's relentless.

After dropping her home last night, I thought she'd give me a few days off. Wrong thinking. She came back this morning and spent the day calling me over and over and over until she wore me down... I drove her home again.

She's harmless, I know she is, but she's driving me fucking insane. Before I slide my finger across the screen to talk restraining orders with my eldest brother, my phone rings.

It's a Hayes, just not the one I need.

"What's up?" I ask Theo, checking the fridge for leftovers.

"Hey, bro. Listen... you busy tonight?"

My back straightens on cue, his tone unmistakable. He needs a favor, and judging by the hesitancy, he's not happy about asking. I can picture him in his kitchen, one hand bracing against the counter, the other squeezing the life out of his cell phone.

Only one thing gets Theo this bent out of shape: his son.

My heartrate picks up. I've been waiting *months* for this phone call, but just in case I'm misinterpreting, I keep the happiness out of my voice. "Not busy. Why?"

With a deep, exasperated sigh, he spits the words at me. "You think you could watch River for a few hours?"

I close my eyes briefly, smiling like the cat that got the birdy. *Finally.* "You want *me* to take him?" I chuckle, slamming the fridge door. "I guess everyone else is either busy or dead?"

"Well, yeah. Kind of. Shawn just called. Josh is coming down with chicken pox, so there's no way I'm leaving River there. Colt's not answering. Nico and Mia are in Europe, and—"

"I get it. No need to list everyone who *can't*, bro. You know I'll stay with him. Bring him over."

Ever since River was born, an invisible wall grew between me and Theo. I racked my brain many times, wondering what triggered the distance, and the only explanation I came up with is that Theo doesn't trust me with his son.

It's not very plausible. I'm great with kids: responsible, caring, and fun. Ask Logan. I'm the first point of contact whenever Noah needs babysitting.

Theo never let me babysit, no matter how many times I offered. He tenses like a fucking guitar string whenever I steal River from Thalia at Mom's get-togethers.

I don't understand his problem, and I think it might be time to air the laundry. Though not right now. If I piss him off, he won't bring my nephew over.

Besides, there's one more possibility I can test tonight—he might think I won't handle River's tantrums; he's a screamer.

While that does scare me, considering he can go for an hour without a break, I want to spend time with him.

What kind of a brother would I be if I said *no* to Theo while I sometimes ask Logan to bring Noah over for a playdate just because I miss the kid?

"You sure?" Theo checks in a careful tone. I hear a note of relief there, mixed with uncertainty.

"I'm sure. We'll be fine, bro. You think Mia woke Nico whenever Logan brought Noah for a sleepover?" I rant, hoping to calm him down as I pace to the bedroom. "Nope, she put him in my room if she needed help or a power nap."

Noah loves me most, no doubt about it. I'm the favorite uncle by a landslide. We've got the same dynamic as Logan and Shawn's kid, Josh. Everyone else ceases to exist when Josh spots Logan, or Noah spots me. Mia used that to her advantage, sneaking into my room around seven in the morning after being up with Noah for a few hours.

He never liked Nico much—can't blame the kid; not many people do. Instead of waking him, Mia woke me. She started by casually lying beside me and *accidentally* falling asleep while Noah crawled over my face.

By the third or fourth time, she walked in, got under the comforter, muttered *your turn*, and we fell into a routine. It's a good thing Nico trusts me, or I'd have stopped breathing thirty seconds after the first time he found his girl asleep in my bed.

"Okay, thanks, Cody. We'll drop him off in an hour."

"Sure. Just hold on a sec," I say, checking in a box under the bed for toys. "Bring a few toys, alright? I don't have anything age appropriate here."

Though if River is anything like Noah, he'll be happy playing with my car keys or wooden spoons.

I cut the call, falling face-first onto my bed. I love my nephews equally, and I'm excited to spend the evening with River, but... I'd be lying if I said I'm not one bit concerned.

River isn't as mellow as Noah. Not as easily entertained from what I've seen thus far. He's six months old, almost over the big crying sprees, but still has his moments. I bet my entire portfolio he'll be ugly crying as soon as Theo and Thalia close the door behind them.

He's not half as easygoing as Noah was at his age. That kid ate, played, then slept. No tummy aches, no crying. No fussing. Low maintenance, just like Logan. At least, according to Mom.

River, on the other hand, is everything but low maintenance. I'm about to find out just how good I really am with kids.

I grab a quick shower, finish the lasagna from last night, and then my sister-in-law arrives, pushing River in his stroller.

I take it as a good sign that River doesn't start crying when we're alone ten minutes later. He grins his two-tooth grin, banging a tiny fist on some colorful sound-making toy before moving to another five minutes later.

"This is going great," I tell him, then wrinkle my nose at the foul smell. "Oh, come on, man. Our first time together, and this is how we're starting? Your mommy was *just* here."

He giggles at the faces I'm pulling as I grab the things I need out of the bag Thalia packed. It's not like I've never changed a diaper before. I have. Plenty of times.

That doesn't mean I enjoy it.

"Next time, don't wait until Mommy leaves, alright? She's better at this than I am." I clip his onesie back in place, and he immediately drags his foot up to his mouth. "Don't chew your toes. That's not cool. You hungry?"

Since I'm not getting an answer, I haul him into my arms,

grabbing the gooey baby food Thalia brought. Twenty minutes of airplanes and... *puff,* our fun uncle–nephew time ends abruptly with sudden tears.

Five, ten, twenty minutes. My keys, wooden spoons, plastic cars, and anything that passes for a toy litter the living room rug, but none catch River's attention.

Disappointment fills my stomach. Failing isn't something I take lightly, but sometimes the only thing left is admitting defeat.

I'm about to wave the white flag and call Theo when someone knocks on the door. It's probably him and Thalia. I wouldn't be surprised if they stood outside this whole time, spying.

Shit. I won't get to babysit the kid ever again.

I fling the door open, my long hair only half in the bun, after River ripped a few strands out. It hurt but kept him entertained, so I let him.

It's not Theo, Thalia, or any other member of the Hayes family standing at my door. It's not even Ana whom I'd welcome with open arms if I was given a choice between her and my neighbor straight from hell.

My eyes slide down Blair's frame, taking in her oversized tee, boyfriend jeans, and bare feet with a cherry-colored pedicure to match her manicure.

I don't think I've ever seen her cover so much skin. She always strolled the school corridors in inappropriate dresses, showcasing her spectacular body.

Yes, *spectacular.*

I'm cynical, not blind.

The few pounds she gained since getting kicked off the cheerleading squad did wonders on her former stick-person figure.

She's got curves.

Sensual, seductive curves. A waistline slim enough that I'd

circle it with both hands, ass juicier than a peach. Perky breasts top out the brain-melting hourglass figure.

Legs to her fucking armpits.

Not that she's flaunting any of that, but I have every inch of her body committed to memory. At least those inches she proudly showed off. There are a few inches I haven't seen. Inches I was dying to see when she showed up at college on her first day as a freshman.

Her long, brown hair frames her face, highlighting that pouty mouth, button nose, and full cheeks. I can hate her all I want, but there's no denying the facts. Blair's always been my type of gorgeous with a head-turning combination of dark hair and blue eyes. Always a looker. Always commanding attention.

And now, wearing cute jeans and a plain white tee, she's fucking stunning. Too bad the beautiful exterior's only skin deep. She's rotten to her very core.

Also... too bad my dick doesn't care about her personality.

I'm rock fucking hard. *Again.*

"Sounds like you need help," Blair says, breaking the tense silence as she peeks under my arm at River.

He sits on the rug, cute face wet and pink. I raise a questioning brow instead of slamming the door in her face.

"*Your* help?" I give a derisive snort. "That's the last fucking thing I'll ever need."

Her demeanor dims, hurt veiling her features. "He'll cry himself sick, Cody. He's been going for twenty minutes."

"No shit. I was here the whole time." My head's about to pop, which might be why I'm dumbfounded enough to still be talking to Blair. "I've got four nephews, so I've seen it all. I'm not fucking new to this."

"I'm not saying you're new," Blair retorts. "I'm offering help."

"I'd rather crash Theo's date."

Folding her arms over her chest, she lifts her chin, shepherding the hurt until it's almost hidden. "Would the crown fall off your head if you'd stop acting so hostile? I want to make things right, but you're not even giving me a chance to apologize—"

"I don't give a shit about your apologies. They don't mean a thing when they're not fucking honest, and you don't know what honesty is. Leave me the fuck alone."

Regret strikes me square in the jaw when her defensive shell cracks, exposing her hurt she tried to hide.

I hate her. I can't stand her, but acting like an asshole puts me on her level, and no way I'll meet her there.

River starts awkwardly crawling toward us, his motor skills exceptionally well developed. Noah didn't start moving about until he was ten months, lazy as his dad, but River has been attempting to crawl for a month already.

"Listen..." I say, exhaling a long breath while hauling River into my arms. "He's dry, fed, and keeps tossing the water bottle away. He's just fussy like his dad. He'll be fine."

"Or he's tired," she points out.

"No. I put him in bed three times. He crawls right out. Put some earplugs in. Theo's picking him up in two hours." I'm about to slam the door but stop when I realize bouncing did the trick. River's quiet. A triumphant smile stretches my lips. "See? He's fine."

Not waiting for another word from Blair, I shut the door. My smile dissipates the instant River's mouth curls down, and *three, two, one...* the concerto resumes.

"You have to be fucking kidding, little man," I groan, watching his big, brown, teary eyes glued to the door. "You're killing me here. We were doing so well."

Testing what I already know, I grab the handle. Blair's still in the hallway, facing my condo, arms crossed.

The triumphant smile that took real estate across my face a moment ago now adorns her lips because... what do you know? With a tiny hiccup, River falls silent, staring at Blair like she's a fucking godsend. She's not. I bet she's got ties with the devil.

"You like girls better, huh?" I run a gentle hand across his cheeks, wiping the tears. "You sure take after Daddy. Grandma said he only liked girls when he was your age. Nothing wrong with that, but choose them wisely. Some will break you ten different ways."

I step aside, gritting my teeth as I gesture for Blair to enter. This is *not* fucking happening right now. Theo's lucky I love his kid, and can't bear to see him cry.

He's also lucky I love his wife and understand she needs time off, or else I'd be bursting into the restaurant and dumping River on their table.

I look at Blair when she outstretches her hand toward him.

"Hey there," she coos softly, making the little traitor show his two new bottom teeth.

"Noah was never this loud," I admit, handing River over before closing the door. "He slept a lot until he turned one."

"Noah is Logan's son, right?"

"First-born," I confirm. "Eli's on the way. Any day now."

Her eyes remain on River as she boops his nose with her finger. Swallowing the bitter taste coating my tongue at letting in the girl who did nothing but hurt Mia her whole life, I temporarily put my hatred on hold.

It's been almost a year since Mia was assaulted. She dealt with the trauma. Made peace with the past, forgave her enemies, and used the bad things that happened to toughen up.

I don't share her worldview that everyone deserves a second chance. An apology and admission of guilt is not enough to wipe a slate clean.

I blamed myself last year. I've worked through it since, but the memories sometimes steal my breath. If I'd gone after Mia right away, if I didn't let her out of my sight, if I paid more attention... everything would be different.

That evening changed a lot of people's lives.

Blair's included. At least she keeps swearing it was an eye-opener. I'm not buying her remorse, and I'm not buying those meaningless *sorrys* she's spewed for months. Granted, she hasn't done anything hurtful since then, but it doesn't mean I'll forget her sins.

"You want something to drink?" I ask when she sits, bouncing River on her knee.

"Tea if you've got any."

I nod, grateful for a five-minute escape.

My whole body is crawling now she's close. I don't want her here, but kicking her out equals upsetting my nephew, and I love him more than I hate her.

Taking my sweet time with the tea, I glance over my shoulder whenever River coos or giggles. He's grinning at Blair, eyes big, round, and sparkling.

Kids are amazing. Carefree, innocent. They don't judge or overthink. They take the world as they see it and trust their gut when it comes to people, the survival instinct helping them along.

It's painful to think that, one day, River will grow up. He'll lose his innocence. He'll see the world for the fucking shitshow it is.

I steal glances at Blair, too, racking my brain. She's a year younger than me, but I've known her since she was five. We went to the same schools, and Blair's pompous, spotlight-loving personality made her less easily overlooked than Mia.

While I didn't notice Mia until high school, I sure noticed Blair. Spoilt, arrogant, rich bitch. The mean girl, always on top of the food chain, surrounded by worshippers, both boys and girls.

That's not the same girl who's sitting on my couch, playing peek-a-boo with River, whose ecstatic screams pierce my eardrums. This girl is different, somehow.

I can't put my finger on what changed. I don't think it's her smile. I've seen that a thousand times.

Maybe it's her clothes. She's not one false move away from her dress accidentally rolling up to flash half the student body. At some point, the guys made daily bets: *what color thong is Blair wearing today*?

Black, usually. Sometimes red. Never white.

"You got kids in your family?" I ask, setting the cup on a tall side table far from River's reach.

My tone's frosty enough to freeze an ocean, but I ask because I can't deal with awkward silence.

"Not yet. Soon, though. My cousin is due in October."

"Boy or girl?" Kids seem the safest topic, given the situation.

I don't want us to talk, but it's not as challenging as I imagined since she seems the polar opposite of the Blair I'm used to.

"A girl. You don't have any nieces yet, right?"

"Not for the lack of Logan's praying. I'm pretty sure he's ready to sell his soul for a daughter." *Maybe you can hook him up? I'm sure you and the devil are besties.*

Blair shifts her arm, circling River's back so he's safe in her lap, then covers her eyes with the other hand, playing peek-a-boo again. "Are they planning another baby soon?"

"Not that soon. Cassidy barely had time to breathe between Eli and Noah. We had a good chat with Logan about giving her a break before knocking her up again."

"I bet she could use a year off."

Every sentence Blair speaks lacks her usual superior confidence. Her voice quakes at the edges—something I've never heard—and I can see her trembling, as if she's trying to hide that she's afraid to be in the room with me.

"That's the problem," I say, purposely losing the disdain from my tone. It works only because I face this unsure-of-herself girl and not Blair the bitch. "She's as baby-crazed as Logan but doesn't want to be pregnant at their wedding. Once that's out of the way, I expect another pregnancy announcement by the end of the year."

Just like that, the topic changes from kids to the upcoming wedding, and somehow, the conversation flows without a hitch, question after question for over an hour. A few times, she looks ready to start apologizing or explaining the past, but she pinches her lips, gently shaking her head as if she doesn't think the moment's right.

It isn't. Not just because River's here, but mainly because I don't give a shit about her excuses. Nothing she could say would change what I think of her.

Nothing.

At some point, River crawls further over her until his head rests against her shoulder and he nods off.

"I think you'll be fine for a while," she whispers, gently stroking his back. "Where do you want him?"

"Stroller," I say, wheeling it closer. "He moves in his sleep too much to leave him on the couch. He'd end up face-planting the carpet."

"Better safe than sorry." She gently transfers River from her arms to the stroller, then covers him with a fluffy blanket. "Feel free to knock on my door if he wakes up."

I won't.

Blair initiated every interaction between us since we moved into the building, and that won't change. Still, I suddenly find myself out of rude comments, and when my lips part, I sound far from hateful.

"I bet you'll hear him first."

"I bet I will."

I hold the door open, watching her cross the corridor. "Blair?"

She turns, worrying her bottom lip, probably expecting something nasty because, save for tonight, that's all I've been to her for a long time. "Yeah?"

"Thanks."

Those blue eyes give a tiny spark, and an uncertain smile twists her lips. Her whole face lights up, her features prettier than ever before.

I don't like what it does to me, that smile.

I'd much prefer my dick turning hard since there's not much I can do to control that brainless organ. But my dick's been up the entire time she sat in my condo, and now, on top of that inconvenience, I feel like someone took a baseball bat to the back of my head.

"Thank you for letting me help."

SEVEN

Cody

The neighborhood is one of the fancier ones, not far from Nico's house. I've been here a few times, but it's been a while. Brandon Price is only throwing the graduation party because, just before he took Mia to Europe, Nico categorically declined my, Conor, and Colt's pleas to throw the party in his garden.

I drive past the line of cars adorning the curbs and enter the driveway of Brandon's villa.

Well, his parents' villa, Brandon's not moving out until he returns from his around-the-world trip next year.

Large, modern villas, ostentatious cars, and immaculate lawns as far as the eye can see—feels familiar.

People crowd the place like they did Nico's driveway whenever we threw a party. It looked different while we were hosting and purposely overlooking the mayhem. Now, seeing the thick crowd flocking toward the back garden, I'm surprised Nico ever let us throw any parties.

In our defense, at least we didn't let people roam the house. There's no such rule here.

I step onto the gravel, lifting my head when someone calls my name. Justin hangs out the top floor window with Finn, red cups in hand.

"Where are the other two?" Justin hollers.

"Colt's on his way, and Conor's getting here later," I say, fetching a case of Corona from the trunk.

I'm not a fan of the beer Brandon imports for his bangers, so I came prepared.

"Cody!" Mikaela yells, waving me over from the front lawn where she's loitering with her friends.

She took the cheerleading captain position last year after Blair got removed by a majority vote.

"You look like you've had one too many already," I say, heading over. "You need coffee."

"You're such a buzzkill sometimes, babe. Loosen up. It's your last college party *ever*!"

"Which is why I want to remember it, not spend the evening napping on the pool lounger."

She sticks her tongue out because that's precisely what happened to her at Halloween. She fell asleep before ten o'clock.

"Do me a favor tonight," I say, tossing my arm over her shoulders to tug her closer. "Don't take any pills, okay?"

She pouts, playfully pushing me away. "What did I say? Buzzkill! Seriously, Cody, why so tense? You should loosen up a bit, babe. Wanna hand?" She wags her eyebrows, a cheeky smile lighting up her face.

I smack her ass hard enough to sting. "Behave. Toby would have my balls if he heard that."

"Why yours? I'm coming on to you here."

"He'd find a way to lay the blame on me, don't you worry."

Mikaela is Nico's best friend's little sister, and after Toby picked her unconscious ass up from one too many frat parties, he asked me, Conor, and Colt to watch her.

It's not easy. She's an unattainable wild cookie. Nothing like Mia. Looking after Mia was a breeze compared to this. Thankfully, our role ends tonight but Mikaela's got another year before she graduates.

I bet Toby's already scouting another babysitter. Ever since he became a father, he's extended the role to Mikaela as well as his actual kid, even though she's not one anymore.

"You know where to find me if you change your mind," she chirps, kissing my cheek.

I leave it without a comment. It's all a harmless joke, anyway. Mikaela has her eyes on a different prize, but she enjoys the banter and I'd be lying if I said I didn't.

Leaving her there, surrounded by a veil of friends, I walk up to the wide-open front door, pretending I can't see the freshman pushing his hand under a girl's skirt a foot to my left. I wouldn't ignore it if she showed any signs of distress, but she's not opposing. Quite the opposite. Her fingers are tightly clasped around the bulge in his jeans.

Nothing new. Scenes like this are the bread and butter of college parties. At least all those I've ever been to.

More people fill the entryway, kitchen, and living room, the place bursting at the seams. Kelly-Ann dances on a table, a guy I don't recognize grinding behind her, groping her boobs. She takes a swig straight from a bottle of vodka, a loud cheer ripping through the crowd when the guy spins her around and shoves his tongue down her throat.

That girl is all about the show. She may look hammered

after a few sips but she's got a real high alcohol tolerance.

I make my way further into the house, greeting the throng of familiar faces. Brandon's sprawled on a large, snow-white sofa in the secondary living area that overlooks a massive pool in the garden.

Two babes hang on his arms, one grinding against his side. I don't know either, but they look young enough to have freshly graduated high school.

I cast a quick glance around, searching for Blair, still unsure whether I want her here or not. I've not heard her leave her condo today, but that doesn't mean she didn't. It's not like I press my ear to the door all day, tracking her every move.

"Cody!" Brandon booms, grinning as he pushes the chicks aside. "Shit, man. I half thought you weren't going to show." He glances at the case of beer I'm holding, two wrinkles denting his big forehead. "You brought beer? There's plenty of that here, man. Corona included. I know you don't drink the imported stuff I like." He summons his minions with a flick of his wrists before grabbing the case.

A second later, I've got an ice-cold bottle in hand, and Brandon's pulling me into an armchair, his face twisted into an uncertain look.

"Listen, we gotta talk about Blair. I know she lives across the hall from you." He falls silent as if waiting for permission to continue his monologue.

I expected this conversation, so I urge him on.

"I know I've got no right to ask a favor, but..." He rakes his fingers through his gelled-up hair, "...can you leave her be? She's dealing with enough shit. She doesn't need you or your brothers making things worse."

I watch him, my teeth clashing behind my lips. Blair and

Brandon grew thick as thieves this past year. I always thought they were just fuck buddies. Rumors have been flying around since she was a freshman that Blair was in love with him, dreaming of a relationship, and he's kept her close, enjoying easy pussy.

Convenient—that's what everyone called their weird relationship. It made sense, but since last year, or rather—since Brandon started earning his place back in our circle—I saw their relationship in a brighter light. The way he defends her paints a different picture than casual sex.

At some point, I noticed the protectiveness, the worry in his eyes whenever I caught him looking at her. It reminded me a lot of what my brothers look like whenever they watch Mia.

It's safe to assume I sport the same look.

While I don't rule out the sex-only relationship between Blair and Brandon, since neither dismissed the rumors, I think there's more there. They're friends. Very close friends. Whether sex is on the table, I don't know, but there's definitely mutual respect.

The fact he's talking to me about her now proves the point. He'll be traveling the world in less than a month, but he's making sure Blair's covered.

He knows that of all the Hayes, I hate her most. He also knows I've not fully forgiven him for what happened to Mia, yet he boldly risks pissing me off to make sure I keep my hostility toward Blair on a leash.

I did a pretty damn good job of that while she played with my nephew last weekend. I even said *hey* when we were both leaving the building on Wednesday. I don't see how tonight or any other day should be different.

I'm the bigger person, and I'll be damned if I don't make

people aware of that.

Squeezing his neck, Brandon continues, sensing he won't be getting any words from me on the subject of Blair Fitzpatrick. "You must've said something if she decided not to show up today. She promised she'd be here." He stares in contemplation at the floor before peering up at me. "I want her here."

"It's your party. I don't decide who you invite."

"Promise you won't storm out if she comes."

A scoff leaves my lips. "Stop acting stupid, Brandon. I'm not a fucking drama queen."

He pushes all air from his lungs, his shoulders slumping in relief. "Alright, good. You think you could keep an eye on this place while I get her?"

I scan the thickening, drunken crowd. "Can I kick out anyone who gets on my nerves?"

"Anyone but Blair," he confirms, rising to his feet. "I shouldn't be long."

He pats my shoulder and walks away, leaving me in charge of babysitting his guests. Thankfully Colt arrives ten minutes later with our little sister, her excitement palpable as she stamps a kiss on my cheek before beelining for the garden.

"Alright, alright!" Justin booms, entering the living room. "We'll play a game. Remember our very first college party?" he asks Colt and me as he plops down on the couch. "That game was fun."

"You mean the R-rated seven minutes in heaven?" Colt scoffs. "I think we're a bit too old to play that now, man."

Justin's smile fades, then returns brighter when Finn slams a glass salad bowl on the table.

"We're playing. With or without you." He takes his watch off, settling it in the bowl.

Justin does the same, and within minutes, at least thirty watches are added. We were fresh out of high school last time we played this. While a quick fuck with a random girl in the closet sounded fun back then, it doesn't now.

I know most girls from college now. There's a lot I wouldn't mind getting hot and bothered with, but just as many I'd never touch.

"I'm out," I say, closing my palm over my watch so Justin can't snatch it off. "You have fun, though."

When I'm in the mood for sex, I choose the girl instead of leaving it to fate. Besides, I'm definitely *not* in the mood after my earlier encounter with Ana. One stalker is quite enough.

She stopped by again like she has done every day since she found out where I live. I stopped answering her calls and texts, leaving her standing outside all week. But today was different... she got inside the building and knocked on my door.

Massaging my temples, I push the memory of our conversation aside. I yelled...

I fucking hate yelling at women, but Ana left me no choice.

Needing a distraction, I head to the kitchen for two more Coronas. By the time I'm back, Conor's there with his girl, and Colt's missing his watch.

"Come on, Cody." He points at the bowl. "This is our last night of stupidity. Come Monday, we're no longer students. Life starts. What have you got to lose?"

My lips part, but words don't come because he's right. I have nothing to lose, and it's not like I never fucked a girl I barely know. Maybe a quick deed will help me work out the frustration seizing my muscles.

With a deep, defeated sigh, I pass him one beer, then flick my watch off, adding it to the pile.

"That's what I'm talking about!" Finn yells, handing Vivienne the bowl. "Mix it up a bit, will you?"

She grins, elbowing Conor. "Give me your watch."

He cocks an eyebrow, but like a good boy, he obeys, only placing his on top after she's mixed the others.

"I pick first," she announces, snatching Conor's TAG Hauer off the pile with a cheeky smile. "Now what?"

Finn cackles beside us. "Now you have seven minutes to fuck in Brandon's coat closet."

At this point, I think she'll back out, but to my surprise, she grabs Conor's hand and follows Justin to the closet by the main entrance.

"Someone time them!" Colt shouts.

"Okay!" Finn calls over the music pumping in the garden and the excited chatter around us. "Girls, if you wanna play, step out of the crowd."

At least twenty rush forward. Some sober, some tipsy, some barely holding their weight—those won't be allowed to play. No way anyone's touching a girl too drunk to know what she's consenting to.

Not after what happened to Mia last year.

The whole campus saw the video, and not a single girl has been inappropriately touched since. Too bad it took Mia getting hurt for some of those fuckers to stop thinking with their dicks.

"What's going on?" Brandon asks, arriving with Blair.

My whole body immediately stiffens.

Now this girl... *this* girl I've known my whole life. I have no idea who the girl playing peek-a-boo with my nephew was, but it wasn't the Blair I know. It was an act, a façade now entirely ripped away. She's back to her usual slutty, bitchy self.

It's a relief if I'm honest. The uncertain, cute-tee-and-jeans-wearing Blair has been horning into my thoughts way too often this past week.

Technically, she's showing less than she usually does at these kind of parties. Her boobs normally spill from the flimsy confinement of a deep cleavage dress, but tonight, there's none of that. Her dress is a long-sleeved turtleneck, so her boobs aren't on display. *Technically.*

In practice, the gold, shimmering scrap is so damn short her sky-high legs are bare, the hem an inch over her butt. It's so damn tight I can count her fucking ribs.

How a girl so thin—even though she gained weight lately—can sport that chest is a mystery. Her boobs aren't big. Quite small, actually, but so perky and perfectly round I could spend hours lost between them, I swear.

She sits opposite me, beside Brandon, and once our eyes lock, I'm fucking glowing.

My skin's itching.

My mind's reeling.

God, I fucking *hate* this girl.

But my dick doesn't. It never did.

A twinge of self-consciousness passes through her, evident by the little shudder in her shoulders. Something like hurt clouds her face before she marshals it, nonchalantly turning her head the other way.

Good job riling me up at the start.

I wish this was my party so I could show her the door like I did on Halloween.

Brandon's burning gaze idles between us as he swallows hard, torn between loyalty and ass-kissing.

My fingers tighten around the neck of my beer. Like I said, I'm the bigger person, and I'll be damned if I don't make everyone aware, so instead of storming out like Brandon predicted, and like I'm dying to, I meet his unblinking gaze.

"You want in?" I motion toward the bowl.

Relief shines in his eyes before a smile widens his face. "Seven minutes? Fuck yes!"

"Couple number one is already getting lucky in the closet," Colt says, draining half his beer. "About done now, too, so get this moving along, Finn."

"Alright!" Finn jumps to his feet, studying the waiting girls. "Remember the rules! No whining, no quitting, no swaps. You get who you pick! If you're not willing to take the risk, step back." He stares down the guys next, with the same conviction in his eyes. "Same goes for all of you. Anyone who breaks the rules gets a bottle of Patrón and won't leave until it's empty."

"Oh, shut up already," Mikaela chuckles, stepping out of the line. "I'm drawing first." She closes her eyes, tilts her head back, and rummages through the watches, pulling out a silver one on a blue suede strap.

A guy steps in—Mick Harris—his smile brighter than a camera flash as he takes Mikaela's hand, leading her out of the room. Good job Toby can't see this, or he'd fuck up every person in the vicinity.

I'm supposed to keep the girl safe, but who she lets between her legs is none of my goddamn business, so I stay put.

Conor returns with his *Little Bee* a moment later, a satisfied gleam in her eyes, his dick hard in his pants. I bet a hundred they'll be out the door within thirty minutes since he obviously got her off and saved his load for later.

The bowl empties slowly. Finn approaches another girl once the last couple returns, and I'm hoping my watch is next so I can be done before the closet becomes a biohazard.

"You want another beer?" I ask Colt, setting my empty bottle aside. "I'll go grab a smoke, too. You coming?"

"I don't think so," he says, motioning his chin at Anastasia, who holds his watch between two fingers.

They had a casual thing going until she fell in love with some doctor around Christmas time. The grin splitting her pretty face as she beckons Colt with her long, manicured finger says it didn't last.

"At least you know what you're getting yourself into," I say, squeezing his shoulder.

"It's been a while. Maybe she learned something new."

"One can hope."

I rise to my feet in sync with him, but we go our separate ways as I navigate outside, where most of the party is happening. Six stands behind his console on a makeshift stage by the pool playing an original song he recorded with Mia last month.

At least two hundred people dance, make out, and drink in smaller and larger groups. Some seniors lurk in the shadows, either getting high, ogling the topless girls playing volleyball in the pool, or both. Taking a moment to enjoy this last night of irresponsibility, I pull a cigarette packet from my back pocket, light one, and lean against the wall, watching the crowd.

Nothing will be the same come Monday. My best years are over and the real work begins.

The real life.

While part of me can't believe I'm no longer a student, a bigger part is glad it's over. Maybe I'd have a different outlook on life if I hadn't watched my brothers starting families these last few years. The happiness and bliss they all share.

Maybe I wouldn't feel like I'm missing out.

"Hey, hey," Rose chirps, materializing out of nowhere to

lean against the wall beside me. "Having fun?"

"Can't complain. You? How many of those have you had?" I point at the red solo cup she's clutching with both hands.

"Just three, *Dad.* Tastes like water."

I mess up her hair. "You know I'm the last one to nag. Just checking if I should haul your ass back to my place later and leave a bucket by the bed."

"Is that an invitation?" She elbows my ribs. "I wouldn't mind crashing at your place tonight. I was staying with Conor and Vee, but they need more than seven minutes. I didn't pack my earplugs, and I bet they'll be at it as soon as we step through the door."

"Yeah, better if you stay with me. I'll tell Conor before his balls turn blue."

She chuckles, tiptoeing to kiss my cheek. "Thank you. If I'm not too hungover, I'll make you breakfast."

"Deal. Go have fun. Let me know when you're ready to head back."

With a tight nod, she crosses the lawn, joining her friends, and I go back inside, grabbing three bottles of Corona while passing through the kitchen.

EIGHT

Blair

"I don't want to play," I tell Brandon when he sets the bowl in my lap for the third time, pleading. "Take it away."

"Oh, come on, loosen up. Everyone's playing, babe."

"Everyone but me." I squeeze my wine glass, tipping back the last of it.

"What's wrong, Blair?" Mikaela asks, arms folded, eyes drilling into mine. "You're too good for a bit of fun? Better than all of us? Don't be such a buzzkill. Grab a watch, and we'll go dancing when you're done."

Peer pressure at its finest.

I shouldn't give in, but neither Kelly-Ann, Mikaela, nor a single other girl said a word to me since I arrived. That's how influential the triplets are. Their mere presence reverts me to the public enemy chair. Besides Brandon, Justin, and maybe Finn, no one will risk speaking to me. They're too worried they'd get on the wrong side of the Hayes brothers.

It's scary how much power a surname holds. How much respect it evokes.

"Deal or no deal?" Kelly-Ann clips expectantly, arms akimbo, brown irises burning into my blue ones.

It's stupid, but I consider playing. Life is so fucking lonely without friends. I still have a year in college... I don't want to spend it alone. They're throwing me a bone, readmitting me to their group if I play like everyone else. If only for one night.

This past year was torture, even though Brandon kept me company. Now he's not just graduating, he's leaving Newport to travel, and I'll be lonelier than ever.

"Forget it," Mikaela huffs. "She won't do it."

She starts backing away, and the girls follow, leaving me at a table full of guys who only tolerate me because of Brandon.

My guts threaten mutiny.

My throat constricts.

Alone reverberates inside my head, summoning the bitter guilt that's plagued me for months. I only got a small taste of loneliness, but it was enough to break me...

Mia spent her whole life without friends until the triplets found her. All because of me and... Jake.

Loneliness is the least I deserve, but I can't stand it.

Sucking in a harsh breath when Mikaela shoves the bowl into Finn's chest, I cave. "Give it here." The words are out. Too late to reconsider despite the heavy weight settling in the pit of my stomach. "I'll play."

A chorus of *oh*s and *ah*s fills the air as the girls turn around, applying their brakes when Finn holds the bowl out with a knowing grin.

"Eyes closed," he reminds.

Pinching my lips together, I do as instructed and dip my

hand into the bowl, swirling the watches until my fingers brush a leather strap with three rows of tiny holes along the whole length.

I close my fingers, pull it out, then open my palm. It's a nice watch. Looks brand new. No scratches on the face, the strap stiff and smooth.

"Fuck," Brandon snaps beside me.

I turn, but instead of looking at Brandon, my eyes move further, higher, and find Cody in the doorway, glaring at the watch I'm holding, his jaw ticking dangerously.

Oh no... no, no, *no*. My heart pounds in my chest. A cold slither travels down my spine, and blood whooshes in my ears.

This is not happening...

It's bad enough I caved under pressure. What the hell was I thinking? No matter how fine I tell myself I am, I don't have the balls to let someone feel me up in the closet.

But I didn't think about the reality of participating. I focused solely on winning my friends back.

"Fuck indeed," Colt agrees, a humorless chuckle falling from his lips. He sits in a wing chair, his hair messy after seven minutes in the closet with Anastasia.

"Whose watch is it?" someone shouts from the crowd.

"Cody's," Finn supplies. Uncertainty paints his face, but since no one is exempt, he plucks the courage to remind Cody of the rules. "Big boy pants, man. No swapping, no whining. Hate-fucks are awesome."

The image of Cody's big hands holding my hips as he thrusts into me from behind, pinning me against the wall, is the last thing I need, but my mind floods with more, fashioning a short, looped erotic clip.

His calloused fingers cuffing my wrists.

His warm breath in my ear.

That mountain of a body pressing against me. The sound it would make, slapping into mine after pulling back... Looks like there is someone I'd allow to grope me in the closet.

Slowly, Cody pushes away from the doorframe, his face unreadable. "Conor," he says, not gracing him with a look as he hands Colt a beer.

Conor jumps to his feet, disappearing out of view, his steps measured like a man on a mission. Apparently, he understood exactly what Cody wants. The triplets have this nonverbal way of communicating I've always found fascinating.

I know why Cody hates me. I do. I hate myself more, but the disdain in his eyes as they lock with mine, cuts me deeper than I care to admit.

Regardless of the consequences, he won't lock himself in the closet with me. He'd rather fuck the ugliest girl on the planet than poke me with a six foot pole, and that... it hurts.

My high school crush has been regaining momentum. It's been growing faster since he allowed me inside his condo last week. He even visibly relaxed after half an hour of conversation.

I took it as a victory, a huge step away from the hatred. Now it feels like I took ten steps back.

The room is so quiet... no one speaks, and if not for the music pumping outside, you'd hear a pin drop as everyone's eyes flicker between Cody and me.

"Not happening," he seethes, holding his hand out, captivating me with a venomous stare. "My watch."

I pass it over, careful not to brush his palm with my fingers, or I'm sure I'll burst into flames. Humiliation warms my cheeks, spreading lower.

Inhaling a calming breath, I recenter myself, activating defensive mode, as I tilt my chin up. "Not even if you were the last man on earth."

Loud *boo*s fill the room, broken up by excited howling.

"Looks like you two are getting shitfaced tonight," Justin hollers as Conor slams a bottle of tequila and two shot glasses on the table. "You don't leave until this is empty."

My palms grow damp. I'm not a big drinker. I enjoy wine, but nothing stronger, and the bottle of Patrón between us is the biggest I've ever seen.

"How much is in there?" I whisper to Brandon, my stomach churning. Bile leaps in my throat even though I haven't had a single shot yet.

I should've eaten something before coming over.

"Too much for you to handle half," he says, running a hand down my back. "Don't worry, I'll get you in bed when you pass out. You're staying with me tonight."

That's not much consolation. I never got black-out drunk and don't want to start now.

"Justin, make sure they're drinking, and..." Finn glances around the room, extending the bowl of watches toward the girls. "Who's next?"

A blonde I don't recognize steps up, but I don't pay attention to her watch-picking. My eyes are on Justin, who pours us the first shots.

"Lemons?" I ask, straightening my spine. "Salt?"

"Coming up," Kelly-Ann chirps, eyes sparkling with mischief. "Girl, you're getting trashed! This'll be fun!"

I very much doubt that, but Mikaela sitting beside me makes me feel better, until she glances at Cody, every seductive trick she knows in full use.

She's into him.

Everyone's into him, Colt, and Conor. Since the latter now has a girlfriend, most girls infatuated with him turned their attention to Colt and Cody. They could snap their fingers and a harem of willing girls would materialize at their feet.

"Had I known we'd be playing this game, I would've memorized your watch, babe."

Conor lets out a short laugh. "Your brother would cut off his dick if it got anywhere near you, Mikaela."

"I think he'd rather it was Cody's dick than say... Brandon or Justin's."

"Wouldn't touch you if you begged," Brandon fires back. "You're too catty for me, sweetheart."

"Take Rose home with you," Cody tells Colt, ignoring the ongoing exchange. "I told her she could stay with me tonight."

"She's staying with us," Vivienne says, sitting in Conor's lap, his fingers doodling over her thigh.

That's another thing all Hayes have in common apart from good looks—their love language. They're incredibly clingy with their girls, always touching, kissing, hugging...

"Better she doesn't hear you fucking in the next room," Colt chuckles, messing up Vivienne's hair before Conor immediately corrects it. "I'll take Rose, but not before you're done here, Cody. I have a feeling you'll need to be carried out."

"And whose fucking fault is that?" Cody snaps, grabbing a lemon slice from Kelly-Ann before she's even set the plate on the table. "Let's get this shitshow on the road."

With that, he tips his head back, swallowing the tequila, and I follow his lead. I don't know what would happen if we refused to drink. We won't, so there's little point in wondering. Cody will drink because his word is sacred, and I because bailing would give my friends more ammunition.

Justin pours another round, then another, but the bottle remains stubbornly full.

We've barely put a dent in, and I'm already tipsy. The shot glasses are big, Justin pours to the brim, and the tempo doesn't help. It's only been fifteen minutes.

Instead of hitting the mellow, blissful tipsy, I hit the other kind: tense, wary, scary, but the girls stay close. Their audible support is the most I've had from them in months, so I cling to them, downing shot after shot.

If a bottle of Patrón is what it takes to truly earn my friends back, then a bottle of Patrón it is.

Once it's Justin's turn to fuck someone in the closet, Cody takes over as our bartender.

My eyes snap to him when after filling his shot to the brim, he pours me half as much. Without using any words, he tells me to keep my mouth shut. At least, I think that's what his stern look means.

I give him a small thankful nod, a warm feeling spreading through my veins.

He's being *kind.*

Toward *me.*

It might not be much, but knowing he's willingly cheating, lowering my doses, is another huge step forward. While no one pays us attention, I mouth *thank you*, slapping the tequila at the back of my throat.

We keep going. Shot after shot at a steady pace. Brandon makes me wash down the alcohol with water and stuffs me with absorbent snacks, but by the tenth shot, I'm past my limit.

I feel sick. Dizzy. The room is spinning, and I see double when my eyes land on Cody. He's not as drunk even though he drank almost twice as much. No wonder. He's twice my size at least, that huge tank-like body of his soaking up the alcohol much better than mine.

I used to think Nico was the broadest, largest Hayes and, while Nico is taller, Cody's gym routine ensures his biceps put Nico's to shame. They're huge. Just like his boots...

A warm flush heats my cheeks, followed by a tiny giggle tearing from my chest. If I have more tequila, I'll pass out, puke, or land in ER with alcohol poisoning.

Or... I'll make a pass at Cody.

My tiny giggle has his eyes snapping to my mouth, and that warm flush spreads through me, giving me a fever.

"Come on, girl!" Kelly-Ann squeezes my shoulders, snapping me out of my lustful fog. "You can do it! You're halfway through. Just a bit more."

The room kaleidoscopes as she shakes me from left to right. "I don't think—"

"No way," she clips, morphing from friendly to judgmental. "You had a choice. Fuck Cody or drink tequila. You chose tequila, so suck it up."

"He chose," I hiccup. "I didn't choose anything."

Cody's gaze remains burning into my eyes once Kelly-Ann stops rocking me, and the blurriness clears. There's something in his stare that electrifies my entire body. The abyss of his black pupils melts me from the inside out. I'm not far off crawling to him under the table.

At this point, I'd let Cody hate-fuck me whichever way he pleased. Closet, bed, table, I don't care, as long as it means no more drinking. I'm about to tell him, but when I blink, he's gone. He probably went out for a smoke.

My head pounds, my stomach so full of Patrón I feel it sloshing back up to my throat, the vile taste coating my tongue.

I squint, searching for Finn and the bowl of watches. He's in the corner, chatting with Justin.

"Can I pick again?" I ask Brandon, as he comes back from his seven minutes. "I can't drink anymore. I'll pass out."

"You want to play? You're drunk, babe. You're not thinking straight."

"I won't be thinking at all if I keep drinking," I say, doing my utmost not to slur. "Please, let me play. I promise I'm fine. Not that drunk."

"Yeah, she's a-okay, babe," Mikaela purrs in Brandon's ear. "I've seen her drunk, and this isn't it. Let her play. She'll be better off getting an orgasm than alcohol poisoning."

Kelly-Ann nods in agreement, but Brandon doesn't look entirely convinced. It takes a few more lines of encouragement from the girls for him to check with me again, his gaze unfocused. I think he's as drunk as I am.

That's good. Works in my favor.

"You're sure?" He trades a glance with Justin when I nod, and one short, nonverbal conversation later, Finn approaches, holding the bowl out.

I grab the first watch and haul myself up as Alan Turner steps out of the crowd. I think he's grinning, but the black spots dancing before my eyes make it hard to tell.

The alcohol rushes straight to my head, every step making me feel twice as drunk.

A warm hand clasps my upper arm, the hold firm but gentle as Alan leads me to the closet. My feet—no longer in heels—drag across the floor. I step in something wet, then something sharp, the pain only registering for a fleeting second before everything goes dark.

NINE

Cody

I should've fucked her.

I *wanted* to fuck her. Why wouldn't I? She's pretty. Gorgeous, spellbinding, and... Finn had a point. Hate-fucks are great, but I wouldn't be able to look in the mirror tomorrow if I touched Blair.

I wouldn't be able to look Mia in the eye. *Remember the girl who made you cry a thousand times, Bug? I fucked her.*

Yeah, not happening, even though getting my dick wet would've been so much better than throwing up behind the house every time I head out for a cigarette.

No, I'm not *that* drunk. I'm just being smart about this, emptying my stomach every three to four shots means I won't get shitfaced before the end of the bottle.

It's something Shawn told me years ago—whenever he had too much to drink at a party, he shoved two fingers down his throat when he got home, ejected the alcohol, and woke up fresh as a daisy the next morning.

I think I'd rather suffer a hangover than keep on retching into the bushes with cramping stomach muscles though.

Fuck this. I'm done.

I'm going home.

College is over. If *this is* how my last night of recklessness is supposed to go, I say to hell with that.

Back in high school, I never turned down a challenge. We all do stupid shit as teenagers. It was fun back then, but I feel nothing more than a fool right now.

So what if I refuse to drink more?

The guys will holler for a while, then get over themselves by tomorrow. Even if they don't? Who fucking cares?

I won't see most of those people again after tonight.

With the resolution to flip them a bird, I head inside, pausing in the living room doorway. Colt's not there. Neither is my drinking buddy but Kelly-Ann's giggling in Brandon's lap, and Mikaela's about to start stripping. I should deal with her, but...

One thing at a time. I have myself to deal with first.

"Is she done?" I ask Brandon, motioning my chin to where Blair sat a moment ago.

If she bailed first, I'm off the hook. I can head home without telling my friends to fuck themselves.

"She decided to play," he explains with a drunken chuckle.

It takes three heartbeats for his words to sink, then they hit like a bucket of ice-cold water and I'm suddenly sober.

"What?!"

"She picked another watch," Finn explains like he thinks I didn't understand. "She's in the closet with Alan."

"Are you out of your fucking mind? She's wasted. What

did we say about touching drunk women?"

"She talked sense. She's just tipsy, man. She knew what she was agreeing to. Leave her be. She didn't want to drink anymore, so either this or—"

"Or *what*?!" I boom, getting in his face, my heart racing as the memory of Mia—not drunk, but drugged—stabs my mind. "Or fucking *what*, Finn?"

"Hey, chill out. What the fuck is your problem?"

To be perfectly honest, I don't know the answer to that question, but a biblical kind of wrath sweeps me head to toe as I glance around the room at the many familiar, drunken faces.

This is ridiculous.

What the hell was I thinking?

Am I overreacting or do they need some sense knocking into their heads?

I get that this is the last hurrah for all seniors. The last college party ever, time to be stupid, but there's a line you shouldn't cross.

Sometime in the past couple of years, I changed. Grew up, and now, standing in Brandon's living room, watching people I've considered friends for years, I realize I won't miss ninety-five percent of them.

I blame my brothers for this sudden maturity.

I'm three months shy of twenty-two. It's still okay to be reckless, but I no longer think in those categories.

I think about the hangover tomorrow and whether I'll have the strength to play with my nephews when we go to Mom's for the monthly get-together. I think about Cassidy and how she might go into labor any minute, so it'd be nice to be fucking helpful. I already called dibs on babysitting Noah while they're at the hospital.

What if her water breaks tonight? She's two weeks from her due date, so it might happen. How the fuck will I help if I'm drunk off my ass?

"Fuck you," I tell Finn, stomping away.

Blair pops into my head when I spot a freshman manning the coat closet door, his gaze focused on his phone's stopwatch. It tells me Alan's been in there with Blair less than two minutes.

I shouldn't give a shit. I should walk straight past the gathering, but I won't let the fucker take advantage of Blair when she's got two glasses of wine and ten shots of Patrón inside her. Leaving her goes against my basic instincts.

I hate her with every fiber in me, I swear, but I won't let that asshole prey on her.

"Move," I bark at the kid.

He looks up, scrambling away with a sheepish look. Either he knows I'm unpredictable or sees it in my eyes. My muscles bunch, a biblical kind of wrath searing through my veins.

A few sharp gasps fill the air when, rather than coaxing Alan to open the door, I kick it open.

My temper goes from zero to death row at warp speed. Alan has his dick out already, one hand clasped tightly around the base as he flinches away from me, terror in his eyes.

Blair's on the floor, gold dress bunched to her waist, eyes closed, chest rising steadily, black panties on display.

She's unconscious and that motherfucker...

My bones shake. I'm practically fucking levitating with anger. I've not felt this unhinged since I pulled Asher off Mia two years ago. A jigsaw of reality and memory sends a shockwave through my mind.

"You piece of shit!" I seethe, steering out the first punch.

My elbow falls back, then shoots forth, my clenched fist

landing neatly on target. His nose breaks.

"Cody! What the fuck are you doing?!" Colt booms.

I don't listen.

I don't stop, ramming my fist into Alan's jaw, clutching the prick's t-shirt in my other hand. "She's fucking unconscious!" I bellow, hauling him up when he starts slipping from my grasp. "You want to fuck her when she doesn't even know what's happening around her?!"

Another whack to his head, powerful enough to give him a contusion.

"Did you touch her?!" I demand, holding him against the wall, my fingers squeezing his throat. "Did you fucking *touch* her?"

He'll be hospitalized if he did.

"Cody, calm down," he sputters blood, trying to cough. "I wasn't going to fuck her, man, I swear, I—"

"Your dick's hanging out, *man*!"

Colt enters the closet and yanks me back hard by the bicep, murder on his mind as he shoves me out.

I don't say a word. We could argue all day over which of us has a shorter fuse, but we'd never reach a consensus. The wrath dancing in his eyes isn't for me. It's aimed at Alan, Finn, Justin, Brandon, and every other person who watched him lock an unconscious girl in the closet to fuck her.

Colt doesn't wait for explanations. He unpacks a punch that undoubtedly loosens a few of Alan's teeth. "Be fucking glad you're getting a kicking instead of handcuffs."

"Stop! Just stop!" Alan yelps, shielding himself behind his hands. "I was jerking off! Fuck, man! Come on, you know I'd never touch her this drunk! She couldn't drink any more. She needed an out!"

"You can give a girl an out *and* keep your dick in your pants," Rose snaps, stopping at my side. "Come on, let's get out of here. I've got her purse."

I cock an eyebrow, surprised that Rose is helping Blair. After learning about Mia's bullying, she conducted her own investigation on campus and discovered more than she bargained for.

Blair became Rose's enemy number one, so her assistance is a shock.

Not as much as my own actions, though.

Without thinking, I elbow Colt out of the way, tug Blair's skirt until it covers her ass, then haul her into my arms.

I've never touched her. Not once since I've known her, but now that I have her safely tucked against me, something shifts inside my chest.

She's... delicate. Fragile. Weighs nothing at all. A feather in my arms. Her skin is soft, warm, and smells like coconuts.

I always considered her tougher. That godawful attitude, sharp, rude tongue, and sophisticated exterior making her seem more resilient, but now that I hold her, she feels breakable. So vulnerable I automatically curve her into me further. Shield her from everyone's gaze.

"Come on, I'll drive." Colt nudges my shoulder. "I only had one beer."

I step out of the closet, cradling Blair, her pale cheek nuzzled into my pec. Filling my lungs to the brim, I glance at Rose. "Grab my hoodie, sis."

She runs to the living room, returning with my hoodie and Brandon in tow.

"What are you doing?" He's swaying as he glares at me. "She's staying here."

"No way in hell," Rose clips, shoving a finger in his chest. "You're disgraceful. You should be fucking ashamed."

"Rose." Colt takes her arm. "Save your tongue. He won't remember it tomorrow."

"I'm not that drunk," Brandon opposes, taking hasty steps toward me. "Blair's staying here."

"Take one more step, and you'll end up like that," Colt warns, nodding to Alan in the closet, covered in blood, dick tucked back in his jeans. "Seriously, man. Don't fucking test me."

I don't wait for another challenge. Turning around, I take Blair outside, then deposit her into the back seat of Colt's Mustang. It's a two-door car, so it takes effort to arrange us in the back. I mold her small, unconscious frame into my side, draping my hoodie around her.

"This is not happening," I mutter when Rose gets in and buckles up. "It's all your fault," I snap as Colt grabs the wheel.

"How is it my fault?" he says.

"Who told me to put my watch in? You did."

Colt shakes his head, reversing around the people lingering in the driveway. "How was I supposed to know Blair would pick your watch?"

"Oh fuck off and stay there. It's *your* fault."

Rose laughs first, then Colt, and in the end, I join in.

What a fucking mess.

TEN

Blair

A loud bang pulls me out of sleep, cutting through my groggy mind and falling like a hammer against my skull. Instantly, my head pounds as if it were a real hammer blow.

The acrid, vile taste of tequila is enough to draw the bile up my throat. I wince, my mind foggy, my body so heavy it feels like I'm trailing an anchor.

And I'm not even up yet.

Images flash through my mind, a montage of disjointed memories. Brandon's smirking face, Kelly-Ann, or maybe Mikaela, shaking me from left to right, Cody pouring Patrón. I remember downing it with ease at first, and then... nothing. A black hole.

Another knock pierces my thoughts, and I panic.

How did I get home?

Did I come back alone?

Did I do something stupid?

I can't remember, and the dull ache along my temples isn't helping me focus. Neither are the shivers shaking my body under the covers, my skin clammy like I'm dying of the flu. I take a deep breath and slowly open my eyes, squinting against the bright sunlight streaming through the window.

With the third thunderous knock, I tear myself off the pillow, standing on unsteady legs, the quick motion sending a sharp pang of pain through my skull. My stomach churns so hard I think I'll hurl all over the place.

"I'm coming," I rasp, my voice distant, the room spinning harder with every step. "I'm coming," I try again, but even I can barely hear it.

"It's open," I hear Cody say in the hallway. "Go right in. She's probably still asleep."

I groan. I'd rather be left to wallow in my misery alone.

"Shit," Brandon yelps. "You scared the hell out of me, man. Listen, I..." He trails off, his words heavy with guilt. "Finn told me what happened last night. I can't remember a thing. Thanks for getting her home safely. How is she?"

"She was okay when I put her in bed."

My heart lurches, swelling enough to break a rib, as mortification and relief wash over me. Cody brought me home.

He took care of me.

I study my shivering hands, frowning when I notice I'm wearing a hoodie. *Cody*'s hoodie. It's soft, warm, and many sizes too big as it falls to my mid-thighs.

"I shouldn't have drunk that much," Brandon mutters.

"No, you shouldn't have, and you shouldn't have let Alan lock her in that fucking closet."

A flashback hits me. I remember Alan smiling, his watch... his hand around my waist...

Feeling nauseous, I wrench the door open, staring at Cody across the hall. He looks like I feel—pale, dark circles under his eyes, and clearly still feeling the effects of last night's Patrón.

"I guess she's up now," he says, arms folded over his chest. The way he looks at me sends my pulse racing. "You good?"

The tension between us resumes, more potent than last night. It's evolved into a palpable energy, a whip of raw, bright red electric current coiling us tighter and tighter together.

I shake my head, prompting another jarring ache in my skull. "What happened?"

"I'll tell you inside," Brandon says. "Come on, babe, I'll make you breakfast. You look like shit."

"Knock if you need the other side of the story," Cody clips. Then he flicks his eyes to Brandon. "Don't fucking lie to her."

It's not just how he says it—full of warning and threat—but how he roves my frame, his gaze burning into me like the thrill of a stolen kiss. It's a hard-to-read look. It could be anything from concern to anger to desire. I can't tell which, but I can hope.

His dark eyes linger where the hem of his hoodie meets my thighs and a flush creeps up my neck.

Does he want it back?

I tug at the collar to check there's anything underneath. Thankfully, there is. The dress is bunched at my waist, but still there. I shove my hands under the hoodie to readjust the fabric, but Cody cuffs my wrist, kindling a smoldering fire within me.

"Don't," he says, his voice low and body tense. "Keep it."

Does he likes how it looks on me, or does he recall dressing me in it last night? Just as I'm starting to float, an unpleasant realization surfaces, like a sharp, stinging slap across my cheek.

He doesn't want the hoodie back because I wore it. Because it *touched* me... He'd bin it the moment I'd hand it back.

Another wave of regret, guilt, and hurt twists my stomach, the shame only amplified by my hangover. This is what Mia must've felt when Jake and I called her *cootie Mia*. Dirty. Humiliated. Unwanted.

Karma's finally caught up with me.

I pinch my lips, swallowing the tears. I deserve to feel unwanted, humiliated, dirty... I deserve much, much worse, but it hurts so much.

Brandon shoulders past me, heading straight for my kitchen. He's out of sight, but Cody's not. I can't make my vocal cords work. My eyes won't meet his burning gaze. All I can do is retreat and close the door...

***

"Better?" Brandon asks after I emerge from the bathroom, showered and dressed.

He moves around the kitchen with ease, perfectly content playing cook as he flips eggs and bacon on the stove and pours me a glass of cold orange juice.

Even when I don't deserve it, he's always there for me. Apart from a very dark time last year when he was too busy. Too busy to hold me when I cried.

"Tell me what happened last night. I can't remember anything after the fifth, maybe sixth shot."

He dishes out breakfast, and the aroma of sizzling bacon and fried eggs roils my stomach as I sit at the kitchen island, my hands resting on the cool marble.

"You don't?" He pauses the task, narrowing his eyes before finally adding *shit* in a whisper tinged with concern.

"Tell me about Alan," I say, my mind racing with worst-case scenarios. "Did he—"

"No," he interrupts. "I swear, okay? He didn't touch you." His expression turns serious. "I'm sorry, babe. I shouldn't have let you play, but you sounded fine, you know? You made sense. You didn't slur much."

Relief comes first, quickly replaced by shame and regret. "It's okay. It's not your fault. I should've stayed home like I planned all along." I down a few vitamin and pain pills, hoping they'll alleviate the pounding headache. "So Alan took me to the closet but didn't touch me?"

Brandon nods. "I spoke to him today. He said you slumped to the floor as soon as he closed the door... Cody kicked it down a minute later."

"What? Why?"

"He went for a cigarette before you asked to play, and you weren't at the table when he came back. I told him you were with Alan, and he got pissed." A small smirk curves his lips. "I've seen Cody lose it a few times, and last night was easily top five. Alan's got a broken nose and two black eyes to prove it."

"He *hit* him?" I gasp, covering my mouth with a trembling hand. "No way."

"He didn't just hit him, Blair. He made a fucking punching bag out of his face. Colt stopped him before it got too ugly."

My head spins. Cody coming to my rescue doesn't make sense. He hates me. He could've left me there so I'd get exactly what I deserved, but... he didn't.

The idea of him caring, even in the slightest, is comforting and unsettling in equal measure.

"He scooped you off the floor, and when I said you're staying with me, he was squared up to break my jaw too."

I narrow my eyes as he mindlessly spears the food on his plate. "What's on your mind?" I ask, sensing something heavy hanging unspoken in the air.

"Nothing, just..." He trails off, his gaze flickering from me to the doorway. "Is there anything you want to tell me? You know I won't judge."

I don't like the look on his face. "About what?"

He pushes his plate aside to lean forward. "You and Cody, what else would I mean? I was drunk last night, but not fucking blind, Blair. I saw how you squirmed whenever he looked at you. What's the deal?"

My fork freezes midway to my mouth. "There is no deal. He's barely said three sentences to me since I moved in." That's not entirely true, but I won't tell Brandon about that night with River. It feels personal. A small secret between us. "Even if I was squirming, it takes two to tango, and you know damn well Cody wouldn't touch me with a ten-foot pole."

"That's just it... I was drunk, sure, but I know what I saw. Every time I looked at Cody, his eyes were fixed on you. Every single time, Blair."

The room feels suffocating as if the walls are closing in. My mind races with the memory of Cody's dark eyes tracing my every move and dropping to my mouth time and time again. I thought I imagined it last night, but if Brandon saw it...

No. It can't be. And even if it was, we were both drunk.

It doesn't mean anything.

Brandon carries on talking about what happened last night, mentioning Colt and Rose, but my mind swirls around the same question: *why*?

Why did Cody care what happened to me? Why did he come to my rescue? Why did he bring me home? Why did he give me his hoodie?

The only person who can give me the answers is right across the hall, so when Brandon leaves two hours later, I pluck the courage to knock on his door.

"What did he tell you?" Cody demands after opening the door, his eyes scanning my face for something.

Annoyance, maybe.

He's not moving. His towering frame barricades the entrance. "Let me rephrase that. How pissed off are you with him?"

"Why would I be? It wasn't his fault. I asked him to let me play again."

He furrows his brow. "No way you remember that."

"Doesn't make it any less true. Brandon doesn't lie to me, Cody." I meet his eyes, my stomach somersaulting when Brandon's words come back.

He made a fucking punching bag out of his face.

"I have a question..." I take a deep breath, steeling myself for the next words. "Why did you help me?"

His eyes narrow, scrutinizing my face for a second. "What do you mean *why*? You'd rather I left you there?"

"No, of course not," I stammer, feeling stupid. "I'm grateful, but I don't understand. You hate me, Cody." I pause, waiting, but he doesn't speak, leaving the ball in my court. "I came to say thank you, so... thank you."

Since he doesn't say anything back I make to leave. The embarrassing silence is all the invitation I need. But then he speaks again, his voice low and measured. "There needs to be balance in the world. We can't all be vile."

That stings. Hell, it hurts. The quick, purposeful once-over he gives me speaks volumes: he doesn't mean Alan. He means me. I'm vile.

And he's not wrong.

I don't know what to say and can't understand why he helped me last night. He hates me so much I can taste it in the air. I have no idea what to say, so with a nod, I turn to leave, but he grabs my arm, his grip tight, stopping me in place, the touch of his skin firing electric shocks through my nerve endings.

"It wasn't *your* fault," he says, his voice low, firm, and shaking with anger. "Brandon should've never let you go with Alan."

There's so much conviction in his tone I almost let myself believe he means every word.

"I should've stayed home in the first place, so yes, it is my fault." I gently shrug him off, despite craving him closer than I already have him. "I don't understand why you helped me."

"Are you fucking kidding me? You think hating you means I'd let some fucker hurt you?"

I don't see why he wouldn't. An eye for an eye.

"I deserved it, so—"

His hand grips my jaw so fast I yelp when he backs me against the opposite wall, towering above me. "Don't ever say or even think you deserve to be raped just because you were a bitch your whole life," he seethes, tone layered with a hint of darkness. "No one deserves that."

He looks dangerous. Like he's on the verge of lashing out, and I'm the first thing within reach, but there's a softness in his eyes telling me he'd never hurt me.

My eyes prickle under the intensity of his gaze. With one look, he dismantles my defense wall, and I'm coming apart at the seams. My heart pounds and my mind unleashes its deepest locked-away fantasies, heading straight for the gutter. How would it feel to be at his mercy? Naked in his bed. Ready and begging for his touch. Would he be rough or gentle? Would he take control or let me lead?

I bite my lip, heat rising to my cheeks. He notices my reaction. His eyes darken, sending a delicious shudder to my core. He loosens his hand on my chin, and his thumb traces a slow path along my jawline, making me melt under his touch.

"You're letting it define you," he says, his voice low and gravelly. "You're letting your mistakes define you, B. Use them to guide you."

I nod, trying to focus on his words, but all I can think about is how I want him to keep touching me, to explore my body with those rough hands. The chemistry crackles in the air, but he'd never cross that line, no matter how palpable our desire.

A single tear rolls down my cheek, and his eyes follow the movement. "I'm sorry," I whisper. "I—"

"You've apologized a million times already." He throws my words right back at me, his tone no longer soft or consoling but annoyed. "Stop apologizing. Start noticing the lessons and learn."

He lets me go. Pushing away from the wall, he leaves me alone, breathless, and wanting more.

When I find enough strength to make it back into my condo, there's a message waiting on my phone. One I desperately didn't want to receive.

Dad: Early dinner on Friday. New client. Be ready at four. Two braids, no makeup, red Mugler dress.

And just like that, I know it won't be like lunch with Mr. Anderson. His calm demeanor, steady voice, and respectful distance were a far cry from what I'll face on Friday. Mr. Anderson was polite. Didn't touch me. He was perfectly content talking about art, politics, and every other subject my father ensures I keep up to date with.

This time, I won't be so lucky. After years of this, I can judge who I'll be conquering based on my father's instructions. Whoever his newest client (read: victim) is, he enjoys young women. Too young.

Illegal, hence two braids, no makeup, and the corset-styled red mini dress. It's modest at first sight, but the semi-sheer panels and deep scoop neck make it very inappropriate, even for a woman with my cleavage. My small boobs look twice the size and almost bounce out with every step.

With a deep sigh, I text him back, before he has a fit.

Me: Of course.

ELEVEN

Cody

I can't shake Sunday out of my head.

Almost a week of replaying the look that crossed Blair's pretty face when I pinned her against the wall. The surprise and twinge of arousal in her deep blue eyes. The softness of her skin. How fucking sad she was and how quickly that sadness melted away under my touch.

And damn... she looked so fucking good in my hoodie. So damn sexy with her makeup smudged, hair disheveled, big eyes bright.

I shake off that thought. Girls always look super hot in their boyfriend's clothes. Nothing extraordi—

A sudden onset of migraine splits my head in two. *Boyfriend?* Fuck. That's not how I meant it. She just looked good in my hoodie. End of story. Period. Comma. What-fucking-ever.

The black, soft fabric swished around her thighs, hiding enough skin it could pass for a dress. A far more modest dress than the one she had on underneath... yes. Good thinking. *That's* why I couldn't stand the thought of Blair stripping off my hoodie. Because I'm a gentleman and didn't want her flashing her firm butt at Brandon.

God, I'm so full of shit.

I know I'm toeing a line I cannot cross. I imagine things that should never enter my mind, but the more I fight the visuals, the more frequent they become. All because of that night when she came over to help with River. I saw a different side to Blair that night, and got a few more glimpses during the graduation party.

The uncertainty as she watched me, realizing my watch was in her small hand. The gratitude when instead of pouring her a full shot, I poured half.

I can't stop thinking about how she felt, curled in my arms, when I carried her out of Brandon's house. How my temper raged out of control knowing Alan had her alone in the closet.

Someone's hands on her body shouldn't bother me, but the mere idea of anyone touching her has me running around in fucking circles.

Sweat trickles down my temples, stinging my eyes as I sprint up the stairs, heart galloping in my chest. Every muscle in my body screams in agony, protesting the grueling day of construction work. Last summer's gig under Logan's watchful eye was a cakewalk compared to what I got myself into now.

I thought managing a team would be easier since I'd have hands on deck for heavy lifting while I delegate tasks.

Yeah... it doesn't work like that.

Ninety percent of my team are newbies, clueless greenhorns with no idea what they're doing. Logan insists on making me work my way up the ladder, just like he did.

And I get it.

I've had enough handed to me on a silver platter, and my career is something I want to earn. But I never anticipated how challenging it'd be to train my team while trying to manage everything else.

I have skilled workers specializing in plastering, tiling, and bricklaying, but they're not there to handle the grunt work. That's the young guys' job and most of them are either college dropouts or fresh out of high school.

As they grapple with the ins and outs of construction work, I hold their hands at every turn. I work my ass off, teaching as I go. Three months of hard work with Logan and three years of construction management classes in college are finally paying off.

I may be young but I can teach these guys a thing or two.

Once they get the hang of things, it'll get easier. But for now, I'm drenched in sweat, covered in dirt, and every inch of my body aches. A bath and a few cold beers have been calling my name for three hours now.

With that goal in mind, I climb the last flight of stairs to my condo. As soon as I emerge in the corridor, I stride with purpose, key in hand.

And I'm gritting my teeth, pushing down the sudden prickle of annoyance.

There she is again, like a bad smell that won't dissipate. The queen of all things wicked, standing in the way of my peace of mind. I constantly remind myself that I hate her.

I do. I really do, but I'm also dying to touch her again.

Dying to see how she'd react.

That's wrong for so many different reasons.

We've exchanged a few casual *hey*s in passing since the party, but nothing more than that. Any interaction beyond *hey* would be a mistake.

Still, I wait for her to acknowledge me. An unyielding tightness grips my throat, irritation mounting.

I'm losing sight of what's right. I shouldn't even talk to her, so why does the lack of that fucking *hey* drive me up the wall?

Why isn't she saying it? Have I done something to annoy her? is she pissed off? Does she expect me to take the lead?

I can't decipher her thoughts, and the uncertainty gnaws like a woodworm on the papermill of my mind.

I won't say *hey* first. No way.

I fucking won't.

We're not friends. We're not even friendly. I hate her.

With that little reminder, I open my condo just as Blair's keys jingle to the ground. Turning to close the door, I find her kneeling on the carpeted floor, shoulders sagged, a tiny shudder shaking her frame.

My own shoulders square back, tension knotting my guts.

I think she's—

A whimper slips from her lips, confirming what I already know. The thought of tears streaming down her face sets my nerves on edge. Her nails are white as she grips the keys, trying not to drop them again, fighting to keep herself composed, her hands trembling.

An icy shudder sweeps across my skin: goosebumps. My eyes narrow, lips fall apart, but... words don't come. What the hell would I say?

Are you okay?

She's clearly not, and I don't give a fuck why. I really don't. Honest to God. I *don't.*

If that were true, though, I wouldn't still be here, hand on the handle, door ajar.

She finally finds the right key and gathers herself off the floor. The red dress she wears is as inappropriate as Blair herself. Combing her long dark-brown, almost auburn hair behind her ears, she inhales deeply, pushing the key into the lock, her movements slow and deliberate.

"Show's over," she half whispers, half chokes, and the defeat coating her words ices my blood. "Goodnight."

Without a backward glance, she disappears inside and slams the door shut, the *bang* knocking me out of my trance. I shut my own door, ignoring a twinge of guilt.

Maybe I should've said something. Maybe I should've asked if she needed help.

Or maybe you should see a shrink.

Maybe I should. Looks like I'm losing the plot here.

Let her cry. She deserves whatever caused her tears.

I fucking *hate* that girl.

Tossing my keys into a ball on the narrow side table—something I've copied from Nico's house—I shimmy out of my jacket, hanging it in the coat closet.

The temperature outside hit eighty degrees today, so not jacket-wearing weather, but the early morning rain had me jogging back to grab one as I headed to the site.

I'm not usually one to take a bath, but my muscles burn so badly a quick soak will do me good. I grab a beer, set up my laptop for the Formula One pre-practice show, and get into a tub full of hot water.

Too bad that not even the bliss of cold beer sliding down my throat as my muscles relax can stop my mind drifting to Blair's tearful voice.

TWELVE

Cody

Muffled yells seep into my otherwise peaceful condo while I spread out on the couch, watching the Singapore Grand Prix practice session, my hair damp as I text back and forth with Mia.

Her favorite driver hit the wall at the third turn... she's not pleased with my comments.

I sit up, eyeing my door as if that'll let me hear better, but I can't make out any more sounds.

Bug: That was unfair! Your guy pushed him off the track. If this was the race, he'd get a five-second penalty.

Me: He left him enough room.

Another sound reaches my ears, and I sit up again. It's hard to make out, but someone's definitely shouting. A man judging by the baritone. The words are muffled, nothing but gibberish hitting my ears. It's clear where they're coming from, though—Blair's condo.

I mute the TV, trying to hear better.

"Get out! Get out now!" Blair wails loud enough to carry through the walls.

And *bang*! Something heavy hits the ground. Glass shatters. Then again, and again, and my heartrate soars.

I dash to the entryway as the noises intensify. Through the peephole, I spot a man in a suit standing in Blair's doorway.

"Enough!" he barks, the word laced with brutal disdain. "You're acting like a fucking child, and that won't fly with me. You should know better by now. I'll pick you up tomorrow at eight. Wear what I gave you, and fucking behave. Tonight was unacceptable." He slams the door, marching down the hallway, shoulders squared, fists clenched.

Without thinking, I yank my door open. The guy turns, his eyebrows furrowing.

"What the hell's going on?" I ask.

He shoots me a scowl, his lips meshed into a hard line until his eyes spark with recognition. He reins in his temper, face turning neutral faster than I can blink. "This doesn't concern you, Mr. Hayes."

So he knows who I am. Of course he does. Fucking perfect. It'd be great if I knew who *he* is. He looks young. Thirty, maybe thirty-five, and vaguely familiar, but I can't place him.

"I think it does concern me, considering I live next door."

"My apologies for disturbing your night," he drawls, weighing every word like a British aristocrat but without the accent. "It was a genuine misunderstanding. Please give my best to your brother."

Which brother? dances on the tip of my tongue. I have six, and they each have about six million friends. It's not easy to guess who he means, but a quick appraisal of his bespoke suit hints that this guy has more money than common sense, which suggests he's friends with Nico. That would explain why he looks familiar. I must've seen him with my brother somewhere.

Not waiting for anything else on my part, he bobs his head once in a respectful gesture and stalks away, disappearing behind the corner.

I stand there, wondering whether I should check on Blair. There was something in her voice... a sense of despair that's hard to ignore no matter how much I want not to give a shit.

Seems I'll always give a shit if a woman's hurting.

You'll regret this, I think as I take four steps and stop before her door, quietly knocking three times.

Nothing.

Complete, utter stillness. Not one sound from inside, even though I know she's there. Gritting my teeth, I knock again, my knuckles barely tapping the wood.

Nothing.

She probably doesn't want to talk, but at least I fucking tried not to be an asshole. With a clear conscience, I turn back toward my condo when her door creeps open.

Anger simmers in my chest as I take her in. The tears streaming down her cheeks are like an invisible hand gripping my throat.

She's bleeding. Crying. Choking. A helpless, barefoot mess dressed in red. She's not wearing a bra. The almost see-through fabric of her dress is so thin I can make out the exact shape of her areolas. She covers herself up as best she can using both arms, but all it does is add to her vulnerability.

Her complexion matches that hooker-styled dress, cheeks

glowing either from anger or the effort it took to smash half her glassware. A used-to-be-white, now soaked, crimson rag is wrapped around her left hand. Blood marks her cheek, neck, forehead...

More seeps from two small cuts on her knee, oozing onto the marble floor littered with shards of glass.

She's barefoot, for fuck's sake. One false move and she'll slash her small foot wide open.

"This isn't a good time." She swats her tears away, lifting her chin a little higher to come across composed.

It's not working. She looks so fragile I think she'll crumble to that deadly floor if I look the other way.

I've never seen her like this. Bitchy attitude and superior aura stripped away to reveal her raw form. I've known this girl for almost twenty years, yet I've *never* seen her so human.

So fucking real.

She cries. She bleeds. She's sad.

Not a trace of the confidence she usually projects. Instead, she's like a porcelain doll tipping over the edge of the shelf.

She needs someone to catch her before she shatters alongside all that glass.

For the first time, I see *her*, not the spoilt, arrogant side she meticulously nurtures around people. The one she blatantly showcased at the graduation party.

Faint freckles pepper her small nose, not a trace of them across her rosy cheeks. I didn't know she had freckles. She hid them under a heap of concealer for years. And why?

They're fucking beautiful.

My heart pounds like a jackhammer. I want to wipe away her tears, hold her close and make everything okay. The anger that burned my stomach earlier is replaced with what feels dangerously close to protectiveness.

Fresh tears brim in those deep, dark blue eyes staring at me, a whole angry ocean of truths and secrets begging to be uncovered behind them. She's mindlessly chewing her swollen, raspberry-pink lip, and I'm glued to the spot, my racing thoughts like F1 cars when the lights blink out.

Blair swats another tear away.

A Sisyphean task... more spill, trailing down her chin.

"Can you go?" she pleads, wrestling to keep it together, as she wipes her nose with the back of her injured hand.

Her voice cracks, hitting me in the chest like a battering ram, shattering my resolve to leave her here alone.

I should. This is none of my business. Whatever upset her, whatever happened, whoever that asshole was... *not* my business.

If anything, I should be elated she's a snotty, hurt mess, getting a taste of what she did to Mia.

But elation is nowhere in sight. I'm filled with unease, my insides tying in knots because... I can't stand seeing a woman hurting this way.

"I'm watching the Spanish GP practice," I blurt out, giving her a seemingly innocent reason to come with me. *Let's watch TV, my hurt, sworn enemy.* I could ask if she wants to Netflix and chill and it'd be just as fucking bad. "You like F1?"

Who the hell am I?

A tense, silent moment passes. She scrutinizes my face, waiting. I don't know what she's waiting for. Laughter? Some trickery on my part?

Maybe. Probably...

"I like Spain," she whispers, inhaling a shaky breath.

"That'll do."

I should head straight back to my condo alone, but—knowing damn well it's a bad idea—I step forward, cuff my fingers around her arm, and take her with me.

I don't know what's happening, but touching her now feels different. It's charged with a different kind of energy.

The rag wrapped around her hand is soaked with blood, little red dots splashing against my tiles, carpet, and hardwood floor as I drag her behind me without a word.

She needs a proper dressing. I have no idea where her first aid kit is, so it's easier to take her back to my place.

Rationalizing won't help you, man.

I'm aware. Hyperaware that I've been rationalizing around her since day one, but so far, I'm failing miserably at hate.

"Sit," I say, pointing at the couch once I've closed the door behind us. I grab a hoodie from my wardrobe, handing it over, knowing damn well it's the second one I've given her within two weeks. "You want a drink? I've got wine, beer—"

"I could do with something stronger," she admits quietly, pushing her arms into the sleeves.

The only stronger alcohol I have is half a bottle of gin Vivienne left here after our post-unpacking impromptu housewarming party.

I whip up a gin and tonic and grab the first aid box.

"You don't have to do this," Blair says when I hand her the glass, taking a seat beside her.

"I know." I wish I didn't feel the compelling need to help, but there's no stopping as I perch a cushion on my knees, place her hand on it and carefully unwrap the rag, dropping it onto the coffee table. "You've not cleaned it," I say, spotting a few shards glistening in the long cuts. "Drink."

She does. As she takes the first sip, I grab tweezers and pluck the glass, my stomach churning every time she hisses.

I hate her. I know I do, but I'm not the kind to get a kick out of knowing she's in pain.

"Crystal glass?" I ask, dabbing the excess blood so I can see what I'm doing.

"Among other things."

I pull out the last piece, the longest of the four spread on the coffee table, then grab a washcloth, cleaning around the cuts as best I can. It doesn't look like she needs stitches, so the wound-closing strips I have should work fine, as long as we stop the bleeding, otherwise they won't stick.

"Bottoms up, B," I order, fetching a wooden spoon.

"Why?"

"You'll need all the anesthetic you can get. Drink."

Once she downs the last of her gin and tonic, cringing and shaking off the alcohol kick, I give her the spoon.

"I need to put pressure on the cuts to stop the bleeding. It'll hurt like a motherfucker for a moment, so bite down hard."

She sticks the handle in her mouth, sinking her white teeth into the wood, and nods once, her eyes closing.

A quiet whimper is the only sound she makes, but it's enough to chill the blood in my veins as I press a fresh gauze to the cuts, not daring to look up in case more tears stream down her cheeks.

I count down from one hundred before peeking under the gauze to check. "That should do it."

She spits out the spoon, placing it on the coffee table, the handle bearing her toothmarks and my mind goes straight to imagining those marks on my shoulders.

"How do you know this?" she asks.

"What? First aid? Six brothers, four nephews, and..." I push a long breath down my nose. "Mia. She has a clotting deficiency, so stopping the bleeding is a priority whenever she cuts herself. You learn a lot when you've got no other choice."

Tucking a few loose strands of hair over her ear, she gently touches her hand to mine as it wipes the dried blood from her other one. "Thank you."

"I'm not done yet. I'll get you another drink and you need a proper dressing."

Something in her eyes tells me she'll argue, but it dissipates with a resigned nod. I grab a bottle of Corona from the fridge, then make her a double gin and tonic.

"Who's your favorite?" Blair asks, eyes on the TV after she accepts the glass.

"Ferrari, of course." I unmute it, listening to the reporter say the first session has just resumed after a half-hour break thanks to Mia's driver hitting the wall. "You know anything about the races?"

"I've watched a few with Brandon. He got into it when he found out Mia's dad is a team principal."

"Don't," I warn. Fierce protectiveness detonates my every cell, forcing my mind into high-alert mode. "Don't talk about her."

Blair immediately shrinks in on herself, her hand shaking in mine as I close the longest cuts. "I'm sorry."

The atmosphere shifts to uncomfortable. I want her gone as soon as physically possible. She shouldn't fucking be here.

I grab a bandage, wrap her hand, secure it in place, then clear the table, strutting over to the sink.

The reporter on TV mentions another red flag, and this time my favorite driver's name falls from his lips. I turn to watch the replay, chuckling when my phone pings on the breakfast bar, a message from Mia.

Bug: Karma. Works fast today, don't you think?

Me: It would be a ten-second penalty in race conditions.

Bug: Why? He left him PLENTY of room.

I flick to the Hayes group chat.

It's no longer strictly for me and my brothers. Rose joined, and after complaining about the sausage fest, we added the girls, too, and then Colt created another chat titled exactly what Rose complained about—*Sausage Fest*—so we could give each other shit without the girls knowing.

Me: Who's at fault?

Colt: Your guy.

Nico: Your guy or I'm not getting any tonight.

Mia: See? Told you.

Rose: I don't know what this is about, but Mia's right.

Me: You little traitor. Wait till you need a place to crash.

Rose: Shit. Fine, I'm Switzerland. Sorry, Mia.

Conor: Your guy, bro. He cut in and paid the price.

Me: Fine. Gangbang me, why don't you?

A sea of laughing emojis follows, making me smirk, tossing the phone aside before shoving the first aid box back in the cupboard. Blair hasn't said a word for five minutes. In fact, she's made no sound at all, so I know she's still here. I would've heard her leave however stealthy she was.

"You want another—" I start out of sheer stupid politeness, then cut myself off when I look over my shoulder.

She's asleep, her head resting where the back of the couch meets in the corner, hair obscuring half of her face, the empty glass about ready to slip from her grasp to the floor.

No fucking way.

No way she's staying here.

I lean out to touch her, shake her by the shoulder to wake her, but I stop short of her soft skin. She's exhausted. Dark circles under her eyes, ashen cheeks, and a pained expression betray she's battling nightmares.

The lone lock of hair on her cheek dares me to brush it away. My fingers linger in the air, and just as I'm about to pull back, I change my mind. My heart batters my ribs when I gently guide the thick, silky tangle behind her ear, my thumb grazing her soft, clammy skin.

I yank my hand back like she's a live wire. The tips of my fingers tingle as I blink at her sleeping face.

It's nothing. I'm just not used to seeing her so... helpless.

Life would be easier if I were born a self-centered dick. It would be a handy quality tonight. Instead of fighting an internal battle over waking her, I'd just throw her out.

She probably wouldn't be here because I wouldn't have cared enough to check who was shouting earlier.

But I'm not a self-centered asshole, and I don't shake her awake. No, I shoot myself in the foot, grabbing a blanket from the back of the couch and draping it over her small frame. It's just for a few minutes. She can sleep while I cross the hall and open all the doors so I can easily carry her to bed.

Her doorhandle gives way, letting me into the kitchen where the lights are on. Glass litters the floor, stained by drops of blood marking the route to the sink. I can walk around it to get Blair into her bedroom, but... what if she wakes up, tiptoes over for a glass of water, and steps on the broken glass?

"I should've been an asshole," I mutter as I grab the broom, sweeping the floor. "I bet it's so much easier not to give a shit," I add when I'm on my fucking knees with a wet rag, wiping the blood, then cleaning around the sink before triple-checking I've not missed anything. I open the door to her bedroom and go back to my place, ready to scoop Blair off the couch, but...

I halt *again*.

She changed positions, no longer half-sitting. She's curled right into the corner of the sofa, her head resting on the cushion, the blanket covering everything south of her nose.

For a moment, I stare at her, weighing my options, my temper flaring again. She shouldn't be here. She shouldn't look so fucking vulnerable, chipping away the hatred I've felt for years.

With a long, defeated huff, I head back to her place, lock up, and then lock myself inside my condo with a girl who's so toxic she'd put arsenic to shame.

I stand in the living room, my feet refusing to move because... I can't go in my bedroom and leave her sleeping so close to the door.

If anyone breaks in, she's alone.

I know she lives by herself, and I definitely know she can handle shit, but I physically *can't* leave her sleeping on the couch unattended. It goes against my every instinct. No matter how insane she drives me, she's under *my* roof and under *my* care.

"You stupid prick," I whisper, squeezing my neck.

I strip my mattress off the bed, drag it to the living room, then move the coffee table to push the mattress flush with the couch, quiet as I can.

You're going to heaven, for fucking sure.

I better be, or I'm going to be pissed.

For another ten minutes, I get ready for bed, silently walking back and forth between my bedroom, the living room, and the bathroom. I doubt I'll get one minute of sleep with Blair under my roof, but it's not like I have better things to do.

With nothing left to keep me stalling, I crawl under the comforter, crossing my hands under my head, and stare at the ceiling, mentally calling myself every name under the sun.

How did I get into this situation? Why was I born with this fucked-up moral compass? Why can't I just kick her out?

I've got no answers, but the questions keep coming until my mind finally drifts off.

It feels like five minutes later, my eyes pop open, a heavy weight settling in my gut. A sense of unease washes over me, but I don't immediately realize why my insides roil like a stormy sky. The room is dark and seemingly silent until a stifled sob pierces my ears. Sniffling breaths follow quickly, each punctuated by a shake and the sound of a sleeve wiping tears.

Blair's back is to me, her body curled in a ball, one hand pressed to her head, fingers tangling her long locks, digging into her scalp as if trying to hold herself together.

I've not shut the blinds earlier. The glow of the streetlamps pours inside, illuminating the living room enough to make out how she trembles under the dusty-blue blanket.

She draws in a long, shaky breath, her other hand shifting. Even though I can't see her face, the soft sounds she makes paint a vivid picture: she's biting her fist to muffle her cries.

The effort she puts into staying quiet is fucking palpable, her body taut with tension as she fights to hold back sobs that threaten to break free.

I don't give my rational thoughts a moment. I don't stop to remember *who* this girl crying on my couch is or what she's done over the years to the girl I've considered family since the first day I spoke to her.

Regardless how much I hate Blair, I can't lay here pretending I don't hear how much she's hurting.

I sit up, lean over her, and coil one arm around her middle. She jumps at my touch, her breathing hitching in surprise, cries temporarily halting while I slide her off the couch and onto the mattress beside me.

She's flat on her back for a moment, staring at me with wide, tear-filled, fearful eyes, not one word out of her mouth.

I don't speak, either. I doubt she'd tell me what nightmares plague her mind, and I know words won't ease her pain. She doesn't need me to listen.

Lifting the comforter, I pull her closer, slipping an arm around her before I tuck us in.

It's not enough.

I guide her right hand over my chest, a surprisingly steady rhythm under her fingertips.

Slowly, almost like she expects to be pushed away, she curves into me, burrowing her face into my neck. She grasps a handful of my t-shirt before fresh tears leave a damp trail on my skin.

I don't know *how* I know this. Whether it's from her shudders changing tune from desperation to cautious relief, her muscles relaxing despite the tears, or if I have some sixth sense about me, but I know she was never held like this.

No one ever offered her comfort just for the sake of it. Just to help her cage her demons. No one gave her a shoulder to cry on without a hidden agenda, always expecting something in return.

It's obvious in the way she clings to me, full of caution and surprise, like she can't believe this is happening.

Me neither... for so many different reasons I don't know which matters most. She shouldn't fit this well pressed against me. She shouldn't make my chest inflate as she relaxes, her body no longer wound up tight. She shouldn't fucking be here.

The thought has my arms unconsciously tightening around her frail body. I don't want her here. I can't stand her ninety-nine percent of the time, but the thought of letting her go drops something heavy in my chest.

Minutes go by before I realize my fingers are brushing her soft hair up and down. The longer I do this, the more her body lets go of the tension it's been holding.

Her breaths even out. Her frantic grasp on my shirt turns into a gentle hold as if she's allowing herself to be vulnerable in my arms. Her tears slow while my mind repeats the same questions.

How long has she been hurting like this?

Who hurt her?

How many times has she cried herself to sleep?

I don't know. I'll never know, but for now, I hold her a little tighter, offering a safe haven from whatever plagues her mind, but it's not until dawn that she finally falls asleep.

THIRTEEN

Blair

The first thought that filters through my sleep-hazed mind isn't my predicament. It's how warm Cody feels with his big arms cradling me close. I can't remember the last time someone held me like this.

I've been hugged, but those were quick, fleeting moments. Casual, friendly... nowhere near this intensity. His grip is almost possessive. *Protective*. Like he's drawn a circle around us, keeping out the rest of the world.

I've never been this close to him, and despite the voice in my head shouting that this is a terrible idea, I take a second to savor the moment. It's like I was custom-made to fit molded into his side, my nose brushing his neck, my head on the pillow. He's asleep, his chest rising and falling softly.

My fingers grasp his t-shirt above the calm thump-thump of his heartbeat, almost lulling me back to sleep.

But my memories of last night settle in, reminding me

why I'm here. The surreal bliss disintegrates, tainted by my father's words.

After Dad took over the conversation with his newest victim, I excused myself from the table and sat at the bar for a while, letting them talk. Then, feigning a migraine in front of Dad's bodyguard, I left.

I didn't think I needed permission. Dad never calls me back into action once he's talking business.

Unfortunately, Mr. Simons is not as easily outmaneuvered as my father hoped. After the initial business chat, he told Dad he'd think about his proposal, then went to find me, eager to finish our *conversation*.

The way my father said *conversation* painted the picture—he knew Mr. Simons couldn't care less about small talk.

I shut my eyes, blocking the humiliation.

My father, instead of protecting me from harm, wants me to spend today on the yacht of an older man who he knows tried to slide his fingers up my skirt during dessert. I feel sick at the thought.

Granted, Dad said he'll join us, but that won't help me.

He won't help me if Mr. Simons decides he'd like to show me the lower level or his private suite. My father won't disagree. He'll pretend he doesn't realize Mr. Simons' ill intentions.

A stiffness fills my chest, and I stop breathing, pushing down the oncoming tears. There's no point in crying. I have no choice in the matter, and thinking about what lies ahead won't help. I need to suck it up. Bide my time. It's just one more year.

I've been through worse than this. As long as I don't fight, it won't be as bad as three years ago.

Cody's wristwatch tells me I have less than two hours to prepare. While I'd much rather stay here, safely cocooned in his big, warm arms, I know my father will lose his mind if I'm not ready and waiting.

Moving one inch at a time so I don't wake him, I sneak out of Cody's makeshift bed, and the second I pull myself away I miss the protective bubble. The addictive illusion of safety... as if nothing could touch me as long as he's with me. As if nothing could hurt me again.

He looks so peaceful with his eyes closed. A stark contrast to the disdain—aimed at me—that usually twists his features. I reach to touch him, brush my fingers across his stubble, or map out the contour of his lips, but I stop short, my fingers hovering inches from his skin.

He wouldn't want this.

Despite his kindness, he still hates me, and that thought pushes me to get moving. I'm too afraid to face him when he wakes up full of regret for letting me stay. For comforting me while I cried.

Quietly, I grab my keys from the coffee table and leave, heading across the hallway.

After a quick shower, I shimmy back into Cody's hoodie and decide that pretending nothing happened is not the route I want to take.

He deserves a *thank you* at the very least, so I whip up a quick batch of madeleines and make breakfast. I know he hits the gym daily. His body is a sight to behold, toned to perfection, so he must be on a healthy, protein-packed diet.

With that in mind, I opt for avocado and cherry tomatoes on toast and a strawberry and yogurt milkshake.

I fill a small tray, adding a few warm madeleines, and take it to Cody's condo, certain he's still asleep.

But he's not. The second the door opens, I stand face to

face with his broad, muscular chest, damp hair, and sweat-pants. He's on the couch, cup of coffee in hand, the makeshift bed nowhere in sight, and the living space neat and tidy.

His eyes snap to me over the rim of his cup, one brow slowly arching upward and knocking me out of the stunned silence. "Morning," I say, taking a few steps in before nudging the door shut. "I'm sorry I didn't knock. I thought you'd still be asleep."

His gaze flicks over the breakfast tray, and my face, before he examines his hoodie and my bare feet.

A blush creeps onto my cheeks, but I don't backtrack. I head straight for him and set the tray on the coffee table, aware of the silence ramping up the tension in the air.

His quiet intensity makes me squeamish, his usually expressive face now unreadable. I can't tell what he's thinking. He doesn't look disappointed, but he doesn't look pleased either.

"Thank you for last night," I say, twining my fingers in front of me. "And I'm sorry about this," I add, tugging the hem of his hoodie. "I shouldn't—"

"How are you feeling?" he interrupts. His concerned tone a big contrast to his emotionless expression.

"I'm fine."

"Fine..." he repeats, testing the word.

I'm a far cry from *fine*. Not only because of the day I'm facing, not only because my life is an absolute mess, but also because I spent the night cuddled into Cody, which awakened emotions I have no right to feel.

Things were easier when he acted like I was invisible. At least then, I didn't know how safe he could make me feel.

"You want to talk?" he asks, his gaze unyielding as he stares me down. "Believe me, with six brothers, there's nothing I haven't heard by now."

I very much doubt that.

"Who was that man last night?" he continues, throwing me off track.

He doesn't know my father? How is that possible? Nico is my dad's favorite person. The golden goose, as he calls him. He multiplies his money at an ungodly pace, and he might just be the one person my father respects.

I would've bet my right arm Cody knew him.

"I don't want to talk, but thank you for offering." Better he stays in the blissful land of ignorance. "I'll let myself out," I add when he remains silent.

And it hurts like a bitch when he doesn't stop me.

***

Mr. Simons stands on the deck, wearing a crisp white shirt and navy trousers. He greets us with a charming smile, kissing my hand lightly and turning to my father with a curt nod.

His eyes are back on me in a heartbeat, tracing my moves, roving my body, and latched onto my boobs with hungry intensity. A procession of ice-cold centipedes creeps up my spine, their frosty feet leaving chills in their wake, making me shudder, which Mr. Simons mistakes for a good sign, his blown pupils finally tearing themselves away from my chest to lock onto mine.

"Welcome aboard, Miss Fitzpatrick," he purrs once my father stalks toward the bar where a young man reaches for a tumbler. "It's a pleasure to have you here," he adds in a smooth baritone, then turns as a woman in nothing but a bikini approaches.

She looks much younger than him. Thirty, maybe not even that. Boobs, lips, cheeks, ass... all fake.

Must be one of his mistresses.

"This is my lovely wife, Annabelle." Mr. Simons gestures toward her with a fond smile.

It's good that I don't have a drink yet, or I'd choke. I didn't expect a man like him to be married. She's beautiful despite those fake lips. Blonde hair cascades down her back in soft waves, her body sculpted into a fantasy, skin beautifully kissed by the sun.

"It's a pleasure to meet you," I say, trying not to let my relieved sigh sound too obvious.

Surely, he won't try anything with his wife around...

It's not often that I actually get touched inappropriately. Most men are perfectly content to stare and make innuendos. Some invite me for a drink to show me off like a trophy, and some don't pay me any heed at all.

But...

There is always a *but.* Always an exception to the rule.

While most highly situated men my father uses to multiply his money wouldn't dare risk a scandal by feeling up a barely legal young woman, some don't have scruples. The richest, the billionaires... they consider themselves above the law. Above socially acceptable behaviors, etiquette, and manners.

Some try to cop a feel. Some try more than a hand on my knee or fingers brushing my nape.

And by the look of Mr. Simons, and all I read about his sketchy, full of sexual assault charges past, he is most certainly one of those men. Those who think a stuffed wallet means they're free to do whatever they want.

The saddest part is that it's true. They can do as they please. With influential friends and enough money for bribes, scum like Mr. Simons walk free despite multiple rape accusations. Every time one made it to court, the charges were dropped... probably because his entourage paid the women a lot of hush money.

Thankfully, I've been a part of my father's schemes for years, and I developed a few tricks to keep myself relatively safe.

We spend a couple of hours on the deck, enjoying breakfast. No inappropriate comments fly above the table. Nothing but polite conversation, but things take a turn when I excuse myself to use the restroom.

I don't hear Mr. Simons until his hand clasps my wrist and he shoves me against the wall of the narrow corridor.

Flashbacks creep up, flooding my mind with memories I buried long ago, and my breathing falters.

"I thought you were never going to stand up, sweet cheeks," he says, dipping his head into my neck, inhaling deeply, one hand moving to grip my waist, the other on my thigh. "You look spellbinding. I missed you last night... Where did you go?"

"Headache," I utter, clawing my way back from the abyss of dark memories, fighting to tether myself in the here and now, or I won't be able to protect myself.

"I can't stop thinking about you, and when I saw you today in this..." He trails one hand down between the valley of my barely there breasts, his voice low and husky as he whispers filth in my ear.

My skin crawls when his fat fingers slide up my thigh and he pushes two digits under the hem of my dress, audibly groaning.

"Fucking perfect," he rasps. "I can't wait to see all of you."

"Mr. Simons," I whisper, gently pressing my hands against his chest, blood whooshing in my ears. "Your wife could come down any moment. My *father is* here. We can't."

It takes a few lingering heartbeats for his horny mind to assess the risks before he grunts his disapproval, inching away enough to lick the shell of my ear.

"You're right," he huffs, yet in the next breath he oozes care, however artificial. "I wouldn't put you in that predicament. Nothing to upset my sweet little girl, but..." He leans back further, his lips hovering over mine, eyes searing through me. "Just one touch." His tongue peeps out, moistening his lips as he slides one finger up and down my pussy. "Let Daddy check how soft you are."

I'm drier than the Sahara, but his eyes flare as if he's found the fountain of youth between my legs.

If he calls himself *Daddy* again, I'll projectile vomit in his face, I swear. Considering everything my father does, how he used, abused, and neglected me my whole life, Daddy kink is the last thing I'd ever indulge in. It reminds me of everything bad that I've suffered at my father's hands.

Not a turn-on in the slightest when the word *Daddy* evokes memories of his fists ramming into my mother's stomach whenever she was delusional.

Footsteps echo around us, approaching fast, the distinct click of heels betraying it's his wife. I think someone's watching from above, saving me before this scum forces me to kick him in the balls.

Gideon Fitzpatrick would not be pleased if that happened. He'd confiscate my car, credit cards, and turn my life into a living hell for the foreseeable future, but I'd rather take that than let Mr. Simons fuck me against the wall of his luxurious yacht.

"Impeccable timing on that woman," he rasps, licking my ear. "Next time, sweetie, no one will interrupt us. I'm out of town for a few weeks, but I'll take you somewhere nice when I return. If you behave, we'll go shopping, and Daddy will treat you to a designer purse."

I can barely swallow the vomit threatening to spill from my mouth as he stamps a sloppy kiss on the corner of my lipstick-stained lips, then quickly retreats in the opposite direction from the approaching footsteps.

Dashing into the bathroom at the last moment, I lock myself in one of the stalls, my insides reeling.

I've wondered how my father finds these wealthy, powerful degenerates for years. Since he started using me as bait, I have *worked* twenty-nine men. All held some position of power in society: lawyers, bankers, detectives, politicians... rich, entitled, filthy perverts happy to feel up a young girl. Happy to blatantly flirt while their wives stand nearby.

What is it about money that makes those men feel superior? By this point, I'm fairly certain most of the daredevils grasping at me know my dad's game. They know he flaunts me in their faces, offering me like a sacrificial lamb, and they happily participate, taking whatever they deem fit.

Most are content with fleeting touches: a cheek rub here, a thigh squeeze there, an inappropriate comment thrown between the lines.

Eleven of the twenty-nine men I worked for my father had their hands on my thigh or boobs. Four touched the most intimate parts of my body. One stuck his dick inside me.

I was seventeen. Senior year in high school. A day much like today. Beautiful weather, a yacht, and a sixty-three-year-old businessman from Europe.

I don't know what deal my father struck with him. But I do know he sat on the deck while that scum gave me a tour. I was *underage*... I didn't expect how it ended. Not in my wildest dreams would I have thought the sick fucker would touch me without permission. I mean, my dad was right *there*... I felt safe, so I followed the man.

I've never felt safe in my dad's presence since.

The old fuck pressed me against the wall of the huge, elegant bathroom on the lower deck, covered my mouth with his hand, lifted my skirt, and punched my V card, not caring about the tears trailing down my face.

The longest three minutes of my life.

Once done, he adjusted his pants, threw me a towel, and strolled up the stairs as if nothing had happened.

Dad found me a moment later.

It's the only time in my life that he looked genuinely concerned. Mostly because he didn't realize I was a virgin, and the blood smeared over my thighs flipped his stomach. He gave me space after that. Almost four months without requesting my presence at those stupid banquets. He arranged my therapy and showered me with gifts in between making all kinds of threats, so I wouldn't rat out him or the European businessman.

I never went to therapy, and Dad didn't care enough to check. Instead of working through the trauma, like I should've done, I tried to bury the memory of that brute by sleeping around with college guys on *my* terms.

The one good thing that came out of that night was that I stopped bullying Mia. I'd always done it searching for a voice, wanting to be heard and seen because I was invisible in my own home. With a mother who was either hallucinating or heavily medicated and a father who did his utmost to avoid us, I was always on my own. Ignored, powerless... accused of horrid things by my sick mother since I turned five.

Making fun of Mia gave me an audience. People saw me. Listened to me... but when I was raped and stripped of control in the most brutal way, I realized that I'd inflicted exactly the thing I'd been running from my whole life on Mia.

Isolation. Humiliation. No power. No voice...

When my father summoned me to another meeting months later, I was much smarter. Much stronger. No longer a naïve teenage girl. Whenever anyone gets too close, or the situation looks like getting out of hand, I play them like my father plays me.

Turns out most of those men are somewhat decent. They take what I'm willing to give, but back off if I express concern.

Obviously, I have to be smart about it so they don't storm out or cut my father loose before he gets what he wants.

"Not here, Mr. [insert name here]."

"My father could walk out at any moment. This isn't safe."

"Your wife is one door away."

Excuse after excuse. So far, they work. I've been touched. Three men—four including Mr. Simons—have been bold enough to push their grubby fingers under my skirt and over my pussy, but other than the European pedophile, no one else raped me.

I've dealt with what happened. It didn't leave any lasting damage on my mind—probably because, half the time, I don't even believe it happened. After the therapy, I blocked it from my mind, but it took a long time before I had a healthy sexual relationship.

Once I can't hear any footsteps, I exit the stall, wash my hands, lips, and every part of my body Mr. Simons touched, then head back on deck. For the rest of the day, I stay in plain sight. I don't drink any more, so I won't have to use the restroom and risk Mr. Simons following me again.

But when my father drops me off at home, I feel dirty.

Violated.

I head straight for the shower, scrubbing myself clean until my skin turns pink.

FOURTEEN

Blair

Under strict instruction from my father, I enter the high-end suit store, feeling out of place.

The plush carpet cushions my steps as I walk further in, taking in the grandeur. The walls are lined with rows of neatly displayed suits in different shades and textures. Crystal chandeliers glitter from the ceiling, illuminating pristine white walls and highlighting the luxurious fabrics.

A heady mix of fresh linen, leather, and cologne assaults my olfactory nerves.

For the first time since my father "employed" me to flirt with people he's manipulating, I'm allowed to wear something other than red to a banquet he's planning.

No date has been set, but he barked over the phone this morning that I should be prepared. Instead of red, I'm supposed to wear white. I didn't question it because he's allowing me to choose the dress I'll wear.

"Don't get smart with me, Blair. You're choosing the dress, but if it's not like the others I bought you, you'll fucking regret it."

So the style still stands—short, slutty, but I can pick the right size and not sheer lace. That's a win, so I eagerly got in my car and drove to the mall.

Another thing I didn't question was his order to come here and buy him a crisp white tie. Heading straight for the correct rack, I stop, catching sight of familiar, broad shoulders and dark hair in a bun.

He's on the phone, flipping through the shirt rack. Three already hang from his pinkie—black, powder blue, and cream. I'm rooted to the spot, wondering what sick game karma is playing.

Is it not enough that we live across the hall from each other? Now I'm bumping into him outside our limited, gated community?

Taking a deep breath, I step aside, hiding behind a tall rack of suits, my stomach bottoming out. Knowing he'll be heading toward the changing rooms, I wait until he disappears before I scan the shelves for a white tie.

My gaze lands on a pale yellow tie, and I immediately wonder how it would look against Cody's tanned skin.

There's a shirt in the exact same color on the rack he was just at. God... why am I doing this to myself?

It's a stupid, *stupid* idea, but before I know it, my feet carry me toward the changing rooms, yellow shirt in hand.

The dusty-gray curtain of the one occupied room is drawn shut, and I hesitate. I shouldn't do this. I really shouldn't, but...

Inhaling and holding a sharp breath, I push the shirt through the tiny gap, heart in my throat.

Every time we meet, every time I see him, my crush grows

tenfold while he remains unaffected. Not entirely, sure. The way he looks at me sometimes is a dead giveaway that he finds me attractive, but he's not as affected as I am.

My body tingles, my mouth turns dry, and I'm a ball of nerves whenever his dark eyes meet mine.

"Try this one," I say, immediately regretting my decision to play personal shopping assistant to the man who weakens my knees. "For Logan's wedding," I add as a form of clarification because it's been three seconds of deafening silence, and I just stand here, gawking at the gray curtain, one hand in Cody's changing room.

I all but jump out of my skin when his warm, calloused hand wraps around my wrist. A surprised gasp escapes me as he pulls me into the cramped space.

He's wearing a pair of charcoal slacks I've not seen him pick out, the button and zipper undone, revealing his snow-white boxers. A cream shirt is draped over his back, his muscular chest inches from my face, scent assaulting my senses.

"Yellow?" he questions, still gripping my wrist.

I fight to maintain composure, but his proximity is almost unbearable. I can feel his breath on my face, and my knees melt. "It'll look good on you." He's too close, and yet not close enough. "Trust me."

"That's wishful thinking," he clips, but instead of telling me to leave, he shrugs off the cream shirt, tossing it aside, unfazed by my presence.

My eyes can't help but shamelessly rove the broad expanse of his chest while he's distracted by the yellow shirt. I should leave, give him privacy, but I'm rooted to the spot, and my thoughts drift to what it would feel like to run my fingers over his toned trapezoid muscles.

"You got somewhere to be?" he asks, a hint of amusement lacing his tone.

I snap from my daydream as he flings the shirt on, covering my new favorite view.

He studies himself in the mirror, ironing the fabric with big hands. "You're right. It looks good." Our eyes clash in the mirror. "So? Are you in a hurry?"

"Not really. I need to buy a dress, but that won't take long."

"You're looking for a dress in a suit shop?" A small smile plays at the corners of his mouth like he thinks I purposely followed him.

"No, I came in to buy a tie for my father."

He narrows his eyes but doesn't share his thoughts. "You don't usually shop alone. Where are your friends?"

"They're busy." I step closer, reaching up to adjust the collar of his shirt, my fingers brushing his warm skin. "What do you think?" I ask, undoing one button and smoothing out any creases, my hand pressing the fabric against his chest. "I think it suits you. You could wear it for the rehearsal dinner."

He considers my words for a moment before speaking. "I'll make you a deal. Since you know what will look good on me, you'll help me with everything I need for the wedding weekend, and in return, I'll judge which dresses you look good in."

My jaw almost hits the floor. He wants me to help? He's willing to spend time with me? It's a small step toward forgiveness, but it feels like a massive victory.

"Do you know what color dress your date's wearing?" I ask.

Cody's eyes meet mine in the mirror, a jolt of electricity idling between us. The small space suddenly feels too intimate, and I step back, walking into the gray fabric.

"No idea. I've not asked anyone yet. Why?"

"I thought you'd like your tie to match her dress."

"So I'll buy a tie when I find a date, and she chooses her dress. I need a white shirt for the wedding, any tie will do." He undoes the small buttons, and I can't help but watch as the fabric unfolds, revealing his bare chest.

"Okay. Wait here," I mumble, successfully tearing my eyes from his muscles writhing as he moves, the wetness between my legs growing increasingly uncomfortable.

Stumbling back, I leave, and five minutes later, I'm back with more shirts, suits, and slacks. I watch Cody try on the different clothes, admiring how perfectly they fit him.

"What do you need a dress for?" he asks, watching me in the mirror as he shrugs on the third shirt.

"My father's work do. He throws elegant banquets whenever he needs to butter someone up."

"So you need something elegant," he muses. "I know just the place. It's in Huntington Beach, so we'll take my car."

"Thank you, but I don't need help. I've got strict instructions on what to buy."

Damn it. Why is talking to him so effortless? My filter goes out the window, everything I usually hide now exposed.

"Your date decides what you'll wear?" he asks, his fingers fumbling with the shirt's buttons.

I step in to help. "My date?"

"I assume you're going with someone since you said you've got instructions on what to wear."

"Oh... no date. I'm on my father's arm."

His eyebrows bunch together for a second. "Why? Where's your mother?"

Grief spreads across my skin like a rash. It's been over a year, but I doubt my heart will ever stop feeling like it's snapping in two whenever I think about her.

"She's dead."

Regret casts a shadow over Cody's face for a moment of awkward silence before, "I'm sorry, I didn't know."

"Don't be sorry. It's better this way. I'm sure she's happier wherever she is than she was here." I try to keep my voice steady, but my eyes prick with tears.

Swallowing hard and diverting the conversation, I help Cody shimmy into a suit jacket. "Now *this* looks good," I praise with a forced smile.

"That it does. I think I've got everything I need. We'll grab a quick coffee, before I return the favor."

A quick coffee? Here? At the mall where anyone could see us sitting together? The idea of him willingly getting seen with me has the cogs in my head pinwheeling.

What the hell is he playing at?

"Like I said, I don't need help," I mutter, bailing on spending more time with him even though it almost kills me. "Thank you for offering."

"Who'll tell you if you look nice?"

"I'm not supposed to look nice. I'm supposed to look—" I stop myself in time, worrying my bottom lip.

"What are you supposed to look like, Blair?" he asks softly, brushing a strand of hair behind my ear.

My heart races at his touch, and I fight the urge to lean in. "It doesn't matter. I don't want you to come with me, okay?"

His determined gaze hitches my defenses back up. I said too much already. I need to leave before I give him too many clues. Cody's smart. Perceptive. I piqued his curiosity and he's not the type to drop the subject.

He stands before me in his shirt, jacket, and boxers, and I

know better than to let my eyes wander. I was very, *very* careful not to glance at his cock this whole time.

Ignoring his inquisitive stare, I take the opportunity to flee. He won't chase me without pants.

***

Five hours later, after buying the dress and spending three hours at the psychiatric ward, I'm back home.

Cody's car is parked in its usual spot, and knowing he's home makes me clutch the shopping bag with my whoreish white dress tighter, like he'll jump me, steal the bag, and check what I bought.

"Answer me!" I hear Ana scream as soon as I climb the last flight of stairs.

Cody's outside his condo, feet bare, back leaning against the wall, with Ana on her tippy toes slamming her open hand against his chest, her face bright red, hair in disarray.

"Is there someone else?! Are you cheating on me?!"

"I can't cheat on you," he huffs, squeezing the bridge of his nose. "We're not together. We were *never* together."

I'm frozen in my spot, unsure whether to go back down or hide in my condo.

"Don't say that. You don't mean it!"

Condo, I decide, taking a step forward. I halt again when Cody's eyes snap to mine.

"Shit," he breathes, his expression morphing to annoyance.

A cold shiver seizes my body, and I turn on my heel. He's obviously not happy I can hear their conversation. Maybe they need a few minutes of privacy, and even though I have every right to go into my own home, I'm retreating, so they can talk this out.

"Fuck... Baby, wait!" Cody calls after me, his tone loaded with something I don't understand. It sounds almost like he's afraid. A bit desperate. "Don't leave. I can explain."

I come to a complete stop, my eyes wide as saucers, I'm sure, and not just because he called me *baby.* Not just because his rushed footsteps approach but because my whole body tingles.

One word, but it's enough to knock me off my damn feet. I turn to Cody, stunned into silence by his determined gaze. My heart threatens to burst when he grips me by the waist, dips his head, and presses his lips to mine.

It's a peck. Nothing more. Just one hard, unyielding peck, but the softness of his mouth, and the warmth of his body against mine is enough to send a delicious shiver surging through my entire structure.

I tremble in his arms. Emotions accelerate the hot blood in my veins, overwhelming my senses as he pulls away, his deep brown eyes locking onto mine with a sort of diffident, tentative amazement.

"Jesus..." he whispers, lifting both hands to my face.

Just as it dawns on me that this kiss is a show for Ana, Cody's mouth is on mine again.

And it's not just a peck this time.

His fingers caress my cheeks as his lips claim mine before his hands slide down to lift me off the floor, hauling me into his arms with the avidity of a musician seizing the perfect melody. My legs have nowhere to go but around his waist. His hand clasps the back of my neck and I can't escape.

I don't want to escape. Not now, not ever.

There's so much power in his kiss. So much raw intensity in his touch as he slams me against the wall, one hand supporting my butt, the other tangled in my hair, pulling my head back to deepen the kiss, his whole body pressing into me.

I whimper, surrendering to his inaudible demands.

His hard cock juts against me and I arch into him, craving the contact. It's as if a switch flipped inside his head, removing any resolve he had left.

His hand moves from my neck to my back, then the side of my face, the kiss greedy, desperate... like he's trying to consume me, like he's imprinting himself on me, and I lose my goddamn mind. I'm powerless to resist.

A low hum starts inside me, growing louder with every flick of his tongue, and when he sinks his teeth in my bottom lip, pulling gently with a low groan, my body responds in kind, my hands fisting his hair as I kiss him back with equal fervor. I swear I'm seconds away from coming apart. Seconds from orgasm, and he's done nothing more than kiss me.

But as quickly as it all started, it ends.

Ana's teary voice breaks the moment, penetrating our bubble. "You're such an asshole." She storms past us, whacking Cody's back.

Her hastened footsteps retreat, and once she rounds the corner, my feet hit the floor.

Cody steps back, running a shaking hand down his face. The silence is deafening. I can't bring myself to look up to him, knowing what I'll see will hurt.

Pushing a long breath down his nose, he grabs my bags off the floor, handing them over. "I shouldn't have done that," he says. "I... I didn't think. It was an impulse. I ran out of ideas how—"

"It's okay," I cut in, calming myself as I push off the wall. "A favor for a favor, right? You helped me with Alan, I helped you with Ana. Hopefully, she got the message." Forcing my feet to move, I trot away, head down, hand in my purse, searching for keys. "Goodnight."

"Blair..."

"Goodnight, Cody."

FIFTEEN

Cody

She closes the door behind her, and I stumble into my condo.

What the fuck have I done?

The idea struck me like lightning, powerful and unshakable. I didn't plan on using Blair to send Ana a message, but I also didn't know what else could stop her obsessive stalking, short of calling Shawn for help.

And when Blair appeared just as Ana accused me of cheating, I took it as a sign. Fate showing me the way. *Maybe seeing me with someone else will stop her fixation?*

Deep down, Ana's a good person. She's just lost, struggling to find her way. As much as I'd like to help, she takes every kind word the wrong way. I'd rather hurt her feelings than mess with her future by filing a restraining order.

What I didn't expect was how quickly my dumb idea would backfire. I thought I could stamp a quick kiss on Blair's lips and get on with the show. *Baby, Ana was just leaving. Nothing happened,*

I swear. Please don't go, I'll explain everything... blah, blah, blah.

I took an acting class out of boredom in high school, so I knew I could pull this off, but the moment I kissed Blair, my entire body spasmed. One taste of her sweet mouth and I couldn't fight the urge to explore deeper.

The softness of her lips against mine, the smell of her perfume, the surprised little gasp she let out, and her delicate fingers tangling in my hair, reeling me in as if she needed me as much as I needed her...

Desire seared through me, and I snapped, sinking into her mouth like a fucking savage. Consumed by primal desire burning within me. The need to possess her, to feel her body beneath mine... Jesus *fuck*. My hands ached to touch every inch of her body. I couldn't get her close enough, so I hauled her into my arms and pressed her against the wall, almost fucking afraid she'd disappear.

The heat between us erupted like lava. I was drowning in her, my hands mapping every curve and dip of her body.

Visuals of the new Blair in those cute t-shirts and jeans, baking cookies and cuddling into my chest raced to the forefront of my mind. Mix that with my undeniable arousal, and hatred got lost in translation.

Thank fuck Ana was still there, snapping me out of the trance with a whack to the back, or I probably would've tried to fuck Blair against that wall.

Considering how eagerly her body responded to my touch when she kissed me back, I don't think she'd say *no*.

There's always been this electricity between us, sparking just below the surface. Hatred laced with lust, a potent combination I thought I buried long ago.

Turns out it was just laying dormant, biding its time. I

suppressed the desire, and it reared its head when I let my guard down.

Fuck!

The feel of her in my arms, ready, melting, willing... yep, I'm going straight to hell. No number of good deeds can save my ass.

My hands shake as I stand in my living room, glaring at the couch. Part of me wants to barricade the door with it, along with all the other movable furniture, so I can't storm out and cross the hallway to Blair's apartment.

I don't trust myself not to go after her right now.

The memory of her soft curves against me, her sweet mouth, that breathy gasp hitting my ears... perfection. The pull between us is undeniable. It's a drug I can't get enough of. I'm already addicted.

God, I'm so fucking screwed.

I open the door and stomp out of my condo, heading straight for hers, my heart pummeling my chest.

My mind's in a tumult. Knocking doesn't occur to me until I'm already inside, my feet carrying me straight to her bedroom.

I don't know why that's where I aim. Whether my intuition, the sounds emanating from there, or something else guides me, but I'm suddenly right there. And I stop.

Moving, breathing, thinking.

Her scent wafts in the air, a stimulating mix of vanilla, jasmine, and arousal. Coupled with the eyeful I'm getting, it's almost enough to bring me to my knees.

She lays on her unmade bed, the room dimly lit, the curtains drawn. My eyes adjust to the soft glow of the lamp in the corner. The tiny summer dress has slid off her shoulders, her small, perky breasts on display. Pink, puckered nipples stand to attention, begging to be bitten.

Blair's head is thrown back, her eyes shut tight, the hemline of her dress bunched around her wasp waist. Her legs are bent at the knees, feet digging into the crumpled sheets, a purple wand between her bare thighs.

The pulsating vibration echoes throughout the room, accompanying her breathless moans and gasps. Her hips move, back bows off the bed, as she firmly presses the wand against her pink, swollen clit with both hands.

She's fucking magnetic.

The gold, tanned skin of her thighs quivers in anticipation. Knowing that our kiss triggered this sends a rush of smugness through my veins. If I needed confirmation that she thought the same as I did when we kissed, *this is* it.

I don't believe in God, but there must be something out there because holy... she's spectacular. I can't decide if I want to join her or stare until she comes.

My dick hardens in no seconds flat, straining against my pants, begging to be released. I'd go wild if I got my hands on her right now. I'm already losing touch with reality. Lust and want writhe inside every atom of my body.

My balls pull tight when another breathless moan ricochets off the walls. I could easily come in my pants just watching her thrash on the bed.

A veil of hair scattered across the pillow surrounds her flushed face, and a few locks tangle in her earrings. She circles her hips, pressing the wand closer like she just needs the right angle to set off the climax. Just a little more friction.

Friction she can't seem to find.

I'm rooted to the spot, my legs like lead weights. I don't know if she heard me come in. If she did, she hasn't let it show. It's not like I kept quiet. Either she's lost inside her fantasy, deep within the moment, or she's aware of my burning gaze, and putting on a show.

And if that's true... should I fucking join her? God knows my cock is more than ready.

But I can't move. And I can't peel my eyes off her.

A whimper breaks free as her hips gyrate. She's mindlessly pressing a small button on the handle, increasing the intensity, pressing the wand harder against her clit, eyes shut tight.

She moves it left, right, in small circles, desperate for that orgasm. I can tell she's close. She has been since I walked in, but it's not fucking happening.

Seconds pass before her desire turns to annoyance, then nervousness, her moans of pleasure now turned to defeat.

Her skin heats, her back arches further off the mattress, toes curl, and she pumps her hips harder, but no matter the effort, she's stalled on edge, her mind putting up a roadblock.

And then, as hard as she tried, she gives up, throwing the wand to smash against the wall. Draping one arm over her face.

Slowly she tunes herself back in to reality, and as if she feels my burning gaze, her eyes open, clashing with mine. She doesn't speak, and neither do I as we stare each other down, a silent declaration of want and need. Her cheeks heat and she squirms, pressing her thighs together.

"I won't tell if you don't," I say, shattering the quiet, the words laden with promise.

Her eyes never leave mine, burning with the intensity she had inside her seconds ago before it abruptly went off.

Now it's back twice as powerful. Twice as bright.

And when she answers me with a tiny nod, the dam bursts. Tangible heat between us erupts as I surge forward, my knees hastily digging into the mattress. I crawl over her, and she meets me halfway, our lips clashing in a hot, urgent kiss.

It's an all-consuming wildfire, tongues dancing, teeth nipping, breaths mingling in an intoxicating mix of desires. She tastes like sugar and spice, cherry candy and everything tempting.

Her fingers dig into my hair, pulling me closer, deepening the kiss as we battle for dominance, her trying to crawl on top while I try to pin her down. Our hands and legs tangle and suddenly, with a soft gasp, Blair's on the edge of the bed, then off it just as fast, pulling me with her as we fall off in a web of sheets, never breaking the kiss.

I hover above her, our bodies pressed together, shared desperation tearing through us. Fuck, it's only been twenty minutes since I tasted her, but it feels like an entire lifetime.

"You taste like cherry candy," I say, gripping her thigh to yank her fully under me, my elbow by her head supports my weight even though I want to sink and feel every inch of her.

"Did you watch?" she whispers, her cheeks glowing with alluring embarrassment. "How long were you standing there?"

"Long enough to see you were doing a lousy job." I move my hand to her ankle, then brush my fingertips up her smooth skin to the inside of her thigh.

A soft shudder shakes her, and the red of her cheeks fades to pink. "The toy is new," she admits, each word growing in confidence. "I'm not sure how to use it properly... I don't think it's very good."

"I think it's just fine, but it's not what you want today, is it?" I nose a line on her jaw, my hand camping close enough to her pussy that I'm almost brushing it with my fingers. Almost but not quite. Not yet. "Ready to cross some lines with me, B?"

Our breaths mingle as she reaches to brush those delicate

hands up my arms, feeling every muscle, awe replacing embarrassment. "Are you?"

I grip her wrist, settling her small palm over my hard cock. "What do you think?"

"Are you sure you want this?" She squeezes me gently, tearing a guttural groan from my chest, and the fire in her eyes rekindles. With measured strokes, her hand glides over my cock, making it jut against the zipper. "You'll regret it tomorrow."

I pull us back onto the bed, Blair flat on her back while I hover over her, and she immediately grabs hold of my cock again.

"My sister-in-law once told me it's better to regret things you have done than things you haven't, and you..." I angle my hips, grinding into her palm, "...I definitely want to *do* you." I dip my head, gliding my lips up her neck, marking every inch with open-mouthed kisses before speaking in her ear. "You're tense, B. Looks like you could use an orgasm or two to take the edge off."

"Since you're so kindly volunteering..."

I grip her wrist again, moving her hand under my t-shirt, then take over the teasing, touching her thigh, up, up, up until my fingers caress around her pussy.

I love how warm she is. How her eyes hood over, and lips part in an inaudible gasp. Long nails dig into my shoulder blades as she tries to pull me down, hungry for my lips.

I give in a little, kissing and licking the seam of her mouth, a hot ball of pure need swelling behind my ribs. She hooks her fingers in the belt loops of my jeans, pulling me to where she needs me most.

"You want me to touch you?" I ask, not moving an inch. "Look at me."

She obeys, pumping confidence into her gestures as she drags my hand back to her thigh. "Yes, please."

"You had anything to drink today?" This time, I move straight for the prize, sliding my fingers between her pussy lips, locked in some alternate dimension when I check how wet she is.

A soft moan falls from her parted mouth, and her head hits the pillow. I've not pushed one digit inside her yet. Not touched her clit, but she's back on edge, humming beneath me.

"I asked you a question."

"What?" Her skin heats once more, but it's not shame this time. It's arousal. "Oh... n-no," she mewls, gripping my t-shirt with both hands. "No, I didn't drink."

"Good." I locate the small button on the apex of her thighs, gently rolling it under two fingers. "Birth control?"

"No, please stop talking."

That earns her a gentle slap of her clit. We're not done with the questions yet. If she thinks this is a turn-off, she should see what a fucking turn-off a teenage pregnancy scare is. I lived through it once in high school, and I'm not doing it again.

"Condoms?" I ask, slowly playing her clit like I would a guitar.

"No, I don't have any. Do you?"

"Not on me."

"Just... pull out, okay?"

I cock an eyebrow. "Pull out?"

She bucks her hips, inching away from the mattress, looking for more friction. "God, Cody... stop teasing. You should've sent me a survey before you came over."

"Shut the fuck up," I whisper into her mouth. Rubbing her a bit faster. "This is important, B. I'm not getting you off until you answer the questions."

She groans, rolling those aroused eyes at me. "What a waste."

"A waste?"

"You had the best opportunity to end that sentence differently, and you blew it." She grips my shoulders to yank me down. "Say it again."

"Shut the fuck up."

"And take that dick like a good girl. *That*'s how it ends."

A small smirk plays across my lips. "You're not a good girl. You're a brat and I don't like brats, so you need to lose that attitude." I bite her earlobe, then nose a line down her cheek. "I like the idea of you taking my dick."

"I'd be full of it now if you'd just. Stop. *Talking*."

I slap her pussy again, harder this time, making her jerk, her eyes wide, but she soaks my hand, so I know she loves it.

"Watch your mouth. We're not cutting corners. I want consent. Audible consent to fuck you."

"You have it," she sighs, her hips urging me to work her faster. "Permission, consent, do what you want."

"What I want is for you to understand I won't be gentle."

"I can handle a hate-fuck, Cody."

"Good, because that's *exactly* what it'll be." With a low groan, I sink my fingers into her pussy, stroking her G spot hard and fast. "Now pretend you're a good girl and come for me."

All the tension in her body ebbs away. She melts into the bed, giving up control and dropping the fake, confident mask she's been wearing for years.

At least I think it's fake.

I don't pump my fingers long. Less than a minute is enough to tip Blair into the abyss she's been teetering on since I entered.

She vibrates beneath me. Her loud moans cease, the orgasm stealing her voice. My hand is soaked she's so wet. When the pressure increases, realization dawns and I yank my fingers out, looking down just in time to catch the sight.

"You didn't tell me you're a squirter," I rasp, the words strained because fucking hell... it's the hottest thing I ever saw.

"I... I didn't know I could do that... I'm so sorry." She throws one hand over her face, hiding away and trying to shut her legs, denying me access.

She *never* squirted before?

Well, shit, and here I was, thinking my ego couldn't possibly get any bigger, only for Blair to double its size.

I triggered her squirting.

"Sorry?" I pry her arm off her flushed face. "What the fuck are you sorry for? That's hot, baby girl." Pushing my hand back between her legs, I groan at how wet she is. "Show me again."

"It's not gross? Are you sure?"

I push my fingers inside, stroking her G spot again. "I'm sure. Now relax. I want another one."

With a small nod, she grips my shoulders, gliding her hands higher until she cinches my neck, tugging my hair as I work to bring her higher.

She just had an orgasm, but the next one's close behind, her body still not mellow enough. I dip my head, sealing her lips with a kiss, working her up even more, and that fucking kiss...

It's a replay of what went down in the hallway. A complete loss of inhibitions. Our tongues fight for dominance, mouths come together in a rushed rhythm, and Blair mewls, her thighs slapping closed to lock my hand between them.

She's back to the putty version of herself. Adjusting to my

pace, giving into my dominance as if allowing herself to let go of the fight that fuels her is all she craves.

"Almost there," she mumbles, angling her head back and exposing the porcelain column of her throat. "Cody, I—"

"Come," I cut her off, sucking a bit of flesh above her pulse, not hard enough to mark her but hard enough that her eyes burst open in shock. "Now, B. Show me how good it feels. Let go."

And she does, her chest rising and falling faster as she pulls down quick, erratic breaths. The orgasm hits, the pressure pushing my fingers out, and her legs shake as she drowns the sheets.

I've watched enough porn to know this isn't over.

Pushing my fingers back in, I pump fast and hard while she's still in the throes of orgasm, and the wave retreats only to gush back stronger.

Blair's moaning, gasping, muttering something incomprehensible, her nails drawing long lines down my back, legs shaking so hard her feet float above the soaked sheets. I've never seen a woman this lost in the moment, fueled by nothing but desire. She's still quivering, beads of sweat forming along her hairline, blue irises almost swallowed by black pupils.

"That's so fucking hot," I say.

I could force another out in seconds, but her skin's clammy like she's not far off passing out.

"And so intense," she half gasps, half whispers when I glide my fingers between the swollen lips of her pussy.

Bracing both hands against my pecs, she finds enough strength in her frail body to push me back until I sit on my calves.

Her delicate hands go straight for my zipper. She pulls it down, flips the button, and urges me to help as she hauls my jeans down my thighs. My cock springs free, the head red, precum beading at the tip.

"Are you always walking around commando?" She locks her fingers around my shaft, maneuvering to lay on her belly.

"I jumped out halfway through the shower when Ana battered at my door, screaming the place down," I say, weighing every word because Blair's hot breath is right there, fanning my cock, her hand deliberately pumping up and down.

"Consent to put your cock in my mouth?"

I laugh. Well, try, but it comes out desperate because she uses her thumb to massage the underside, and after watching her writhe on the bed for the past fifteen minutes, I'm not far off shooting the load from this tiny move alone.

"I might fucking die if you don't," I groan, and as soon as the words fully roll off my tongue, she licks me balls to tip, my whole body jerking with the motion.

"Is Cody Hayes losing his cool?" she teases, rising a little higher on her elbows as she smears the growing bead of precum around the head. "Do you want to know a secret?" she whispers, peering up to meet my eyes.

I freeze because *now* I realize there's one standard question on my list I didn't ask. It seemed such a fucking stretch considering Blair's reputation that I didn't bother, but now, looking into her beautiful eyes, a cold chain closes my throat.

No, no way she's a virgin.

According to hundreds of rumors, she fucked half the football team, for crying out loud.

"I do want to know a secret."

With a tiny smile, she parts her lips, then quickly bows, swallowing my cock all the way down.

All the way.

The head hits the back of her throat, then slides deeper, and before long, Blair's bottom lip touches my balls.

My mind can't comprehend how she fits eleven inches there, but my body responds in kind, growing that much hotter because *one, two, three...* and she lifts her head, releasing me with a pop.

"I don't have a gag reflex," she says, beaming at me from under thick eyelashes.

And she's back on my shaft like it's a lollipop, and she can't get enough, her fingers toying with my balls in time with her head bobbing up and down.

Sweat coats my back, the orgasm so fucking close I won't last much longer, and this is *not* how I want to finish the evening.

I want her pussy, but instead of yanking her off me, my fingers tie her hair, and I look down, loving the sight of her swallowing me all the way.

The image of her kneeling, lips parted as she lets me deep-throat that pretty mouth flashes on the back of my eyelids, and I almost lose it.

"As amazing as this feels, I want your pussy, B."

She claws my thighs, swallows me once more, and freezes for three long seconds before she comes up, wiping the corner of her mouth with one finger. That sultry, heated look in her blown pupils flips a switch inside my head.

I grab her by the waist and sit her in my lap, her legs locking around my back. It's intimate, this position. We're face to face. Her nipples brush my chest, and when I take her lips, she weaves her fingers through my hair, grinding her hips to slide her wet pussy along my cock.

Moving one hand under her butt, I lift her enough to get us in position. A small, satisfied whimper rips into my mouth as she inches down my length.

There are so many contradicting emotions running through me I can't decide which takes the stage until she yanks my hand from under her butt and drops in one quick motion.

We both let out a moan. My muscles pull taut, her wet, tight pussy gripping me like a vice, pulsing along my shaft like she's on the verge of coming undone.

"That feels so good," she breathes, trying to rise, but I grip her hips firmly in place.

"Don't move. Give me a minute."

She remains still, but her soft, warm lips brush my ear, and she bites gently, sending a pleasant sting through my entire body.

"Fuck..." I groan, my cock jutting inside her, muscles spasming to rein in the overwhelming need to offload. "Jesus, B... you're so fucking wet."

"That's supposed to be a good thing," she whispers, skating her mouth along my jaw.

"It's the best thing, I promise."

Testing the waters, I lift her hips up slightly. The angle is perfect. Too perfect, but with a deep breath, determination, and a few unsexy thoughts, I keep my orgasm in check, pushing it down enough that I won't come the second we up the tempo.

"Take charge. Ride me."

She arches back like she's about to show me the time of my fucking life, and gasps, rising on knees buried in the mattress either side of my hips. She rises so high my cock almost springs free, nothing but the tip left inside her, and then she falls, impaling herself on me in one long thrust.

Bruising her lips with a deep kiss, I marvel in the feel of her locked in my arms. I'm fucking drunk on the intense craving for her body even while I'm balls-deep inside her. I pull her flush against me, and our brakes snap.

It's frantic the way we move in sync. Loud, too, with her gasps, and moans, and my growling every time she sinks. We claw for control, taking and giving at the same time.

"My turn," I say when her moves gradually slow like her legs lack the strength to keep going.

Both hands under her butt, I move her onto her back so I can fuck that sweet, tight pussy like I really want to.

But as soon as she lays under me, her tiny summer dress still bunched at her waist, those small boobs covered in goosebumps, candy-hard, pink nipples standing to attention, the merciless fuck loses its appeal.

I wanted to imprint myself inside her. I wanted her to feel me for days every time she sat down, but I can't find it in me to use her body like that. She's so pure in this moment, her eyes full of trust, arousal, and bliss, her fingers ghosting my skin like she's worshipping every inch.

So I return the favor.

I move my hips back then forth, driving myself home, bottoming out inside her, not relentlessly pounding her like she's nothing more than a cum drop.

Because she's not.

There's more to Blair than I let myself see. More than just Blair the bully. There are deep emotions and layers to her personality, secrets she guards, hurt she harbors, regret that gnaws at her mind. I see it. I notice because I finally look past my own fucking hatred, and now...

I want to use her, but I also want to please her.

Sex is suddenly way fucking different to what I had planned. It's hot, fast, and hard but not insensitive.

If anything, we both fight to touch as much as we can.

Kiss like we're losing our grip on reality. Speak with gestures instead of words. Every stroke of her tongue against mine sets my mind alight. Every sound she makes, every sound *we* make, pulls me deeper into our bubble.

And when she comes beneath me, shuddering, moaning, clawing my back... I fuck her until the pressure is too intense and I pull out, spilling across her stomach as she squirts all over the bed sheets.

"That was... overdue," she sighs, amusement coating her words as she brushes her hair behind her ears and looks down at her hot body. "What a mess."

I roll onto my back, my chest heaving, ears ringing, cock at half-mast still. I'm waiting for the awkwardness to creep up. We both lost our minds tonight, crossing lines we were never meant to cross.

Well, *I was* never meant to cross.

Blair doesn't share my sentiments. She's not stabbing anyo-ne's back by giving in to me.

Inhaling a deep breath, I push those thoughts aside for a few more minutes. I'll have plenty of time to torture myself once I leave her bed.

"You should invest in waterproof mattress protectors and thick, chunky towels," I say, leveling my breathing.

"Why?"

"It'll be easier than changing your sheets every time."

"I doubt you'll want to repeat this, so no point getting pre-pared," she sighs, not a trace of sarcasm or hurt in her words.

That's... not what I expected.

She's not hoping for another round. She knows even this was never supposed to happen, and that's all she's getting.

Girls always act cool about a one-night stand before it happens, but most grow attached during sex, and by the time we orgasm, one night is not enough.

At least as far as my experiences go.

But Blair... she's not pining. Not fishing for more, and... Fuck, I'm confusing even myself. I never enjoyed girls who clung to me longer than agreed after I'd had them, but the indifference radiating from Blair—the same one I always projected—has my panties in a fucking twist.

It almost feels like *rejection*.

For the next minute or so, I rationalize, calming my racing heart and mentally revitalizing my limbs. Once my breaths lose their irregular edge, I sit up and take a moment to admire the wet sheets and Blair's still-naked body.

Ribbons of my cum adorn her stomach, boobs, and neck, a sight to fucking see.

She stares at me, nothing short of content bliss in her heavy, hooded eyes. She looks ready to fall asleep.

"You need a bath," I say, getting to my feet.

"Is that a subtle way of saying I smell?"

"It's a subtle way of saying you need to relax your muscles and wash my cum off your stomach." I enter the bathroom, halting with my hand on the doorknob. "You smell delicious, B. Sweet like candy, you taste like it, too."

She doesn't respond, but the shy smile I get in return is everything. I turn the faucet to fill the tub, pour some bubble bath in, then clean myself up, and go back to the bedroom, where she's on her feet, the spaghetti straps of her summer dress back in place, the bed stripped of the sheets.

"Get in the tub. If you're sore tomorrow, take another bath in the morning, okay?"

Her eyes widen, but she quickly wipes the surprise off her

face, nodding once. "This was fun."

I smirk, crossing the room to kiss her lips one last time. "That it was, but don't forget I fucking hate you, B."

SIXTEEN

Cody

With a deep breath, I pull my phone out, typing a message to my brothers. I need one or more of them here to keep me in check. Even if they won't know they're helping.

It's been less than twenty hours since I had Blair, and I'm itching to go over there and do it again. I can't stop recalling how she looked, sounded, and tasted. How well we snapped together. How mind-blowingly good the sex was.

I thought I'd get my fill if we worked out years of pent-up sexual frustration in bed. Turns out I've not even scratched the surface. She's on my mind non-stop. The need to grip her waist, impale her on my cock and watch her ride me is so intense I already jerked off twice today.

I could knock on her door, bend her over the kitchen counter, and have her squirt time and time again all over the tiles, but I can't give in to this.

If one night has me this desperate for another, things will

get worse if I cave.

I need my brothers here talking shit, complaining about whatever the fuck they want because it'll keep me occupied, but before I send the text, there's a knock on my door.

Shit. I was so busy thinking of ways to stay away from Blair I didn't once think she'd come over for more. I have no doubt she's outside my door, and my mind fucking soars.

Need and want battle with reason and common sense. I can't do this. I can't start a no-strings, casual fuck fest with Blair. Right?

Right.

Then why are my legs moving, and why is my heart climbing up my throat like an alpinist ice-axing their way up a sheer cliff face?

My brain skips ahead, imagining what's about to go down. Blair in *my* bed tonight. Naked. Panting. Moaning. Loving every fucking thing I planned in the last two seconds.

"It's happening!" Logan grins when I open the door, a big bag flung over his shoulder and little Noah beside him. "You alright, Cody?"

I was so convinced I'd see Blair that I need a second to snap out of the shock and swallow the bitter pill of disappointment.

Disappointment that it's not her.

And disappointment that I lost my sense of right and wrong so fast. That I considered establishing a regular fucking schedule with the girl who did nothing but harm to one of my favorite people.

It's true what they say.

Men think with their dicks regardless of age.

"Hey, yeah, I'm fine. I just... wasn't expecting this today.

Babies rarely come on the due date, right?"

He chuckles, handing the bag over. "Almost is the keyword here." He messes up Noah's hair before hauling him into his arms. "You're staying with Uncle Cody tonight, alright? You'll have fun."

"So much fun," I agree. "I have your favorite cookies and lots of apple juice."

That's about the only thing this kid drinks the last few months, since Cassidy stopped breastfeeding him. Try giving him water, and he'll spritz it in your face.

"Is Cass in the car?" I ask, stepping aside to let them in.

"She is. The contractions are still far apart, so I thought I'd drop Noah off before things get crazy." He points to the bag I dropped on the breakfast bar. "I packed enough for three days in case Eli takes as long to get out as Noah. If you need help, Nico and Mia said to tell you they're a phone call away. I called Gareth already, so don't worry about work. He'll take over your team tomorrow and Friday if needed."

Gareth is Logan's right-hand man at Stone and Oak. He started out working construction and now whines about sitting behind a desk delegating work. I bet he'll enjoy getting his hands dirty again.

"You're rambling, Logan. Chill. We'll be fine. It's not my first time, bro. Nico's still got the spare car seat?"

He nods, setting Noah down when he starts wriggling in his arms. "Okay, Daddy's got to go now." He kisses his head, then taps his nose. "Have fun. I'll come and get you when your little brother's here."

"Bye, bye," Noah cheers, cuddling a plush t-rex to his chest. "Bye, bye."

"Don't give Uncle any trouble."

"Bye, bye!"

"Alright, alright!" Logan chuckles, raising his hands. "I'm going."

A minute later, we're alone, and a cheeky grin twists Noah's face a second before he drops his plushie and bolts for the snack cupboard in the kitchen.

You wouldn't know he only started walking two months ago with how fast he runs.

"I should've checked with your dad if you had dinner."

"Pasta!"

"You ate pasta, or you want pasta?"

He yanks open my dry-food cupboard and pulls out a plastic container filled with penne.

"I take it you didn't eat then. We're cooking, huh?" I set the container on the breakfast bar, then pull out a foldable highchair from the coat closet. "Deal, I could eat, but you're doing the dishes."

"No!" Noah yells with a giggle, banging his hands on the highchair tray.

"I knew you'd say that." Grabbing a handful of wooden utensils and a plastic bowl, I set them before him, keeping the drummer entertained while I prepare dinner.

***

"Your mommy won't be happy about this, so you need to promise you won't tell her," I say, wiping Noah's face for the third time since we entered the building.

I don't know why I bother. It's not like he's clean. The chocolate ice cream in his hand melts, dripping onto his hand, t-shirt, and—since he's in my arms as I climb the second flight of stairs—my t-shirt, too.

Noah grins, licking the ice cream, and his face is dirty again. I don't bother wiping it again, stuffing the wet wipe in the back pocket of my jeans as we emerge on the third-floor hallway.

Since he woke up at six am, I've changed his clothes twice. Logan packed enough for three days, but it's not even been twenty-four hours, and I've burned through half the supplies.

"Hey," I hear as I pop the key in the lock. Doing a one-eighty, I halt face to face with Blair.

God, she's fucking beautiful again, dressed in black sweat-pants and a matching t-shirt stained in white powder. There's more on her forehead, her hair in a bun, a few locks kissing her shoulders.

I open my mouth to reply, but Noah shuts me up, stuffing my face with his ice cream, then bursts out giggling.

Wiping the chocolaty goo off my lips and beard with the back of my hand, I maneuver him over my hip. "You could've said *enough*, you know?"

"No!" he cheers with a broad smile.

"Close. We'll practice later. I love you, but don't feed me your food, okay?" I turn back to Blair. "Busy morning?"

"Why do you ask?"

"You've got..." On instinct, I step closer, wiping what I think is flour off her skin. "You're baking cookies?"

"Cookie!" Noah cheers, bouncing in my arms. "Cookie!"

"Yes, madeleines. I can bring some over later. I just need to run to the shop. I'm all out of sugar."

The words are out before I can stop to think why this is wrong. "I've got sugar. You mind finishing in my kitchen and watching Noah for ten minutes? I could use a shower, and this devil can't be left unattended."

Lies. Filthy lies.

Noah's fine spending a few minutes alone if he has enough toys. Also, I had a shower while he was still asleep, but... I don't really know what.

There's not one explanation in my head for why I just asked her to spend time with me.

Not one excuse.

Maybe curiosity.

She's in sweatpants again. A rare sight. Blair Fitzpatrick never once came to school without a face full of makeup, a perfect outfit, and bling. She's not wearing any of that now, and it's like staring at a brand-new person.

Her cheeks heat, eyes darting to my lips before shifting to Noah. "Will you help me with the cookies?"

"No."

"He'll help when it's time to eat them," I say, opening my condo. "Come in."

"Let me grab everything first."

"You need a hand?"

She looks me over. "Yours are full. It's okay. It's just a few small things. Won't be a minute." She disappears into her condo as Noah pinches my nose.

"Juice," he says. "Juice!"

"I can't wait until you speak full sentences."

He speaks a lot already for his age. Mom said neither my brothers nor I started talking until we were around two, so Noah must take after Cassidy. He's sixteen months and has a vocabulary of about twenty words. He mostly shows me what he wants, but I bet he'll be talking my ear off in no time.

Leaving the door ajar, I take Noah in, and by the time he's got a sippy cup, Blair's back with baking trays, three bowls, and an array of spatulas and ingredients.

"I'll try not to make a mess."

"You can try all you want," I say, washing my hands under the kitchen faucet. "Noah won't share your sentiment. I'll grab a shower. Help yourself to whatever you want."

With a tight nod, she lifts Noah into the highchair, and I head to the bathroom for the quickest shower in the history of mankind.

Ten minutes, and I'm back, dressed in clean—for now—clothes. They're filling the baking trays with batter. Noah grins when Blair helps him, guiding the tablespoon in his hand. Seeing them working together, his tiny hand engulfed in hers, makes me ache in a way I don't understand or even want to think about.

There's not as much mess as I expected, though if I collected the batter from Noah's t-shirt, the counter, and the floor, we could make another tray of madeleines.

Leaning against the wall, I watch, taking a moment to appreciate how beautiful Blair is. She should throw away all the slutty dresses she owns and embrace how good she looks when she's not even trying.

Soft strands of hair dance around her face, her cheeks flushed from the oven, giving her a rosy glow. I prefer this side of her. The carefree girl with a big, genuine smile. She feels real. Not like the other one—the rude, self-centered bitch.

"Is everything okay?" she asks, peering up at me. "I'll clean this up in a minute. We're almost done."

"I'll clean it up. You're baking, I'm cleaning."

"Done!" Noah exclaims, flailing the spoon around and spattering everything in sight with batter.

"Yes, we're done. Now let's go wash your hands."

He protests, banging the spoon against the marble countertop, but Blair scoops him up, tickling him until he giggles.

"I'll sort him out. He needs a change of clothes, too," I say as she passes him over.

By the time I've changed him, Blair's cleaned the kitchen, and the warm scent of vanilla and sugar emanates from the madeleines in the oven.

"It smells amazing in here," I say, watching Noah climb onto the couch. "How long before they're done?"

"Not long now." Her features soften when she looks over at Noah. "Looks like someone's tired."

He lays on the pillow, eyes closed, t-rex tucked under his arm. I wish I could fall asleep that fast. It literally takes him thirty seconds.

"So?" she questions, her tone reserved. "On a scale of one to ten, how much do you regret the other night?" An apologetic look shadows her face when I don't answer and she gives a tiny shrug. "One of us had to bring it up, don't you think?"

"I don't."

"You'd rather pretend nothing happened?"

"No. I was answering your first question, B. I don't regret it, to be honest, it was a long time coming."

Relief floods her face. "So we're okay? I mean, not okay, obviously. You still hate me because of Mia, but—" She applies the brakes, her guilt-ridden eyes snapping to meet mine. "I'm sorry. I can't turn back time, Cody. I'll never be able to right my wrongs, but I want you to know I regret it all..." She heaves a heavy sigh, pushing off the counter like she's about to flee.

That familiar pang of protectiveness jabs my heart again. She looks so resigned, so hurt, humiliated, and fucking sad, a stark contrast to that façade of arrogance and disdain she presents to the world. I hate this look on her almost as much as the resting bitch face.

Extending my hand to stop her leaving, I pull over a bar stool, gesturing for her to sit, and once she reluctantly does, I grab two cans of Coke from the fridge.

"We're not okay," I say, my voice firm but far from rude. "I don't know if we'll ever be okay, but I want to hear your story. Why did you do it? Why did you bully Mia? Was it her looks? Those pink dresses riling you up? How shy she is? Smart?"

Blair's eyes drop to the can as she twists the tab, her fingers twitching. Her silence feels like a thick, oppressive wall between us before she finally speaks.

"I don't want to make excuses, Cody. It's inexcusable. I'm just not a good person. Let's leave it at that."

That's been my go-to explanation since I found out about the bullying. Plausible and fitting, but... I've had time to get to know Blair a bit these past few weeks. There's a different side to her. A hurt woman sheltering behind a mask. She's full of kindness that she mostly refuses to show. Full of smiles and full of tears.

"You're not all bad. There's good in you. I don't know how much because you hide it so well, but I see you with my nephews, B." The fear in her eyes subsides, so instead of pushing her to share things I'm not even sure I want to hear, I change the subject. "What are your plans for the summer?"

Her features soften, relief slumping her shoulders as she checks on the madeleines.

"I don't have plans," she admits.

"No job? Won't you be bored at home?"

"My dad needs me at short notice a lot, so any paid work is out of the question. I do a bit of volunteering."

I cock an eyebrow, genuinely surprised. I wouldn't have guessed Blair had it in her to be selfless. "Where?"

"At the hospital. I spend time at the psychiatric ward, reading, playing chess, and just... offering a companion, I guess. A lot of those people are very lonely."

Now isn't that a revelation. I've known this girl for years. At least, I thought I did. Turns out there are many layers to her personality that she's been meticulously hiding. The best parts of her are never on display.

"Why the psychiatric ward?"

"Call it sentiment. My mom had schizophrenia," she says, and the oven dings, letting us know the cookies are ready.

There's a sadness coating her words reminding me her mother's no longer here.

She inspects the cookies through the glass before pulling out the tray. "She died last March," she adds, grabbing one cookie then quickly dropping it to pinch her ear. "Hot."

"No shit, you just took it out of the oven."

A sweet smile lifts the corners of her lips and... what the fuck is happening inside my chest right now?

I don't like this girl. Not one bit. But for reasons I'll never understand, that tiny smile while her eyes teared up has my heart beating faster.

"They're best when they're still warm."

"Warm, not hot," I agree, grabbing a glass serving bowl and a spatula to transfer the cookies. "I'm sorry about your mom."

"Don't be. She had a horrible life. Maybe death will be kinder."

My eyebrows pull together, but she doesn't elaborate. Sensing she doesn't want to share, I change the topic again.

"So you play chess?"

"I do. I'm pretty good, too. It was the only thing my mom

liked when she had good days, so I got fifteen years of practice."

Fifteen years. Shit.

She was five when her mother got sick. I doubt she remembers her before the illness. I don't know Blair's father. Never seen the guy, which, now that I think about it, is fucking odd. I don't recall anyone ever showing up for Blair's cheer practice. No one picked her up from school or came to see her perform...

Shaking off the undesirable sense of sadness on her behalf, I cross the room and pull a chessboard from the cabinet. On my way back, I tuck Noah back in, moving him closer to the backrest of the couch before he takes a dive.

"Alright, show me what you've got."

I set the board up on the breakfast bar and she eyes it while I snatch a cookie from the bowl, the condo filled with an aroma just about as sweet as the heaven melting on my tongue.

I know what she's thinking; she's wondering why I'm keeping her here. I'm wondering that, too.

Why have I invited her in the first place?

Fuck knows. I can't explain it. Hatred still sizzles beneath my skin, but there's something more there since she spent the night crying in my arms. Empathy.

She's obviously been going through a tough time for a while. Losing her mother couldn't have been easy, no matter how little contact they had. She died last year, just as Blair was left with no one in her corner. Everyone turned their backs on her after what Mia went through, and—

What if her mother's death triggered the bullying again? Blair left Mia alone in college. Didn't bother her until after the Spring Break party in... *March.*

"You know what, let's get it over and done with now," I

say, needing to find out more because things just don't add up. "We'll have to go there at some point anyway. Tell me about the bullying. Don't give me excuses, just the truth."

She squares her shoulder, moving her e-pawn two spaces after I moved my f-pawn up by two. "Okay, you're right. I've been trying to apologize and explain for a long time."

I believe that. Blair's tried to approach Mia on multiple occasions this past year, but she's hardly ever alone, always under our care, and when we're not there, the football team guys are looking out for her. The few times I caught Blair lingering nearby, she was too afraid of a backlash to approach.

Since she moved in across the hall and started interacting with those little *heys* here and there, I've grown increasingly curious about it. All the more after she spent the evening here with River and me.

There's something disturbing about how she can spin on a dime from this caring person before me to the A-grade bitch I know so well.

There are two sides to Blair Fitzpatrick. What's even more disturbing is how she keeps her vulnerable side buried, always on guard even among those she considers friends.

The nagging question returns: who is she playing?

Them or me?

"I bullied her because she was an easy target," she whispers, firing a fucking bazooka with the first sentence. "She was weak, quiet, closed-off. Never talked or fought back... seeing her cry gave me a sense of power."

It's a hard pill to swallow, but despite how furious her words make me, at least I know she's telling the truth. Instead of playing the '*I was just a kid and didn't know any better*' card, she's exposing her darkest secrets. Not many people openly admit guilt like this.

I bet not even Brandon knows.

I bet she never told anyone.

"It made me feel like I mattered," she continues quietly, sliding her can from hand to trembling hand across the counter. "It started in kindergarten. The first time Jake made her cry, everyone started listening... following him. It was amazing. Such an easy way to have friends, to be heard and seen...

"I started doing the same, picking on her by his side because I loved the strength it gave me. I know it sounds messed up, but that's how it was. Other girls looked up to me, said and did nice things, and..." Her voice cracks, prompting me to look up.

I've been staring at the oven all this time, watching madeleines bake. Tears well in Blair's eyes, nose pink, chin quivering.

I'm not far from snapping and kicking her out. She has no right to look this vulnerable and hurt. She deserves to feel like shit for what she's done, but the concern spearing my insides stuns me into silence.

"I didn't realize until senior year in high school that I was projecting onto her all those years. What I did to her was the thing I was running from myself," she adds in a whisper.

I move my g-pawn up, grinding my teeth before I trust myself enough to ask. "Running from what?"

"That's not important. I told you I won't make excuses." She wipes her wet cheeks with the back of her hand. "When college started, Jake wasn't there anymore, but my friends stayed even though I stopped taking shit out on Mia. The respect I'd earned over the years lingered. People still saw me, still listened when I talked, so I left Mia alone." She glances at me, holding my gaze as she says, "Once you took her under your wing, bullying meant going against *you*, and... I had the biggest crush on you when I saw you in college. Hurting the girl you were so protective of wouldn't win me any points, but..." She pinches her lips, eyes welling with tears again, and she gently shakes her head like she's done.

Like she's refusing to say another word.

"Keep going, B," I encourage, hiding any trace of the mixed emotions tearing me apart. "You got this far."

Shutting her eyes tight, she inhales a calming breath. "Brandon fell in love with her. He didn't realize it, but I did. I knew that if he made it work, I'd lose him, and I couldn't lose him, Cody. He's the closest thing to family I have."

"Family? You've been sleeping with him on and off for years. Now you're friends, even though he's a shitty friend at best, and you call him your *family*? That's messed up."

"He's had my back through thick and thin. Well... almost. He's a little lost and immature, but he's got a good heart, even if his head is sometimes screwed on the wrong way."

"You're evading. If you don't want to answer, say so."

"I'm not evading. I'm explaining." She sighs, shifting her queen to h4, and I get the most genuine smile I've seen from her. "Checkmate."

"What?" My eyes drop to the board. "How?"

She points to the diagonal e1 to h4 that exposes my king. "You're not good at this. This is the fastest checkmate you can perform in chess."

"Looks like I need a few lessons."

"Anytime." She beams, but her smile slips off fast. "Sorry, I didn't mean to—"

"Mondays and Thursdays?" I cut her off because I don't want her back in defensive mode.

I want *this* girl. She's... nice. Fun. Beautiful and caring. She's a good person.

Her eyes widen a little, but she smiles, her shoulders relaxing as she nods. "That'll work." She grabs another cookie, handing one to me as well. "And about Brandon... I know there were rumors flying around campus, but we were never a thing. Neither casual nor serious nor a one-night deal."

"Never?" I echo, not comprehending the information fast enough. "*Never*? Why didn't you do anything about the rumors?"

"I started them, Cody. Brandon's the only person I trust. He knows things no one else does, and I needed him."

"So you told everyone you were sleeping with him so other girls would steer clear?"

She nods, her cheeks hotter by the second. "Not many girls dared stand in my way back then. I fueled the rumors, but they only worked because Brandon never wanted more than sex until he noticed Mia. My mom died the day before the Spring Break party, and he wasn't there for me."

"So you took it out on Mia," I say, connecting the dots. "She did nothing wrong, Blair. Brandon's the one who hurt you." I don't realize I've slammed my fist on the counter until she flinches, her eyes filling with fresh tears. "You humiliated her. You *burned* her hair! How fucked up is that?!"

"I know... I—" She clamps her mouth shut, tears spilling down her cream cheeks as she slips off the bar stool. "I'm sorry, Cody. I... I don't have anything but apologies, and I know they don't mean anything, but they're sincere." She pushes a long, shaky breath past her lips, glancing at the oven. "I didn't realize it was so late. I have to go, but thank you for today and, and... take the next batch out before it burns," she rambles, backing out around the corner until I hear the door slam shut.

"Fuck." I run a trembling hand down my face. Way to keep

my cool. "Well done, asshole..."

Admitting her sins that blatantly couldn't have been easy. She opened up to me, showed her rawest form, unearthed things she probably has a hard time thinking about, let alone confessing, and making exactly *zero* excuses while doing so. She laid the hard, cold truth down... and I snapped.

As I do wherever Mia's concerned.

I get up to follow Blair, but one glance at the couch stops me taking half a step. I can't leave Noah alone.

Flexing my fingers, I ball my fists repeatedly to purge the tension and influx of unpleasant emotions from Blair's confession. The hard-to-stomach memories and the protectiveness I've felt toward Mia since I saw her struggling with Asher.

To this day, I don't know what triggered the response. I was never interested in her, never saw her as anything more than a little sister, but the need to defend her engulfed me. No matter how much time passes, no matter the fact she's engaged to my brother, I still feel responsible for her.

Guilt smacks me across the face as Blair's confessions swirl round my head, my challenge-loving mind deciphering the clues.

"Such an easy way to have friends, to be heard and seen..."

The fleeting mention of her mother's schizophrenia, and how death might be kinder to her than life. How she weighed every word to make sure nothing she said could be interpreted as an excuse. How she looked like she'd resigned herself to a life of guilt and regret, not worthy of any good moments.

Heard. She wanted to be heard and seen...

I grab a packet of cigarettes from the kitchen drawer and head to the balcony, surrounding myself with thick, white clouds. It helps center my mind, clear the clutter, and focus.

Three deep drags, and the web of information, the scraps Blair threw my way, unravels, creating a simple but bone-chilling picture. A *reason.*

She bullied Mia to feel like she had an ounce of power and control in this world. Living with a mentally ill parent had to be a nightmare. To top it off, throughout all the years I've known her, Blair's never mentioned her father.

And the fact I don't know the guy speaks volumes about his involvement in his daughter's life.

Was Blair alone with her mother all those years?

Did she watch her die?

I don't know much about schizophrenia other than what I've seen in one episode of *House M.D.* If it's anything like that, then a five-year-old girl would've been properly messed up after witnessing her mother's mental breakdowns.

The more I think about her words, the more sense I find and the more empathy I have for the little girl who watched her mother wilt away. The more I understand why she stood by Jake Grey's side, taking her hurt and frustration out on Mia.

"It doesn't fucking change anything. She could've stopped, she could've..." I zip my mouth, though I admit I get why Vee talks to herself.

It really helps center the thoughts.

The cold, harsh truth is that Blair's confession does change a fucking lot. And... she did stop bullying Mia for a while. I don't know why, but now I've got to know her, I think she tried to do better. Be better...

"Shit." I toss the cigarette butt in the ashtray and head back inside.

I should've never let Blair get this close. We're at the friendly neighbor level, I think, but that's still way too fucking close.

“Juice,” Noah’s voice brings me back to here and now, his big brown eyes staring from where he sits on the couch, wide awake. “Juice.”

“Sure, little bud. Give me a sec.”

And just like that, the negative emotions disperse, leaving nothing behind. That’s what my nephews do to me. They bring a sense of order, peace, and bliss. Hanging out with a kid is easier. They don’t have a care in the world, and I let myself off the hook for a few hours.

SEVENTEEN

Blair

The chess lessons never happened. I stood outside Cody's apartment for ten minutes last Monday, my hand falling to my side every time I tried to knock.

Afraid of facing him, I tucked my tail between my legs and fled. It was too easy to forget how much he hates me after he saved me from Alan, held me when I cried, and made me come so many times I lost count.

Amazing sex, closeness, fleeting conversations, and possessive touches... but the thing I loved most was spending time with his nephews.

River is a cute baby. Loud but adorable.

And Noah... Noah might just be the cutest kid in California. I love how curious and gregarious he is. Not a shy bone in his body.

I guess he takes after his dad. Logan's the most ostentatious of all the Hayes.

I grew up surrounded by them. I was five when I saw the triplets at school. Six when Dad started doing business with Grandad Hayes after inheriting a large piece of land that's now an office block. Twelve when Nico took over the role of my father's stockbroker, and fifteen when Dad took me to my first Monica Hayes charity gala.

Cody didn't bring up the chess lessons again when I passed him. He hasn't said anything other than *hey* this past week, and I'm too chicken to start a conversation even though he infests my mind daily.

It's for the best.

Those few encounters we've had so far didn't do me good. I've replayed our conversation for days, scrutinizing my every word, hoping he didn't think I was trying to make excuses for who I've been my whole life.

I let my guard down around him without thinking, and not just with the words. No one except Brandon ever saw me like Cody did when I baked madeleines. No makeup, no pretty dress or jewelry.

Nothing to hide the ugly.

I don't leave my condo unless I look the part I play, but my mind didn't go to *get yourself sorted out* when I ran out, hearing him talking in the hallway. Lack of sugar was a lousy excuse, but it worked.

It feels so natural not to pretend around Cody. So natural to be me. The *real* me, not the Blair I created to deflect the past.

It also felt fucking amazing to lay all night tucked against Cody's side with his long fingers tangled in my hair, the bulk of his warm body holding me close.

It's the safest I've ever felt—in the arms of a man who despises me for what I've done to Mia.

Him and me both.

Ana sits outside Cody's apartment when I come home from a shopping spree with Kelly-Ann. Holding a few bags of lingerie, I stop dead in my tracks, unsure which way to turn.

I bet she remembers Cody pinning me against the wall, devouring my mouth last week.

This is bound to be awkward.

Moving the bags into one hand, I fish my key out, my feet aching from six hours in heels. It's funny how quickly your feet get used to comfortable shoes.

I used to spend hours in heels every day, shopping with the girls or meeting up after school to gossip in our favorite restaurants and cocktail bars, but I've not been out much lately, so spending a few hours in Louboutins warrants a soak.

"Hey," Ana chirps as I reach my door, not an ounce of hostility in her voice. "Do you know where Cody is?"

I look her over, wondering how Cody would expect me to act. Play dumb? Pretend there's something between us to get rid of her? Looks like the kiss did nothing to scare her away, so I guess that strategy wouldn't work.

"I'm not sure," I say.

"Oh, that's okay. I didn't think you would."

It's bizarre how calm she is, but I shake the moment off, reminding myself she's been stalking him for weeks. This eerie friendliness isn't that odd. I push my door open, but her soft, apologetic voice glues me to the spot.

"I'm sorry things didn't work out."

I should've asked Cody what my role is here. It'd be helpful to know what he expects of me where Ana's concerned. "I'm not sure what you mean."

"You know... you and Cody. When he kissed you, I assumed it was serious."

It's not serious for obvious reasons, but my curiosity piques. How would she know it's not serious? She's not been around. I would've noticed her lingering outside his condo or the building.

"You spoke to him?" I ask. "When?"

"Oh..." Her face falls, cheeks heating a touch. "He didn't tell you you're over? I'm so sorry, I figured when he called me that things didn't work out and he needed a distraction."

"He called you?"

I'm aware I'm stating the obvious, but I'm so taken aback my mind can't do anything smarter.

Why would he call her? She's obviously unhinged. He used me to get rid of her and now... what? He changed his mind?

"Yeah, he told me to come over tonight. He didn't say what time, though. I've been waiting for an hour."

My chest tightens, an unpleasant feeling sinking its claws into my bones—jealousy.

I have zero right to feel that. Cody and I are nothing more than friendly neighbors. Though we've not said anything other than polite *heys* I despise since the night Noah stayed with him, so *friendly is* probably no longer true.

"Why don't you call him and check when he'll be back?" I ask. A small voice in my head whispers that she might be lying.

"No, it's okay. I think he's out with his brothers, and he doesn't like being disturbed. I don't mind waiting."

Still unsure what to think, I decide it's none of my business. I shouldn't be nosy. Closing the door behind me, I drop my bags next to it, slip my heels off and sigh in relief.

I need to grab a shower just in case I get a last-minute invitation. I won't, but what's the harm in being prepared?

Mikaela's organizing one of her famous pool parties. I haven't been invited this time, but a small part of me blindly hopes she'll change her mind after a few drinks.

She's been throwing those parties since her sweet sixteenth. No boys, just girls gossiping, dancing, and drinking. The party used to take place at her parents' house, but once their son—Toby—eloped a few months ago and had a baby, they moved to Europe, leaving Mikaela under Toby's care.

And that's where the party is —at his and his wife's house... the wife who so happens to be Mia's older sister, Aisha.

Sometimes it really sucks that the Newport ecosystem is so small, and everyone knows each other. Aisha would drown me in the pool if I showed up, and I'm sick and tired of the silence my condo offers.

Showered and dressed, I sit at the breakfast bar with a glass of wine, drinking it like water to unlock my tense muscles.

After another moment of considering Ana, I decide a looney stalker warrants a heads-up. If she's here because he told her to come, no harm done, but if she's here to ambush him, Cody would probably want to know.

~~*Me: Ana's waiting for you and wondering where you are because you told her to come over and you're not at home.*~~

Nope... I sound jealous, so I try again.

~~*Me: It's not nice setting up a fuck session and*~~

I don't finish typing that one. It's worse than the first. Taking a deep breath to calm down and suffocate the jealous monster inside me, I send something simpler.

Me: Ana's here.

A few moments pass before *delivered* changes to *read* under my message, and the three dots start dancing. They don't dance for long because next thing I know, he's calling.

My chest erupts in tingles, then a hot flush sweeps me from head to toe, my heart picking up pace.

If Ana's right, Cody's with his brothers. Why is he calling instead of texting? I swipe my shaking thumb across the screen.

"Did she do anything to you?" he asks, his anger tainted with a twinge of worry that has my heart singing.

"No, she just said you told her to come over."

He releases a deep breath and butterflies take off in my stomach because that breath sounds a lot like relief. "I didn't," he says forcefully, like he's making sure I believe him. "Fuck, she's really asking for that restraining order."

"What's going on?" I hear one of his brothers in the background, Theo, if I'm not mistaken. "Who's that?"

"My neighbor," Cody grinds out. "Letting me know my psycho stalker is at my door again."

And just as he says it, there's a loud bang on my door.

"I have to go," I say, my finger hovering over the end call button as I reach for the handle.

"Wait. Don't talk to her, okay? She might be all smiles and kindness, but Shawn says those are the ones who suddenly snap and go batshit crazy."

"I got a notification you spent eight hundred dollars at Victoria's Secret!" my father booms, shoving the door wide open in one hard kick. "Who the fuck are you dressing up for?"

Words stick to my throat as Gideon Fitzpatrick towers above me, nostrils flared, hand raised like he's about to smack me.

I've seen this so many times. The memories of him in this exact stance, wearing the same malicious sneer, as he took his anger out on Mom whenever she hallucinated, threaten to bring me to my knees.

My breath falters in my lungs, my body stiff, unmoving as I wait for him to strike... Not until he pushes a gush of angry air down his nose and his hand falls to his side do I inhale deeply, feeling like I dodged a bullet.

But my mind riots almost instantly when I realize I'm clutching my phone and Cody's still on the line.

Shit, shit, shit.

I kill the connection before my dad notices, but he's too busy gathering my shopping bags and storming into my walk-in closet. I hear the wardrobe doors and drawers clattering until he returns, the bags filled with every piece of my lingerie.

"Who are you sleeping with?" he snaps, little torches swimming in his eyes. "*Who*?!"

"No one, I swear... I went shopping because Kelly-Ann—"

"Spare me the bullshit Kelly-Ann story. I don't care, but you better not be dating some fucker behind my back because I will find out, and if you're whoring around while you're working for me, there'll be hell to pay."

He wasn't always like this. Until last year, he didn't give a damn who I date or sleep with, but then Grant Bailey happened. A twenty-seven-year-old, smart, caring man I met at a coffee house. We hit it off and started casually dating. Nothing too serious, but I enjoyed spending time with him.

It was right about when Dad was looking for an accountant he could manipulate into doing the books the way he commanded. He staged dinner with him and his associate to talk a bit of business, and, doing my job, I flashed the accountant my pussy at the table. His hand went to my knee, and that's when his associate joined us.

My fling, Grant.

It was a nasty evening. My father was—rightly so—accused of using me as bait, so I had to lie through my teeth, making up a story that I was the one who wanted to meet him because I'd heard so much about him from Grant, and had seen him somewhere or other and developed intense feelings.

Thankfully, he was very handsome, so the lie got swallowed, and my dad was off the hook. But from then on, I wasn't allowed to date or have a sexual relationship with anyone because *we are not risking the same situation ever again.*

"I'm not seeing anyone, I promise," I add again, quickly diverting his attention away from my personal life. "Are we going somewhere? Should I get ready?"

He clamps his jaw tight, teeth gnashing as he pacifies himself. "You have two fucking minutes to get dressed."

With a tight nod, I scurry toward my bedroom. I've pissed Dad off enough lately, and I'm not willing to face the inevitable consequences.

Once I fit into one of the many red dresses and slide my feet into heels, I glance in the mirror, staring into my dark blue irises surrounded by a smokey eye. Red lips, tight dress, layered necklaces, diamonds... Blair for the world.

I wish I didn't have to do this. It felt great to wear sweats or jeans with Cody, not an ounce of judgment in his eyes...

With one last touch of mascara, I join my father in the living room, hyperaware that I'm currently *not* wearing panties since all of mine are in the bags he's holding. I checked, but he even went to the extreme of picking out my lingerie from the bathroom hamper.

"You want a dick, Blair?" Dad snaps, his lips curling into a mocking smile. "I've got one you can have."

With that, he yanks the door open, where wide-eyed Ana sits with her back to Cody's.

"Are you okay here, sweetheart? Are you waiting for someone? A boyfriend, perhaps?" my father coos at Ana. "Cody Hayes, correct?" he adds, eyeing the door she's resting against.

Behind his back, I softly bob my head, praying that she confirms. Her lips part, but she says nothing for a second, until she swallows like she's making room for words.

"Yes, sir. Cody Hayes."

"You got yourself a keeper there, sweetheart. I'm sure you heard *nothing*, but I apologize for all the screaming."

The implied threat in *nothing* is not lost on Ana. He stares her down, acting concerned and apologetic, but I know his eyes speak volumes as he waits for her to nod in confirmation that she'll keep her mouth shut.

Satisfied with her cooperation, he grips my upper arm in a gesture that could easily be mistaken for affection if he weren't gouging his fingers into my flesh so hard it hurts.

"You'll leave bruises," I whisper when we round the corner.

"Be glad I'm not leaving a black eye. Maybe if you got a beating like your crazy mother, you'd stay in your place."

Once again, the memories his words summon almost turn my knees to jelly. I'm not half as scared of his threats as I was when Mom was alive. He never hit *me*, but he took Mom's meds whenever I misbehaved, then beat her up when she started hallucinating.

He won't hurt me, though. Not while he needs me to play my part. Bruises on my arm can be easily attributed to wild sex. A black eye or split lip, not so much.

"Where are we going tonight?"

"Strip club. Simons pulled out. I've got a new guy, probably an even better fit for what I have in mind..."

EIGHTEEN

Blair

Cody steps out of his condo when I shove the key into my lock. It's after midnight, and I smell like smoke and stripper perfume after spending too many hours watching women writhing around poles while my father talked business with his newest victim.

The man didn't pay me any heed. He barely even looked at me when I arrived, too busy salivating at the much bustier and curvier girls than me working the poles.

But I wasn't excused until my father shook hands with the man, his smile dazzling, fucking blinding in all its flakiness. Tonight must've been the fastest deal Gideon Fitzpatrick ever closed. I bet the fat envelope he slipped into Mr. Whatever's hand helped speed the process, but it's unusual for my father to willingly hand out bribes.

The deal must've been one he couldn't afford to lose. Still, giving money away isn't a decision Dad takes lightly.

"Where were you?" Cody asks, his icy tone demanding my attention. "Who was that asshole screaming at you earlier?"

My body ignites at the sight of his sweatpants hanging low, bare feet, and bare chest. Since the night we spent together, I've been walking around hot and bothered whenever he invades my mind. I wake up drenched in sweat from intense dreams and finish the job using my purple wand. I've mastered using it, but it's nowhere near as good as Cody.

My cheeks heat more, filthy thoughts on display as I watch him tug from a bottle of Corona, glaring at me like I've killed his pet snake.

"I don't know what you're talking about," I lie.

Playing dumb probably won't work on him, but I can try.

He scoffs, shaking his head, clearly disappointed in my answer. "Ana said he dragged you out of here like a fucking dog, Blair. *Who* was he?"

"It's none of your business." I turn to go inside, but Cody leaps forward, gently cuffing his fingers around my wrist.

"I'm making it my business, B." He steps closer, backing me against the wall.

"Who was he? Your boyfriend?"

Blood sings in my ears. God, he sounds... he sounds *jealous*. Possessive. Territorial with how his fingers sink into my flesh, hard enough to send a message but not hard enough to hurt.

"Stop asking questions. Please."

"I'm not forcing you to answer." He moves his hand to trace the line of my hip, looming over me, his brown irises dancing across my face and body, two lines creasing his forehead when he takes in my dress. "You look..." He pauses, scrunching his nose like he caught a bad stench. "You look better in jeans."

"So polite," I mock.

Or try to mock, but my words come out as breathless as I feel when he's crowding my personal space, the heat of his body engulfing me whole.

He's so damn *big*.

I'm not short. Five-six is not short. Add my three-inch heels, and we're close to eye level, but his broad chest and big arms make me feel like small prey. "You wanted to say I look like a whore. I know. No need to point it out. I own a mirror."

"Then why do you dress like this?"

"It's none of your business!" I drop my gaze, hiding from his scrutiny, and another thrill passes through me at what I discover.

He's hard.

And I'm so wet... Feverish with need, dazed by his presence, desperate for another night. Desperate to nip this topic in the bud and stop him asking uncomfortable questions.

"The lines we crossed two weeks ago aren't as significant as those you're trying to cross now." Without thinking, I run my fingers along the obvious bulge and squeeze gently, but he grabs my wrist, forcing my hand away. "Stop asking questions, Cody. I promise I'm not worth it. Take a step back, and... if you want to cross lines, stick to those we already crossed."

Feeling bold, I wriggle my hand free and move it back where I started, though this time I slip my fingers inside his sweats and grasp the base of his thick, warm shaft, pumping slowly.

He falls forward, bracing one arm on the wall, eyes hooding over as his primitive need takes center stage.

"Should I stop?"

"Fuck no," he groans, thrusting into my touch. "Good job derailing the conversation."

I watch a restless muscle feather his chiseled jaw, my blood growing hotter, my mind skipping ahead to him using me to get off. I love how quickly he can lose control and seize it back whenever he wants.

Rising on my toes, I lean in, my warm breath fanning his ear. "I'd do this faster with my mouth."

With another low groan, he loops one arm under my butt, hauling me into his arms, a beer still in the other hand that he promptly sets aside as we step into his condo.

"I've imagined fucking that sweet no-gag-reflex throat of yours since you swallowed me down. You got anything to say?"

A small smile twists my lips when he sets me on his bedroom floor, ever so carefully. I shimmy out of my dress straps, tugging it down to expose my boobs.

"Don't come in my mouth."

"The only place I'll come will be your pussy." He drops a pillow by the wall. "Lose the heels and kneel."

I find it incredibly endearing that he's worried about me bruising my knees. I don't know why that's so sweet, but the soft dom vibes I'm getting from him make me melt.

I whip my hair over one shoulder and look up, loving the sight of Cody's strong thighs and long, thick cock proudly standing to attention, begging for my touch.

"You're sure you're okay letting me do this?" he asks, his voice low, hoarse. The sentence ends with a groan when I angle my neck so it's easier for him to slide in. "Words, B."

"Yes, I'm sure." Giving him a quick reminder of what my lips feel like wrapped around him, I swallow him down and slip him back out, looking up. "Do your worst."

He grabs my hand, setting it over his thigh. "Tap out if I'm taking it too far."

"I won't."

His nostrils flare, and his patience wears off.

I might be coming across as experienced, but the truth is, despite having a lot of meaningless sex, I've gone down on two other men total, and I never allowed either of them to use me the way I want Cody to use me.

Seeing the abyss of his black pupils, hearing his breath falter, those low, primitive groans... it's unlike any euphoria I've experienced. It's addictively freeing, letting him do as he pleases.

I feel *safe* despite handing over control.

Maybe because he's fixated on consent. Or because of those soft dom vibes and how his eyes lose their hard edge when he looks down at me... or maybe because I'm so into him I want all he offers.

He slides in all the way, legs bucking as he sucks in a harsh breath. I love when he does that. I love those audible, primal sounds he can't control.

"You really don't have a gag reflex," he says, staring like I hold the answers to life's most important questions. "Fuck, baby... you're beautiful on your knees."

Slowly, he pulls out, then slides back in, my cheeks purposely hollow, my tongue curled to lick the underside as he sets a pace. Another pleasant sensation spreads inside me when Cody cradles the back of my head, so it won't bang against the wall with every thrust.

I'm shaking, grinding my thighs together, searching for a bit of friction the faster he pumps, chasing his climax. The guttural moans falling from his lips drive me incoherent.

I can't get enough of how he watches me, his eyes glazed over. I'm the one who leaves him this desperate, this *satisfied.*

The salty, pungent taste of him coats my tongue, precum

leaking every time he hits the wall of my throat, sliding further until I swallow him whole.

Again and again... the faster he pumps, the slicker my thighs and the harder I suck, ravenous for that moment when he stops fighting his orgasm and lets it consume him.

"Fuck," he growls, easing up, both hands softly cupping my face as he pulls out. "I won't come unless you come with me, B."

Helping me up, he spins me around, pins my open palms to the wall, and locks my wrists in his grip. With the other hand, he yanks my dress up.

"Are you always walking around commando?" he grinds out, throwing back the question I asked him the first time we fucked. He follows it with a stinging slap on my butt that makes me wetter. "Where the fuck are your panties?"

"Stop asking questions," I plead, my voice catching when I feel his cock slide across my pussy. "Either fuck me or get your hands off me."

He rests his forehead against the back of my head, gripping my hips. "Keep your hands on the wall, B." A groan of approval resounds when the head of his cock juts against my entrance. "On your toes for me."

I rise as high as possible when he slams into me, making my whole body spasm. "God, this angle..." I throw my head back, arching into his hurried strokes. "So good."

"That it is. It'll be even better when you start squirting." He ups the pace, pumping in and out faster against my G spot with measured precision, and before long, his arm circles my waist, holding me upright. "Good girl, don't fight it. Soak me."

The orgasm hits, blurring my vision, and the pressure of my squirting pushes him back.

"Best thing ever. One more, okay? Give me another." He

drives himself home hard and fast, beckoning another orgasm to the surface within seconds.

I tremble like an uncoiled spring, wave after wave of small orgasms assaulting my senses, the floor wet under our feet, the room hot, stuffy, and reeking of sex.

"Such a good fucking girl when you want to be," Cody whispers, pressing his hand between my shoulder blades until my back is almost as level as a table. "So obedient. So fucking submissive... You know what I like, don't you, baby?"

He gathers my hair, wraps it around his wrist, and drives into me fast. The sound of his hips slapping against mine as he hate-fucks me is the most erotic thing in the world. Our moans, gasps, and sucked-in labored breaths mix in the air, tuning out reality until it's just us. Just *him* working himself into me, every stroke designed as the sweetest punishment.

I feel the telltale change of impending climax in his movements. An injection of panic seizes my muscles because he didn't grab a condom, but just as I part my lips to remind him, he pulls out, painting my back with warm jets of cum, his hips jerking in sync with the quiet curses falling from his lips.

"Shit," he pants, slapping my sore butt—gently this time. "Looks like we've got a fucking problem here, B."

I tense immediately, but his soft lips stamping the nape of my neck counter it.

"I already want to do this again," he admits, and with the last lingering kiss on my skin, he turns me around. "You think we can keep this up for a while without you catching feelings?"

His cum trickles down my spine, pooling at the base where his arm circles my back, firmly holding me to him. Unable to stop myself, I brush back a strand of his dark hair that fell out of the bun.

"You're asking if we can casually fuck until we're both sated, then stop without me ending up stalking you?"

"That's exactly what I'm asking."

I wish I could say my heart didn't speed up at the prospect, but that'd be a blatant lie. I already caught feelings. When he held me all night, helping me cage my demons without even knowing how much I needed that comfort.

But I can put a cap on those feelings if I get amazing orgasms and a bit of closeness in return.

"Under one condition," I say, mindlessly tracing patterns on his pec. "One we probably share anyway."

"Fire away."

"No one can find out."

He narrows those brown, gorgeous eyes. "I know why I'd rather keep this between us, but you... What's your reason?"

"You ask too many questions." Rising on my toes to peck his lips one last time, I wiggle out of his embrace, stepping into the bathroom. "Take it or leave it."

He follows, wetting a fresh washcloth under warm water before gently cleaning my back. "I should start using condoms, so I'm not making a mess of you every time, but I really don't want to miss how good it feels when you're squirting all over my cock."

"I'm making a mess of you. It's fair you make a mess of me, too."

I don't add that it's fitting since I'm a huge mess inside. Instead, I grab another washcloth and wipe his cock. It's still at half-mast and probably wouldn't need much attention to rise back to full glory.

"So?" I drop the cloth in the sink. "Do we have a deal?"

He tries to kiss me, but I arch away, knowing damn well I

need to set some boundaries if we're going to participate in extracurricular activities. Kissing was okay when I thought one night was all I'd get or when I thought, just a few moments ago, that this was the last time we'd fuck, but if it's going to be more regular, kisses are out of the question. I love his mouth too much to risk it.

"We're supposed to be working out the sexual tension," I say when he cocks an eyebrow. "Kisses are intimate, and intimate might turn problematic."

"And sex isn't intimate?"

"Not the way we just did it."

He smirks, lifting his hands in defeat. "Fine. Have it your way. No kissing. Anything else?"

"Yes. No interaction outside the bedroom. No more cookies, no helping with babysitting, no helping with shopping. No more questions. Let's not blur the lines, okay?"

He grinds his teeth, probably not happy about the no-questions part. The whole point of him cornering me out in the hallway was so he could learn about the things I refuse to share. I hope to take my dirty little secret to the grave.

And that's why I'm imposing the no-questions rule. My crush on Cody is something real, but I know better than to think or hope *we* could evolve into something real. There's too much ugly history, baggage, and hurt that can't be overlooked outside feral, primal, bedroom lust.

Sex is physical. While it can lead to emotions, if we set iron-clad boundaries, we'll get what we want from this arrangement without risking too much.

I get to feel in control of my body. Since my traumatic first time, I've used sex to erase the feel of the sixty-year-old pervert's hands on me. I never enjoyed it the way I enjoy it with

Cody. His insistence on communication and consent helps tear down the walls my mind built that fateful night.

I worked through the trauma mentally with my therapist, and now, thanks to Cody, I'll work through it physically so that one day I won't dread the idea of commitment.

And, obviously, sex with Cody is a fantasy come true. A fantasy I was too embarrassed and scared to dream about since I laid eyes on him my first day of college.

I'm not sure what Cody wants out of our deal. He can have any girl he wants, but right now he wants me, so why the hell not?

"You're driving a hard bargain," he says, lifting his hand to toy with my nipple. "But I think a step back is a good idea, so yeah, let's revert to *hey*s and replace the talking and working through our bullshit with sex."

I try not to get hung up on the spite in his voice. He's annoyed he won't find out who the man he heard over the phone is, where I was tonight, and why I'm not wearing underwear.

"You're pouting," I say, dragging my nails along the underside of his stiffening cock. "Want me to work that frustration out of you, baby boy?" I inject enough sarcasm into the endearment to drive my point home.

His teeth gnash between his lips. "You don't like it when I call you *baby girl*?"

I love it. I always cringed when I heard guys call their girls that because, from the observer's point of view, it's just so lame, but the desire coating his voice when it's aimed at me... not lame at all. Nothing sounds lame on Cody's lips.

But again, pet names fall on the wrong side of the line. "Save it for someone special," I say, looking down because his cock swells in my palm, the tip leaking precum once more. "I think you're ready for round two."

"I think I am," he agrees, gripping my hips and setting me by the sink, his fingers finding my clit. "Are you sore, B?"

"Not one bit."

"You're about to be." He smiles darkly, guiding himself in. "Tap out if I'm too rough."

I gasp and cling to his broad shoulders when he slams into me. "Like I said. I can handle a hate-fuck."

"Good..." he breathes in my ear, bottoming out inside me. "...hate fucks are suddenly my favorite."

NINETEEN

Cody

The new arrangement with Blair works better than I initially anticipated. Not that I was thinking clearly when we made the deal. I'm not thinking clearly now, recalling one morning last week that she spent sprawled over my breakfast bar while I feasted on her pussy, making her squirt three times before we moved to the bedroom for round two.

Guilt gnaws at me whenever she's not around to distract me from my thoughts, but I ponder calling it off ten times a day, feeling like an asshole for indulging in Blair, of all people. I feel even worse when we're together, and I can barely keep myself from dipping my head to take her lips in mine.

I'm not lying to myself, though. I know I won't call it off. Not yet. I've not had my fill. One second of remembering what she feels like coming beneath me, and calling it off seems like a felony. Besides, no one knows.

No one will know unless either of us decides otherwise,

and sex with Blair is something out of this world. When we're alone, she's not on guard. No masks, no pretending, no fake smiles, or bitchy attitude. She's pliant and submissive, or demanding, depending on my mood.

She's perfect and I have no control around her.

I'm weak.

There, I fucking said it. I'm weak.

No matter how bad I feel about fraternizing with the enemy I can't stop this.

What Mia's eyes don't see won't hurt her, and this meaningless arrangement with Blair might just stop my obsessive, compulsive protectiveness toward my brother's fiancée.

There is nothing healthy about it. Neither for me nor her.

I almost blocked her relationship with Nico because I was so fixated on keeping her sheltered. Thank God he doesn't give up easily. By his side, Mia blossomed from a timid, afraid of her own shadow, sweet little girl to a still sweet but confident young woman.

She doesn't take his bullshit like she did at the beginning. She stands up for herself. She's *fine*, and I need to stop walking on eggshells wherever she's concerned.

Try as I might, I couldn't fight the feral need that consumes me whenever Blair's close. I stayed away for two weeks after that first time, running around in fucking circles before I snapped.

Making our sexcapades more regular didn't cross my mind until I painted the delicate skin of her back with my cum and realized that was *it.* Done. Over.

The last thing I wanted was for it to be over.

But it's just sex. Nothing more.

When she set the rules while standing naked in my bathroom, I almost said *no way*, remembering the man who screamed at her while we were on the phone. I'm not sure but I think it's the same man who screamed at her the night she slept in my arms.

I need answers because I didn't like that guy's tone. Derogatory, spiteful... that's no way to talk to a woman.

Even if that woman is Blair.

I had time to think about everything she told me while Noah napped on my couch. I spent two weeks overthinking our every encounter, unearthing the little things she said, the things she only implied and... I'm having a hard time hating her as much as I did before.

I still hate her—pinky promise—but it doesn't come as effortlessly. I have no trouble fucking her brains out, though.

But while we're acting like perfect strangers, I wonder what she does when she's not with me, alone in her condo. I wonder if she thinks about me. I wonder if she cries herself to sleep.

I wonder why I fucking wonder.

"Who the fuck are you dressing up for?!"

Those words come back and hit me a few times a day.

Is that guy dangerous? He sounded like someone who wouldn't have an issue smacking a girl about, but I've been scrutinizing Blair's body every time we have sex, and so far, not a single mark on her perfect skin.

Not one bruise, cut, not one sign someone touched her against her will. And you don't ask a guy to face-fuck you if you went through that kind of trauma, so there's that.

Another thing about our little dalliance that surprised me is the weight these rules took off my shoulders. Instead of obsessing that I'm doing a stupid thing with the girl I should never touch, I accept us for what we are—physical.

Primitive, desire-driven, great sex.

Blair made sure it's impersonal. A dirty deed. No chats, no kisses, no way we could crave more. We severed the connection sprouting between us before it properly took root. The same connection that had us digging through the piles of crap in our past. We channeled that effort into testing our limits in bed.

I found zero in Blair so far.

Despite going overboard more than once, she hasn't tapped out yet. On the other hand, she found one no-go with me when her finger ventured too close to my asshole. To say I jerked away would be an understatement. I jumped out of bed, my chest heaving, eyes shooting fireballs her way.

I don't hate for the sake of hating. I tried many things over the years, learning what makes me tick. I could get on board with cock rings, vibrators strapped to my shaft, or even—though I'm not a fan—edging, but a finger in my ass is *not* my jam.

Blair, on the other hand, almost fucking purrs when I coat my fingers in her arousal and toy with that tight back entrance. I'm yet to push my dick in there, but she comes twice as hard when I slip the tip of my finger past the ring of muscles.

I adjust myself in my chair because my cock's growing hard just thinking about going balls-deep in her ass to make her squirt.

It's been two weeks since we made the deal, and we've had sex eighteen times (not that I'm counting). July is here already, hellishly hot. Five more weeks until Logan's wedding, four until the bachelor party I'm here to plan with my brothers.

Too bad planning the night's strippers and booze loses the battle for my attention with Miss Fitzpatrick. I can't push her out of my head for five fucking minutes lately.

Just this morning, she knocked on my door at five thirty, two hours before I normally rise on a Friday, sucked me off in the shower, then pushed me onto the bed and rode my face.

She tried sliding off when she was about to come, but hey, we're testing limits, so I held her in place, and almost fucking drowned as she came.

I thought I wouldn't enjoy it considering scientists have yet to decipher the squirting phenomenon. I thought it'll be like a golden shower—

A lightbulb moment has me snatching my phone from the table to text Blair. Sex talk is the only talk we are free to engage in, so I'm not crossing any lines.

Me: Got one more. Golden showers.

B: Isn't squirting the same thing? You didn't protest this morning.

Me: It's nothing like that. Tastes sweet like your pussy. Smells like your pussy too. Cherry candy.

She sends back a rolling-its-eyes emoji because she thinks it's dumb that I claim she tastes like candy. *That's impossible, Cody.*

Like I don't know that. Of course it's impossible, but I love her taste, and when I say she tastes like cherry candy, it's because it's my favorite flavor and hers is on par.

"What're you smirking at?" Colt asks, joining me at the table, fashionably late, his hair freshly cut into the signature style he's had for years.

Seems like everyone in this family took punctuality lessons from Logan. I've been sitting at this table for ten minutes, and even though we said seven and it's five past, no one but Colt is here yet.

"Nothing. A message I got," I say, erasing the chat before tucking my phone into my back pocket. "Where is everyone?"

"Shawn pulled up just as I was coming in. I don't know about the rest. You been here long?"

"Not really. Ten minutes tops."

His eyes quickly sweep the table. "Why haven't you ordered a beer?"

"I was waiting for all of you."

"You never do that." He narrows his eyes, crossing both arms over his chest. "Alright, spill. You obviously spent the last ten minutes texting some chick, so out with it. Who is she?"

"I'm not texting any chicks. I've not got rid of Ana yet, so I'm taking a break from pussy."

"You gonna try a dick?" Shawn asks, approaching our table with his husband, Jack.

"My friend has a massive crush on you, Cody," Jack says, pulling another table closer since we won't all fit by the one I chose, and Nico apparently failed to let the staff know we'll need a table for eight. "I can give you his number."

"Tell him I'm flattered but I'll stick with pussy. As soon as I find one less unhinged than Ana."

"Has she been in touch again?" Shawn asks, waving the waitress over. "Why didn't you call me?"

"I got rid of her. She's not doing anything harmful. I'm sure you can't file for a restraining order just because someone gets on your nerves and doesn't understand *no*."

"Evening, boys," Kathy, the waitress, says, pulling her notepad out of her breast pocket. "What are we having? The usual?"

"Yes, babe. The rest are on their way so grab theirs too, alright? Except Logan. We're planning his bachelor party, so he's not coming. Oh, and could you grab us something to nibble on? I get the feeling we'll be here a while."

"Sure thing," she chirps, sending Colt a smoldering look we all catch.

As soon as she saunters back toward the bar, the attention swings from me to my identical brother.

"Nico's gonna be pissed when he finds out you're fucking his staff, bro," I say in a hushed tone.

"What else is new? He's always pissed."

"True," Shawn chuckles. "But maybe tell your girl to keep it on the down-low if she doesn't want to lose her job. Back to you though, Cody. I don't like this Ana thing. She sounds obsessed, and from experience, I can tell you it never ends well."

"I'll be fine. She's not been around since—" I push the air from my lungs, applying the brakes before I let it slip that Ana's not been around since she caught me sneaking out of Blair's condo last week. "Since I yelled at her."

The questioning looks triggered by my tripping over my words dissipate in a flash. They know I break out in hives whenever a situation forces me to raise my voice at a woman.

The only girl I ever snapped at without remorse is Blair, but now things between us have escalated, the regret hits every time she's such a good girl and lets me paint her tanned skin with my cum or slide my cock deep into her sweet mouth.

Conor and Theo arrive when the waitress sets our order on the table, but no sign of Nico. He's never late, at least not this much, so we're getting restless. Theo grabs his phone ten minutes later, putting it on loudspeaker.

Nico answers almost immediately. "Five minutes, Theo. Order me a beer, will you?"

"Already waiting."

As promised, Nico shows up five minutes later, his cheekbone swollen like he's been fighting. Not one of us would bat an eye a year ago, but since he found Mia, Nico stopped throwing his fists left and right, so this is interesting.

"What happened?" Jack asks, gesturing at his face. "Who pissed you off?"

"Better question would be who I pissed off." He sits beside me, snatching his beer and draining a third. "Mia's not happy with me."

"She *hit* you?" Theo's eyes widen before he bursts out laughing. "And she actually did some damage with those tiny fists? Shit, bro. I knew I liked her the moment I saw her."

"She didn't hit me. Well, not in my face. She threw a few punches at my shoulder. I was teaching her to drive and she panicked when the green light came on. Instead of slowly accelerating, she fucking floored it. We were in the Merc, and that thing spins like nobody's business, so the car shot forward, did a one-eighty, and my head slammed the side window."

"Is she okay?" I ask, my fingers flexing in and out of fists. "Is she hurt?"

"She's fine, relax." He waves me off. "Not a scratch on her. She's pissed off, though."

"Stop forcing her to drive. She won't learn because she doesn't want to learn," Shawn cuts in. "It's not like she needs to drive, right? Rose can take her to college."

"I don't think she'll let me teach her again."

"Good. Leave her alone, and let's get started," Shawn says. "I remember Logan mentioning a tiger when we were planning my bachelor party. Are we doing that?"

"Can't say I know where to rent a tiger, but we can paint Ares with orange stripes," Theo, the best man, says with a grin.

"He was all talk back then because he didn't have a girl," he adds. "Now he's whipped, and I bet he won't even want to leave Cassidy alone for the weekend."

"Tough shit," Colt says, waving the waitress over for another round. "He's coming. Voluntarily or not."

"Okay, so no tiger, what about the guest list?"

"I've got one penciled in. It's a bit long. Almost eighty." Theo pulls a piece of paper from his pocket, passing it to Nico.

"Eighty?"

He shrugs. "I only included people I know they'll invite to the wedding, but I'm sure we can prune this a bit." He crosses his hands, staring us all down. "What? It's not my fault Logan's friends with half of fucking Newport."

Nico skims the list, pulls out a pen, and starts crossing off names. Before long, the list is shortened to fifty-two guys and we're left with no choice but to ask Logan to join the next meeting and narrow it down further.

While Jack and Shawn argue about hotels and casinos, my phone vibrates in my pocket, and I head outside for a smoke to check the message, not dumb enough to do it at the table under my brothers' scrutiny.

It's just two words.

B: Not tonight.

My eyebrows pinch in the middle. She's canceling plans we only made this morning?

I guess I can't expect her to be at my beck and call and a break might be a good idea, but it doesn't feel right. We've been fucking multiple times a day, and most of those times Blair initiated, beating me to the punch.

Me: Okay.

It sounds harsh, like I'm pissed off, and truthfully... I am. I clench and unclench my fists, annoyance dancing at the edge of my mind. I was looking forward to tonight. Got her favorite wine and planned to feed her Chinese takeout before letting her leave.

Even if she'd throw a fit that I'm *breaking the rules!* which she probably would.

Colt joins me outside, leaning against the wall a few steps to my left, pulling his cigarettes from his pocket.

"Feels like we're losing touch," he says, staring into the sky. "Conor's with Vee most of the time, you're locked in your condo, I'm working my ass off..."

"That's normal. We had to grow up sometime, but I don't think we're losing touch."

"Yeah? Because not so long ago we couldn't go a day without talking through anything that happened, and now look at us. You didn't even tell me Ana's still stalking you."

"Nothing new happened, Colt. Not so long ago, you were trying not to share every tiny detail of your life with us, and now you're pissed off that I'm not whining about Ana every time she shows up?"

He grinds his teeth, knowing damn well I'm right. "I don't want you to feel you can't talk to me just because we don't live in the same house, okay? There's suddenly distance between us and I don't like it."

"I know we can talk. If there's something worth mentioning, I'll call."

"You sure there's nothing you want to mention now?"

My heartbeat accelerates. There's no way he knows about

my deal with Blair. No way. We've not been caught or even near-caught—

Fuck! Ana...

If she blabbed, I'm screwed. What do I tell him? How do I explain myself? What excuse can I conjure? I'm not great with making shit up on the spot, so I drag out the silence, racking my brain and coming up empty.

How do I explain that the Blair we both know and hate hides a different girl inside? One that's kind, helpful, and broken. One that needs someone to believe she means every word when she apologizes. Someone to hold her when she cries and kiss her when she smiles.

Colt wouldn't believe me.

"You got something to ask?" I huff, no clue what to say if he gets it right. "Ask away, Colt. Don't play games."

I don't think Ana called Colt to tell him she caught me with Blair. Why would she? They exchanged maybe ten sentences total since the night in *The Ramshack* last year.

Ana doesn't know anything about Mia's bullying or why this dalliance with Blair could hurt me and the people around me if anyone found out.

I take a deep breath, cooling my jets.

"Fine," Colt says, pushing away from the wall, looking annoyed. "Blair. What's happening, Cody? First you hate her, then you knock out Alan. Now you're MIA most of the time."

He doesn't know shit.

He's just fishing for information in true Colt fashion. If he knows I'm fucking Blair on the side, he'd call me out on it.

"Don't throw Alan in my face. You know why I did that. You knocked him out for the same fucking reason. I would've been pissed off regardless of who he had in that closet.

Nothing to do with Blair."

At the time, I believed it, but things changed quickly. Well, not that quickly. Blair and I have been neighbors for almost two months, and she's been spending hours upon hours on my cock for two weeks now.

We don't talk unless it's related to sex, but I'm learning so much about her while she's under me and even more right after when we lay in bed, coming down from the high. Silence, gestures, facial expressions... all speak volumes.

I've not realized this until I saw her leave her condo last night, but somewhere along the line, I learned how to figure out where she's heading based on what she wears. Short, tight, colorful dresses when she's meeting her friends. Red, hooker-styled ones when I don't think I want to know where she's heading. Skinny jeans that look painted-on and pretty blouses when she's volunteering at the hospital, and... anything goes when she's with me. Sweats, jeans, shorts, pj's.

I like her best when she doesn't give a crap about her clothes and makeup. When she lets her guard down, peels off the disguise, and isn't forcing smiles or overthinking her words.

"Fine," Colt says, butting his cigarette on the ground. "I believe you, but..." He pins me with a pointed stare that I know well: *I've got you.* "Come talk to me if anything changes."

"I will," I say, half absent from this conversation, my mind whirling around Blair's whereabouts.

I didn't see her leave today, so I don't know what she was wearing or where she went that was so important she can't stop by for sex.

"I mean it, Cody. I'm here for you, alright?"

"I heard you the first time."

TWENTY

Cody

Sometimes I worry my head isn't working the way it should.

Setting aside the fact I stayed up on Friday until I heard Blair come back so I could deduce where she went by her outfit, I've been thinking about Ana daily.

By the way, I'm ninety-nine percent sure Blair was with her friends based on her blue sequin dress.

But Ana... I worry about her. Up until her brother's suicide, she was the most laid-back, carefree girl I ever came across. Always laughing, never taking things seriously. Not even sex, which was refreshing, if I'm honest. No pressure.

I should be happy she's done stalking me, done hanging outside the building, but when she was here, I knew she was okay.

Well, not okay, but not doing anything reckless.

Now I'm left wondering.

It's been almost a month since she was last in touch. Anything could've happened, but I can't text her without fueling her obsession.

A knock on my door halts my internal tug-of-war. Setting the knife aside, I cross the condo. Blair's there, looking unsure of herself, both hands behind her back, nose scrunched.

And she's wet. Hair, clothes, face... soaked.

"Is it raining?" I ask.

"In my bathroom," she confirms. "I slipped while cleaning... grabbed the pipe to steady myself, but something cracked, and now it's sputtering water everywhere. I can't turn it off. I know this crosses a line, but it's Sunday—"

I chuckle, halting her rant. "How about you say *Cody, could you please fix my shower* instead of rambling on? We're neighbors, B. Neighbors help and your neighbor happens to be very good with his hands."

A cute blush creeps up her cheeks. "As he proved many, many times." She winks, the blush dissolving into a smile. "Could you please fix my shower before it floods the petty woman downstairs?"

"I can." I invite her in, then retrieve my toolbox from the coat closet. "And Karen's not only petty, B, she's old, miserable, and bored."

"Her name isn't Karen, but it sure fits. You know she keeps leaving fake parking tickets on my windscreen whenever I'm not parked perfectly inside the lines?"

"All she leaves me is her phone number," I joke, earning myself a whack on the shoulder. "Hey, it's not my fault you park like you need extra-strong glasses. While I fix your shower, can you finish the lasagna? Mix the spinach with the meat, layer it all, then shove it in the oven."

She spins on the balls of her bare feet. "You can cook?"

"I can cook, clean, fix showers, and locate the G spot."

"Aren't you a package deal?" She struts toward the kitchen, leaving a wet trail behind.

"Lose your clothes, B. Slip into one of my hoodies." I motion at her wet jeans. "Or just strip. Your call."

The last thing I see before I lock her in my condo is two wrinkles lining her forehead. Yeah... I shouldn't have offered my clothes. I shouldn't have joked, either, but whatever.

Arriving at the scene in Blair's bathroom, it's not half as bad as I imagined. The water' s spritzing, and the pipe is loose, but it's not a full-blown geyser. Most of the water falls back into the basin, so there's minimal risk of flooding Karen.

Too bad. She'd have something to do.

Thankfully, the pipe isn't bent, just snapped out of place. Despite it only being a five-minute job tightening the valves, my t-shirt's soaked when I head back across the hall.

"My brother should be shot on the spot for putting that shower cubicle in a modern bathroom. You need an anti-slip mat."

Blair looks up from where she's layering the lasagna and takes me in with a cheeky smile. "Had a little accident, did you?"

I follow her line of sight, finding a wet patch on my groin. "Yeah, fixing showers turns me on."

"I was implying something else, but coming in your pants works better. I guess you had more say in the design than I did. I like your walk-in shower."

"It fits us both. I doubt yours would."

"Should I say thank you with words or gestures?" She rounds the island, purposely bending down as she pops the lasagna in the oven, her sweet ass peeking from under the hem of one of my white t-shirts. I groan at how good she looks in white, a stark contrast to her tanned skin and brown hair.

"You forgot the cheese."

"No, I didn't. I add it closer to the end so it melts but doesn't burn. Unless you prefer it burned."

"Leave it. I don't need a *thank you*, B, but I won't stop you saying it with gestures." I step back to lock the door and yank my t-shirt over my head. "We have forty minutes before the food's ready."

"Thirty," she counters, crossing the room and jumping into my arms, her bare, warm, wet pussy pressing into my stomach. "You're forgetting I need to sprinkle the cheese on top."

"Shameless," I tut, supporting her with one arm, her legs tightly wrapped around my waist. I push the other hand between us, strumming her clit. "No panties."

She moans, biting my earlobe as I carry her into my bedroom. "They were wet."

"I bet they were." Dropping her on the bed, I strip out of my clothes and fall forward, my face conveniently landing between her legs. "Lay back and open wide, baby."

Before she obeys, I'm on her, coating my tongue in the first taste of her arousal.

"D-Don't," she gasps, arching her hips, both hands weaving into my hair when I blow on her clit. "Don't call me that."

I lick her, push my tongue in then out, and in and out until she claws my scalp, her thighs holding me hostage. "Don't call you *what*, baby?"

I suck her clit and the slap she lands on my head isn't half as hard as she intended, I'm sure. "You're breaking the rules, Cody."

Prying her legs open, I crawl higher, locking her between my arms as I dive for a kiss.

I want her lips.

The silent, no-kisses fucks were fun at first but the longer we do this, the more uncomfortable I am when I work myself into her as if she were a sex doll.

Fuck the rules. She either uses her lips to speak or to kiss me.

I miss the mark when she turns her head, my lips landing on her ear. I bite and suck the lobe hard enough that she'll know it's not what I wanted, then yank her t-shirt over her boobs, coming down on them like I'm starving.

"Oh shit, that feels so nice." She grabs my ass, spurring me on, demanding more, faster, harder. "I need you deeper. Please."

"As you wish." I flip her over, cross her ankles, and shove a pillow under her hips. "As deep as I can get," I say, forcing my cock between her thighs. "Tell me what you did all day." With one long measured stroke, I'm in. Fuck... I need a second to catch my breath because this is the absolute perfect position.

"No, no, no," she chants quietly when I pull out and slam back in deeper than ever.

I halt, my heart pounding like a train on the tracks. "What is it, B? Does it hurt? You want to stop?"

"No! God, *no*. Don't stop," she mewls, grasping handfuls of the sheets when I repeat the maneuver. "It's... it's amazing, I promise. I meant... I meant..." Another moan rips from her chest. She arches her spine so hard I think it might snap. "God, that's so good."

"I know." I grasp her hair, pulling back until she's perfectly positioned for a Spiderman kiss.

But as soon as I move in, she jerks away, driving me fucking feral. In slow, methodic moves, I sink into her, taking my annoyance out on the delicate skin in the crook of her neck, kissing and nipping the same way I want to kiss her lips.

"Keep talking," I encourage, leaning back on my calves.

"What did you mean?"

"That I won't tell you about my day."

"Fine." I pump faster when her walls pulse around my length. "I had breakfast with Conor and Vee." My thigh muscles scream the faster I drive into Blair, watching my cock disappear in her pussy, fitting so well. "She made waffles with maple syrup..."

"Shut up," Blair pants, the orgasm hitting her so hard her legs shake, and her back arches off the bed. "One more," she pleads. "Please, I need another one."

"When have I ever left you with one orgasm?" I chuckle, breaking another rule to kiss a line up her spine before changing position so she can take what she needs.

She scrambles to straddle me, and fuck... she's sexier when she takes me in my t-shirt than she is when naked.

How's that possible?

Naked flesh should win over t-shirts, but the mess of Blair's hair framing her flushed face, how the soft fabric grips her small boobs, how it bunches around her thighs, giving me glimpses of my cock sliding in and out of her... it's close to fucking perfection.

"They're sickening," I continue my story, recalling Vee and Conor serving breakfast, those lingering looks, smiles, how great they fit... "Conor's whipped and Vee—"

"All your brothers are whipped," Blair utters, knotting her fingers on my nape. "Why are you telling me this?! You're breaking the... *oh*." Her eyes roll back into her head when she finds the right angle. One that lets her grind her clit over my abdomen as she cants her hips, getting us off. "You're breaking the rules."

I am, but I don't care. Either we morph these sex sessions

into something less clinical, or I'm out because she's reduced it to jacking off. Fun, but not half as satisfying. The longer we do this, the more detached she is.

"Vee's as whipped as he is." I grip Blair's jaw, spreading my fingers under her chin from one ear to the other as I lean in...

She throws her head back, and I miss again.

Jesus fuck!

"She wants a cat..." I ramble on, kissing, nipping, and sucking the soft, warm skin. Her tight pussy grips my cock harder with every move, another orgasm nearby, "...but Conor wants her pregnant—"

"What are you doing, Cody?" Blair snaps, freezing in place to glare at me. "Why are you talking? *Stop* talking!"

I wrap an arm around her back, weaving my fingers into her silky hair and exercising subtle control as I bring her closer, our kiss a breath away. "Make me."

Her eyes flicker to my lips. A wild storm of emotions—anger, irritation, confusion, and *relief*—crosses her pretty face.

And finally, something shifts. With a swift exhalation of air, she surrenders, bridging the distance between us, her soft mouth meeting mine.

I take over immediately. The dam holding intimacy at bay bursts, and we lose it the same way we lost it when I caught her playing with the purple wand.

Every stroke of my tongue is returned with a hunger deep within her. It's as if she wanted to break this rule since she set it in place, craving the taste of rebellion.

I bite her lower lip, tugging gently, igniting a very different kind of fire than the primal lust burning within us.

Shit... maybe her rules had a point. She's addictive, and this is definitely the wrong side of the line. Intoxicating tension electrifies the air, inflating my chest, and yep... *definitely* the wrong side of the line.

But the *wrong* side feels so fucking *right.*

And when we're done and sitting at the breakfast bar in my kitchen, devouring the lasagna, talking about Conor's fixation with babies, Logan's bachelor party, and Karen's pettiness... that feels right, too.

TWENTY-ONE

Blair

The venue is the one my father enjoys most. An elegant private room at the back of the Country Club—owned by none other than Nico Hayes.

He's the only influential person my father hasn't manipulated in Newport Beach.

I'm sure it's not for the lack of trying.

Although, as he manages my father's money, maybe Dad doesn't dare meddle in Nico's business.

The fleeting thought fills me with a warm, fuzzy feeling because I associate Nico with the portfolio my father set up in my name a few years ago. An award, a prize for the years of serving his needs. I'm supposed to gain access to it once I graduate.

Unless it's a lie my father conjured to ensure I obey every command. A carrot on a stick he can hold over my head.

The private event room is relatively empty. Less than thirty people sporting fake smiles and real diamonds. Apart from my father's associates, there are a few new faces in the crowd, including the man from the front page of the *Newport Gazette* that Dad handed me on our way here.

He didn't answer when I asked why my workload had tripled since I moved out of his house three months ago.

I haven't worked this many men in such a short time since I turned eighteen. Looks like Dad's squeezing the most out of me before my twenty-first birthday. Once I can access the portfolio, he'll lose his bargaining chip.

Casting a quick glance around, I examine the man I'll be flirting with tonight. He's in his fifties with a head of silver hair, an unlit cigar in his mouth, and an expensive suit hugging his tall frame—Archibald Duke—the chair of the Orange County planning committee.

Last year, spurred by whispers of an upcoming highway project, my father bought a substantial tract of land from an old-time farmer. He offered double the market price, betting on the highway rumor enabling a big payday.

As fate would have it, the highway plans fell through. Now he's stuck with overpriced land and a huge dent in his wallet.

Dad didn't explain his next move, but using the Planning Commissioner must mean he's trying to flip the land to residential. If he gets the green light, he can sell it to a developer without breaking a sweat.

And I bet he already has a developer in mind: Stone and Oak. Since Logan Hayes took the reins two years ago, they've been buying land like it's a Black Friday sale.

Logan's a visionary. The best architect in Orange County. A skilled businessman, too. Rumor has it that he doubled the company's revenue within two short years by taking the bold risks his grandfather refused to take.

"Smile," Dad barks in my ear, snaking his arm round my waist to lead me further into the room, greeting people as we pass. "Everything is set up. When I give you the signal. Do what you do best."

Plastering a convincing smile to my lips, I let him walk me around the room, my job well defined: a silent coquette.

I scan the men my father introduces me to. Over the years I've got this down to a T, learning what makes men like my father's associates tick. I lick my lips, smile, and bat my eyelashes.

My dress rolls up with every step, and I tug it down just enough to cover the bare minimum.

"Sweetheart, meet Mr. Duke," my father says when we finally make it across the room, stopping before the star of the evening.

He's alone. No woman hanging on his arm. The man he's been speaking to for the past five minutes bobs his chin and walks away, offering a fleeting sense of privacy in a crowded room.

"Mr. Duke," I say, my voice sweeter than sugar. "It's a pleasure to meet you. I've read so much about your recent success."

"It's Archibald, my dear. I insist." He dips his head to kiss my hand. "Your father's told me a lot about you, young lady."

I don't breathe while he talks to me about college and some sketches my father apparently showed him. Once the oxygen deprivation has done enough to create a fake blush, I subtly take a breath.

"Well, thank you, Mr..." I purposely trip over my words, biting my lip. "I'm sorry, *Archibald*."

"I would love to hear more about your volunteer work," he says, dropping his gaze to my breasts before it roams lower, eating up every inch. "It's admirable, Blair. Your father is very proud that you're spending time at the hospital."

Bullshit. My father is only proud of the eight digits he sees when he logs into his bank account.

But I play my part as expected, faking smiles as I run a gentle hand down his arm. "Of course. I'd love to."

"Can I get you a drink?" He glances from me to my father. "You're old enough to drink, sweetheart, aren't you?"

"Barely," my father huffs, wearing the mask of a concerned, loving, but not-so-strict parent.

If those masks we both wear were tangible, we'd have quite the collection between us.

"One drink won't hurt, but just one, sweetie." He shoots Archibald a stern look. "Keep her safe. I need to find Richard."

"Take your time," Archibald says, offering me his arm.

Hook, line, and sinker.

Just like that, I'm strutting toward the bar with Archibald Duke by my side. I'm usually a wine kind of girl, but at my father's banquets, I need something stronger to take the edge off the humiliation coursing through my veins. With a glass of neat whiskey each, we head through the patio doors, taking a seat on a bench by a large fountain outside.

I answer Archibald's questions on volunteer work for a moment, but it's clear from his lustful gaze that his mind is elsewhere. In the gutter, most likely. I bet he imagined fucking me ten different ways by now.

"What brings you here tonight?" I flick the ball to his court, playing dumb.

He drapes his hand over the back of the bench, gently sweeping his fingers along my nape, curling my hair behind my ear before he says, "Your father has quite the proposition for me."

"I should have known. It's not often these events are attended by such powerful people as yourself."

God, this sounds so bad. Anyone with half a brain would immediately know I'm playing him, but I melt Archibald's brain by crossing my legs as I speak.

His eyes widen, pupils dilate.

It's a brief show, but he sure noticed. I'm not bare tonight. Even after the shopping spree with Kelly-Ann, my father didn't confiscate my card, so I've bought new underwear, but a flash of the lace between my legs is enough to thicken Archibald's blood.

My skin breaks out in goosebumps when he moves closer, turning his body around like he's purposely giving me a better view of the bulge in his slacks.

My stomach churns painfully. Bitter bile slicks my esophagus. I swallow hard, or else the contents of my stomach will end up decorating his expensive suit.

I hate this.

I hate that he's imagining me naked right now.

I hate that he's touching me, even if it's just his fingertips on my neck. Still too much contact. Contact without consent.

I'm not afforded the privilege of consent in this setting.

"You're a very clever young woman," Archibald rasps, his voice thick as he incredulously readjusts his hard dick. "I'd love to hear more about you."

"Ask away. What would you like to know?"

"Let's start with why a beautiful young woman like yourself comes to these events on your father's arm."

Fear quickens my heart.

Can he see through my ploy? Am I slacking? My ears ring when I picture the wrath I'll endure if Archibald figures out he's being used.

"I'm not sure I understand your question."

"Why are you here with your father and not your boyfriend, sweetheart?"

"No boyfriend, I'm afraid." Drilling the point further, luring him in with vulnerability, I add, "I wasn't meeting his expectations, so he found what he was looking for somewhere else."

Archibald grabs my chin, forcing my eyes to his. The unexpected move tears a surprised, a little frightened gasp from me.

"You exceed expectations." He weighs every word, eyes falling to my lips. "You're beautiful, Blair. If your *ex* didn't see that, it's his loss, not yours."

Another forced timid blush as I look away, abusing the vulnerability card. "Thank you, sir."

"None of that, sweetheart. It's Archibald. Boys your age wouldn't know what to do with you anyway." He doesn't need to elaborate on his implication.

Dropping his hand from my chin, he sets it on my thigh, grazing my skin with his thumb. I tremble under his touch, and he takes it as a good sign, inching his fingers higher.

If only he knew it's fear shaking me like a leaf, not arousal. I don't want his grubby hand anywhere near me, let alone three inches from the hem of my dress.

The door behind us opens with a click, rattling a wave of relief through me as Archibald's hand twitches away.

"That was close," he whispers in my ear.

"There you are." My father's voice breaches the warm evening air. "I've been looking all over for you."

I jump to my unstable feet, wobbling on five-inch heels. "I'm sorry, Dad, I—"

"It's my fault," Archibald cuts in, turning to look at my father. "We lost track of time, Gideon. She's an extraordinary woman, your daughter."

I look over my shoulder, where my father nods, his features soft, almost proud. He's a great actor. "That she is. Could you give us a second, Blair? We have business to discuss."

I rise to my feet, holding my empty glass. "I'll grab another drink. Would you like anything?"

"Whiskey, if you don't mind, sweetheart," Archibald says, his hot gaze stalking my every move.

With a tight nod, I retreat inside, tugging my dress down every three steps and avoiding eye contact with all the men I pass.

Now that Dad's taken over, I'll be okay.

Going on the track record of these banquets, as soon as my father starts talking business, I'm off the hook.

My job is done. Just a few nights of crying myself to sleep left. I'll be fine.

I'm always *fine.*

I head into the restroom, splashing my face with cold water. My phone is on silent, but I check the screen, hoping I'll see a reply from Cody in reply to what I sent before my father picked me up: *Text me after your brothers leave.* They have another bachelor-party-planning session tonight. The last one ahead of the party weekend.

We've been over the line since the shower incident two weeks ago. We talk about things we aren't supposed to, kiss during the deed, kiss when we're parting ways, and... I fell asleep in his bed the other night when he took a quick shower.

I woke up around four in the morning, entangled in his arms, his t-shirt clinging to my body. A t-shirt he must've gently slipped over my head after I nodded off because I was naked when he left me in bed.

I panicked and snuck out, worried the atmosphere would be awkward in the morning. Cody didn't mention it or explain why he'd let me sleep in his bed, and I was afraid to ask.

Unfortunately, there's no messages waiting on the screen. It's almost ten, so Cody's either still with his brothers, or not in the mood for sex. I tuck my phone away, focusing on the task at hand as I exit the restroom, heading to the bar.

Like a well-behaved, obedient daughter, I order Archibald and my father a drink, deliver them outside, then sit at the bar with a neat whiskey in hand, my mind racing.

"You look like you don't want to be here," the bartender says, resting his elbows on the counter. "And like you hate whiskey."

"I don't usually drink whiskey," I admit, swirling the amber liquid in the glass.

"I'll get you something better."

He whips out the shaker, pouring, shaking, adding, mixing, pouring again, until a tall green cocktail glass stands before me.

It's tangy with a sweet kick, and I smile for the first time since entering the room over an hour ago. "Thank you."

He moves away to serve an older woman with short, bright red hair, but once he's done, he comes over to chat.

I wish I could just sneak out, but I know better than to make the same mistake twice. Disobedience will cost dearly, so instead, I spend an hour and a half talking to the bartender whenever he's not serving.

But just as he's about to start mixing me another drink, my father arrives, a storm cloud over his head.

"We're leaving," he seethes through gritted teeth, gripping my elbow to yank me up.

"Is everything okay? Did—"

"Zip it, Blair," he snaps, maintaining a neutral expression all through the Country Club until he can shove me into the passenger seat of his car. "You can't fucking help yourself, can you?!"

I shrink in on myself, watching the speedometer climb as Dad drops the pedal to the floor, speeding out of the parking lot.

"I don't know what you're talking about. What happened?"

"*You* happened. You're nothing but a problem. I wish I never fucking had you!" He bangs his fist on the steering wheel. "What the fuck were you doing flirting with that lowlife at the bar?!"

"Calm down, Dad, I wasn't... I..." Words catch in my throat, my palms slick with sweat as he accelerates, flying across Newport at almost a hundred miles an hour. "Slow down. Please slow down, you're—"

"Is that your type?" He slams the brake when the lights change at the junction ahead.

Thank God I'm wearing a seatbelt, or I'd break my nose on the dashboard.

"Broke fuckers?" he continues. "He's a *bartender*! A nobody! If you're whoring around, at least have some fucking standards!"

"You told me to leave you and Mr. Duke alone," I stutter, pumping my fists open and closed the same way I've seen Cody do countless times. "I was waiting at the bar until you were done talking."

"You were drooling all over the fucking bartender," he snaps. "Your attention should've been on Archibald the whole time!"

I bite my cheek hard enough to draw blood. Year after year, Dad gets worse and worse. I'm used to being called names. I'm used to the insinuations, yelling, and insults, but tonight is the first time he's admitted he wished he never had me.

Resting my forehead against the cool glass, I stare at the buildings lining the street as Dad pulls away from the traffic lights at half his previous speed. There's no point arguing I wasn't drooling all over the bartender.

Dad's right. I'm wrong.

Story of my life.

He doesn't speak the rest of the way. Not until he's parked up beside my Porsche. "You want to act like a slut?" he snaps, undoing his seatbelt. "Look the part." He licks his thumb then gouges it into my eye, smearing my makeup.

Then he rubs his sweaty palm over my mouth to do the same with my lipstick, before hooking his fingers in my cleavage and ripping my slutty dress open in one tug.

He yanks me closer, tearing out my hairpins to leave my hair a disheveled mess. My eyes sting with unshed tears. I won't fucking cry. I refuse to give him the satisfaction.

Not this time.

"Get the fuck out of my car but leave the shoes," he barks. "And your credit cards."

TWENTY-TWO

Cody

"I don't know..." Conor mutters, staring at the invitations. "This feels too fancy, don't you think?"

Colt snatches one from the box by my coffee table, turning the black and gold card as he trails his finger over the engraved script. "I think it's the right amount of too-much-out-there for Logan."

"Fuck you," Logan booms, a big smile stretching his face.

He shouldn't be here, but he was driving Theo up the wall with his questions, so in the end, we invited him to join the planning committee of his own bachelor party. He's not complained once, so we've not kicked him out yet.

"How many have you printed?" Nico asks from the barstool, his broad shoulders squared, jaw tense.

The cloud over his head isn't because of us, the fact we're holding this meeting in my condo instead of the Country Club or his house, or that we're drinking beer while he's clutching a bottle of water.

The reason is Mia. More specifically that she's out.

Well, not *out* out. She's actually in. At home, but not alone. She's with Thalia, Rose, and Vee, planning Cassidy's bachelorette party. Nothing out of the ordinary, right?

Well...

Instead of choosing the location, gifts, and hotels over a glass of wine, Thalia decided it would be *so much fun* to vet male strippers before hiring three.

It's why we're all stuck in my condo. We didn't feel like going out tonight, and the girls are at Nico's house, watching a dozen guys take their clothes off.

Needless to say, my older brother is barely keeping his ass seated for longer than three minutes at a time. He mostly paces the room, pumping his fists.

"Oh unclench," Theo huffs over his shoulder from where he's pissing off Ghost by tapping his fingers on the glass. "They're fine. They're at *your* house. You've got cameras all over the place and panic buttons everywhere."

Yes, he does. Installed a week after Mia moved in. She accidentally tapped the one under the piano one day while Nico was in the basement gym. The second his phone blipped its distinctive alarm, he practically teleported upstairs, barreling through the house like a fucking wrecking ball.

"We've got fifty invitations. Enough?" I ask, steering the topic back toward the bachelor party, but before anyone can chip in, our phones ping in unison, a message in the group chat.

Nico groans and I laugh, staring at Rose's message. It's a picture of a naked fireman, yellow helmet covering his dick.

"You might want to disinfect the living room," Conor tells Nico. "And buy a new couch."

Me: You know you're not supposed to take pictures, sis?

Rose: No? Too little too late.

"They're having much more fun. Why didn't we order any strippers to check out?"

"Because we're spending the night in Vegas and the girls won't come all this way to dance in your condo, bro," Shawn mutters. "Can we please get this shit organized so I can go home? It's been a long week, boys. I'm exhausted."

And so we do. We organize the guest list, book the hotel, flights, and VIP booths for a few clubs—strip club included. I doubt we'll spend much time watching women grinding around poles when my brothers are so fucking whipped.

When we're just about done, Conor clears his throat, visibly tense as he stares Logan down. "Listen, I wanted to talk to you about something. I wanted to ask Cass at the same time, but it might be better to ask you first, so if the answer is *no* Cass won't need to know a thing, since, now I'm about to ask, I kind of think it's a dick move."

Logan runs a hand down his face, smirking at Conor. "You always did know how to start a conversation by immediately shooting yourself in the foot. What's going on?"

"I promised Vee a year before I propose—"

He's drowned out by a booming choir of *no ways*, *holy shits* and *fucking hells*.

"You've been dating six months, Conor. Slow down," Shawn says. "Why so soon?"

"What am I supposed to wait for?"

"Nothing," Nico cuts in, glaring at Shawn. "Life's too short to wait around."

"Agreed. I got married six months after I met Thalia," Theo says. "I don't regret it, but... what does your proposal have to do with Logan and Cass?" He turns to rummage through my chilled drink cabinet, pulling out a bottle of champagne.

"He wants to propose during the wedding weekend, right?" Colt asks, leaning back in his chair. "I'm with you on this one, bro. It's a dick move."

Logan cocks an eyebrow. "Why is it a dick move?"

"Because it's your day. Yours and Cassidy's. Who do you think the attention will shift to if he goes down on one knee?" Jack chips in. "Sorry, Conor, but that's how I see it."

"No, it's cool. That's what you're all for, a bit of fucking honesty. Alright, I'll revert to my New Year's Eve proposal idea."

"Hold on a minute." Logan yanks his cap off, running a hand through his mess of dark hair. "It's my wedding. Don't I get a say in this? When do you want to do it?"

"After the rehearsal dinner. The whole family will be there, so I thought it would work okay."

What he's not saying aloud, but we all know by now, is that Vee loves this family like her own. We all thought Mia would be Mom's favorite with their shared passion for music, but Mom and Vee connect on a different level. It's fascinating to watch sometimes. And because Vee's mom died, I think Conor's trying to include her in our family as much as possible.

What better way than letting us witness their engagement?

"I have to run it by Cassidy, but I don't see an issue. I don't think she will, either," Logan finally says.

"I'm with Logan," I say, accepting a champagne flute from Theo. "You got the ring yet?"

"Yeah, I—"

"You should've fucking called us before you went shopping," Colt groans, folding his hands. "Can you return it?"

Conor's eyebrows bunch in the middle. "You haven't even seen it yet!"

"Doesn't matter. Your taste in jewelry is... really fucking bad," Nico says. "The only good-looking accessories you buy are watches."

"It's a nice ring," Conor huffs, pulling his phone to show us the picture. His face immediately falls when we cringe. "What? What's wrong with it?"

"What's right?" I chuckle, patting his back. "Come on, seriously? is that the biggest diamond they had?"

"No, they had seven carats, but it was square. This is six. The bigger, the better, right?"

"The diamond doesn't have to reflect the size of your dick," Logan chuckles, drying his champagne flute.

It takes another half an hour of innocent banter before Conor settles on a prettier and far less obnoxious ring.

Nico's out the door the moment we call it a day, and Colt follows suit. Within the next half an hour, everyone but Theo leaves. He lingers, nursing his beer, staring into the distance like he's got something to get off his chest.

"I'm sorry," he finally says.

I look over my shoulder, checking whether someone's hiding on the patio, but no. We're alone. My eyebrows knot in the middle, not a clue what he's apologizing for.

"You'll have to elaborate." I rest both elbows on my knees. "What's going on?"

"I'm sorry I didn't want you to babysit River."

"You didn't? Good to know... mind telling me *why*? Am I untrustworthy or something?"

"No, it's not that. It's fucking stupid, Cody. I got an earful from Thalia about it already, so spare me."

I toss back the last of my beer, setting the empty bottle on the coffee table. "You're not explaining much, bro. Out with it."

"I was... jealous."

A semi-horrified scoff of amusement saws past my lips. "Jealous? What the fuck do you mean? When have I ever given you a reason to be jealous? I don't even tell your wife she looks nice when—"

"I wasn't jealous about Thalia, Cody," he says, cringing before a long sigh leaves his lips. "I told you it's stupid. You've always been great with kids. Josh, then Aiden, but Noah... you' ve got something special with him. It's almost like he's yours. I didn't want you babysitting River because I thought you wouldn't give him the same attention."

As grateful as I am for his honesty, I'm fucking offended. I love all my nephews equally. But kids don't take to everyone equally. They don't pretend, so if they like you, they like you, and if they don't, you're fucked.

"I don't favor Noah, Theo. He favors me. I'm Logan's first point of call because Noah enjoys spending time with me best. I treat him the same way I've always treated Josh, and yet I'm not Josh's favorite uncle, Logan is."

"Yeah, I know," he mutters, nervously toying with the bottle. "Like I said, Thalia already did the talking."

"She said you have to apologize?"

He lets out a laugh, relaxing a bit. "You know she did, but it would've occurred to me at some point. Especially because you did great with him."

"I had help," I say, and *oh fuck* blares inside my head before the words are out.

"Help?"

Running my fingers through my hair, I busy my hands re-doing my bun. "Yeah, a friend stopped by when River was crying, and helped me calm him down."

He must notice I purposely omitted a pronoun. I'm not proud I let Blair in that day. If I hadn't, I wouldn't be where I am right now—very well acquainted with her gorgeous body.

Not wanting to make this a big deal, which it will be if I tell Theo because he's a fucking gossip, I don't bother explaining.

"I get the feeling you don't want to share, so I won't push, but you know where I am if you need to talk."

"Nothing worth sharing."

"Yeah, if you say so," he sets the bottle aside. "I better go pick up River. Mom's probably pulling her hair out by now."

"She had seven of us, and we were all different. I doubt there's anything she can't deal with."

"I'm sure, but—"

"You miss him already," I chuckle, walking him to the door. "Call me if you need a babysitter. I mean it."

"I know and I will." He pats my back, stepping out of the condo with a stupid grin. "Put a word in for me with Thalia next time you see her, alright?"

I burst out laughing, but it dies on my tongue when I notice Blair. She freezes midway into the hallway, eyes jumping between Theo and me. A second before he follows my line of sight, one eyebrow raised, she dashes round the corner.

"You alright, Cody?" he asks, still frowning. "You look like you've seen a ghost."

"I'm good, just... never mind." I shake it off as if I had a hallucination or remembered something I didn't want to remember. "Say hi to Mom and Dad."

"Do it yourself," he huffs, backing away toward the staircase. "Mom's complaining she only ever sees you at the get-togethers these days. Make an effort."

"I will."

He turns the way he's heading, lifting one hand in a silent *see ya* as he disappears behind the same corner as Blair.

I listen, waiting until he sees her and freaks the fuck out, but other than retreating footsteps, the building is completely silent. She must've gone upstairs.

A minute passes. Then another, and I'm still rooted to the spot in my doorway, waiting for her.

Eventually she peeks around the corner like she's checking the coast is clear. Her face falls, chin wobbles, and my veins fill with red-hot fury.

I'll kill whichever fucker laid a finger on her.

She's barefoot, her stockings ripped at her thighs, dress torn at her cleavage, barely hiding her areolas. Her hair is messy, and her makeup doesn't look any better: red lipstick smeared up to her ear, black mascara river deltas traversing her cheeks.

A cold, icy dread settles in my stomach. I need whoever did this right here, right now. I'll fucking kill him, I swear.

"What happened?" I ask, my voice raw, the anger stirring within me almost impossible to rein in. "Who did this to you?"

She pinches her lips, a futile attempt to keep her emotions in check as she steps further into the light to cross the hallway, tightly clutching her keys

"Don't brush me off, B," I warn, gripping her elbow. "Who hurt you?"

The way she jumps away from me turns the lava filling my system to ice. I grind my teeth, shoving the dark scenarios away, but it's useless. They scramble to the front of my imagination, driving me insane.

"I'm fine," Blair whispers, the words strained, voice brittle.

"Turn around," I hiss.

She shakes her head, pushing the key into the lock. I have half a mind to spin her around myself, but after her reaction to my touch I'm second-guessing my every move.

"I'm fine, Cody. I promise," she insists, barely keeping her composure.

"Fuck! Baby... *turn. Around.* Please." The desperation in my voice is pitiful, but in this moment, I couldn't care less because... shit... I don't think I hate her anymore.

She stills. I watch her entire demeanor change before my eyes. She squares her shoulders, lifts her chin, pushes out her chest and locks herself like that as she turns to face me.

If you ignored her eyes, she's a good enough actress to have you convinced. She's putting on a performance worth a standing ovation, but her eyes, those damn blue, sad, beautiful eyes, give her away, swimming with fear and humiliation.

"I'm fine," she repeats with a conviction that would fool anyone but me. "Goodnight, Cody."

"No." Instinctively, I reach to stop her turning away, but freeze before I touch her. Scaring her is the last thing I want. Closing my fist, I let my hand fall to my side. "Talk to me, B."

"There's nothing to talk about," she snaps, hurt morphing to anger. "Leave me the hell alone, okay?" She turns around, poking my chest with her long finger, fresh tears cascading over her nose. "We're not friends. We're nothing! I don't need your pity!"

"You're not *nothing to* me," I grind out, adding something I never thought I'd consider. "I'm across the hall if you change your mind. I'll leave the door unlocked."

"I won't come. We're done. I can't do this anymore."

I'm rendered speechless, and she uses that moment to flee. With visible stiffness in every move, she enters her condo, slamming the door shut while I'm reeling.

We're not done.

She can't mean it. She's shaken up, doesn't trust me, and needs space. That's all it is, but the protective instinct roaring within me hates the very fucking concept of space right now.

TWENTY-THREE

Cody

I can't sit still. The image of Blair—disheveled and broken, her clothes torn, makeup smeared, shoulders sagging—is ingrained into my psyche like a millennia-old cave painting that refuses to fade.

It'll haunt me forever, along with this all-encompassing feeling ripping me apart. A feeling I know so damn well: the overpowering need to protect. Maddening concern. Bloodthirst.

Whoever touched her... whoever laid one fucking finger on Blair would end up six feet under if I got my hands on him now. It's intense this feeling, raging like a thunderstorm.

Restless and fuming, I busy myself with mundane tasks to stop from barging inside Blair's apartment and demanding answers. I discard the beer bottles my brothers drained, straighten the cushions, feed Ghost, unload the dishwasher... I do anything and everything that springs to mind in a vain attempt to push aside the worry eating me alive.

Did someone hurt her? Did they touch her against her will? *Who* the fuck dared to touch her? Why? Where?

Until about eleven o'clock, I'm hoping she'll come over, but once midnight strikes, I accept she's asleep. Which summons a brand-new reason to cross the hallway.

I want to hold her. Mold her to my side and chase away whatever demons torment her fragile mind. But I can't.

She doesn't want me there.

That's not how this thing between us works.

One foot after the other, I drag myself into the bathroom, shower, then get in bed.

Not that sleep wants to take me. I'm still fucking reeling.

I shouldn't be. I shouldn't give a damn, but I do, and it drives me wild. Even more so because I can't erase how easily she switched into this other girl. From displaying her vulnerabilities to shutting them off within seconds.

From the girl I want to spend time with to a girl I can't stand.

Ever since she showed up at my doorstep when River was crying, I've wondered where this unfamiliar side of her came from. The girl who bakes cookies, wears jeans, and sometimes smiles with her eyes. She's a stranger.

Was a stranger. I've not seen that girl once at school, and since I met her, I've wondered if it's a front. A new trick to weasel her way back into the spotlight.

One day I'm certain it's not a front, that the girl in tight dresses, flashy makeup, and vile personality is a mask, the next I'm not so sure. I've known the vile Blair for years, but it's been less than three months since I met the caring, cute, beautiful Blair.

The constant second-guessing drives me insane. It's scary to think she's pretending when she's with me, but it's fucking petrifying to think she's not.

I don't know when sleep finally takes me, but I do know when it lets me go. It's when the mattress dips, informing me I'm not alone.

The dim glow of LED strips illuminates Blair's tear-streaked, frightened face as she perches on the edge of the mattress.

She closes her eyes, shuts them tight as if blocking reality, then swallows hard, her body tense. She might be bracing to say something, but the fact she snuck into my bedroom in the middle of the night and now sits here, steeling herself for the worst, tells me more than words ever could.

She needs this. Needs *me*.

When I mentioned leaving the door unlocked, I thought she'd come to explain what the fuck happened, not crawl into my bed.

It doesn't matter what I thought. She's here now. I'm sure it took a great deal of back and forth before she gathered the courage to come over. To put herself on display, risking rejection in the most intimate way.

"I'm sorry," she whispers, blinking her eyes open to meet mine, her vulnerability clear in the near dark. "I didn't mean what I said. I... I—" She pinches her lips as if trying not to cry. "I don't want to be alone."

The turmoil whipping me into a frenzy all evening subsides. The world sharpens into focus. The fog and the static buzzing in the back of my mind dissipate, replaced by a clarity I haven't felt in a long time.

"Come here," I whisper, lifting the comforter.

More silent tears slide down her pale skin, her shoulders hunch, relief visibly rattling through her. Without hesitation, she slides into bed beside me, a bit stiff and guarded, unsure how much I'll allow.

A whole fucking lot.

"Thank you," she mutters, settling awkwardly on her back, leaving enough distance for another person between us.

She's already in my bed. We might as well not build a pillow wall between us like teenagers.

"I said *come here*, B," I coax, lifting the comforter higher. "Either your head on my chest or my chest to your back."

She turns to the side, staring at me with big, wide eyes like she can't believe the offer.

To be honest, neither can I. I'm stepping over the line we drew, the one she fights much harder than I do not to cross.

It's so far behind right now I can't even see it. And I should. There's a reason that line was in place. Mia.

One person, but her hurt is enough to detest Blair. Enough to kick her out, bolt the door, and not give a damn but... Blair's a puzzle. She's more than meets the eye.

Her past is full of hurt, a sick mother, a missing father, fake friends, and her present... fuck knows what it is. From the little she said, the little I've seen, it's far from good. Far from simple.

My internal battle comes to a screeching halt when, in a heartbeat, she's on me, moving closer with such urgency she'd knock me over if I were standing. Her small body fits against mine, and the second I feel how fragile she is, every reason this is wrong ceases to exist.

I pull her into me, my arm around her waist, chin resting on her head, hugging her hard enough that there's not a breath of space between us. My chest is heavy, my mind chaotic, but not one muscle feels tense. I love having her this close.

I love that she feels safe with me.

Letting out a long, steady breath, she melts into both me

and the mattress—a clear sign she trusts me to soothe her.

And knowing she does... stirs up feelings I can't name.

Or maybe don't want to.

"I need to know if someone hurt you," I whisper, my fingers spread over her belly, holding her in place so she can't run. "If they touched you without consent."

She's quiet for a while but remains pliant with my thumb brushing her belly button. She doesn't run.

I wouldn't let her. She shouldn't be alone.

"Not like you imagine," she finally replies.

That doesn't help me much. It's an honest answer, but not clear, and my mind races, inventing more questions. Someone did hurt her. Touched her without permission, but not like I imagine.

And what do I imagine?

The worst, obviously. Anyone who saw her in the hallway would imagine the worst.

"I'm fine, Cody," she adds quietly. "Karma's leveling the field. I did worse than what I'm getting."

A tightness settles in my chest. She doesn't show this side often. Whenever I get a glimpse of this resigned girl, I'm fucking reeling. She believes she deserves all the suffering life has in store. She takes it, not even trying to draw a line between the person she was and the person she's become.

"What are you doing, B?" I ask, feeling her tremble. "You want to be miserable for the rest of your life? Live in the past? Never move forward?"

She's silently drawing a pattern on my chest, her whole body pulling taut the longer she's lost in her head. I don't realize she's crying until the first tear puddles my chest. She swats it away, inhaling a shaky breath.

"I don't know how to fix it," she whispers, her voice full of self-inflicted torment. "I can't."

"No, you can't. You can't change what you did, but you can admit you were wrong. You can apologize and forgive yourself for not knowing things before you learned them."

She burrows further into me, gripping the sheets and wrenching like she's trying to transfer the pain ripping her apart. "I don't deserve forgiveness. I haven't done anything to deserve it."

I gently nudge her onto her back, propping myself over her as I cradle her face in both hands, looking down into those tearful blue eyes. "You've done two of those things, B. You admitted you were wrong. You apologized to me and you tried apologizing to Mia. It's my fault you never had the chance. I'm sorry for that."

"Don't be. I wouldn't let me apologize, either."

"Stop," I whisper, brushing her tears away. "Stop punishing yourself. You've grown. You learned. You're a better person than you were back then."

She shakes her head, eyes closed to block my words, but both hands hold onto my t-shirt as if I might disappear.

"You told me about the bullying. You told me about your life. You haven't made a single excuse, but I know..." I dip my head, pressing my forehead to hers as a pained sob rips from her chest, making mine swell. "I know you weren't cruel for the sake of being cruel, baby. Why can't you see that? It was a defense mechanism against your own hurt."

"That doesn't make it okay! The reasons don't matter!" she chokes, moving her hands to my neck and threading her fingers into my hair. "I didn't know I was projecting until I was older."

"Exactly." I drop a gentle kiss on her forehead. "And when

you realized, you stopped. You learned. I said a lot of shitty things to you, B, but you forgave me, didn't you?"

She slowly opens her eyes when I rise on one elbow, tucking her back. "There was nothing to forgive. I never blamed you, Cody. I know you're a good person, and I—"

I press a finger against her lips before she says she deserves to be hated, hurt, and cast aside. She keeps saying that and it's not true. No one who so blatantly admits their mistakes deserves to be judged solely on those mistakes.

People are the best defense lawyers for their own mistakes and the harshest judges of the mistakes of others.

Blair's the opposite. She's her own judge, jury, and executioner. She ruled herself guilty. A life sentence of sabotaging her happiness. Even though she doesn't believe she deserves anything good, she's not just waiting out her time. She's growing as a person. Learning how to be better.

"You see good in me, but not in yourself? This is where you go wrong. You think your feelings, past, and everything *you* endured doesn't carry any weight? That none of it left a mark?" I ask, trying to show her she's being too hard on herself. "You're not a bad person. You're aware of the wrongs. You think you're inflicting justifiable punishment on yourself, but you're taking it too far." I kiss her forehead, then flip her so my chest is flush against her back. "Enough, baby. Time to take a step forward."

She says nothing else, but we're both wide awake. The delicate aromas of the mango in her body lotion and coconut shampoo waft the room, keeping me eerily calm. I hope her scent will soak my sheets and pillows. And more than anything, I hope she'll still be here in the morning.

TWENTY-FOUR

Blair

A knock on my door makes me jump off the stool, crossing the room faster than I usually move at this hour. It's barely past six, but I'm nursing my second coffee, already showered and dressed.

I haven't slept much. I've been replaying everything Cody said last night, the sincerity in his voice, the soothing delicacy of his touch. He really believes I deserve another chance.

He's got a heart as big as Mia's.

I almost let it slip that, in a moment of unexplainable courage, I visited Nico's house three days after the graduation party, when they'd returned from Europe, and apologized to Mia.

I can thank Cody for that courage, but I don't want him to know what I did. He might take it the wrong way... he might think I did it because I want more from him than we agreed.

I do, but that's not why I faced the man made of pure wrath—Mia's fiancé.

It was what Cody told me the day after the graduation party that ignited my new sense of courage and helped me knock on Nico's door.

"You're letting your mistakes define you, B. Use them to guide you."

I did.

Nico let me in, Mia listened, and even though her huge heart allowed her to move past my cruelty, the weight didn't drop off my shoulders. Knowing Mia had the strength to forgive me made me feel worse because she's so pure. She didn't deserve what she got from me, and the regret and guilt amplified.

I pull the tie out of my hair, combing the braid out with my fingers as I expect it's my father standing outside with another round of demands, much harsher today thanks to last night.

But instead of Dad, Cody's there in his boxer shorts, the expanse of his chest stealing my breath.

"You're not leaving my bed twice without a word," he grumbles, running a hand down his face like he's trying to rub off the sleepiness.

"There's nothing to talk about. I'm sorry I—"

"No," he clips. "No bullshit, B. I thought we were past that now. You can't crawl into my bed in tears, expect me to hold you, then disappear without a word."

I step back instead of forward. "I'm sorry, I won't do it again, I promise."

With an exasperated huff, he grabs my waist, slings me over his shoulder, and carries me into his apartment. He lays me on the bed, pulling the comforter to my chin.

"I'm not saying I don't want you coming over when you need me. I'm not pissed off because you came. I'm pissed off because you left. You're obviously going through some shit, and I..." He grips his neck, squeezing hard. "I want to help, okay?"

He crawls in and draws me against his chest. "Tell me what happened last night. Where were you?"

"Thank you for caring, but there are things I don't want to talk about. I know what you thought when you saw me last night, but it wasn't *that*, okay? I'm fine." I fling one hand over his torso, snuggling into his side. "You're crossing more lines, Cody."

He presses his cheek to my head, and I feel his jaw clamp tight, an internal battle stealing his attention from the determination he exuded moments ago. Using that to my advantage, I distract him further, sliding my hand down his chest until my fingers find the outline of his big, hard cock.

"You can't keep evading," he growls, arching his hips into my touch as I jack him off slowly. "Talk to me. I'll listen."

"So will my therapist," I counter, and dip my head, planting open-mouthed kisses on his neck.

"You're in therapy?"

I nod, tracing my lips along to his ear. "I thought she could fix me, but... it's been a year, and I'm still broken."

"You're starting to piss me off," he grumbles, his fingers ghosting my back, the touch possessive, firm but affectionate. "You're not broken, B."

"Careful there," I say, arching back enough that we're at eye level. "You sound like you're forgetting you hate me, Cody."

"What if I don't want to hate you?"

"Then I don't want to fuck you." I kiss his jaw, inching toward his lips, then sit up, yanking my top over my head.

Cody's on me in a flash, his big hands palming my small breasts. He circles his warm mouth around my nipple and sucks before tending to the other the same way.

"Show me how much you hate me," I whisper.

He sucks harder. The sharp sting travels straight down between my legs when his tongue joins the fun, soothing the ache.

"You're cheating," I say, wrapping my arms around him as he kisses his way up between the valley of my breasts, pinning me to the mattress with his body. "No kiss—"

His lips come down on mine, restless, hot, demanding. "Lose that attitude, shut the fuck up, and take what I give you," he murmurs, spreading my thighs to make room for himself. "You'll talk, B." He nips my lip before stealing another long, hot kiss. "You'll tell me what happened last night."

"No. I... I..." I swallow a harsh breath when he pushes my panties aside, quickly dipping two fingers inside. "That's not fair."

"Fair? You don't play fair, so don't expect it from me." He dips his head again, the kiss as feral as our first. "Scream, kick, fight me all you want. I. *Don't.* Care. You'll talk."

"God, I hate you." I don't mean it. And the words don't ring true. It sounds like I mean a different four-letter word.

He flips me onto my belly, tears my panties off, and falls on top of me, his boxers long gone. His cock slides between my soaked lips, teasing, promising an orgasm.

"That's good. Hate me more." His chest is flush with my back as he moves inside me, supporting his weight on both elbows to not squish me into the mattress. "Where were you last night?"

"Out..." I moan, grasping the pillow with both hands.

He slams into me harder, gripping my hair in one hand to lift my head off the pillow. His lips hover over mine just long enough to sink his cock deep into me while his tongue plunders my mouth.

"So sweet," he whispers, biting my lip, the pace of his thrusts enough to send me hurtling toward the edge but not enough to summon the orgasm to the surface. "Where were you last night?"

"I told you. Out."

He lets go of my hair and sits back on his calves, driving into me hard until I'm shaking, almost coming, but then he eases off, before pulling out completely.

"Out *where*?"

"This is blackmail! Very cruel, horrible, awful—" I swallow the rest of the sentence when he curls one arm under my waist and hauls me up, settling me over his cock, my knees digging into the mattress either side of his hips.

"Choose a safe word, B."

"What?"

"Choose a fucking safe word. Anything you wouldn't normally say during sex." He lifts my hips, impaling me on his dick, eyes boring into mine. "Red? Pineapple?"

"Checkmate."

A smirk curves his lips. "Checkmate it is. Use it when you want me to stop."

"Stop talking or stop touching me?"

"Both. When you use your safe word, everything stops."

My smile slips off my face, but I don't stop moving, his big hands guiding me to slowly rise and fall. Mine wrap tightly around his neck as I cling to him, not wanting to miss a second of having him so close.

"I don't want to talk, Cody. Please, don't make me talk. I just want you inside me. Don't use sex against me. Keep hating me, keep hate-fucking me."

"I'm afraid you don't make the rules here, B." He skates his lips across my collarbones. "I'll hate-fuck you ten ways to Sunday once you stop acting like a brat. I'm not using sex against you. I'm using it to shut down your firewall." He grabs my nape, guiding my lips over his for a soft kiss. "I'll edge you. I'll make you submit not because *I* want you to tell me what the fuck happened but because *you* want to tell me." He kisses me again, nipping my bottom lip. "You're just scared."

"You're wrong," I breathe into his mouth, inching away.

He slaps my butt. "I don't think I am." Pinning me in place, he takes over the torture as he slowly, oh so slowly, hits my G spot with shallow thrusts. "Where were you last night?"

"I don't like this." I hide my face in the crook of his neck, and he immediately wraps his arms around my back, holding me close while we move in sync.

"That's okay," he coos. "I don't like this either." He flips me onto my back, crawling over me, and the deep, urgent thrust almost sets me off. "But what I don't like more is seeing you cry. Who did you go out with?"

"None of your business."

"Same guy that was here when you broke your glassware?" he demands, driving into me faster, the orgasm like a teasing wave at the shore, coming and going, coming and going, never quite reaching far enough to flood the beach. "Same one who yelled at you when we spoke over the phone?"

This isn't the first time Cody's denied me the release. I don't mind that part, but couple it with the questions, with his angry and concerned at the same time tone, and the way he looks at me... my armor starts to crack.

I shut my eyes tight, blocking the oncoming tears, blocking his words, and the memories, but it's useless.

Everything comes crashing down. The last thing I hear before my mind jams up is Cody's next barked question.

"Same one who picks you up when you're wearing red?"

Every suppressed emotion I've ever bottled up, hiding behind fake smiles, and a fleeting sense of control, resurfaces, hitting me from all sides at once.

Cody disappears. His bedroom, too.

My head turns into a giant screen. The images flick so fast. My mother losing her mind, hallucinating, my father ramming his fists into her head, the degenerates watching, touching me against my will since I was twelve. How I preyed on Mia, then cried under my bed when Mom screamed that I killed Dad. Blood on my thighs, hands on my hips, filthy words.

Hundreds of broken scenes, a projection of the worst moments in my life. Of my *whole* life, because there was no happiness in it. Not real happiness. Artificial, manufactured. Fake.

Just like the face I show the world.

Cody rocks me gently in his arms, my head under his chin, his arms around me, my nails clawing his flesh so hard I've left long, red lines.

I broke the skin.

A powerful shudder shakes me as reality re-emerges. My face is wet, and I'm naked under the comforter Cody's tucked around us. I've never had a panic attack in front of anyone other than my father. The last one happened when I hurled those glasses across my kitchen at him.

"There you are," Cody breathes in my hair, his hold tightening around me when I try to move. "It's okay, calm down. It's me, baby. I've got you."

"I'm fine," I rasp, swallowing the tears and prying myself away. "I'm sorry, I... zoned out."

"Blair," he utters, taking my chin between his fingers to turn my face his way. "Does it happen often?"

"Nothing happened."

This has gone too far. Cody's too perceptive, too clever and he *cares* enough to dig deeper, to ask questions.

"You had a panic attack, B. That's not *nothing*." He cushions his fingers round my wrist, dragging me back to him. "Talk to me. Tell me what's going on."

Against all reason, I curve myself into him, hiding my face in the crook of his neck. He smells of sex, cologne, smoke, and me. Soothing. Heady.

My negative emotions fade with his every word. It doesn't matter what he says. It's his voice that calms me down. He could be reading the phone book for all I care.

"I did," I answer truthfully. "I hurt me."

There's a long pause, his muscles tensing until he's wound up so tight he might never unwind. "Will you ever answer any of my questions?"

"That's not part of the deal."

"Fuck the deal," he whispers in my hair. "You want me to break someone's neck? I'll do it. Tell me who hurt you."

He shouldn't care. I'm not worth it. Not worth his attention or the rules he's breaking.

My lips part. I want to tell him we're done. Over. No more sex. Not even a *hey* in passing, but I can't push the words out.

Cody's my first taste of calm and safe. My first taste of normal. I don't pretend when I'm with him. I don't feel I have to, and that's scary. Scary and addictive, so instead of closing the gates, I take the cowardly way out, leaving them open.

"Checkmate," I say, bracing both hands against his chest to push him away.

He doesn't oppose, lifting his hands so I can move away, every next word sharp as a bullet. "Next time you need a shoulder to cry on—" He pauses, teeth gnashing between his lips, anger dancing in those deep, brown eyes.

I know what's on the tip of his tongue: *don't come crawling to me*, but with a long exhale, his shoulders slump, and something else comes out.

"You made it clear you won't tell me what's happening. All you're after is a good fuck, so fine, we'll stick to that, but if you need help... if anyone hurts you... I'm here, B. Come to me, okay? I'll help."

The hurt in his voice cuts me so deep it briefly steals my breath. He cares and I... I'm pushing him away.

It's better this way. I don't have anything good to offer.

TWENTY-FIVE

Cody

The bachelor party guest list ends up being thirty-two men long. *Thirty-two* guys in the wild of Las Vegas for two days straight. I don't know if I want to remember every minute or blackout and not know a thing because I just know I'll make a shitload of bad decisions.

I've been on edge since Blair texted an hour ago with yet another *not tonight*. She's avoiding me, but I can't figure out why.

We were fine after she used the safe word. I stopped by her condo on Monday after work, and we spent three hours in bed, but on Tuesday, without explanation, she sent a text saying *not tonight*. She did the same yesterday—today, too.

Three days, no explanation. I'm crawling out of my skin, fighting my every instinct so I can give her space.

It'll be easier once the bachelor party sets off in a rented luxury bus that'll not only take us to Vegas, but chauffeur us around the city all night. My mind will be occupied, no time to think about Blair's silent treatment.

But... we need to leave first, and with my brothers acting like a bunch of whipped pussies, it might be problematic.

The messages in the Sausage Fest group chat come more frequently every hour. Colt and I, the last Hayes brothers left with unclouded judgment, have been putting fires out since five am.

Theo had his panties in a twist first because they're all leaving their kids with Mom, and he wasn't sure she could handle five boys.

Colt: She had seven of us, bro. Five is a piece of cake. Dad's there, too, and Grandma is coming over to help. Relax.

Theo: She was thirty years younger, Colt. She only had four to deal with. We were self-sufficient before the three of you arrived. River's not an easy kid.

Logan: Neither were you. And you're even worse as an adult.

It took more than those messages to calm him down, but once Theo was under control, Nico asked Shawn to break the law and get Mia a gun permit. Since I'm not in the best mood, instead of being reasonable and helpful, I'm an annoying prick.

Me: Get her a bulletproof vest while you're at it, Shawn. Two bodyguards with vicious dogs, a satellite phone for emergencies in case she's out of range, and one of those panic buttons she can wear around her neck.

My brothers join the fun, quicker than lightning, when there's a rare occasion to put Nico in his place.

Shawn: I don't have a spare bulletproof vest, but I have proper body armor. Will that work?

Conor: Yeah, that's good. Don't forget a holster for the gun, a few knives, and maybe a smoke grenade just to veer on the side of caution.

Logan: She'll need silver bullets for vampires too, bro. And a survival kit in case there's an apocalypse. Flashlights, water, batteries, canned food. You know, the essentials.

Nico: Fuck you all.

There's a pause in the incoming messages. Long enough that I'm starting to wonder if we took it too far, but then *Nico is typing* appears at the top of the chat.

Nico: Fine, assholes. Just a can of pepper spray if you can, Shawn. But make sure it's light and the range is good. Damn, will you all be fucking sorry if zombies take over the world tonight.

Another hour goes by before the shit hits the fan again.

Logan sends a picture of Noah's t-rex. Eli's grasping its tail in his small palm, and Noah stands beside the crib, crying.

Conor: I got you two of those last year. Where's the spare?

Logan: No idea. Can't find it.

Conor: Fine, I'm on it. I'll finish up in the office and stop by the arcades on my way home.

It's barely lunchtime, and I've done little more than stare at my phone most of the morning. It's a good thing my team's finishing off the construction site we've been working on since I started in May. They're clearing the equipment before we hand over to the interior design team next week, so not much for me to do, or Logan would be busting my ass for wasting work time on personal matters.

We're close to the city center, so I hit a café for a sandwich and a coffee, choosing a table by the window, my phone face up, the chat on because there's another meltdown.

Theo: Come to think of it, pepper spray isn't a bad idea. Plenty of crazy in this world. Get one for Thalia, Shawn.

Logan: Make it three.

Conor: Fuck. Fine, get one for Vee, too.

At this point, I'm done. What a bunch of absolute crybabies. Theo leads the pack on this one because Thalia's the toughest, and she definitely doesn't need pepper spray to keep herself safe. She'll keep the girls safe, too, but—

The image of Blair all disheveled, makeup smeared, clothes torn flashes before my eyes and... shit.

I think I finally get why my brothers act the way they do. I'd feel so much better if B had a can on her.

I snatch the phone, sending her a short text.

Me: Care to tell me what's going on? Why are you avoiding me?

My foot taps against the floor while I wait for the reply,

ignoring the messages coming in to the Sausage Fest chat.

B: I'm not avoiding you.

My clenched fist slowly uncurls on the table and the muscles in my jaw relax, making me realize I've been mindlessly grinding my teeth while waiting for her message.

Me: Fine, then come over tonight. No questions.

The reply comes back, so does the tension. It seizes my muscles so hard they cramp. The involuntary reflex also makes my fist clench, and since I'm holding the phone, the screen cracks. A hairline fracture in the bottom left corner, but it's enough to skyrocket my temper.

B: I can't. I'm sorry.

I look up to the ceiling, muttering under my breath. *Kick me when I'm down, why don't you?*

Three days is a long time to think. Last night, to keep myself occupied, I worked out Blair and I have been sleeping around for eight weeks. *Eight* weeks. Two months of sex. I've not had a relationship this long with any other woman in my entire life. Not even Ana came close.

During those two months, she's texted me variations of *not tonight* a dozen times, but *I can't* hits differently. Given the situation, it feels like a gentler way of saying *we're done.*

And knowing we're done, that I won't see her, touch her, *kiss* her drives me to the brink of a nervous breakdown.

Two months, but I've not had my fill yet. Not even close.

If anything, I want more.

Boy, am I in trouble.

Without thinking, I let the hurt rippling through me take the stage. She should have the guts to tell me the deal is off the table.

Me: If we're done, it'd be nice to know before I go to Vegas so I don't keep my dick on a leash all weekend for nothing.

I regret it as soon as I press send. It sounds so fucking wrong... like she's just a good lay. Like I don't care about anything other than sex.

I shouldn't care.

Jesus... *what* have I gotten myself into?

Or better yet, *why*?

It's not like I didn't know any better. I kept the attraction simmering beneath the surface, suppressed and denied, for a long time. *Just desire*, I told myself. But deep down, I knew the undeniable truth. I knew it when I carried Blair, wasted and unconscious in my arms, out of Brandon's house after the graduation party.

I knew it when I held her close to my chest, wrapped in my hoodie, in the back seat of Colt's car.

Fuck, I even knew it when I kissed her and stalked into her bedroom with one goal in mind: fuck her senseless.

I knew, but I ignored it. Belittled the intensity of the magnetic pull between us.

I thought I was safe. That I had it under control.

After all those years I saw Blair parading the school corridors in tight dresses, the rumors, and her reputation... I was certain I could keep it physical. I had to, considering everything she did to Mia.

Just sex. Great, intense, raw sex.

But now I'm absolutely fucking screwed. Trapped in a whirlwind of emotions, a damn hurricane tearing through my mind. The text I just sent her might be the lowest I've ever sunk, but shit can always get worse.

When her reply arrives, it's definitely worse. Ten times worse.

B: I can't because it's THIS time of the month, but good to know where you stand. Feel free to use your dick whichever way you deem fit.

How about I accidentally catch it in my zipper as punishment? If I thought I felt bad for texting the idiotic line before, it's got nothing on how I feel now.

***

Five hours later, with three boxes of takeout food stacked in my arms and a paper bag dangling from my wrist, I knock on Blair's door, still in my work clothes.

Shower can wait.

I've got some serious apologizing to do. I never guilt-tripped a girl for being on her period. Had I known, I definitely wouldn't have done it this time.

The door opens, Blair's pretty face contorts into a scowl as she looks me over, one eyebrow raised. "What do you want?"

"I'm sorry," I say, stepping closer, not close enough that she won't be able to shut the door in my face though. "I'm having a shitty day and I took it out on you. I didn't mean what I said." I lift the takeout boxes higher. "Pizza, Chinese, and Italian. I didn't know what you'd want."

The two wrinkles on her forehead even out, vulnerability peeking through the cracks of her composure.

"No one has ever apologized to me," she admits quietly. "Thank you, and I'm sorry, too. I should've told you I'm on my period instead of tiptoeing around the subject." She glances at the bag hanging from my wrist. "What's in there?"

"I'll show you if you let me in."

Her combative stance across the threshold wavers, and she opens the door further, stepping aside. "We're not having sex tonight, Cody."

"A true sailorman will cross the red sea, baby. Orgasms help with cramps, you know?"

"I'm the one with a vagina here, so yes, I do know. Do you know what also helps? Heat packs, pills, and candy bars. I don't feel sexy right now so no orgasms. It's gross." She closes the door, staying in the same spot as I dump the takeout boxes on the kitchen island.

"It's not gross. It's normal. I'm not here for sex, B, but I could make you squirt in the shower so it's less *gross*."

"I'll pass, thanks," she says, scrunching her nose, eyes glimmering softly. "So? What's in the bag?"

"Take a look."

TWENTY-SIX

Blair

Candy bars. Lots of candy, a scented candle, a bath bomb that smells like coconuts and vanilla, tampons, pills, and even some lame rom-com. *That's* what's in the bag.

A period survival kit.

I peer up at Cody from where I stand looking at the contents spread before me.

"What is it? Did I forget something? I can run out and—"

"You bought me tampons," I whisper.

He cocks an eyebrow, scrutinizing the box. "Do you not use tampons? I can go buy pads if you want."

"No, this... this is perfect." My hands tremble as I place every item back in the bag, my thoughts in overdrive.

Cody crosses the room then hauls me onto the counter, both hands gripping the marble edge as he beds his elbows, staring at me. "What's wrong?"

Needing something to do with my fingers, I wrinkle the

hem of his black polo shirt.

My heart pounds a wild rhythm of hope and fear. This is so much more than just being friendly. It's intimate, personal. Something a boyfriend would do, not a man who labeled himself my enemy.

He shouldn't be here. As much as I want him to spend time with me outside the bedroom, he shouldn't. He's not doing us any favors. We're tiptoeing on thin ice, and it's more like stomping when he acts considerate and helpful. Tender, sweet, *caring*.

When he looks at me like he never wants to look away.

He tilts my chin, searching my face. "Words, baby. What's wrong?"

"Nothing. It's just... this is the nicest thing anyone's ever done for me," I admit, meeting his piercing gaze. "It doesn't feel like you hate me anymore."

The lines we drew are blurring, evaporating, and I'm scared because... I think I'm in love with him, and now... everything has to stop.

We were doomed from the start.

I had feelings for him before he kissed me, and I put up a lousy fight whenever he stretched the boundaries.

I let it happen, falling deeper and deeper while fooling myself I had it under control.

"You should go," I say, bracing both hands against his chest as I slam my walls back up, even though they're full of holes now. It's no longer easy to slip into my unemotional, guarded act. No longer easy to play that part. Not around Cody. "Please," I whisper, everything inside me rioting as I say, "I... I can't do this. You need to leave."

He doesn't budge. If anything, he crowds me further.

"Take it off," he says, cradling my thighs, a tornado of contradicting emotions in his eyes fighting for the stage. "Now, B."

My eyebrows bank in the middle as I look down at my summer dress. He can't be serious. "No. I told you we're not having sex tonight."

"That's not what I want," he seethes through gritted teeth. "Eyes on me, B," he adds, near whispering. "Which one is real?"

"Real? I... which *what is* real?"

"You. Which one of *you is* real? I'm tired of guessing, so tell me. Is *this* real?" He flicks a hand at me. "Or the girl who laughed with me last night? The girl who bakes cookies, plays peek-a-boo with my nephews, and cries herself to sleep in my arms. The girl who doesn't give a fuck about red lips or high heels and doesn't mind me seeing her without makeup? The girl who drinks beer from the bottle, wears sweatpants, and admits her mistakes or *this*." He motions to me again, alluding to the fake act I'm trying to put on right now. The godawful, attention-seeking attitude, crude language, and rude comments. "Which one is real and which is a mask?"

I stare at him, my insides tingling and tying into knots. "You know which one is real."

"I do, but you'd still rather be *this* girl. You're *her* when you go out with your fake friends. *Her* when you wear those red dresses. The only time you're *you* is when you're with me."

I bite my cheek, loving and hating that he sees right through me. That he pays enough attention to notice that the face I show the world isn't my true face.

"You have a year of college left," he continues, hammering his point across. "After that's over, life begins. You won't see most of your fake friends again. They won't give you a second thought two years from now. In five years, most won't remember your name."

He leans in closer, close enough that our noses almost brush. "This isn't you," he whispers, almost pleading, though with a flaring temper laced in his tone. "This is a defense mechanism. An alter ego you created to deflect the hurt. I can't fucking stand *this* girl," he spits out, eyes roving my body up and down before he meets mine again. "But I like the girl who sneaks into my bed when she needs a hug. I like the girl who smiles with her eyes, not just her lips." He takes a pause. Every muscle in his body winds up tight, but his face radiates determination. "I like the girl who trusts me to bear the weight of her hurt. I don't hate her, B. Far from it."

My heart beats out of my chest, the last sentence coating every mental cut and bruise, acting like a balm, cuddling me with more warmth than I ever received.

Cody moves back a step, standing taller, prouder, more confident. "Take it *off*. Bin it, burn it. Stop sabotaging your life."

My thoughts race a million miles a second, my mind flooding with memories of every moment I spent with Cody these past weeks, every fleeting conversation, tear, and time he let me fall apart in his arms.

That tiny brush of my lips against his neck when he fell asleep after dragging me onto the mattress in his condo.

The first kiss *he* initiated and how fast it led to more.

Every smile, every gasp, every blissful minute.

And then it all shifts to the other side of the coin. My father, my friends, the future I dreamed of for so long. The goals, threats, everything I could lose. Everything I suffered, the road I've taken, and how close to the finish line I am.

And then there's the imposing shadow of my mistakes. The hell I put Mia through, how much it hurts to even think about forgiving myself.

Even if I can... Cody's family will never accept me. This is beautiful on paper, but it won't last. Cody will leave.

He'll leave, and I'll be alone. Not even any fake friends to take my mind off those dark thoughts. No money to fall back on. No dreams. No future.

What will I do then?

God, but what if he doesn't leave? What if I really earned a second chance?

Cody cups my face, forcing me to look at him. "Don't disappear inside your head. Don't overthink, B. Take. It. *Off.* Please... If you can't do it for you, do it for me. I'll teach you how to let go of the past. I'll teach you how to be happy."

Inching away, my vocal cords tying in knots, my shaking hands drop to my unsteady legs. "You should try to hate me again. I'm not worth the risk, Cody."

"That's not your decision to make."

TWENTY-SEVEN

Cody

With my heart on my fucking sleeve, I wait for Blair to speak. To *smile*, take off that fucking mask, and be herself: the girl learning how to be happy.

That it's *okay to* be happy despite the past.

I'm in deep. So fucking deep. I have no idea how to navigate these treacherous waters. I miss her. She's right here, but I fucking miss her. I want her. Whether beneath me, on top of me, or nestled into my side... I don't care as long as she's with me.

I should've realized I wouldn't give her up. It should've clicked when I stormed over here after she sneaked out of my bed. But I ignored the signs, the undeniable attraction, and feelings that defy logic because deep down, I knew that once I acknowledged how much I crave Blair outside the bedroom, I'd have to end it.

And now it's too late to get out unscathed. It's too late to get out, period. I'm falling in love with her.

It's as simple and as complicated as that.

The last nail to my coffin was the look of utter disbelief when she stared at a pack of tampons I bought. You'd think I gave her a diamond ring, she was so bewildered.

My pulse triphammers in my neck while she remains silent, overthinking her next words.

It'll hurt like a bitch if she tells me we're done. The mere idea of us being over turns my blood cold. I don't want to let her go. Not now, not ever, and accepting that is both intoxicating and terrifying.

I want to learn more about her. Uncover her protective layers, permanently strip her masks and help her accept every mistake she's ever made. I want to help her move on and embrace how much she's changed. Show her that she's most beautiful when her tough exterior crumbles to reveal vulnerability and goodness. I want her to let go of the blame and believe she deserves happiness.

Happiness with *me.*

I'm teetering on the edge of a dangerous path. Afraid of losing my brothers' trust. Scared of hurting Mia. Fucking petrified of losing them all because I want Blair.

"There isn't a single thing you could do to make us turn on you."

Nico's words echo in the deepest recess of my mind. He said that when Logan admitted he was in love with Cassidy. Logan thought that because Cass was friends with Kaya, who cheated on Nico, it would be an issue.

Logan thought we'd never speak to him again. He thought we wouldn't forgive him...

I wish I could say my situation is the same, but it's not in the slightest. If anyone can help me organize my thoughts and shed some light on how I should approach this, it's definitely Logan.

Blair stares at the floor, but I don't think she sees it. She's deep in her head. God knows what she's thinking about. Is she weighing her options? Wondering if she feels the same way I do? Wondering how to tell me she doesn't?

Fuck. Knows.

I wait because I trust she'll make the right choice. That she'll let go of the blame. That she'll take a step away from the alter ego she's masqueraded as for years.

I wait because I'm falling in love with her.

I want to help her see that her past doesn't define her. Mistakes are a part of life, growing up, and learning who we are. She can right the wrongs if she believes she's worth fighting for.

Seconds pass, each stretching into oblivion, my wristwatch ticking loud and clear. Slowly, Blair moves her eyes from the floor to me, and the weight on my shoulders eases.

It's hard to pinpoint *what* exactly changes that sends relief rattling through me. Maybe it's the way her shoulders sag, how she nervously pulls her lower lip between her teeth, or the uncertainty shining in those deep blue irises.

Maybe it's all that and something else I can't name.

"There she is," I say as I trail my knuckles along her jawline, tilting her chin up. "There's my girl."

The corners of her lips twitch. Not a smile, barely a promise of one, but she's calm, her decision made, and my heart swells three sizes, threatening to burst, when she hooks her index finger in the collar of my t-shirt, tugging twice.

I dip my head, covering her lips with a kiss, slipping my tongue inside the silk of her mouth, tasting, teasing, sealing the unspoken promises. We'll make this work. I know we will.

She scoots closer to the edge of the counter, weaving her

delicate fingers through my hair, the kiss evolving like it did the first time.

Everything holding us back disappears, raw, primitive desire returning, now more potent with the burgeoning emotions behind it.

"This won't be easy," she murmurs between kisses. "There are things I need to deal with, things I need to figure out... things I can't tell you about."

"I'm not asking for miracles, B. I just want you to stop pretending you're someone you're not. Stop living in limbo and start walking forward. I'm not saying it'll be easy, but I promise it'll be worth it."

She trails her fingertips down my scalp, neck, and shoulders, then holds my face in both hands. "You're worth every tear I'll cry, Cody, but I need a few days to deal with my life. A few days to make changes. Until I stand firmly on my feet..." She touches my chest right above my heartbeat, then touches hers, "...this has to stay between us."

Who would've thought *she'd* be the one keeping us a secret? It should be me doing everything in my power to make sure my brothers won't find out, but I've lost interest in keeping our enemies-with-benefits status on the down-low.

I was sloppy. Careless enough to stop locking the door when she came over. One of my brothers could've walked in on us fucking in my kitchen, and I didn't care.

"Deal, but don't make me wait long. I'm not keeping you a secret longer than I absolutely have to."

Her cheeks pale. "Aren't you afraid what your brothers will say?"

"Petrified," I admit.

I could lie to make things easier, but nothing about us is

easy. This is a fucked-up, complicated kind of love. The best things in life are never easy, and I refuse to start with lies.

"Cody, I—"

"You're worth it," I cut in before she says something that'll spike my blood pressure.

"I'm worth losing your family?"

I smile, pecking her forehead. "You don't know my family all that well, but I promise I won't lose them. It might take them time to accept that you're mine, but they will."

"How can you be so sure?"

"I know my family, B. There's nothing I could do that would make them hate me. We give each other shit over anything and everything, but when it matters, we listen."

TWENTY-EIGHT

Cody

We spent the evening eating cold takeout, watching the lame romantic comedy I bought, cuddling on her uncomfortable, navy-blue couch, and making out like a pair of teenagers.

She didn't elaborate on what she needs to take care of before we tell my family about us, and despite the curiosity gnawing at my brain, I decided pushing for answers wasn't the way ahead.

When she fell asleep on the couch, around midnight, I carried her to bed and stayed, cradling her to me all night.

What I didn't do was set the alarm. The bachelor party meets at Nico's at seven am. He's got the biggest driveway, enough space for the guys to leave their cars there all weekend.

The moment I open my eyes and glance at my wristwatch, I know I'm screwed. It's six-thirty already. I'm not showered or dressed. I may have grabbed a shower last night when I went to pack a bag for the weekend, but that doesn't count. I need a shower in the morning to wake up properly.

"Fuck," I hiss, leaping out of bed. "I need to go, B. I'm late."

She grumbles something, tucking the comforter closer to her chin before peeking with one eye. "It's too early."

"It's late for me." I yank my pants on, gather the rest of my clothes, and bend over to kiss her head. "You better not be on your period when I come back." Grabbing her hand from under her pillow, I settle it over my cock, groaning when she applies the right amount of pressure. "This needs taking care of."

She sits up with a half-asleep, dreamy smile. "I know how to make it all better."

"Me too, but I don't have time, B. Behave."

"You're already late. What's three more minutes?"

"You think you can jerk me off in three minutes?"

"If that doesn't work, there's always another way." She wiggles her ass to give me a hint.

Heat detonates behind my ribs. The idea of exploring her this way is music to my ears. Too bad it's not possible. "Seeing that you think I can just slide in there the same as your pussy tells me you never had a cock in your sweet tight ass. We need lube, a plug, and more than three minutes to get you nice and ready."

She hooks her index finger in the pockets of my sweats, tugs my pants down and quickly does the same with my boxers.

"B, we don't—" I shut up when she takes my dick in her hot mouth, twirling her tongue around the head. "Fuck," I hiss, my balls pulling taut, orgasm already building at the base of my spine. "You might be onto something with those three minutes."

She sucks me in deeper, her head bobbing back and forth, long nails gouging into my hips to keep me in place when she swallows me down.

"Good girl, fuck, that's good... a little faster."

I gather her hair, holding it in a ponytail with my fist, eyes on her pretty face. The orgasm gains momentum, hurtling to the surface faster once she grips the base. It's a sensory overload. That stubborn part of my character not prone to giving up or letting someone else win is fighting it, but B knows how to drive me incoherent with need. How to make me lose control.

"Out," is all I rasp before nothing more than my guttural noises fill the room. My throat constricts as the orgasm rattles through me, powerful enough to cramp my thighs.

B arches back in time, working my length with her small hand, milking my warm cum over her chest and throat.

"That was..." I suck in a harsh breath. "Thank you, baby."

I grip her underarms, helping her up when she tucks my cock back in my boxers and readjusts my sweats.

"I like making you lose control," she admits, smoothing her hands down the sides of my sweatpants.

"I hate that I can't return the favor, but—"

"I'm on my period, Cody. I wouldn't let you return the favor even if you weren't late." She smiles, looks curiously down her cleavage, wipes up a fingerful of my cum, and sucks it into her mouth.

One small move, but it drives me feral. I could easily rise again and bend her over the bed.

Her eyes widen in surprise as her finger pops out of her mouth. "It's nothing like I imagined." She dabs her finger again, licking it clean as she looks at me. "You can come in my mouth next time."

"Jesus... What are you doing to me?"

She's careful not to touch her chest to mine as she stamps a quick kiss on my lips. "I'm making sure not one show you see this weekend tops this."

I slap her butt, squeezing hard. "Nothing tops this, B, but you look good in green. I like that you're jealous, as long as you don't take it too far. If I wanted to fuck someone else tonight, I wouldn't have told you I don't hate you." I slap her butt again and drop one last kiss on her head. "Go take a bath. I'll see you Sunday. Call me if you need me."

A smile is all I get before she locks herself in the bathroom, and I exit her condo, determined to grab the fastest shower in the history of mankind.

But that goes to shit the second I yank the door wide open, stalking out of Blair's condo with a bare chest, wild hair, and half my clothes in hand.

It goes to shit because I come face to face with my brother, strutting down the corridor. He halts mid-step, narrowed eyes taking me in.

"I thought you could use a lift," Logan says, weighing every word. "All those cars will be a tight fit at Nico's."

"Am I glad it's you and not one of the others."

He cocks an eyebrow. "If you think I won't give you any shit, you're sorely mistaken, bro."

A small smile plays across my lips despite the atmosphere thickening, tangling, and getting too hot to breathe as I cross the hallway. "I know, but among all that shit, you'll be helpful. Come on, I need a shower."

"Yeah, I bet..." he mutters, following me inside. "Shower first, then I get to call you names, and then you can talk."

"While you're thinking of those names, make me a coffee."

He punches my shoulder on his way to the kitchen while I take a left to my bedroom, Logan's quiet *asshole* hitting my ears as I pull fresh clothes from the closet.

"That's one!" I shout back. "Why don't you take five minutes to remember what it was like when you were in my shoes."

"I wouldn't fucking fit in your shoes, bro," he snaps, annoyed but nowhere near as angry as I expected. "Shut up, let me think, and get a move on. We're late."

"It's *your* party. The guys won't leave without you."

"If you don't start moving, I'll leave without *you*."

Ever since Blair crawled into my bed, I've imagined my brothers' reaction if they found out about us. I wondered how much shouting I'd have to endure, how pissed they'd be on a scale of one to ten, and how long Nico would growl, snap, and avoid me.

How hard would he punch? Would he break my nose or rein his temper enough that I'd only end up with a black eye?

I was jittery and restless when these thoughts overwhelmed me, my stomach tied into elaborate knots, anxiety chewing at the edge of my mind.

But now that Blair's mine, my head is quiet.

Logan just caught me red-handed. I should think of the best way to lie my way out of this, but I don't. No matter what he might say, or if he demands I come clean today, I'm not nervous. I know what I want.

I'm ready to face the consequences.

Once I step back into the kitchen, showered, dressed, and wheeling my small suitcase, the atmosphere makes my skin crawl.

Fine, maybe I am a little nervous after all.

"So?" Logan prompts, handing me a cup. "Are we just gonna pretend nothing happened, or will you start talking?" He leans against the counter, sipping his steaming americano. "I know who lives across the hall, so tell me... what were you thinking?"

"I found her," I say simply, looking him dead in the eye.

"Was she lost in her condo? Cody, I'm a patient person. I have two kids, so patience is necessary, but if you don't start explaining, I can't promise I won't fucking hit you." He sets the cup aside, grinding his teeth, the reaction he's kept in check thus far blowing up in my face.

He's fifteen feet away, but his shoulders tense so hard I can fucking see it. His posture changes from careless to a statue, and along with his posture, the atmosphere shifts, the air heavy, loaded with tension.

"Fuck, Cody," he clips, starting off resigned, but his voice grows sharper with every word. "Blair? Seriously? What the hell were you thinking?"

"I wasn't," I admit, plopping down on the couch. We're not going anywhere until this conversation is over. "I didn't expect it would go this far. There's more to Blair than meets the eye, Logan. She told me about her past, the bullying, why she was doing it, and—"

"She burned Mia's hair! You have any idea how pissed Nico was when he found out? How long it took to calm the fucker down? and you..." He massages his temples with both hands. "You were going out of your way last year to keep Nico from hurting Mia. Now you're fucking around with the girl who did nothing else? That's..." He trails off, clearly at a loss for words.

"We're not fucking around. Not anymore. She's my Cass, Logan." I pump my fists, clenching and unclenching to rid the inferno behind my ribs. He has every right to ask questions. I'm sure it's a walk in the park compared to what Nico will put me through, but that *fucking around* comment just rubs me the wrong way. "She's my Thalia, Mia, Vee... *my* girl," I add to clarify. "I know it's complicated."

"No shit," he huffs, but his tone is gentler as he runs a hand down his face. "Fuck. If this is how you see her... it changes things." He stares at me over his coffee, taking another long sip.

Logan and I have grown closer since I became Noah's favorite uncle. Or maybe it's because I'm no longer an annoying teenager that we get along better.

My dynamic with all four of my older brothers has changed over the past two years, but Logan and I are similar on more levels than we realized.

He gets me. Sometimes pulls thoughts straight from my head like Colt and Conor do.

"Love is always complicated. Name one of us who had it easy?" he challenges but doesn't wait for an answer. "We've all been through shit to get our happy ever after."

"This is as close to you and Cass as it gets, so you're my best hope for support."

"That's why you were happy I caught you sneaking out of her condo, not one of the others, right?"

"Yeah. You're least likely to bite my head off." I crack my knuckles and straighten my spine, setting my empty cup on the coffee table. "Tell me what I'm supposed to do."

"You want *me to* tell you what to do? Don't get me wrong, bro..." he pauses, pulling a dumb fucking face.

It's probably not dumb, but I'm on edge and easily irritable. Sue me.

"Alright, let's backtrack a bit. I need more information, Cody. How did this happen? How did you justify it?"

"Blair's different now. She changed. I know how it sounds, but it's the truth. She had a fucked-up life. It still haunts her, but she's working on herself..." I hide my face in my hands.

It's not easy explaining how much she changed to someone who hasn't spent time with Blair. How what she went through shaped her into the person she is now.

Even I don't know exactly what her life looked like or what bodies she's still hiding in the closet.

It's not easy explaining how much sheer will and character she's shown, never making excuses even though she's got plenty of raw material for one.

How resigned she is to her deluded belief that she doesn't deserve to be happy because she made mistakes.

Everyone makes mistakes. What we do about them proves who we are. Blair's amazing. Strong, beautiful, kind... so fucking fragile. Filled with regret, careful, sweet.

I'm in fucking love with her for every one of those things.

"The point is," I say, peering at Logan. "I get it. I understand her. She's not a bad person."

He mulls it over, scratching the stubble he's growing out. "Does she know how you feel?"

"I haven't told her I love her if that's what you mean. I think it's pretty damn obvious. We were casual for a while and—"

"Ah, ah, ah," he tuts, wagging his fingers. "I'm not done yet. Do you want my blessing? You need assurance that your brothers will have your back?"

"No. I know what I want, Logan. She's mine."

He bobs his head up and down a few times. "Good answer. Means you're serious. I didn't wait for your blessing before I went after Cassidy. I wanted her, and nothing would've changed my mind." He folds his arms across his chest. "So? What is it you want from me? Lay your cards down, Cody. I'm too old to play games."

"Pointers. Advice. What do I tell Nico and Mia? How do I break the news? How do I explain that Blair's not all fucking evil?"

"Well, for starters, don't tell anyone this weekend. I love

you, but if you fuck up my night, I will hit you. You waited however long, so wait a bit longer."

"I wasn't planning on telling anyone today. B asked for a few more days before we make it official. Once I've got the green light... what do I do? Call everybody in like you did or talk to Nico and Mia first? I'm pretty sure everyone will listen, but Nico—"

"Bring her to the wedding," Logan cuts in.

"What?"

A small smirk curls his lips, soothing the furious look he's had on for the past few minutes. Though furious might be an exaggeration. Logan's unpredictable, hot-headed, and ruthless when the situation requires, but his face is soft. He doesn't look intimidating. At least not as intimidating as he thinks he does.

"Bring her to the wedding," he repeats much slower. "Shock therapy. Show her off and deal with the aftermath."

"I don't know... I don't want to put her in the firing line."

He pushes away from the counter, setting his empty cup in the sink. "You're not avoiding that, bro. She'll be on the spot one way or another. You want Nico to listen? Bring Blair to the wedding. He can't leave or avoid you there. You'll say what you want to say." He snatches his keys from the breakfast bar, motioning for me to follow. "Besides, what kind of a fucking wedding would it be if someone didn't get their ass kicked?"

This is the last way I'd plan this, but it's not an entirely idiotic idea. If Logan thinks it's good, I won't question him. Not just because he went through the same thing and wouldn't advise me to do something that could seriously backfire but because I'm selfish. I want my girl on my arm at his wedding.

Looks like it's settled... I'm getting my ass kicked in a tuxedo.

TWENTY-NINE

Blair

With a pounding heart, I inhale a deep breath before dialing my father's number. It rings once, twice, and the call drops. My stomach twists with dread when my screen lights up with a message.

Dad: on holiday. Back Friday.

Not what I was hoping for. We need to talk before Cody comes back. I don't have a plan yet, but Dad being away is not the worst thing. It gives me time to take the first steps into a life without Gideon Fitzpatrick's support.

Me: It's important. We need to talk.

I hit send, give him a minute to read it, then call again. This time, the phone doesn't even ring. Instead, I'm greeted with his voicemail. "*You've reached Gideon Fitzpatrick. I'm unavailable at the moment. Please leave a message.*" I hang up before the beep, frustration and relief filling my jittery mind.

Maybe it's for the best. It gives me a few days to gather my thoughts and steel myself for the inevitable showdown.

Slumping back onto the couch, I stare at my phone, praying that when the time comes to face my father, it doesn't destroy this fragile happiness I've found. And more than anything, I hope it doesn't ruin my relationship with Cody.

He's become my safe haven. My source of joy, security, and calm. Losing him is more terrifying than any confrontation with my father.

I don't know if I deserve him, but for the first time in my life I have something worth fighting for.

Someone worth fighting for.

I spend the rest of the day sorting through my jewelry, purses, and shoes, texting Cody every few hours. They're all hungover and not looking forward to the six-hour bus ride back.

He sent me a picture of the Corona he's nursing at the hotel bar, along with a few words that almost had me whipping my purple wand out.

Cody: Can't wait to be inside you, baby. I've missed you.

As much as I'd like to scratch that itch and give myself an orgasm, I'd much rather have Cody do the honors. He's better at it than I am. The orgasms he evokes are much more powerful.

By the time the bachelor party is in good enough shape to get on the road, it's eight in the evening. Cody won't be back until late into the night, so I send him another text as I head out for food.

Me: I left my key in your mailbox. Let yourself in.

He doesn't reply until I'm on my way back, the aromatic scent of pizza filling my small Porsche.

Cody: That tells me you're planning to fall asleep. Wait for me.

Me: I'll try, but just in case, the key is there.

My good mood evaporates when I park my car and spot Cody's stalker lurking outside, eyes hidden behind a pair of oversized shades.

She's nervously pressing a button on the keypad, probably ringing Cody's place, then paces three steps left and right, arms crossed tightly over her chest.

"What are you doing here?" I ask, my voice far from friendly.

I'm in combat mode, jealousy writhing inside me. If she thinks she can steal my man, she has another thing coming.

She turns on her heel, and my combat stance wavers. There's something almost desperate in her expression. A kind of deeply ingrained sadness I know well.

"Oh, hey, Blair. I was just calling your apartment..."

"You're here to see me?" That's not what I expected. My initial jealousy fades as I gesture toward the pizza box. "I stepped out for food."

She bites her lip, inserting a tense pause. "I need a favor," she finally admits, eyes welling with tears. "Please." Her voice cracks like eggshells.

"Are you okay? What's wrong?" I set the pizza on a nearby bench, giving her my full attention.

"I need to apologize to Cody."

I stiffen at that, the jealous monster rearing its head once more. "Cody isn't here. It's Logan's bachelor party weekend."

"I know. That's why I came tonight." She pauses as if shepherding her emotions. She looks so small and lost it throws me off-guard. "I want you to give him something." She hands me a crumpled piece of paper from her pocket.

"What's this?"

"An apology. I can't face him. Not after everything I did, so I wrote a letter. Read it, okay? I want you to know, and if you decide he should see it, give it to Cody."

"It's not my place to decide what he should or shouldn't see. I'll give it to him when he comes back."

"Thank you." She offers me a small smile, already backing away. "You make a cute couple, you know?"

She doesn't wait for me to respond, turning and marching away, her heels clicking against the sidewalk.

I lose my appetite by the time I drop the bag on the kitchen island.

Ana did say she wanted me to read it...

Before I can talk myself out of it, I sit on the couch and unfold the letter.

Cody,

A letter. How very nineties of me, right?

Maybe in a way, but the truth is, I'm scared to face you. I made a mess of my life. There's a lot I need to get off my chest, and I owe you an apology.

Hopefully, by the time you finish reading, things will make more sense, and you'll understand why I behaved the way I did.

First, I'm sorry for dragging you into my messed-up world. It wasn't fair. You never deserved the crazy you got from me.

I blamed myself for my brother's suicide and, in a twisted way, I started punishing myself. I couldn't deal with the guilt, knowing he could still be alive if I had found time for him.

My brother's girl broke up with him, and I wasn't there when he needed me most. I was so caught up in my own life that I didn't give him the time and attention he needed. He called me the night before he died, asking me to come over... I didn't, and then he was gone.

Everything fell apart. I thought that by setting myself up for your rejection, I could feel a fraction of the pain he did. I'm sorry you got caught in the middle. I have nothing in my defense other than that I wasn't thinking clearly.

I'm sure you've noticed—with great relief—that I've not been around for a few weeks. I've been in daily therapy since I last saw you.

I would probably be stalking you still if my mom hadn't asked me to help clean out my brother's place. Seeing his empty apartment and dealing with all that guilt was too much. I broke down.

Now that I'm in therapy, popping pills, I'm starting to get better. I'm working through that guilt, learning to live again.

I'm sorry for everything I put you through. I'm sorry for the drama and thank you for never filing that restraining order like I know you wanted to.

I hope you can forgive me. Once I'm all better, maybe we can grab a drink and make fun of my stalking.

Ana

***

"B," I hear Cody whisper, softly but urgently, his fingers grazing my cheek. "B, wake up, baby. I need you."

A flutter in my belly pulls me further out of sleep, the anticipation sky-high. Slowly, I open my eyes, finding him sitting beside me, nothing but his silhouette visible in the darkness.

"Hey," I murmur, reaching to touch his face. "I half expected I'd wake up with you already sliding inside me."

"It crossed my mind, but we've not discussed it."

"You have my consent to fuck me while I sleep." I yawn, stretching out before I sit up. "What time is it?"

"Almost three." He grips my waist when I get up, standing me between his legs, his lips kissing the hollow between my breasts. "You're not getting any more sleep tonight."

"Okay, but I need three minutes in the bathroom first."

"Two." He pats my butt. "Not a second longer."

A pleasant shudder runs through me when he slips his fingers under the hem of my night dress, moving the fabric up as they graze my thigh.

"Dirty dream?" he questions, slipping two digits inside me. "You're wet, B."

"That's what you do to me."

He groans, plunging in deeper. "So warm... fuck, I need you on me right now."

I gently tap the back of his head. "Two minutes. Strip, Cody."

Wriggling out of his embrace, I lock myself in the bathroom to brush my teeth and sprinkle my face with cold water. Cody's naked when I step back into the bedroom.

The nightlamp is on, and he sits with his back to the headboard, palming his cock, stroking slowly.

The sight makes my knees buckle.

"Do it again," I order, sliding the straps of my night dress down my arms. It sighs into a heap of blue silk at my feet. Cody pumps his length, his burning gaze fixed on my boobs.

"That's hot," I whisper. "One day, I want to sit and watch."

"That day won't be today. Panties off, B."

Hooking my thumbs in the elastic, my blue thong follows the night dress before my knees dent the mattress at the bottom of the bed.

"Good girl," Cody rasps, his big hand working faster. "Now crawl to me."

Another body-wide shudder shakes me. I'm slick between my legs, every move reminding me how much I want and need him inside. I crawl slowly, my eyes idling between his face and his cock, the head red, angry, and glistening with precum.

"I want a taste," I murmur.

"*Want?* Someone's feeling bratty tonight." He grips the back of my head once I'm in reach. "Lose the attitude and ask nicely."

He tries to drag me in for a kiss, but instead, I dive, taking him down my throat fast.

Oops... I forgot to ask.

"Fuck," he rasps, his fingers spasming in my hair. "Fine. I'll gladly take this kind of bratty, but not tonight. Come here."

He gently pulls me off him and helps me maneuver into position, his hands supporting my butt. We both gasp when I sink, loving how he stretches me slowly.

"Don't move," he whispers in my mouth, holding me still once he's balls-deep. "Too good. You feel way too good, B. I missed you." He forces my forehead against his, taking my lips in slow, biting kisses. "I couldn't stop thinking about you."

"All those boobs you saw didn't distract you?"

He pushes my hips back far enough that just the head of his cock remains nestled inside me, then yanks me close again, the sensation setting off fireworks in my head.

"I prefer your boobs." He pushes me back again, dipping his head to circle my nipples with his hot tongue.

"Mine are small. I'm sure you've seen better."

"They're not yours; they're mine and perfect. Round, sweet..." He kisses each one, then my lips as he grips my waist, flipping us over. "Mine, B. Every inch of you is mine."

He pulls out and thrusts in, hovering over me, the weight of his body soothing me in the best way. Instead of the expected hard, relentless fuck, sex is different tonight.

So much different it has my heart swelling every time he bottoms out inside me. Those brown eyes glued to my face shine with an unfamiliar intensity. Less lust, more affection. Our moves, touches, kisses... different. Deeper. More intimate. More meaningful. Slow, tender, intense.

He cradles my face, kisses my lips, and watches me as if he's afraid I'll disappear.

We can't get close enough.

A smoldering behind my ribs envelopes my heart more the longer I look into his eyes and *see* the emotions raging inside him, and I want—

No, I shouldn't. It's too soon... too dangerous. I should protect myself in case this bubble bursts. In case he leaves once I tell him about my father, or when his brothers decide I'm not worth forgiveness, but... when he touches me like he's worshipping every inch and kisses me like he's trying to show me who I belong to, I stop overthinking, and just feel.

I part my lips, throwing caution to the wind. "Cody, I—"

"I know," he whispers, sealing my lips. "I know, baby."

I feel it in our gestures. See it in his eyes. Taste it on his lips.

This is it. What I never wanted to happen, happened, and now we're both desperate to let the other one know because this... *us*... it's perfect in all its imperfections. It's right.

And well overdue, seeing how fast we fell.

"I hate you more," he says, caressing every inch of my skin he can reach.

That word feels right.

The hate we harbored evolved. So has the definition, at least for us, and we both mean a different four-letter word.

"I hate you so. Fucking. Much," he breathes, pressing his lips to my forehead.

"I hate you more."

THIRTY

Cody

With two cups of coffee and a bag of Jolly Ranchers, I cross the airport, heading into the departure lounge. The symphony of rolling suitcases, conversations, and announcements thunders loud enough that I can't hear my thoughts.

Loud enough to muffle the quiet doubts prickling my mind. I want B by my side, but I'd be lying if I said I'm not worried about my brothers' reaction.

It took a few days to convince Blair she should come. A few long days of chats, sex, declarations, and promises. Maybe the best few days in my life thus far.

It was so freeing to hold her every night, wake up beside her, and come home to find her cooking.

Mundane. Normal. Boring. Fucking amazing.

We spent every minute after I came home from work together. Just the two of us every evening. Well, apart from Monday when I called Ana, asking her to come over, after I read her letter.

My step falters when I turn right toward the cozy couch Blair and I occupied minutes ago and find a different couple there, the guy holding a tumbler of whiskey, the girl scrolling through her socials.

A quick scan of the area tells me Blair's not here. Maybe she went to the restroom, and the seat poachers swooped in.

"Are you Cody?" the guy in my seat asks.

"Yeah. Why?"

He retrieves a napkin from the pocket of his flannel shirt. "Blair left this for you."

Dread shudders through me, throwing my hands into a shaking fit that nearly sends Blair's mochaccino toppling off my black coffee. Quick reflexes save the day as I park everything on the nearest table, before taking the napkin from the man's outstretched hand.

Even without looking, I know she bailed, but I unfold the napkin anyway, my heart pounding a drum solo. The airport logo is ingrained in the bottom left corner, and scrawled in the middle:

Cody,

Please don't chase me. I can't go through with this. We're not meant to be. You're the best thing that ever happened to me, and I don't want to be the worst that happens to you. I should've never let this get so far. I'm sorry.

B.

My stomach drops as I read her words once, twice, and

then again, each striking a more devastating blow. I fight the growing sense of panic... unsuccessfully. It's overwhelming, singing in my ears, whooshing through my bloodstream. The sweat from my hands soaks the napkin, smudging the ink as it crumples, and I feel like I'm suffocating.

She's breaking up with me? Through a fucking *napkin*?

The airport buzz becomes a dull throb, drowned out by my heart thundering in my chest.

A knot twists in my gut, nausea threatening to spill over.

Fuck, this is... love is cruel. I've experienced my fair share of pain but this is the worst kind. My hands shake so hard that Blair's words blur together. My head is a cacophony of thoughts, all colliding and ricocheting, refusing to settle.

This must be how Vivienne feels whenever she's off her meds. I remember how she visualized it one evening over beer—a huge intersection with traffic zooming in from all directions at different speeds, no traffic lights to control the mayhem.

I'm stuck in that traffic jam, thoughts honking and veering, no safe way across.

"We're done," I say under my breath, using Vee's technique of speaking her thoughts aloud.

I should've chosen a different thought because, out loud, this one guts me like a fish.

Feeling the burning, curious gaze of the couple on the couch, I peel my eyes off the napkin. The woman stopped staring at her phone to watch me with accusing eyes.

"How long ago did she leave?" I ask.

"Not long, maybe ten minutes," the man offers.

"She was shaken up," the woman adds, in a judgmental screech. "She looked *scared*."

Yeah, well, dumping your boyfriend via a note on a fucking

napkin forty minutes before flying to his brother's wedding will do that to a girl.

Ten minutes is long enough to leave the building and hail a cab. Instead of chasing her like she told me not to, I grab my phone, dialing her number.

No luck. I should've figured she'd switch it off. The voicemail message twists my stomach further.

With a new sense of determination, I stride toward the exit, ignoring our flight being announced. Screw the flight. I need to find Blair. I need to—

God, I can't fucking breathe. It feels like she pushed an eleven-inch blade into my heart. If this is what Conor felt when Vee tried to leave him, then I owe him an apology for belittling how much this hurts.

I halt halfway across the building, gouging my fingers into the back of my neck. Blair played this smart. She knew I won't skip Logan's wedding. She knows I can't chase after her.

By Monday, when I get back, she'll probably have moved out from across the hall, long fucking gone.

My insides shake, the hurt morphing into seething anger because that's easier to deal with. After everything we've been through, the bullshit we've had to work through to put our happiness first, she turns around and spits in my face.

Good, keep going. It's working. Anger is easy.

Easier for sure. I reread her stupid note, focusing on certain lines that fuel my anger.

I should've never let this get so far.

No. It's me who should've never let this get so far. So out of control. I shouldn't have trusted a girl who dealt hate, abuse, and pain like playing cards her whole life. I shouldn't have trusted she could do a one-eighty and stick in the new lane.

I make myself hate her again until the agonizing pain shredding my heart ebbs enough that I can pull down a breath without worrying my lungs will collapse.

The relief doesn't last long, though, because I know I'm lying to myself.

Another announcement rings from the speakers. Passengers flying to San Francisco should make their way to the gate.

Awesome.

Not only has she dumped my ass, but she's left me dateless for Logan's wedding.

I whip out my phone, blinded by my corkscrewing emotions. With stiff fingers, I dial the number and press the phone to my ear.

"How quickly can you get to the airport?"

***

I'm calmer once the plane takes off. Only a bit, though. The pain is there, throbbing like a raw wound. My chest feels hollow. I'm pretty sure Blair ripped my heart out and took it with her.

During the flight, I have time to decode her note, hunting for the reason she chose to leave today. It doesn't take long before a disturbing idea pops into my head... something triggered her decision.

It makes sense because she was perfectly happy this morning. All pretty smiles, kisses, and a few breathless orgasms. After worrying for days, she was finally looking forward to the wedding, though obsessing over my brothers' reaction.

It was cute how nervous she was, rethinking her dress choice twenty times over, keen to make a good impression.

This morning, she woke up happy, saying she'd follow

my lead, and believed what I told her: *they'll accept this faster than you think*.

I'm not naïve enough to have thought they wouldn't react. I expected explosive emotions, yelling, probably a right hook from Nico, but I know my family. I know my brothers.

We've been through enough over the years. There are seven of us, so life's never boring, but regardless of what happens, we stick together when it matters. Always loyal, trusting the process, and giving each other the benefit of the doubt.

I knew they'd come around once they realized how much Blair meant to me—how much she still means to me. It would have taken a while, but it would happen.

I pep-talked myself all week to the point where I was actually buzzed about seeing their faces when I'd arrive with Blair on my arm.

That's why I didn't tell them who I'm bringing.

Was bringing...

There is nothing you can do that would make us turn our backs on you.

Nico's words casually popped into my head ten times a day, making the prospect of showing off my girl less daunting.

They won't turn on me.

Wouldn't turn on me if B was still mine.

I'd been expecting surprised looks, annoyance laced with confusion and angry curiosity. They'd find the first opportunity for us all to sit alone. With two bottles of vodka and enough answers, they'd stop growling. And then... they'd either forgive and accept or take time out to mull it over.

What's most bizarre is that Mia's reaction worried me least. Again, I had time to imagine every possible scenario, but not one I could conjure ended with anything other than her smile. She loves me. Probably more than my brothers do.

She wants to see me happy. I know she does, so I also know she'd talk through the past with Blair.

Circling back to the point, despite Blair's initial worries, she was genuinely excited about the wedding and meeting my family. We had sex right before we left for the airport. She told me she loves me more than once today, and nothing else she's said or done triggered my suspicions.

Nothing hinted something might be wrong.

She's a good actress, but I don't think she was playing me. Something happened while I was getting coffee. Whether a realization hit her or something else entirely, her decision was abrupt.

Too fucking abrupt, and now I regret not running after her. I should have. If I'd caught her outside the airport, maybe she'd be the one sitting beside me.

But I wasn't thinking straight. It didn't even cross my mind to catch a later flight, or even drive to the venue.

I wish I could skip tonight's rehearsal dinner and follow Blair to demand an explanation. Help her deal with whatever's happening. I can't because Conor will drop on one knee after dinner, and thanks to catching a later flight, I'm not sure we'll make it before he asks Vivienne the question.

It was only when my stand-in date turned up, after I waited over an hour and a half at the airport, that she suggested we catch the next flight and I realized it was an option. By then, it was too late to go after Blair. I'd be risking not making the rehearsal dinner at all.

We're already set to miss most of it as we're running three hours behind.

Selfishly, I hope Colt tells Conor I'm running late, and he'll hold off until I get there because I don't want to miss the moment. Four of my brothers are already engaged or married. I haven't witnessed any of them pop the question. I doubt I'll get to see Colt propose, so this is my only chance to share this with one of my brothers.

***

The flight really did me good.

I organized my thoughts and decided that I won't let Blair go no matter what. Not without an explanation. Even if she says she doesn't love me and, by some chance, it's true, I want to understand what drove her away.

I hurry outside, spurred on by the ticking clock and a spike of adrenaline. We're so fucking late, and it's an hour's drive to Yountville Estate.

I load mine and Blair's luggage into the trunk first, then help my date with hers. Holding the door open for her, I shake the stiffness off my limbs, ignoring the guilt prickling my skin. I organized a replacement plus one without conside-ring why Blair left.

Now, it feels like I'm cheating on her.

Too little too late for a change of heart now, I guess.

With a bit of luck that seems to elude me today, I'll rent another room. If not I'll crash on the floor, or with Rose and her new boyfriend. A little supervision won't hurt her.

The drive to the venue is painfully quiet, my mind spinning, fixated on where Blair is right now, why her phone is switched off, and whether she's safe.

But the incessant whirlwind is forced aside by a race

against the clock when we arrive at the hotel. Once the receptionist checks us in—informing me that they're fully booked—we rush upstairs to change.

Throwing my suit jacket on, I remember the day Blair helped me pick my outfits for the wedding. Looking back, that was when I started falling in love with her. It took all I had not to grip her waist, pull her to me, and kiss her in that small changing room.

The yellow skater dress Blair wanted to wear tonight hangs from the closet door along with the deep blue one she chose for tomorrow. I took them out of her suitcase, so they won't crease, in case, by some miracle, she changes her mind and shows up.

Not even ten minutes after arriving, we're downstairs, and—thank God—we made it in time.

Conor's rising from his chair, and Mia's halfway across the room, heading toward a piano.

As we stop in the ballroom doorway, all eyes turn to us. My brothers' faces a mix of confusion, annoyance, and surprise... more or less what I expected if Blair was on my arm.

But it's not my girl.

It's Ana.

THIRTY-ONE

Blair

Sitting in the departure lounge, I watch Cody disappear toward a café. A tight ball of nerves forms in the pit of my stomach the moment he's out of sight but it's not nearly as overwhelming as I'd anticipated.

Maybe because I faced Nico and Mia. Or maybe because Cody keeps me grounded in the present, calming me with a kiss or a look whenever my hands start shaking.

They're doing it now, and while Cody's getting me a mochaccino, I let my mind flicker back to our past few days together, to the sense of freedom and happiness he evokes. It's in every shared glance, every lingering touch, every sweetly intimate kiss, and mind-bending orgasm.

And it's certainly there every time he murmurs, *I hate you* in that low, tender voice. Each time he says it, another hidden bruise inside me heals a little more.

It's new, this bliss. New, exciting, and addictive. *He* is addictive. The more time I spend with him, the happier I feel.

I pull my phone out of my purse at its quiet ringtone. Anxiety ripples through me as my father's name blinks on the screen. I've been trying to reach him since last week, but now he's calling, I'm tempted to let voicemail keep him from ruining my day.

Keeping it a secret from Cody, I started paving my way out over the past few days. I've not told Dad, but there's nothing he can say to change my mind, so I've been quietly selling my valuables—designer purses, shoes, jewelry—piece by piece, hoping to scrape together enough money for somewhere to live when my father evicts me from my condo.

And he will because this is it. I'm done playing his games. Done sabotaging my life. It's about time he found out.

"Hey," I say, pressing the phone against my ear, eyes scanning the crowd for Cody. "I've been trying to reach you all week. We need to talk."

"We'll talk tonight. I need you at the Country Club at eight o'clock sharp. I'll be heading there straight from the airport so make your own way."

Biting the inside of my cheek, I lift my chin higher, pumping as much conviction into my words as I can. "I'm not coming."

"What? What do you mean you're not coming? And why is it so loud there? Where are you?"

"I'm at the airport."

"Airport? Where the fuck are you going?" he snaps, his tone spiked with casual arrogance that makes my skin prickle.

"San Francisco," I breathe out, my fingers tight around the phone. "Logan Hayes' wedding."

Silence rings between us, stretching so long it prompts me to check he's still on the line. "Are—"

"You're fucking Cody, aren't you?"

I expected anger. Screaming. Insults... I didn't expect him to sound amused.

Taken aback, my palms turn clammy. "We're seeing each other," I confirm quietly, falling silent when his low, dark laughter pierces my ear. "What's so funny?"

"I always knew you were stupid, but you never struck me as naïve, Blair." He laughs again, the sound grating. "Do you really think he'll stick around? That you're more than a temporary hole to indulge in?"

"Cody's not like that. He cares about me, and I'm not—"

"He's not like what? Like any other man keen to fuck easy pussy? You're not Cinderella, Blair, and this isn't a fairy tale. Don't be childish."

"He cares about me," I utter, pinching the strap of my purse between my fingers. "He's taking me to the wedding so I can meet his brothers. How do you explain that?"

"The reason doesn't matter," he says with conviction. "It's the outcome that will crush you. Cody won't stick around. Family is sacred to the Hayes, and you tormented Nico's fiancée for years. You're a vile human being, and Cody will drop you once the novelty wears off. Probably sooner than you think."

I swallow hard, swatting my tears away. Dad's wrong. Cody wouldn't take me to the wedding if he wasn't serious about us.

"You don't know me," I say, my voice quivering at the edges.

"No one knows you like I do. I fucking *made* you. Face it, Blair. The moment Nico snaps is the moment you and Cody are done. You'll be flying back home in tears before midnight." A bang at his end startles me so much I jump. I think he slapped his mahogany desk. "Do you really think he'll choose you over his family? No one would choose you."

First tears roll down my cheek, and more follow, Dad's

words hitting my insecurities with laser precision. "I'm different now," I whisper. "I'm not a bad person. I've changed, Dad. I—"

"Changed?" he snorts, his voice dripping with disdain. "A leopard doesn't change its spots. You're still the same little girl, desperate for attention. Desperate to be seen, and you'll do everything to be seen. You're doing it right now, fucking around with a Hayes of all the men available in this town. I specifically asked you not to get involved with anyone. You had *one* job, and you couldn't even do that. You're problematic, Blair. You're a liability, and you're delusional if you think Cody won't see it."

Every word he speaks, laced with cruel certainty, claws my fragile defenses, shattering the cocoon of happiness that Cody's woven around me.

"He loves me," I stutter, covering my eyes with my hand. "He said so."

"Did he now? And since no one's allowed to lie about that, it must be true," Dad laughs, sarcasm dripping from his tone. "I love you, Blair."

A cold shiver slithers down my spine. "No, you don't."

"No, I don't," he agrees, cold and ruthless. "And yet I said it. Cody says he loves you and he can do whatever the fuck he pleases. You live across the hall! It's convenient. Wake up and smell the roses. Will you really throw away the future you spent your whole life working for? Be real, Blair. Look in the mirror. Admit that you're not worth the trouble you'll cause when you show up at Logan's wedding."

I hate him with everything in me. I hate his tone, the toxic, brutal symphony of accusations he spews, and I hate that he's right.

I don't deserve Cody. I never did, and I never will.

I scoff at my own stupidity. How did I let myself believe I

could make him happy? How is forcing him to risk his family supposed to achieve that?

He'd be crushed if he had to give them up. It's so obvious in the way his eyes light up when he talks about them, how great he is with his nephews, how much he loves Mia...

He won't give them up. Not for someone like me.

Cody deserves more. Someone who's not haunted by the past. He deserves everything, and I can barely offer *anything.* All I have is a truckload of baggage and a trail of bad decisions. The future I can promise isn't easy or colorful.

It's a heartache waiting to happen.

More tears ruin my makeup. It probably resembles a Halloween-worthy costume by now.

I've cried countless times in my life. What's once more?

I love Cody. And, because I love him, I can't let him risk losing his family over me. My mistakes can't mess up his life. Even if he wants me now, it won't last.

My father sighs long and heavy. "Okay, I'll make you a deal. You're less and less useful as the days go by, so here's what we'll do. You lock in Archibald Duke, and you're free to live your pathetic little life. The condo, car, money—all yours once Archibald signs the papers. One last deal, Blair. You won't have to see me ever again."

"Okay," I manage, barely keeping my voice steady.

At this point, I don't care about the condo or the money. I want to crawl into a ditch and stay there, but there's a tiny voice whispering at the back of my mind I can't ignore.

Falling apart is easy. Hold it together, even if only out of spite.

"Good choice," Dad spits out. "One day, you'll be sipping drinks on your yacht, looking back on this conversation, and you'll thank me. Meet me at the Country Club at eight."

THIRTY-TWO

Cody

The engagement ring glimmering on Vivienne's finger is easily the prettiest in the family. Good job he let us help instead of proposing with the monstrosity he bought or Vee would walk the streets wearing an oversized rock and risking being mugged.

With the rehearsal dinner done and the congratulations dying down, Colt pulls me outside for a smoke. Before we even leave the venue, all my other brothers follow suit.

"Jesus, Cody!" Conor snaps, his brows furrowed in frustration. "What were you thinking bringing Ana here?"

"This isn't how you convince her to leave you alone," Colt adds, shaking his head. "Why the hell is she here?"

Shawn steps forward, smacking the back of my head. "Use this sometimes, will you? She's watching you like a lovesick puppy. How the hell do you expect to get a restraining order when you invite her as your plus one?"

"I'm guessing their reaction now is why you haven't told

anyone who you're bringing," Theo says, his voice even, almost amused, as he rests against the wall with a smirk. "You all should shut up and let him speak. What if they worked things out, and she's the next Mrs. Hayes? You'll regret barking at him."

Nico snatches the pack of cigarettes from my hand, pulling one out, eyes drilling into me. "So, what's going on?"

I run a hand down my face, the weight of their judgment a bit much to take in my current state. "Ana's here as my friend."

"A *friend*?" Conor scoffs. "Do you hear yourself? Cody, what the fuck? She's been stalking you for weeks! She wouldn't take no for an answer. You magically forget about that?"

"Damn, she must be good in bed," Theo chirps.

"No, I didn't forget about the stalking, but she apologized and explained she was having a rough time."

Conor rolls his eyes. "You're such a fucking do-gooder, Cody. It's gonna come back and bite you in the ass."

I knew Ana was struggling, but she illuminated the details in her letter and when she came by on Monday.

"She was depressed and couldn't let me go because I was the only person who actually fucking listened to her," I continue. "She's better now she's on antidepressants, and I am not sleeping with her." I emphasize the last sentence.

I'm not sleeping with anyone considering my girlfriend dumped me five hours ago.

For a moment, I wonder whether to tell them about Blair. I'm dying to get this off my chest. I need them... I need them to help me through this.

"Alright, if that's really what it is and you trust her to behave, then fine," Shawn says, kicking himself off the wall as he inhales a drag of his cigarette. "She can stay."

"Excuse me?" My head snaps to him so fast I hear a crack. "What do you mean *she can stay*? That's not up to you."

"Technically, you're right, but you really think I'd let a stalker, possibly a crazy person, stay here with our family and kids all weekend? I'm a cop, Cody. I've seen enough shit to know that would be a bad idea."

I know he witnesses awful things every day, and he's sensitive when it comes to safety, but it riles me up how fucking inconsiderate he can be sometimes.

"Alright," Logan says, staring me down like he's trying to ask questions telepathically. A small shake of my head is all I can give him and, with a tight nod, he continues, "The DJ's staying until one in the morning, so let's move. I need a drink, and I promised Cassidy a dance."

I think that's Logan's subtle way of making sure this conversation is over so I don't start spilling my guts. Good call.

There'll be time for confessions on the flight back on Sunday. Only Nico won't be there to hear my rant, as they drove here to spare Mia the flight. She was on Xanax when they flew to Europe, and Nico was not pleased.

While he should be the first one to find out, maybe it's best if he's the last. Maybe my brothers can help me prepare.

They all head back inside, but I linger in the garden, grabbing another smoke while checking my phone for messages from Blair. I have half a mind to hurl it across the lawn when I find nothing. I tried calling her a few times and I've sent too many texts demanding an explanation, but now I've calmed down, I send a very different message.

One that will hopefully strike the right nerve.

Me: I'm not letting you go without a fight, baby.

Enjoying my time here is almost fucking impossible while I don't know what's happening with the girl I love.

All I need is one text, confirmation that she's safe. She's perfectly capable of taking care of herself but not knowing what pushed her away has me running around in circles.

"When you refused to tell us who you're bringing over, I thought you'd show up with Blair," Colt says, making me jump.

I was certain he followed the others inside...

Fuck, I'm not getting out of this now. Lying is a possibility as valid as playing dumb, but I'm ninety-nine percent sure Colt figured this out a while ago. He was just giving me a chance to come to him first. Which obviously didn't work.

I'm tired of evading his questions. We never kept secrets from each other, so instead of lying again, I pull the breakup napkin from my jacket pocket and tell God's honest truth as I pass it over.

"That was the plan."

What do you know? My voice fucking quivers. When did I become so weak? So *whipped.*

Crazy what love does to a man...

We're not over, though; I need to focus on that before I have a meltdown. I won't let her leave. Not unless she can honestly tell me she doesn't love me and never could.

"That's not what I expected," Colt huffs, squeezing the nape of his neck as his eyes rake the words, his thumb grazing the airport logo. "Why didn't you tell me?" He punches my shoulder hard enough to hurt. "I asked you so many times if you wanted to get something off your chest because I fucking knew."

"I thought way too many times about calling you," I sigh, staring into the sky. "What gave me away?"

He shrugs, raking his hand through his hair. "I don't know. Call it a triplet intuition." He laughs without humor. "Conor knows too. He came to me a few weeks ago, subtly fishing for intel. He thought you'd told me and not him."

"I didn't share because I didn't think there was anything worth sharing until last week. It's not as if I brief you about every woman I fuck. B and I... we agreed to—"

The door slides open, and Conor pops his head out. "What are you still doing here? Your date looks mighty uncomfortable, bro," he says, shooting me a meaningful glance. "What's going on?"

"We were right," Colt says, stretching out his hand to pass Conor the napkin. "You catch up, I'll go grab a few beers, and then you can tell us exactly what happened, Cody."

"Not now," I say. "We're here for Logan's wedding. We can't just vanish. I'll tell you everything when the party's over."

That reminds me... I should talk to Rose about crashing in their room. I bet she'll be thrilled about having her brother breathing down her neck and killing off any funny business.

"Yeah, you're right," Conor says, handing me back the napkin. "But just so you know? I'm pissed off you didn't tell us sooner." He doesn't sound pissed, though. He sounds worried.

"Keep it between us, okay? I don't want this to spoil the wedding."

They nod, and we enter the venue where Vivienne and her best friend, Abby—Colt's date—have adopted Ana into their circle. Dancing is the last thing on my mind, but, I invited Ana here so I shouldn't mope all night. She deserves a bit of fun after the rough few months she's had. With that in mind, I muster the energy to take her hand and lead her onto the dance floor.

***

It's well past midnight before everyone retreats to their rooms, the bride not concerned about catching her beauty sleep. Noah and Eli are staying with their babysitter in a separate room, so Cassidy won't have to keep getting up to feed Eli. I guess the eight hours of uninterrupted sleep she'll have tonight is longer than she's had since Noah was born.

I send Ana into our room and scratch the idea of crashing with Rose. Our room has a wide loveseat, so I'll sleep there. That's if I even make it upstairs before morning. The idea of hitting the bottle until I black out is tempting.

As if reading my mind, instead of beers, Colt joins me in the garden under a chiffon canopy covered with fresh flowers for the ceremony in the morning, armed with shot glasses and Patrón. "I thought you'd appreciate this."

Instead of the chairs flanking a long wide carpet that serves as an aisle, we settle on a raised wooden platform where the piano for Mia's performance will sit. They asked Mom to play throughout the ceremony, which meant focusing her attention on something other than Logan and Cassidy, so she framed Mia.

"Where's Conor?" I ask, watching Colt unscrew the bottle. My stomach cramps at the strong smell of tequila wafting in the air, sending me down memory lane to Brandon's house, and that first time I held Blair in my arms.

"Kissing his fiancée goodnight."

"Close," Conor says, stepping out of the darkness. "I was giving my fiancée a quick goodnight orgasm. She'll be out cold before I make it back, so we wouldn't have had our engagement night otherwise."

"That's not a thing," Colt laughs, offering Conor a shot

glass, then swiftly yanking it back as he reaches for it. "Did you wash your hands?"

"I didn't use hands, bro."

"Touché."

We knock back a shot, their expectant gazes on me.

"I'm in love with her," I admit, pulling out the big guns. "I don't know how or when exactly, but I am." I run a hand down my face, squeezing the shot glass just shy of hard enough to break it. "We agreed to casual sex, laid ground rules—"

"I guess keeping it a secret was one of them?" Conor asks.

"Yeah. She didn't say why she wanted to keep it a secret—"

"That was her rule?" Colt grabs the bottle, pouring another round. "I figured *you* kept it on the down-low because of Mia."

"That would've been my reason if I hadn't got to know Blair better. She told me her side of the story but never made excuses. She owned up to everything..." I crack my neck left and right, staring at the white flowers above.

"What did she say?" Conor urges quietly, raising his shot.

"It's not my story to tell. Blair needs a chance to clear the air with Mia before I tell you what I know. That's if I get her back."

"They already talked," Colt chimes in, and my spine goes rigid as a titanium rod. "She stopped by the day after the graduation party. You didn't know?"

"No, I didn't. Why didn't you tell me sooner? Did they—" I halt, remembering Mia was in Europe with Nico that weekend. "Mia wasn't home," I say quietly. "What did you tell Blair?"

"To try another day." He shrugs, throwing tequila down his throat.

Him and his fucking tension-building pauses. "And?" I urge, my jaw ticking. "Did she come back?"

"Yeah, a few days later. They talked. Nico was with them

the whole time. I don't know what they talked about, but Blair didn't leave in tears, and Mia just said she was okay."

Why didn't Blair mention this? Why didn't Mia?

Blair went to see her way before we accidentally ended up in bed yet never said a word. It's not like she didn't have the time or the opportunity. She could've mentioned it when she told me why she bullied Mia in the first place.

I whip my cigarettes out and light one up, the smoke filling my lungs a plausible tranquilizer.

"Alright, keep talking, bro. I want the whole story," Conor encourages with a hard slap on my back. "How did it start? How did you go from hating her to whipping your dick out."

I get comfortable, resting against one of the pillars holding the canopy over the platform. "I got to know her first. We weren't talking until she helped me with River one day, and then slowly, we built up on that. A sentence here, two there..." Colt takes my shot glass, filling it to the brim before handing it back. "One day, Ana came over," I continue. "While she was accusing me of cheating, Blair rounded the corner. I saw an opportunity to get rid of Ana, so I grabbed Blair, acted distraught that she caught us, and, putting on a show, I kissed her."

Memories flood back. That one kiss—hands down—the best moment of my life. The second my lips touched hers, I was doomed. Cupid, bow, arrow.

"And then?" Colt asks. "Stop daydreaming and talk."

"I don't know..." I sigh. "Something just fucking clicked. It was supposed to be a quick peck, but before I knew it, I slammed her against the wall. We were seconds away from fucking right there in the hallway."

"Jesus," Conor chuckles, running a hand through his hair. "Is this what I sounded like when I complained Vee didn't want to go out with me?" He thrusts another shot glass toward me, downing his own simultaneously with Colt. "Too many details, bro."

"That's *exactly* what you sounded like," Colt agrees, an effortless grin playing on his lips. "And you..." He points at me, "...spare us the details."

"Okay, fine. Fast forward a bit. We agreed to casual sex, and Blair insisted we revert to nothing more than polite *hey*s in passing. No kissing, no sweet talk, no talk at all. We were just supposed to use each other in bed."

"But that backfired, didn't it?"

"Big time. We were casual for a while, but before I knew it, what I didn't want to happen to her, happened to me. I caught feelings. I tricked her into kissing me, locked her in my condo, and didn't let her leave until she ate dinner with me..."

Conor rolls his eyes. Too bad he's not so prone to keeping his stories PG-rated whenever he talks about Vivienne.

"When did you decide to take it up a step?" Colt asks.

"Last week. Just before the bachelor party."

"I fucking knew it!" Conor booms, his voice carrying over the pristine lawn. "You were so fucking happy, and you barely looked at any girls all weekend. Damn, I'm good."

Colt, more composed, raises a questioning eyebrow. "And the wedding? Quite risky bringing her here, don't you think?"

"Yeah, I know, but to be perfectly honest, I was dying to see your faces when you saw us walk in together."

"Oh, thank fuck." He exhales a long breath, looking up to the star-studded sky, theatrically mouthing *thank you.* "I was freaking out you'd kept quiet because you're as stupid as Logan and thought we'd stop talking to you."

We all chuckle, remembering the name-calling that went

down when Logan proudly announced he was in love with Cassidy and would choose her and—unborn at the time—Noah, no matter what we thought.

"Maybe if that situation with Logan never happened, I would've been more worried," I admit, passing Colt my shot glass. "I remember what Nico said, so I know that nothing, least of all love, would make you turn on me."

"Say what you will, but I think we turned out better than they did," Conor muses, raising his shot glass higher as if making a toast. "We learned from their mistakes, didn't we?"

"We sure did." Colt's face softens. "Way to drive the point home, though. Big-headed as always," he quips, clinking his shot to ours. "So what happened today? Why isn't she here?"

The tequila burns going down, warming my chest. Too bad it doesn't dull the ache ripping my heart open all over again. "That's the thing. You've got as much information as I do. B was nervous all week but woke up excited this morning. I left her in the departure lounge for five fucking minutes while I went to buy coffee. She was gone when I came back, and some random guy gave me that napkin."

"Sounds like she got cold feet, bro. She'll probably apologize when you get back. You'll be fine."

I shake my head. "No, it's something else. It's not me. At least I don't think it's me."

"Time." Colt makes a T using his hands. "We need another bottle. Hold on a sec."

However many drinks he had before we started the Patrón are showing in his steps as he zig-zags toward the hotel. He's quick, though, back inside three minutes with two bottles.

"If we drink this, we'll end up sleeping right here," Conor says but still downs his shot with a grin. "Alright, so how does

Ana factor into all this? Last-minute decision? Is she the reason you had to take another flight?"

"Yeah, Blair bolted forty minutes before take-off." I fall back, lying flat on the wooden platform, staring at the flowers, chiffon, and stars. "I shouldn't have brought Ana here. I called her two minutes after I read Blair's note. I hadn't processed what it said, and on our way here, I realized this can't be it. There's something I'm not seeing."

We keep talking while the second bottle of tequila empties at a steady pace. By the time my wristwatch reads three in the morning the world blurs and sways as we stumble into the hotel lobby.

We're trashed.

I can't remember the last time I was this drunk, but I'm feeling a little better now that I got everything off my chest. Now that I *know* my brothers have my back no matter what happens. It's been a while since we had a good heart-to-heart. I fucking missed spending quality time with them. After all, that's what family is about. We stick together through the highs and the lows.

"Fuck, I sure hope we'll be up in time for the ceremony," Conor mumbles while an imaginary tornado in the lobby tosses him about. "I'm so drunk. Vee's not gonna be pleased."

"We'll be golden," Colt slurs, phone in hand.

He stops by the stairs, narrowing his eyes at the screen, his feet spread for balance, upper body swaying wildly.

"What are you doing?" I ask.

"Shut up. I can't see when you talk."

Conor chuckles, resting against the wall, his head down as if eyeing his shoes, but I think he's nodding off.

We're definitely not waking up on time.

I already feel like I'm rolling down a steep hill. The world tips sideways, something hits my ribs, then my head, and many hands grip my arms, hauling me up.

Ah, so I *did* roll down. Not a hill, though. The stairs.

That'll hurt tomorrow.

THIRTY-THREE

Blair

My eyes sting. Concealer and a heap of foundation barely cover the puffiness—the aftermath of a day spent crying. I stop in the doorway of the Country Club's private room, mentally preparing before I step into the elegant, luxuriously decorated space.

A warm golden light spills from the chandeliers overhead, casting a warm glow on the impeccably dressed crowd mingling around me. Polite conversation and the clinking of crystal glasses create a humming soundtrack, but I feel like a hollow shell, a puppet going through the motions. A prop in this performance. My father's done-up doll.

My dress is red as always. It's inappropriate, with its short, shimmery length leaving little to the imagination. And, as always, that's what my father wanted me to wear... another task, another demand in this charade.

Gideon Fitzpatrick is impossible to overlook. He towers over the throng, standing by the bar, exuding an air of authority that immediately draws attention. He's alone, leaning over the counter as he orders a drink.

His gaze scans over me, a satisfied smirk curving his lips as he takes in my attire. "Blair," he acknowledges, his voice dripping with smug satisfaction. "Good to see you're making the right choices. Did you tell Cody first, or did you flee like a coward?"

His snide remark could be a punch to the gut and I wouldn't tell the difference. He knows exactly which words hurt most. Before I retort, we're interrupted. Archibald Duke enters the scene, saving the day, in a way. I'm not sure if I was about to retaliate or break down into pathetic, ugly sobs, but neither would have been good.

Archibald's eyes shine as they sweep over me, a predatory grin taking real estate across his chiseled face. "Good evening, sweetheart," he greets, taking my hand to press a lingering kiss on the back. "You look very nice tonight."

In a well-practiced move, my father finds something in the crowd that requires his immediate attention.

"I'll be right back," he promises. "Five minutes, Archibald."

"Take your time. We'll order some drinks." He snaps his fingers at the bartender as my father retreats. "Whiskey and a glass of your finest white."

"Of course, sir."

Once the bartender turns around, Archibald seizes the moment, resting his grubby palm on my lower back, the gesture serving as a reminder of what he expects tonight.

"*Nice* doesn't do you justice," he says, leaning closer to my ear, warm breath kissing my neck. "You're beautiful, sweetheart. And this dress... a masterpiece."

Playing my role, I smile, thanking him quietly, my attention on the bartender, who takes all but a minute to slide two glasses across the counter.

And once again, Archibald seizes the moment, taking me outside. We sit on the same bench I sat on with Mr. Simons, and I just know tonight will go down the same way.

My mind veers to Cody of its own accord, and the messages I found when I switched on my phone earlier.

Cody: What the hell happened?

Cody: Why did you leave?

Cody: Fuck, B! If you're running because you're scared, I get it, but you could've fucking said you didn't want to come!

And then, an hour after those messages, another one arrived, the tone much different.

Cody: Just let me know you're okay.

The reality of what I willingly, knowingly gave up sinks into my bones. I didn't have time to think it through when I ran. Now, I wonder how I'll face him when he returns. How will I explain myself?

Archibald's touch on my cheek pulls me back into reality. His gaze is gentle, though still aroused, despite the deep eleven marking his wrinkled forehead. "Blair, is everything okay, sweetheart?" he murmurs, his voice a soft whisper. "You've been crying, haven't you?"

"Oh, no, it's just allergies," I lie, getting back in character with a deep breath. "I'm sorry for zoning out. It's been an exhausting week."

"You should relax," he coos, leaning into me.

I watch his long fingers brush the hem of my dress, teasing the fabric higher and higher. My heart pounds like a sledge-hammer, my body frozen, cold, motionless.

He's not wasting time, and I can't react. If I upset him, he'll storm out, my father won't close the deal, and I'll lose the chance to end this tonight.

My father is not a man of his word, but there was something in his voice when he said this would be the last *job* I'd have to complete... something I can't name, but that gave me hope. If I do well, this will all be over by tomorrow.

One last job. One last man touching me without permission.

"Are you always this brave?" Archibald asks, closing in, the whiskey on his breath fanning my cheek. "How many men have you allowed to do this?"

"I..." My mind is reeling.

I think he knows he's being played. I think he figured out what I've been doing all these years.

I'm surprised it lasted this long.

When I was younger, it was no surprise that men didn't brag to each other about feeling up an underage girl, but since I turned eighteen, I've expected my father's manipulations to come to light.

It's been over two years, though, and none of the men I've been made to flirt with since I became legal seem to realize it's just a game I'm forced to play.

Either that, or they're purposely ignoring the signs.

Some probably keep their mouths shut to avoid marital problems. Some might be afraid of sexual assault accusations—which my father would make if anyone dared undermine him—but I would've expected at least a few to warn their friends.

I think Archibald might be one who's been warned.

My palms are sleek with sweat, My heart hammers away, and blood sings in my ears when he pushes my dress higher, savoring the moment until I'm exposed. Nothing but sheer black lace stands between Archibald and an eyeful.

"I—"

"Shh, sweetheart," he coos. "This will be our secret. Your daddy wouldn't be pleased if he knew you were flashing those pretty panties to an old man." His fingers brush my thigh, making camp an inch before the black lacy fabric. His guttural groan has me shaking harder. "Like I said. Boys won't do you no good. You need a real man."

He drags his index finger higher, touching the elastic, then lower to curve between my legs. I shut my eyes, blocking reality, my teeth cracking from gritting them so hard.

Forcing my lungs to breathe, I imagine I'm not here.

No one's touching me without permission. No one's using me to make money. No one's threatening to destroy my dreams or my future.

I'm safe, locked in Cody's arms, his long fingers entangled in my hair. His other hand ghosts along my spine, soothing, calming. My head tucked under his chin as I inhale his scent, his soft whispers tickling my ear.

"I hate you, baby girl. I hate you so fucking much."

But I'm not with Cody.

He's thousands of miles away, and I'm here, my mind jumping from reality to what happened last time things went this far, three years ago.

A pathetic whimper slips past my lips. It's unmistakable, that sound. Distress, fear... but Archibald doesn't stop. He pretends he can't feel how much I'm shaking, how scared I am...

Or maybe that's what gets him off.

He pretends I'm enjoying this, that I'm encouraging him as his finger slowly heads for the prize.

"You need to be very quiet, sweetheart," he tuts, the warm stench of whiskey on his breath making my stomach churn.

I stay still, convincing myself that I can do this and survive... It's just this one last time. Just once, and it's over. I grit my teeth, rationalizing further, but then my phone vibrates in my clutch bag, and I know it's Cody demanding my attention.

It's as if he knows I need him right now.

His face flashes before my eyes, an avalanche of beautiful memories flooding my system.

I can't take this anymore. Not one more second of humiliation, degradation, and fear. No amount of money is worth this. It was when I hadn't known anything better.

It was worth it before Cody showed me what happiness and real, unconditional love feels like.

Before him, only my mother offered me her attention without expectation. Everyone else either wanted something in return or wanted me to act a certain way. My so-called friends stood beside me because they looked up to me, were scared of me, or could use me for money or popularity.

Everyone had an agenda.

Everyone but my mother and Cody.

"Stop punishing yourself. You've grown. You learned. You're a better person than you were back then. I know you weren't cruel for the sake of being cruel, baby. Why can't you see that? It was a defense mechanism against your own hurt. You think your feelings, past, and everything you endured doesn't carry any weight? That none of it left a mark? You're not a bad person. You're aware of the wrongs. You think you're inflicting

justifiable punishment on yourself, but you're taking it too far. Enough, baby. Time to take a step forward."

I deserve to be happy.

I'm not out of the woods, there's still so much that needs fixing, but I'm willing to stop punishing myself. Stop believing I'm not worth a chance.

I am. I can do better. I can earn his family's forgiveness and make Cody happy. I know I can.

My body immediately goes into combat mode, but I stop before pushing Archibald away with everything I have. If I make a scene, I won't have time to get away before my father follows.

I probably won't even reach my car.

A questionable plan forms within seconds. Instead of fighting Archibald off, I force myself to relax as I lean into his gentle touch.

X marks the spot.

He finds the prize, his finger drawing from the fabric-covered entrance up to my mound. My entire body stiffens. The thin fabric of my panties is all that separates his skin from mine.

He drags his finger down again as if looking for wetness that's not there. Spurring him on, I part my lips, letting out an almost inaudible gasp.

"Shh, sweetheart. We don't want to get caught, do we?"

"I can't," I murmur, doing my best not to sound like I'm about to hurl. "I can't keep quiet when you do this."

"This?" He rolls my clit under his finger, then pinches hard, earning a tiny artificial moan. "You're spectacular, sweetheart."

"Could we—" I pause purposefully, rolling my eyes back like I love what he's doing. "Could we please go somewhere else? Somewhere I won't have to be quiet?"

A low grunt tears from his chest. "I'm not sure your father would be happy if he saw us leave together."

Inching even closer, I line his ear with my lips. "He doesn't have to know. I can tell him I don't feel well, and meet you in the parking lot in fifteen..." Another fake needy gasp. "No, not that long... ten minutes. I have a car here, we can go back to my place. I live alone."

"Not your place. I have a spot in town." He pulls his hand away.

I almost cry in relief, but catch myself in time, making a soft, disappointed sound. It does the trick. The corner of his mouth lifts, his eyes darker than coal.

"It's okay, sweetheart," he coos, slopping a kiss on my temple. "Daddy's going to take care of you very soon."

My stomach twists, but I keep my composure intact as he hands me a black business card. There's nothing on it apart from an address. No name, no logo, just the address. Telling me Archibald takes a lot of women there.

"Judging by how he treated you last time you left before he allowed it, I think it's safer if I make an excuse on your behalf," he says, driving his hand down my thigh to stop on my knee. "Meet me there in an hour." He taps the card.

For the first time since I met the man, I feel a tiny bit of gratitude toward him. He just bought me time to pack my things. I'm sure my father will head for my doorstep the moment Archibald leaves this party.

That's what I want. I want him to come so I can tell him it's over. I won't follow his orders any longer but this extra time allows me to plan a little better.

"What color do you like?" I ask, building up on my lie, so he won't have any reason to doubt me. "I'll make sure I wear it."

"Oh, you're gonna be such a treat. I like white." He takes my hand, helping me up. "Go, sweetheart. I'll see you in an hour. Go around the building, don't go back inside."

I readjust my dress, trying not to break into a sprint as I walk away, looking back a few times before I disappear behind the corner.

It's a blessing that Dad couldn't pick me up today, because my car is here. Not even three minutes later, I'm on the road, my hands shaking, heart pumping blood faster.

I'm officially homeless.

It won't take long before my father comes after me. As soon as Archibald tells him that I left because I wasn't feeling well, he'll see through the ploy, and I'll be facing the wrath of all the gods. Not even an hour from now, I'll be homeless. Broke. Discarded.

But instead of feeling defeated, I feel oddly at peace. The only thing left is to get to my condo and pack as many things as I can before my father turns up and starts throwing everything away to intimidate me into cooperating.

I check the clock on the dashboard—almost one o'clock in the morning. My mind immediately goes to Cody, wondering what he's doing right now. The rehearsal dinner must be over. I imagine he's drinking with his brothers. I doubt he told them about us, but I'm sure he'll need a drink.

I don't let my mind linger there too long. There'll be time to think of apologies and how to best explain why I left once this nightmare is over.

By the time I push the key in the lock, I have a plan in place. Leaving my door wide open, I open Cody's apartment. He gave me a key so I could let myself in whenever I needed him.

I need him now.

Why is it that people only appreciate what they have when they lose it? Why couldn't I have seen how misguided my self-punishment was and how much I want to stop it while I was still with Cody at the airport?

Kicking my heels off, I pull out a suitcase, dropping it onto the bed, and empty the documents drawer first. They're what I'll need most. Then it's the money I've been collecting for the past few weeks in case my father cuts me off again.

There's not much there, not even ten grand, but it's enough for a deposit on a small apartment. The rest will keep me afloat while I search for a job.

Jewelry is next. I don't pack everything, just things I got from friends over the years, and a few things I bought without my father knowing. I add the few designer purses and shoes I haven't yet sold, so I can pawn them when I run low on cash. Then, I pack clothes. No red dresses. Just jeans, t-shirts, Cody's hoodies, and a few pairs of sneakers.

It takes less than ten minutes before I zip the suitcase and wheel it across into Cody's apartment. I leave it in the bedroom, along with my phone, then lock the door and peel up the carpet by Cody's door, stashing the key there.

And then I wait.

THIRTY-FOUR

Blair

I'm on my couch when my dad barges in, cheeks red with exasperation, chest heaving as if he ran here.

"Mind telling me what the fuck you were thinking, leaving again when I specifically told you that you're not allowed to leave until I say you can?" He slams the door behind him so hard the windows shake. "You should be fucking glad that Archibald promised to meet me on Monday after he told me he couldn't stay."

"I'm done," I say, without emotion.

"You're done?" he scoffs. "What do you mean you're *done*?"

I point at a suitcase by the couch. It's not the one I wheeled to Cody's condo. This one is full of things I won't miss if Dad won't let me take them—which I expect he won't.

"What is that? Some sort of power play?" he sneers, genuinely amused by my idea. "Stop living in a dream land and look around! You're on your own. You think you can threaten me?

I own you, Blair. You have nothing without me. No money, no home, no car. No college tuition."

"I don't want your money," I say calmly, his words hitting a void. "Take it all. I'd rather be homeless than—"

"You're damn right you'll be homeless!"

"That's okay." I set the car and condo keys on the coffee table, pushing them his way. "I packed a few things, mostly gifts from friends, but you're welcome to check I'm not taking anything you paid for."

He laughs. Loudly. Maniacally.

I'm so detached, so worn out, that it doesn't faze me. He can laugh and threaten me all he wants, but he won't change my mind.

Seeing no reaction no matter how loud he laughs, Dad stops. "You really think he loves you, don't you? How fucking dumb are you?" He looks me dead in the eye. "Wake up, Blair. Life is not a movie. You're throwing away years of work, and for what? A guy who's worth ten of you? Forget Cody! There's six million in your portfolio, Blair! Think about those dreams you'll make come true—"

"Some dreams are worth sacrificing for one that already came true," I say quietly. "I agreed to be treated like I'm worthless because I blamed myself. I thought I deserved nothing but pain for how I acted."

"You're right. That's all you deserve," he seethes, folding his arms across his chest. "So what? You suddenly forgave yourself? Don't play innocent, Blair. You did what I said every time because you fucking enjoy it. You love the attention. You love a challenge, and you love manipulating people."

"Do you really think I love being touched without consent? Being used? Having no say in what happens to me? There's a lot of reasons I allowed this so long, why I never reported you, but none of them are valid anymore."

"What will you report, Blair?" he barks, full of confidence that suddenly wavers as a shadow of fear clouds his face. "It's my word against yours. No one will believe you after I've told them I cut you off. That I took away your allowance. You're a spoilt little girl with a long list of sins. You have no credibility."

"I won't report you. I don't want the money, or the car, not even the house. The only thing I want is for you to leave me alone."

He rakes his hand through his hair, shaking his head. "I can't fucking believe you. You think you're in love? You're not. Love is an illusion. It *doesn't* exist!"

"It doesn't feel like an illusion," I say, peering up at him.

This conversation is pointless. There is nothing he can say that will convince me I'm making a mistake. There's also nothing I can say to show him what kind of monster he became once Mom got sick. Maybe he'll see it one day. Maybe he'll look back at his life and regret the things he's done while blinded by greed.

But that day isn't today because there's not an ounce of remorse on my father's face.

With a deep, calming breath, I muster the strength to get up, wheeling the suitcase behind me. "Goodbye, Dad."

He stands there, dumbfounded, watching me leave. I get as far as the elevator before he grips my arm, yanking me back.

"Where the hell will you go?"

I'll be back here as soon as he's gone so I can grab the other suitcase from Cody's apartment. "That's not your problem. *I* am no longer your problem."

He grinds his teeth. "Of course it's my fucking problem.

What do you think people will think when you end up homeless after Cody throws you out?" He shoves the keys into my hand. "It's your name on the deed and your name on the car registration. I can't throw you out even if I want to. Get back inside, calm down, sleep this dreamy attitude off and we'll talk on Monday."

I open my mouth, but he holds his hand up to silence me and marches away, heavy steps thudding down the stairs.

I gawk at the empty space where he stood a second ago, the whole situation surreal at best. If I had stood up for myself years ago, how different would my life be now?

Slowly, I turn around, wheeling the suitcase back into my condo before crossing the hallway to get the other one from Cody's bedroom. As soon as I step inside and his smell engulfs me, I break down, crying like I've never cried before.

Instead of bursting with relief because I still have a roof over my head, tears well in my eyes.

It doesn't feel like a win.

It feels like a blade through my heart because judging by Dad's reaction, by how quickly he folded, he only used me because *I* allowed it...

I did this to myself.

THIRTY-FIVE

Cody

"Morning." Mia's normally sweet, melodic voice slices through my aching head like a chainsaw. "Did he sleep here all night?"

I cautiously peek under heavy eyelids, squinting against the blinding sunlight streaming through the window. Did someone take a baseball bat to my skull last night?

The room spins wildly, and I clamp my eyes shut, inhaling a steady breath.

"Yes," Ana says in a low, soft tone. "He came back around three this morning, grabbed this..." She tugs something I'm resting my cheek against, "...and fell asleep before I had a chance to cover him with a blanket."

"Fuck," I hiss, my throat dry, tongue like sandpaper. I try to speak, but can only manage a raspy whisper. "Bug... lower, please." I peek again, finding Mia leaning over me, her face blurry and distorted.

"I've got the hangover remedy for you."

"No, Bug..." My head pounds so hard I can barely think straight. This is the worst hangover ever... I should've retched into the bushes like I did at the graduation party. "*Lower.*"

"I think he means your voice," Ana chuckles, quickly slapping a hand over her mouth. "Sorry."

I snap myself upright as if I'm ripping a band-aid. "Oh, fuck. Bad idea. Very, very bad idea," I mutter, steadying myself as the room spins. God, it feels like I've been hit by a fucking truck. "The wedding... did I miss it?"

"It's barely seven in the morning, plenty of time," Mia whispers. "Here, drink this." She hands me a glass and two pills. "Electrolytes and painkillers."

I swallow them down without a question, cool water soothing my parched throat.

"How did you know he's not well?" Ana asks, watching me empty the glass in one.

"Colt texted me last night." She air-quotes for impact. "3C drunk. SOS am." She swaps my empty glass for a full one.

"Have I told you how much I love you?" I rasp, then almost double over and hurl when the smell of her sister's signature hangover remedy hits. My stomach twists like a washing machine on full spin. This is fucking brutal. "I hate this," I tell them, but pinch my nose, chugging until there's nothing left.

This isn't my first rodeo. Mia's nursed me back to health more times than I care to admit, and this magical, disgusting, ginger, lemon, and something-or-other drink is a godsend. Combined with electrolytes, a hot shower, and a big healthy breakfast, I'll be back on my feet, fresh as a daisy in no time.

"You always love me when you're hungover." Mia beams, setting both empty glasses aside. There are four more waiting on a small tray. One pair for Conor, one pair for Colt. "I better go save the other two. Meet me downstairs in twenty minutes." She grabs the tray, backing away, but pauses by the door. "You might want to prepare for questions from your older brothers. They're annoyed the three of you got drunk last night without them."

With a deep groan, I fall back expecting the loveseat to cushion me. It doesn't because I'm not on the loveseat, and now my head really feels like it split open.

Sitting back up, I look around, realizing I'm on the floor, crammed between the foot of the bed and the loveseat. It turns out I used Blair's yellow dress as a pillow, crumpled up and reeking of alcohol and cigarette smoke. My heart sinks, unpleasant memories filtering through my foggy brain.

Pushing them away, I focus on what I *can* fix.

"I'm sorry," I tell Ana, feeling genuinely bad.

Not only have I invited her here as my last resort, but I also neglected her the entire evening, then woke her up in the middle of the night, barging in almost black-out drunk.

It doesn't look like I'll be in any better shape throughout the wedding, so *sorry is* the very least she deserves.

Dressed in her cozy flannel pj's, her pretty face eyes me with a concerned look. "I know you probably don't believe me after everything, but I really am over you, Cody. I didn't come here expecting anything could happen. I came because you sounded really broken. You're a great guy, you know? I hope one day we can be real friends. I guess..." She inhales deeply, her eyes full of sincerity. "What I'm saying is that if you need to talk, I'm here. I'll listen."

"We won't *be* real friends, Ana. We already are. You know why I called you of all people?" The pounding in my head slowly lessens, the pain not as invasive now.

She chews her lip before replying, "Because I'm the only person who'd drop everything and come over?"

I laugh at that. She's a great girl, fun and caring. Just a little lost. The fact we saw each other naked, that we had a sexual relationship for a few weeks doesn't matter. It was fun, but from my side, there were no feelings involved. Us shifting into the friend category isn't all that hard. I don't think Ana had real feelings for me, either. She just needed a friend.

Maybe I would've had a harder time admitting I want to stay in touch with Ana if Blair showed any signs of jealousy.

She didn't. She sat beside me when Ana explained why she acted like a lunatic. The only emotion I picked up from Blair that day was sympathy. She probably could relate given her past, the mistakes, blame, and regret.

"I called you because you may have done some crazy things, but you had the guts to apologize. We all lose our way sometimes, Ana. It takes a great deal of courage and character to admit it." The headache ebbs away further as I carefully gather myself up to sit beside her. "I'll tell you the same thing I told Blair." Draping my arm across her shoulders, I pull her into me. "Forget what you did but remember what you learned."

She nuzzles her cheek into my shoulder, her words thick with emotion. "Can I give you a piece of advice, too?"

"Sure. Go for it."

"If Blair comes to talk, don't send her away. Listen, okay? She must've had a reason to leave you at that airport, Cody. If she comes to explain, don't dismiss her, because you'll regret it for the rest of your life."

I can sense the pain as she speaks, and I intuitively pull her in closer. She's speaking from experience, the regret of not listening to her brother when he needed her most still evident.

"She won't come," I say on a heavy sigh. "I'll find her first."

"Good for you." Scrunching her nose, she moves away from me. "You need to take a shower. Seriously, you stink."

"Yeah. You know it's bad when you can smell yourself," I chuckle, dragging my jelly feet into the en suite bathroom.

***

Showered and dressed for the morning mayhem, I join my family in the restaurant downstairs with Ana. The scent of bacon wafts in the air, making my stomach grumble. Everyone, except the bride and groom, are there, enjoying breakfast and coffee.

Coffee.

The aroma hits me as I sit by the table most of my brothers are occupying and reach across to snag Mia's cup.

She's faster, snatching the tall cup away with a stern look before my fingers come anywhere near it. "Breakfast first," she chides.

"So bossy this morning, baby," Nico smirks, planting a kiss on her head before lasering in on me. "Why weren't the four of us invited to drink with you last night?"

Theo and Shawn are at the other end of the room, chatting with our parents. So, I lean forward, lowering my voice. "I didn't want anything to disrupt the wedding, but I can't keep shit from Colt or Conor no matter what it is. I'll tell you everything tomorrow, okay?"

Nico narrows his dark eyes. I can tell he's plotting how to get the story out of me sooner. Thankfully, with the wedding starting in three hours, and the groomsmen tasks we both have to complete before, he has no fucking chance.

With a tight nod, he leans back, wrapping his arm around Mia's shoulder and pulling her in for a kiss, as if it's the only thing that can calm him down right now.

Which, honestly, it probably is.

"I want the recipe for that ginger thingy," Vivienne tells Mia. "It's disgusting, but it sure works. Conor was ready to party half an hour after you left."

"Disgusting?" Colt protests. "It's delicious."

The waiter brings my breakfast, and I abruptly turn to ask him for a cup of coffee as he struts away. Pain shooting down my side reminds me what I saw in the en suite mirror. "Anyone know why my ribs and back are bruised?" I ask.

"You fell down the stairs," Conor answers, stuffing his face with a big bite of avocado toast.

"Yeah..." I bob my head up and down like a bobblehead on a dashboard at a rally race. "I don't remember that."

Shortly after breakfast the photographer arrives, his camera equipment strapped to his back like a backpacker's survival kit, and I head upstairs to change into my tux, before joining the wedding party downstairs.

Beneath the same canopy of live flowers we got shitfaced under last night, the photographer starts clicking away, directing us into different poses. Whenever the camera isn't pointing at me, my eyes follow the bride and groom. They've been together over two years, but still look as in love as the first time Logan introduced us to her.

The photo session takes an hour, and once we're dismissed, I go inside to grab a glass of water. The temperature outside is scorching, and the staff are setting up big fans that will hopefully cool the guests down during the ceremony.

Ana sits at the restaurant bar in her summer dress, looking

a little pale. She's not in the wedding party, so she didn't pose for the pictures, hiding away in the airconditioned building. Lucky her. I feel like I've sweated my balls off out there and a change of tux would be good.

I pull my phone out like I've done every chance I get since I woke up, but no messages from Blair wait on the screen.

With a peculiar, indecipherable look, Ana touches my arm as soon as I stop by the bar. "Could you do me a favor?"

"Sure, what is it?"

"I'm a little lightheaded. Could you grab my purse from our room? My pills are in it."

The bartender stops beside us, so I order two glasses of water, simultaneously pressing my hand to Ana's forehead.

"I'm not burning up," she says with a smile. "It's a side effect of my antidepressants."

"Okay, I'll grab your purse. Drink your water, and..." The bartender hands over two glasses and I say, "Keep an eye on her for me, alright? She's not feeling well."

"Sure thing, sir."

I climb the stairs, phone in hand, as I send yet another text to Blair while I have a moment. I've already sent her a dozen similar messages since I woke up, but one more won't hurt.

Me: I hate you, baby girl.

I ignore the breakup napkin stashed in my inside pocket as I fish out the key card, pushing the door open as soon as the lock clicks. It closes softly behind me and I stop.

Moving, breathing, fucking thinking.

Sounds familiar? Good, because the girl standing in the middle of the room looks familiar, too.

Her skin has a ghastly ashen tint, dark shadows under her beautiful eyes rimmed pink from crying. Her hair is a mess, tangling down around her face, and her shoulders are hunched forward as if she's shielding herself from harm. She looks up at me, pinching the fabric of the hoodie she's wearing.

My hoodie.

My heart somersaults back in time with my stomach, and a wave of relief knocks out my breath. Jesus... she's *here.* Tears well in her eyes. Some spill while I stand frozen in place. Her usually bright, lively aura seems dimmed, replaced by an air of sadness and defeat.

How did she get here?

When?

Who let her in here?

Ana. It had to be.

The silence between us is suffocating, the tension palpable.

"I hate you more," she half whispers, half wails. "So much more, Cody. I'm sorry."

That's when I start moving. The key card slips from my grasp. I'm three steps away, already charging at her, the emotional turmoil I've been wrestling since she left me at the airport evaporates in an instant.

She's here. She came back.

Whatever pushed her away didn't win the battle.

I crash into her, gripping her by the waist and hauling her into my arms. Our lips meet in a frenzy, hers salty from tears, mine urgent, determined, demanding. The mere sensation of her this close again is enough to make me feel I might burst at any moment. She parts her lips, opening up to me and I delve deeper as her fingers lace through my hair, tugging me closer.

"I'm so sorry," she whispers every time we come up for

air, her voice shaking. "I hate you so much."

"Shh, it's okay, B. It's okay. You're here now. Just... give me a minute." With that, I take her mouth again with the same desperation that's consumed me for the last twenty hours.

"What happened? How did you get here?" I ask, scanning her face for clues, as I set her on the bed.

"It's a long story," she murmurs softly, cradling my face in her hands as I shift her higher onto the bed, my knees sinking into the mattress. "We don't have time for that right now. I promise to tell you everything tomorrow, or even tonight if you're not too exhausted after the wedding."

I kiss her again, savoring the taste of her lips as my hands explore her body. My fingers skim her legs, caress her waist, cup her breasts, and trail down to her hips. I'm fucking drunk on having her back in my arms. Every inch of her missed me as much as I missed every inch of her. It's clear in how she reacts, arching into my touch.

"Cody, we're wrinkling your tux," she mutters, gently pushing me away. "We'll talk later, okay?"

Talking isn't exactly what I have in mind, but she's right, we don't have time.

"Tell me you love me," I whisper, closing my teeth on her bottom lip and pulling until a soft moan escapes her.

"I hate you."

I shake my head, looking down into her deep blue eyes. "No, baby. Tell me you love me. Tell me you'll never leave me. Convince me I'm all you want, and maybe... *maybe* I'll agree to wait for your story."

More tears brim in her eyes, threatening to spill, but she swats them away, then gently cradles my face. "I gave up everything for a chance to get you back. You showed me I'm worth more than I thought possible. You showed me I deserve love and happiness. For those things alone, I will always love you, Cody." She lifts her head, catching my lips with hers, the kiss slow, soothing, delicate. "But there is so much more there. Things I can't name, and probably won't ever be able to."

She pauses, wiping her eyes again before inhaling a deep, sharp breath, and when she speaks again, her soft voice is full of conviction. "I love you. I hate you. I feel everything for you. I feel alive, happy. I'm yours as long as you want me. I won't leave."

It's that one line, *'I feel everything for you,'* that shatters all the doubts I've had since I read that damn napkin.

I love that line because it's real.

It's not a fairy tale, not a happy-for-now situation. No, this is more. It's *everything.* She's mine, she'll be mine through the good and the bad because life isn't just the good moments.

Relationships aren't just the good moments.

There are ups, downs, twists, turns, and so many different emotions that make a relationship worth fighting for. So that one line injects a new sense of hope into my veins.

"I love you more," I tell her before crashing my lips to hers again, the kiss dominating and soothing the way she loves most.

She gave me a sneak peek into her past with her schizophrenic mother, and I did a bit of research into the illness, but I'm pretty fucking sure she'll knock me off my damn feet with whatever else she's hiding.

It doesn't take a genius to realize she went through hell to come back. She looks like fucking hell right now, but as much as I want to hear every single detail, we have a wedding to attend.

No matter what she says, what other demons from her past she's hiding, she's mine. Always mine. I can wait for an explanation a little longer and be there for my brother.

Pulling her up with me, I comb her hair over her ears. "You need to get dressed, baby girl. The ceremony starts in less than two hours. We don't have much time."

She immediately shakes her head. "It would've been okay to show up with me yesterday during the rehearsal dinner, considering Logan had no issue with Conor borrowing the spotlight to propose, but today is all about them. We both know that me walking in on your arm will cause a rift, Cody."

Brushing her thumbs under my eyes, she stamps a sweet, affectionate kiss on my forehead. "I haven't slept since we woke up together yesterday. I got in the car at three in the morning and drove here because I couldn't wait to apologize. Now you know, now that you're willing to wait for a proper explanation... I'm exhausted. I wouldn't last ten minutes outside."

She drops her hands to grip the lapels, pulling me closer. "You have Ana—"

"Baby, the only reason Ana is here—"

"It's okay," she interrupts quickly, her fingers playing with the buttons on my shirt. "I'm not jealous. Who do you think helped me sneak in here unnoticed?" She cups my face again. "Enjoy the wedding. Have fun, okay? I'll take a nap. We can talk when you're done downstairs or maybe tomorrow."

"I don't want you locked in here all day. You don't know my family that well, but believe me, they'd understand if I brought you to the ceremony. Logan and Cass would never consider it as me trying to steal the spotlight."

She smiles gently, her hand resting on my chest. "I'm sure you're right. I've heard so many stories about your family that I believe you when you say they're supportive, caring, and loving. But it's time to return the favor, Cody."

Here I was thinking I couldn't love this girl any more, and she says this and proves me wrong. Who would have thought Blair Fitzpatrick could be so considerate?

I had this girl figured out all wrong.

When she inches away, falling back on the pillow, I move with her. I want to hold her, kiss her, rip her clothes off and drive myself home inside her to remind her who she belongs to, but she needs rest, and I need to be downstairs.

"Go down there and enjoy it," Blair says softly, her hand running through my hair. "I'm not going anywhere. I promise we'll talk. I promise I'll be here when you're too tired to dance, and I promise I'm not jealous of Ana. If anything, I owe her."

We both do.

Pulling the sheets aside, I tap the mattress, urging Blair to get under the covers. "I'll wait until you fall asleep." I curl her into me, her back to my chest, my lips on her head.

It doesn't take long. While I battle inside my head, wondering which question I should ask first, she falls asleep before I can voice any. Tucking her in, I kiss her head, and leave the room, hoping I can clear my mind enough to enjoy my brother's wedding.

THIRTY-SIX

Cody

"Is Ana feeling okay?" Nico asks once the best man, Theo, is delivering his speech filled with jokes and gags.

"She's fine. Why?"

"She's been disappearing upstairs every half hour since the reception started. I thought she might not be well. A stomach bug or something."

She's been checking on Blair for me so I can get send her something to eat when she wakes up. It's almost five in the afternoon, and she's still asleep.

Colt's the family's resident Poirot, but he's too preoccupied with Abby's babbling to pay attention to anything else. Nico, on the other hand, has way too much time, considering his fiancée is spending most of the evening at the piano as per Logan and Cassidy's request.

"She's fine," I say, hoping I sound convincing. "Powdering her nose. She feels a bit out of place here."

Too bad it's not Theo asking. It's easier to lead him astray than Nico. He's way too fucking perceptive, and I'm pretty shit at coming up with lies on the spot, so that doesn't help the situation as Nico drags his gaze to Ana chatting with our grandmother. She's all smiles as she sips her wine.

Yeah... she hardly looks out of place.

His burning gaze moves to me, one eyebrow raised like he's calling my bluff. "Out with it, Cody."

I heave an exasperated breath, knowing damn well I've already lost the fight before it began. Nico won't stop. He's a bloodhound when it comes to family matters. He'll push for details until I tell him exactly what's happening.

"The reason Colt, Conor, and I had a drink last night without you four was that my girlfriend dumped me... and this morning she turned up to apologize."

Nico leans in with a look of genuine concern as he rests one arm on the table, turning his body my way. "What happened, man? You didn't tell us you had a girl."

"I had a few good reasons not to. The main one is that the girl I won't leave, no matter what you all say is—" I pause, quietly chuckling under my breath. "I'm starting to sound like Logan, aren't I? He had a point, though. I love you all, but I'm not letting Blair go."

The muscles in Nico's shoulders tense on cue and his jaw clamps tight. I can almost hear his brain working overtime. It takes a long, tense minute of him processing, rationalizing, or using whatever information he already has to answer his own questions before he looks at me again.

"Blair Fitzpatrick," he states for the record, then falls silent again, probably recalling everything Mia told him about the abuse she suffered at my girlfriend's hand.

"There's more to this story than you know, Nico, I—"

He raises his hand, shutting me up with that and a pointed, furious glare, then takes another long moment to think.

I like that about him. He usually thinks before he speaks.

Although right now, I'd rather have him lash out. The tension's growing so fucking taut I'm uncomfortable in my own skin.

"Nico—"

"Shut. Up," he grinds out, clenching his fists on the table.

So I do. I wait, the clock inside my head ticking as if counting down my last seconds on earth.

"I was nine when you were born," Nico finally says, his tone level, though far from light. "I remember when you took your first steps, when you said your first word... I watched you grow up, Cody. You lived under my roof after you graduated high school. I saw you with countless girls and friends... I saw the kind of people you let close and I know the kind of person you are." He inhales deeply, raking a hand through his hair before he looks me in the eye. "You wouldn't be with a girl who was vile just for the sake of being fucking vile. Give me some credit. The fact you love her tells me—"

"I never said I love her. I just said I won't leave her."

A truly amused chuckle rips from his chest. Still a rare sound even now that Mia lightened his life. "That's the same thing. You're forgetting I watched Shawn, Theo, and Logan fall in love before it was my turn." He drops his heavy hand on my shoulder, squeezing tightly. "You're in love. Don't fucking deny it. Out of all of us, you have the biggest heart, Cody. If *you* love this girl, you don't have to prove to me that she's worth it. I know it. And Mia will too, so instead of hiding Blair upstairs, bring her down here to meet the family."

I didn't realize how scared I really was of his reaction until now. He's once again proved there's nothing in this world that can tear our family apart. I pinch my lips, swallowing the wave of intense emotions burning my throat.

"Thanks, Nico. I meant it. I love her, but it means a lot that you're not throwing punches right now."

The corner of his lips twitches. "You thought I'd hit you?"

"At the very least. I knew you'd support me after you'd calmed down, but I thought the calming down would take longer."

"It would probably be different if Blair hadn't apologized to Mia a few weeks ago."

"I didn't know about that until last night. We weren't a thing when she did that, so don't think it was because of me." I lift my glass, draining half the whiskey. "I wasn't ashamed to bring her out yesterday like I planned, but tonight's about Logan and Cassidy. B can meet everyone tomorrow."

"Well, at least you're smarter than Logan," he says with a smirk. "I'm still annoyed he thought we'd abandon him."

I laugh at that. "So am I. Conor said last night that the three of us turned out better than the four of you. We learned from your mistakes."

"That's how it's supposed to be. It rarely happens, so I'm glad you paid attention." He pats my back, exhaling a deep breath when Mia approaches, the adorable sweet and stern act she's got going on aimed directly at her man.

"It's been half an hour since you promised to dance with me," she says, holding her hand out to Nico.

He grabs it, kissing her knuckles, then passes her hand to me. "We have the whole night, baby. Now grab Cody and distract him. He's been on edge all day."

Dancing is the last thing on my mind, but Mia's cute smile

convinces me otherwise. I take her delicate hand, leading her into the middle of the couple-filled dance floor.

I wrap my hands around her, pulling her close as I dip my head to speak in her ear so nobody can eavesdrop on our conversation. "I love you, Bug."

She laughs softly, gliding along the dance floor with me to the sound of "Swim" by Chase Atlantic.

"I love you too. And I know, Cody."

"I do say it a lot," I agree.

"No, I mean I know you're in love with Blair," she explains with a cheeky smile. "I saw it coming from a mile away. Every interaction you ever had, even when you were rude, there was tension between you. It was a long time coming." She twirls away, flashing me another smile before she comes back, wrapping herself around my arm. "Once she moved across the hall from you, it was just a matter of time."

My hands tighten around her as I pull her in closer. "I never meant for it to happen. I'd never intentionally hurt you, Bug."

"I know. I love Conor and Colt, but *you* are the best friend I ever had. Which is why..." She twirls around my finger with a beaming grin before she leans in. "I'm happy you found what I have. Don't let it go."

"I won't. I don't know what Blair told you, but I'm sure it wasn't much. She's so careful not to sound like she's making excuses, but it would mean a lot if you could give her a chance to explain. There are some things in her past that might give you a little bit of perspective."

Mia smiles, stepping three steps away from me, our hands outstretched, fingers locked together. "Remember how worried you were when Nico told you he was going after me no matter what you said and how we turned out just fine?"

I nod, pulling her back and dropping a kiss on the top of her head. "That's different, Mia. Nico never hurt you."

"No, he didn't. However, you knew what kind of man he was but still allowed him the benefit of the doubt. That's what I'll do for Blair."

How this girl fits her big heart into that tiny body will forever remain a mystery. We glide across the dance floor until we bump into Theo and Vee, and switch.

Then I switch again, and again, until not many women in the room are left that I haven't danced with. Cassidy is in high demand, so it takes almost an hour, two cigarettes and one drink before I steal a dance.

"You look beautiful," I tell her, holding her close.

Not close enough to risk Logan knocking my teeth out. I wouldn't put it past him. His irrational temper tantrums rival Nico's. While he trusts me, he's absolutely obsessed with his wife, so a safe distance is a necessity.

Cass beams at me, the white dress hugging her curves in all the right places as it falls to the floor, trailing two feet behind her, making it impossible to effortlessly glide around.

"Do you think I'm snobbish, Cody?"

My eyebrows meet in the middle. "Far from it. Why? Did someone say something?" I quickly scan the crowd, gauging who'd have the audacity. "Who?"

"No one said anything. Do you think I love you?"

"Well, you better," I laugh, playfully pushing her away before pulling her back in. "Yes, I think you love me..." I glance around, searching for Logan, "...in a very appropriate way," I add, louder. "You think I love you?"

"Yes, but that's not my point. Do you think I'm a bridezilla?"

"Hell no, you're a very mellow bride. Where are all these

questions coming from?"

"So you don't think I'm a snob, you know I love you, and you don't consider me a bridezilla," she lists, as she spins away and back in. "Then explain one thing. Why the hell do you think you'll steal my spotlight if you bring the girl you love downstairs?"

My step falters and then I all-out stop dancing in the middle of the dance floor, holding the bride in my arms. "Who told you?"

A satisfied smirk quirks her lips. "Logan."

"And how the fuck—"

The words fall off my tongue when I look over and spot Logan's shit-eating grin that morphs into two eyebrows punched in the middle as soon as he catches my evil stare.

"Colt, Conor, Nico, Mia... they all know. Did you really think you could keep it a secret for the whole weekend? I mean, yes, it's my wedding, and—" She pauses, rolling her eyes. "*Fine.* Mine and Logan's wedding. The spotlight should be on us today because *this is the best day of our lives...*! Or so everyone tells you." She twirls away, her dress swishing in the air. "You know what the best day of my life was?"

I could guess at a few, but Cassidy doesn't let me get a word out.

"The day I slapped Logan's stupid face in *Q*."

I don't know the story, but I sure want to. It's always fun when my brothers get slapped around by their girls. It brings me so much joy. And it's fun to give them shit for it, too.

"That's when I found my worth," Cassidy continues. "I realized Logan treated me badly because *I* treated myself badly. That day our relationship took a turn. I realized my worth, and so did he." She twirls away again, beaming. "I always wanted an amazing wedding, but seriously, you really think anything can overshadow me in *this* dress? Do me a favor. Turn around and ask your girlfriend to dance."

She pecks my cheek, then spins me around. My chest tightens and my heart contracts until it hurts. But it's a satisfying pain.

I wish I could say it's because Blair looks spellbinding in her navy dress, but it's not that. It's the fact my brothers went behind my back and brought her downstairs without me knowing. It's because Ana, Rose, and *Mia* stand beside her without an ounce of tension in the room.

How did I get so lucky?

"Thank you," I tell Cass.

"Oh, stop it," she whispers, holding back the tears welling in her eyes. "Don't mind me. I've been like this since I got pregnant with Noah. Too emotional." She pushes me forward a step. "Go before you ruin my makeup and Logan ruins your face."

As I start walking, crossing the room toward Blair, the girls make themselves scarce.

"They wouldn't take no for an answer," Blair mutters, her cheeks pink. "Even Logan came upstairs."

"I told you they wouldn't mind." I dip my head, pecking her lips. "You must be starving. Come on, you should eat something and then we'll dance."

She bites her cheek, looking up at me. "I can't dance."

"What do you mean you can't dance? What about all those banquets and balls you went to?"

"I wasn't there to dance," she says, something dark marring her features before she blinks it away, shooting me a coy smile. "Can you teach me?"

She's deflecting, pivoting my attention from the sadness in her eyes. While all I want is to drag her back upstairs to talk, I think we could both use a few hours of not thinking about the hard things.

"I'll teach you." After I stamp a kiss on her head, we knot our fingers together, and I take her to our table, where somebody's added another chair between me and Ana.

I have the best family in the world.

THIRTY-SEVEN

Cody

It's almost five in the morning before I make my way upstairs after spending two hours answering my brothers' questions about Blair. Their drilling skills would be an asset in the forces, for sure. Some of the questions they came up with tripped me over big time.

Together with Ana, B disappeared as soon as the band stopped playing.

As much as I wanted to follow, I had to relay the story to the older four like I had to Colt and Conor the night before. At least this time, I wasn't on the verge of a mental breakdown and it was easier to talk, knowing she was asleep two floors up.

Colt was considerate enough to invite Abby into his room for the night so Ana could sleep in a bed rather than on the loveseat in our room.

I gently push the door open, careful not to wake B, but I step inside to find her sitting on the bed smiling at me, the night lamp bathing the room in a soft, orange glow.

"Why aren't you sleeping?" I ask, pulling my tie off. "You didn't have to wait."

"I thought you'd want to talk, so I stayed up, organizing my head. Are you sober enough to listen?"

Stripping down to my boxers, I climb into bed, resting against the headboard, my heart picking up speed. "I barely had a drink all night, B." I had more than my share last night and didn't feel like waking up with another hangover. "I'm sober."

She makes herself comfortable, sitting cross-legged as she pinches the comforter between her fingers. "Just please... don't get all worked up, okay?"

"When has a line like that ever calmed someone down, baby?"

She nods solemnly, inhaling deeply as if bracing for something nasty. "That man..." she starts, looking up from picking her nails. "The one who was there when I smashed the glasses, the one I wore the red dresses for, the one who screamed at me... he's my father."

"Your father? But he's... he looks really young."

"He's very proud of that fact," she admits. "He's forty-two, but that doesn't really matter. He's a very greedy man. Money is all he cares about, and—" She pauses, taking yet another deep breath and when she starts talking, my skin fucking crawls.

She tells me about the work she's been doing for years, about the men she had to flirt with, about those who touched her, and I'm reeling. With every word, my blood boils further. She tells me about every threat her father used to keep her in line, every time she watched her mother hallucinate because the fucker confiscated her meds, every time she surrendered to his orders.

She's not crying, but her voice breaks like eggshells when

she gets to yesterday.

"You know what the worst part is?" she asks quietly, still sitting in the middle of the bed.

I've tried to pull her into my arms countless times, but she keeps saying she won't get the words out if I touch her.

"Everything about this is the fucking *worst*, B. Jesus..." I get up, too jittery to stay still. "You should've told someone, baby. You should've told *me* when I asked, I—"

"I did this to myself," she whispers, avoiding my gaze. "He called when I was waiting for you in the departure lounge. The things he said... he fleshed out my every insecurity."

She relays their conversation word for word, then proceeds to tell me about the banquet and Archibald fucking Duke pushing his fingers up her dress.

"He's a dead man walking, B," I seethe, shaking all over. "Him and your sorry excuse for a father." Ignoring her protests, I climb onto the bed, and pull her in, cradling the back of her head, caging her in my arms. "You're safe with me. I promise I won't let anyone hurt you ever again."

"Cody—"

"No, don't even start telling me you deserved any of it!"

"It's not that," she whispers, moving away. "You made me realize I couldn't keep punishing myself. I don't want to dig over the past. I want to look forward, and that means letting go of everything I've done, and everything those men did to me."

"They should all rot in fucking jail, Blair."

"Maybe, but neither they nor my father are worth our time. I told him I'm done. I told him I don't care about money, and..." she pauses again, the first tear sliding down her cheek. "He said the condo and car are mine. He folded so fast I realized he's used me all this time only because I *let* him. I didn't fight hard enough."

It absolutely guts me to know what nightmare she willingly put herself through, thinking she deserved nothing but pain. I didn't think I could love her more than I already did, but I do, and my new life mission's just become making her happy. Making her believe she's worthy and making her realize what an incredible woman she is.

"Next time I see your father—"

"You'll do nothing," B interrupts, darting away from me. "Please, Cody. He's spiteful, he'll do something to get back at you or me, maybe mess with Nico's business or worse. Leave it, okay? All I want is for him to disappear from my life."

"He wouldn't dare start a war with Nico, believe me. He'd feel the repercussions for years to come." I kiss her head, trying to soothe her agitated mind. "You love me, B. And that means you trust me."

She falls silent, the weight of her confession dawning on us both. I replay every word she spoke, and the knowledge rips me to shreds.

She really never did have a voice. Couldn't say *no*, couldn't ask her parents for help, couldn't tell her friends...

I hold her even closer, my lips almost permanently glued to her head as I stroke her hair, waiting for her to drift off, but instead, she moves away just far enough to kiss my lips.

And that kiss is as far from a simple peck as it can be. She wants me, needs me inside her.

My first instinct, after everything I *just* learned, is to push her away. My mind screams that she needs time, until I remember she's already had years of dealing with this, months of therapy, and weeks in my bed.

"Promise me something," I say, dragging her onto my lap.

"Anything."

"Promise that you'll never lie to me no matter what you think the truth will do. Not even a tiny white lie."

She narrows her eyes, contemplating my face while her fingers skim up and down my pecs. "You're worried about my head," she muses, a small smile curving her lips. "You think I'm traumatized, correct?"

"In a way, yes. If you need time, we have plenty."

"I don't need time. I dealt with the mental damage before we happened, and you helped me get over the physical constraints." She leans in, kissing the tip of my nose. "I love *you*, and I love our sex life. I'm not coming on to you because I'm trying to forget. I'm coming on to you because I need to remember what it feels like to be truly happy, calm, and safe."

So I remind her, flipping her over, I quickly hook my thumbs over the elastic of her panties and slide them down her legs. I don't bother with the night dress. There's something devastatingly arousing about her wearing clothes when we fuck. My t-shirt works best, but the night dress will do. I grip her thighs, watching her blue eyes hood over, the wanton look on her something to behold.

Taking my sweet time, I kiss the inside of her thighs, nose a line from her pussy to her navel, and not until she squirms, jutting her hips, do I suck her into my mouth.

A satisfied gasp falls from her lips, launching a brand-new flavor of desire straight to my aching cock. I can wait. I need her orgasm more than my own.

"Cody..." she tuts, weaving her fingers through my hair. "A little faster, please."

I lick her, increasing both the tempo and pressure. She tastes fucking divine. I push two fingers inside, my cock pulsing in time with her pussy. She's on edge within minutes. Her breathing pattern changes, her moans become louder, and that's when I stop and move back. Her eyes fly open in an accusatory stare.

"You'll make a mess of the bed, baby, and I'm not spending another night on the floor," I explain, hooking my arms under her back and knees to haul her up. "We'll finish in the shower."

"I don't care where," she sighs, clinging close enough to brush her lips along my neck.

I stand her in the walk-in shower, turn the water on, and adjust the temperature before I kneel. Draping her right leg over my shoulder, I latch onto her clit, slip two digits inside her, and get to work. The pace is nowhere near as mellow as on the bed. I'm done teasing. I want her to come, then come again, then over and over again on my cock until she can't move her legs.

She squirts a minute later, biting her hand to muffle the squeals. Hotel walls are paper-thin, and it's already six in the morning. I'm not as ostentatious as Conor, who didn't mind Colt and me hearing Vee scream down his bedroom while we lived at Nico's. They were loud enough to wake me up sometimes.

I'm less inclined to such theatrics. I'm possessive as fuck over those sweet sounds B makes. They're for my ears and my ears alone. All of her is just for me. No one can watch or listen.

"One more, then—"

"Later," she pants, her thighs quivering. She unhooks her leg and gently tugs my hair, signaling she wants me to stand. "Let's see how strong my man is."

With a graceful *hop*, she's in my arms, her legs wrapped around my middle, arms holding onto my neck. "Press me against the wall and have your way with me."

I smirk, tucking a few wet strands of dark hair behind her ears. "You need a hate-fuck, baby?"

She nods, biting her bottom lip. "I want to feel you every time I sit down tomorrow. Maybe even the day after."

No more encouragement is necessary. I press her against the tiles, my hand cradling the back of her head to break the impact. I slam into her as soon as she's pinned to the wall. She yelps a resounding "Yes!" and sinks her nails into my back.

"Remember your safe word, B, and don't let anyone overhear us. I won't be happy if you wake anyone up."

"I promise I'll be quiet."

"Good girl. Lean your head on my shoulder and bite down if you can't keep it in."

Pulling my hips back, I drive myself home, sinking balls-deep in one sharp thrust. Then again, and again, harder, and faster, spurred by Blair's almost soundless mewls in my ear, and her nails carving long lines down my back.

She does a beautiful job of keeping quiet, and an even more beautiful job of branding me with a big, stinging hickey when we come in sync. I bet it'll be sore as long as her pussy.

Still wet, and now utterly boneless, she clings to me as I carry her to bed and tuck her into my side. It's light out, the clock showing half-past six in the morning.

***

Sunday passes in an utterly uneventful blur. By the time we dragged ourselves out of bed it was past lunchtime, and most of the guests had already left. Dressed, packed, and fed, we got on the road in Blair's Porsche, with Ana tucked in the back. Six hours later—thanks to a lot of restroom breaks—we arrived home and spent the rest of the evening in my condo.

It's Monday that brings a sliver of closure.

Logan wasn't at all surprised when I texted him late on Sunday, saying I needed a day off after Blair slipped up and told me about her father's imminent visit.

I was itching all morning, hoping he'd give me a reason to break his jaw. While we waited for the fucker to show up, I reviewed her condo purchase documents to ensure the place was legally hers. Once that was out of the way, I called two guys to replace the locks in case her father had a copy of the key.

"Did he call?" I ask B, watching her unpack a suitcase. "It's getting late."

Just as she opens her mouth to answer, a faint knock resonates in the hallway. It's not on Blair's door, though, it's on mine.

My muscles seize painfully as I cross the kitchen, flinging the door open. Instead of Gideon, like I expect, Nico turns to look at me. He hasn't casually dropped by since... ever.

He never arrives unannounced, and never for chit-chat, so the cold shiver sliding down my spine is warranted.

"What's wrong?" I ask.

"Invite me in, Cody. Your girlfriend's dad left my office twenty minutes ago. He was... *disturbed*, to say the least."

I refrain from pointing out that it's seven in the evening, and he shouldn't be working at this time. Instead, I hold the door open to let him in.

Blair's in the bedroom doorway, her cheeks pale as she takes the bulk of my brother in. "Hey," she says. "Is something wrong?"

"Your dad stopped by Nico's office," I explain, gesturing for her to come closer as Nico props himself against the breakfast island. "Go on, bro. What did he want?"

Blair grabs two Coronas from the fridge, popping the caps, her hands trembling softly.

"First, he apologized for Blair 'crashing' Logan's wedding. Said he understands how much distress it must've caused me and Mia, and tried promising he'd deal with her in due course."

"How did he know I was there?" Blair asks, pouring herself a glass of wine, her voice small, face flushed.

"Logan's socials are full of pictures from the wedding. People were posting all weekend, tagging him and Cass. You and Cody were caught on quite a few."

"What did you tell him?" I ask, pulling a barstool out for B to sit.

There's a slight pause, and when he speaks again, a rare note of humor coats his words. "That the past is just that. Past. It doesn't matter now you two are together."

"I'm guessing Dad wasn't happy about that," B says, already halfway through her wine.

"No, he wasn't," Nico confirms. "To cut a long story short, he spent over two hours trying to belittle you, your relationship with Cody, your feelings, and your remorse, all while adding in quite a lot of shit to try and piss me off."

I smirk, imagining the situation. Nico has a very short fuse wherever Mia's involved. He's opinionated and snaps faster than the naked eye can register when anyone disrespects his family but, despite that, he can be surprisingly well composed when he knows he's being manipulated.

"I guess it didn't work."

"You guess correctly. However, Gideon worked himself up rather quickly, and instructed me to cash in his largest portfolio and deposit the money in a Swiss bank account."

Blair stills beside me, wide-eyed. "That makes no sense,"

she whispers. "You're the only person he respects and the only person he trusts with money. Why would he—oh," she gasps, suddenly enlightened as she whispers, "Punishment..."

"Punishment?" Nico questions, one eyebrow raised.

"He closed my portfolio. The one he promised I'd get for my twenty-first birthday. He's threatened to do this for years," she explains absentmindedly, a tiny, disbelieved chuckle escaping her. "He really thinks I'm like him. He thinks leaving me high and dry will somehow hurt me, and I'll come crawling back."

A moment of deafening silence ensues, my older brother mulling her words over, either reading between the lines or recalling whatever Gideon told him. I can almost hear his brain working. He pierces Blair with unyielding eyes, trying to coalesce something solid. While he's thinking, I top B's wine glass up.

"He blackmailed you with that portfolio," Nico finally says, all humor gone from his voice. "I guess the rumors were true."

"What rumors?" Blair whips her head up, peering at him over the rim of her glass. "What have you heard?"

"That you were interested in the old, rich, influential men your father worked with." He runs a hand down his face. "I guess it was never a matter of preference or *choice*."

Blair doesn't respond, but I feel her demeanor shift as shame and dread take over.

"So? Did he say what his plan was now?" I ask, but Nico's not looking at me. He's focused on my girl.

"Blair," he urges and waits until she lifts her eyes. "Your father set up your portfolio during our first meeting. It's in *your* name. Only you can withdraw the money and..." He pauses, something dark and heavy passing over his face.

It almost looks like *pity*. Blair's not as hung up on the *and* as I am, she's shellshocked by *only you*.

"It's mine?" she asks quietly, eyes big, round, and tearful. "He didn't take it away?"

"He can't," Nico insists, letting out a long sigh. "You've had right of access since the day you turned eighteen."

Her stool scrapes the tiles as she springs to her feet, spilling her wine. I reach out to grab her, but she shrugs me off, shaking all over, eyes full of tears.

"I'm okay, I just... I need a minute," she chokes, rushing into her bedroom.

The door closes with a click and Nico zeroes in on me, the quiet intensity of his gaze like an invisible pole probing my brain.

"Did she tell you what Gideon made her do?"

I bob my head, chugging the last of my beer.

"How bad was it?"

Everything Blair told me about her *work* resurfaces. She didn't go into detail, but it was enough to draw a bone-chilling picture.

"No one was there to help her when she faced her own version of Asher and Jake," I say, knowing damn well Nico will understand *rape* without me having to spell it out.

His hands ball into tight fists as he regains his composure, squashing the memories of his girl's sexual abuse.

"You should go see how she's doing," he finally says, pushing away from his casual lean against the cabinets. "Call me when she decides how to proceed with the money. And tell her Gideon's set on moving to Europe by the end of the month." He squeezes my shoulder, a silent gesture of reassurance. A nonverbal confirmation that he's available if we need any help. "I'll let myself out."

With a tight nod, I turn the opposite way, finding Blair in

bed, curled under the comforter, silent tears streaming down her cheeks. Her eyes are shut tight, a clear indication words aren't what she needs right now.

The first night she spent crying in my arms comes back to the forefront of my mind. I loved how she curled into me and held onto my t-shirt while silently falling apart.

Despite our mutual hatred, she trusted me even then. She embraced her emotions and let her tears dry at their own pace.

I sneak under the comforter, pulling her into me, ready to put her back together when she's done crying.

Her tears dry much faster tonight than they did all those weeks ago. She clings to me, no longer afraid I'll push her away, and feeds off whatever calmness she finds in my arms.

"Can you promise me something?" she murmurs a while later, her fingers drawing little hearts across my chest. "Don't go looking for my father, okay? He's not worth it."

I clench my jaw, the cogs in my mind whirring. Since we came back yesterday, I imagined breaking the fucker's nose a thousand times. Holding back all day wasn't easy, but he was supposed to show up at some point.

But he's not coming and B's making me promise I won't go looking...

And that goes against my reflexes. He hurt her. Intentionally used her as bait. His own *daughter*. A few broken bones are the least he deserves.

"I don't want him anywhere near you, B. I'll just talk to him. Let him know he should stay the fuck away if he values his life."

She smiles. Fucking *smiles* into the crook of my neck. "He will stay away. Now he knows Nico doesn't mind us being together, he won't risk a scandal. He knows he can't intimidate me anymore. That if he tries poking, I have enough stories to bury his reputation." She sighs heavily, rising on her elbow to look me in the eyes. "Why do you think he's moving to Europe? It was always his retirement plan, but now that he's facing a backlash, he's removing himself from the picture."

"Coward," I mutter, wrapping one arm around her back.

"He always was," she admits, then stamps her lips on my forehead. "When I wake up in the morning, I want it to be the first day of the rest of my life, Cody. A life I fully intend on spending with *you.* I want to draw a line and start over but I won't if you can't start with me."

A part of me screams *hell to the no.* Gideon should hear a few hard truths. He should fucking hurt, but... at the end of the day, what will screaming and throwing fists accomplish? Nothing much. He's too rotten for any of the things I'm dying to tell him to make an impact, and bruises heal.

What won't change is the weight on Blair's shoulders. Not until we start moving forward instead of looking back and standing still. She deserves smiles. She deserves to feel safe and loved and that *will* make a difference.

I take her face in my hands, pulling her in for a soft kiss. "Okay. I won't go looking for him."

The smile she gives me has my heart squeezing like a sponge. It's the most genuine smile I've seen on her to date; I want to give her reasons to smile like this every day.

"I love you," she whispers, maneuvering us back into a tangle under the sheets.

"I love you more."

EPILOGUE

"B! Baby, I know you're busy, but if you don't move that sweet butt we're gonna be late!" I shout from upstairs.

She said *just five more minutes* twenty minutes ago. Most other days, I'd call off whatever we had planned so she could indulge her passion, but that's not possible today.

"I'm coming!" she huffs back, her soft footsteps padding up the stairs. "Why the rush? We still have almost an hour."

"It's an important evening."

"So you keep saying."

She doesn't bother asking why. She's tried a few times, but my reply is always the same: *it's top secret, B. Patience.*

While I rummage through the closet for my favorite t-shirt, Blair locks herself in the bathroom. The shower starts running making me groan for two reasons.

One, she's not exactly quick in the shower with all that long hair and we *don't* have much time. And two... she's there, all wet and lathered up, and my dick hasn't seen action for five days.

Two years together and she still doesn't let me touch her while she's on her period.

I busy myself picking out a watch to match... nothing, really. I'm all in black so any will do, but looking over each and every one keeps me from barging into the bathroom and stroking my cock while I watch her soaping down that body.

Two *years* and I'm still out-of-control hungry for Blair on a daily basis. I can eat her out first thing in the morning, sink my cock into her tight ass after she orgasms and I'll want her again by lunch time.

Madness.

Perfect, addictive, blissful madness.

Twenty minutes later, when we should be leaving the house, B emerges from the bathroom. She's dressed, dry hair up in a ponytail, and delicate makeup done.

"You look beautiful, you know that?" I say, my eyes roving her from head to toe.

She rolls her lips, biting back a smile. "It's the dress."

"Yeah, the dress is pretty, but you're prettier." I cross the room to where she's putting her earrings on.

The summery, spaghetti strap dress—Blair's very first design in the flesh—rolls up her tanned thighs. Not on it's own. My finger might've helped a little.

Since the day her father disappeared from her life, shortly after Logan's wedding, B started living to the max instead of merely surviving every day. Once she graduated, she immediately started a fashion design company. Twelve months, endless sleepless nights, and a lot of determination later, she's wearing a dress she designed.

And it's gorgeous. Something I'm sure Mia will want in her

collection, though not in black. Delicate, flowy fabric swishes around Blair's knees. Tiny, cherry blossom patterns tone down the black fabric, making it look cute but edgy. Modest neckline, perfect fitting, and a bow under the bra line.

Once B's business operation outgrew her condo, I bought a house and converted the double garage into a studio. We only moved in last month, but Blair's already filled the shelves and racks to the max: while I painstakingly unpacked the rest of the house.

Oh the *joy*.

Thankfully, the Hayes came on a rescue mission and we were done inside two days.

"You haven't kissed me today," Blair says, angling her head.

I have, but apparently a simple peck after work while she was busy sewing doesn't count. Or maybe she didn't even notice.

I don't mind. I love finding her by the sewing machine after I come home from work. I love the smile on her face when she shows me her new designs or tells me about the independent boutiques emailing her about selling her work.

She's determined to make a name for herself in the fashion industry and I couldn't be prouder. A girl who two short years ago didn't believe she deserved a meaningful life, now spreading her wings and living to the fullest.

And I get to watch. I get to share that life with her.

"Let me fix that." I dip my head, sealing her lips. Nothing aligns my mind as fast as B's kisses.

She sighs softly, leaning into me as I slip my tongue inside the silk of her mouth, our breaths mingling, mouths coming together, bodies pressing closer and—

I pull away when she bites my lip. She knows that gets my cock begging for attention.

"You want me to drive to Mom's house with a boner?" I ask, brushing a few stray locks behind her ears. "Or would you rather I get my fill really quickly?"

She trails her hands from my neck, down my chest, and lower still. "Just letting you know we're in the clear."

"My dick sure got the message, baby." I grip her wrists in one hand before she makes the situation worse. "Stop teasing. You should've said we're in the green zone before you got in the shower, baby. Fucking you was all I could think about while you were in there, but as much as I want to, we don't have time. We' re in for a treat tonight. I don't want to miss that, so behave."

She puts on a fake pout. "Whatever's happening must be ridiculously important if you're forfeiting sex."

"See? You get it." I stamp a kiss on her forehead. "Now, can we please go?"

***

My father, together with Mia's and Vee's, takes charge of the barbeque. It's not uncommon for Mom to invite them over for a get-together. It's also not uncommon for three grown-ass men to burn the meat. Instead of committing to the task, they chat and bicker like teenagers, and the cooking part slips their attention. One time, we ended up ordering pizza because the meat they cooked was inedible.

I don't bother offering my help. Blair and Vee already have me on kitchen-to-garden food-transfer duty along with Conor and—if he gets his ass here on time—Colt. The girls are setting the table and Theo's in charge of the makeshift bar while Shawn and Jack entertain the kids.

"Shit," Conor huffs, looking out the living room window.

"I need to get out there. Too many kids, not enough adults."

The ratio is about three and a half adults per kid in this family, but Conor's eight-month-old twin boys require constant supervision. There's only two of them, yet they're *everywhere.*

"Yeah, go on. I've got this," I say, hugging two crates of Corona to my chest. Food can wait. We need fuel first. "Imagine what it'll be like when they start walking."

Conor lets out a half laugh half pained groan, hurrying outside to where the twins have attached themselves to Jack's legs.

I get back into the kitchen, eyeing the last case of beer. One trip outside is better than two, but no way I can stash it on top of the two I'm already holding.

Shit. Two trips it is. Colt's getting a whack across his head as soon as he shows up. Not only should he be helping me, but Mom's already jittery he's late. Logan's not here yet with Cass and the boys, but Logan being late is not news. We'd be more concerned if he showed up on time.

Colt being late, on the other hand, has everyone on edge. He's not particularly punctual when we go out drinking, but he's always on time for Mom. And he fucking knows tonight's important, so he should be here by now. It's already well past four and he's a no-show.

"What's wrong?" Blair asks, following me into the kitchen as I return for the third case. "You look tense."

She doesn't realize how important tonight is. Technically Colt doesn't either, but I did *hint* at it. You'd think he'd take that hint and get here on time. It's a rarity we need to spell shit out to one another. Conor figured it out no problem, though given the looks he's been sending my way since I got here, he might've misunderstood.

I think he expects an engagement announcement.

It's probably overdue by now, but B and I have chatted extensively about our future plans. We will get married. And we will have kids, maybe not next month but it is happening and we're both in agreement. I could pop the question right now, but I know B's main focus is her career, so for now, I'm supporting her along the way by giving her all the time she needs.

"I'm fine, baby," I say, opening the fridge to check how many trips it'll take to transport all the damn food the women in this family have prepared. "Just pissed off at Colt. He's skipping the *helping* part—again."

B laughs softly, pulling two salad bowls from the top shelf. "There's twenty people here, Cody. I think we can manage without him."

She's right and wrong at the same time. Sure we can set up the table without his help, but he'll miss the news if he doesn't get a move on and I know he'll fucking regret it.

"I know," I say, catching her wrist to tug her closer.

One kiss before we get back outside where the whole family—minus Colt—is already by the table. Even Logan's made it, with his two and a half kids; Cassidy's pregnant again, her four-month bump proudly displayed. Logan hides all her baggy clothes whenever he knocks her up so everyone can immediately see she's a two-pack. Fucking caveman.

Colt gets another thirty minutes to show up, but once we all finish devouring the first round of grilled meat, time's up. Nico rises from his chair, a flute of champagne in hand like he's about to make a toast.

"While we're all here, I have some news," he says, pulling Mia up. "We've decided to call off the wedding."

A chorus of gasps rises over the table, and to be perfectly honest, my stomach sinks too. I didn't expect *that.*

They've been planning the wedding for months.

Blair grabs my hand under the table, gouging her long nails into my skin. I gently flex my fingers around hers.

"You're not getting married?" Logan asks, eyebrows drawn together. "Why?"

"We are getting married," Mia corrects. "Just not this year."

"Jimmy," Nico urges, grabbing the attention of his soon-to-be father-in-law who doesn't look one bit pleased. "As promised, she finished college," he says, setting his flute aside." So I hope this..." He moves Mia in front of him, his big hands flattening her swing dress to reveal her small baby bump. "...is good news."

Endorphins hit, obliterating that sinking feeling in my stomach. I've known for three weeks and keeping this a secret was fucking torture. Same as not holding my hand across Mia's tiny bump every time I saw her.

Everyone is silent for the first three, maybe five seconds. My mother reacts first with a quiet elated whimper that snaps everyone out of the shock.

"I'm going to be a grandpa?" Jimmy asks first.

"Surprise." Mia beams. "And... it's a girl."

"No fucking way!" Logan booms. He's trying really hard to look pissed off, but he's smiling so wide his mouth's not far off splitting in half. "How far along are you?"

I chuckle under my breath. Him and Cass are still waiting to find out if baby number three is a boy or a girl because the baby was facing the wrong way during the last scan.

"A couple of weeks behind you two," Nico admits.

While everyone gets up with congratulations, I remain seated. Once I get my hands on Mia, there's no way I'm letting her go quickly just because someone else is waiting in line.

"You knew," Blair whispers, angling her head to speak in my ear. "Why didn't you say anything?"

I stamp a kiss on her temple. "I found out by accident and promised to keep my mouth shut."

She smirks, bouncing her eyebrows. "It's killing you to wait right now, isn't it?"

"You have no fucking idea," I huff, dragging my hand down my face. "Nico doesn't let me hold her anymore. He's gone off the rails but he won't shove me away in front of everyone."

Blair chuckles, nestling her head on my shoulder. "You're both off the rails about Mia."

Yeah... that's true. I love my real sister, Rose, but Mia's more. She's my best friend. And when she went above and beyond to give Blair a chance two years ago, our friendship grew that much deeper. We're living proof that platonic friendship between men and women is possible.

The doorbell rings, announcing the arrival of the last missing piece of the Hayes family. Colt's the only one we're waiting for and with the beeline for Mia still six people deep, I make my way across the lawn, inside the house, and to the main door.

But when I yank it open it's not Colt standing outside with a solemn look on his face. It's a friend of Shawn's from work in full police uniform. A squad car is parked behind him, another cop standing ground by the hood.

"Tim, hey, man. You looking for Shawn?"

He pinches his lips together, an uncertain gloom in his blue gaze. "No, actually, it's you I need." His jaw works for a moment as if he's battling whatever he needs to say. And that's enough for anxiety to invade my mind.

Uncomfortable silence, lack of eye contact and a heavy, threatening atmosphere is never a bearer of good news.

"There's been an accident, Cody," he eventually says, the sentence leaving his mouth slow and heavy.

Everything inside me seizes. Everything apart from my heart that hammers so hard it's fucking painful.

"Colt," I rasp, my voice distant, hands clammy. I immediately know it's Colt because I'm his emergency contact. "Where is he? What happened?"

"Car crash. High speed from what I gathered so far. He was airlifted into the hospital half an hour ago. It's... it's bad, Cody. He's in critical condition. They're operating as we speak, but—"

"What's going on?" Theo's voice comes from behind me, his heavy footsteps clapping like tiny thunder in the empty entryway. "Hey Tim," he adds, stopping on my right and I must look like absolute shit because his face falls immediately. "What's wrong?"

"Colt's in the hospital," Tim reiterates. "They're operating, but it doesn't look good. The steering wheel crushed his chest, damaged his lungs and heart..."

The world tips on it's fucking axis. Shatters around me as the news rips me apart.

Critical.

Damaged heart.

Critical.

Damaged heart.

I don't realize I'm sitting on the floor, my back flush with the wall, my hands shaking until I see Blair's tear-stained face before me, people rushing about in the background.

"Baby, you need to get up," she says, her warm hands on my cheeks. "Come on, he needs you. You need to keep it together."

A big hand grips my arm next and Blair's gone.

Then another hand on the other arm and I'm up, barely

holding my own weight.

"He'll make it," Nico says forcefully, his fingers digging into my bones. "Say it, Cody. Say it and you better fucking mean it."

I swallow hard, closing my eyes briefly to get a hold of the scorching sensation burning through my veins.

"He'll make it," I say and make myself believe it.

I have to believe it.

Thank you

I hope you enjoyed *Too Hard*. I hope you loved the story. It was the most challanging book to write in this series. Colt is next and last.

Love,

I. A. Dice